THE
CALL

by
Chris Ahlemann

Chris Ahlemann
Sept. 23, 1993

Edited and Cover Design
by James Van Treese

NPI

Northwest Publishing Inc.
5949 South 350 West
Salt Lake City, UT 84107

Copyright © 1993
Northwest Publishing Inc.
5949 South 350 West
Salt Lake City, Utah 84107
801-266-5900

International Copyright Secured

Reproductions in any manner, in whole or in part,
in English or in other languages, or otherwise
without the prior written permission of the
publisher is prohibited.

B B / S M 07 26 93

ISBN #1-56901-014-5

Dedication

*To the One whose steadfast love
has given me the courage
to care.*

Table of Contents

Key To Brownsville Map

1. Fitzsimmons House
2. Blacksmith Shop
3. Old Mill
4. Lewis Cabinet Shop
5. Christian Church
6. Chapman's Dry Goods
7. Crawford's Grocery
8. Old Cemetery
9. Crawford's House
10. Bank—Brownsville Banking and Savings Association
11. Spring Grounds
12. African Christian Church
13. Andrew and Claudia's place
14. Central Hotel (Sweet Springs Saloon in basement)
15. Chapman's House
16. Douglas Dry Goods
17. Jane's Millinery & Dress Shop
18. Presbyterian–Methodist Meeting House
19. Train Depot
20. Maple Tree
21. Post Office (after 1871)
22. Jail
23. New Mill
24. City Hotel
25. Bonnie and Randall's House
26. Harvey Fudd's Cabin
27. Fuld and Hoffman's Dry Goods (Smith & Ferguson's Hall upstairs)
28. New Cemetery
29. Kelly's Drug Store

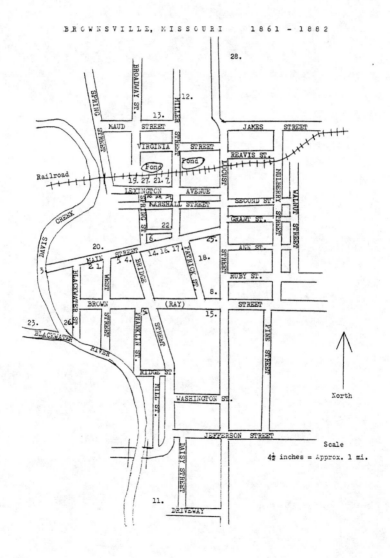

BROWNSVILLE, MISSOURI   1861 - 1882

Scale

4½ inches = Approx. 1 mi.

North

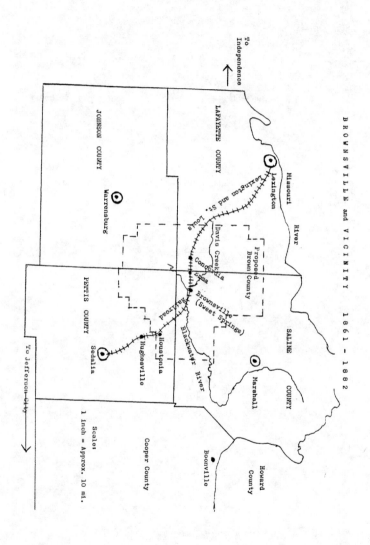

BROWNSVILLE and VICINITY 1861 - 1882

To Independence

JOHNSON COUNTY

LAFAYETTE COUNTY

Warrensburg

Lexington

Missouri River

Lexington and St. Louis

Davis Creek

Proposed Brown County

Concordia

Lyons

Brownsville (Sweet Springs)

SALINE COUNTY

PETTIS COUNTY

Railway

Houstonia

Hughesville

Sedalia

Blackwater River

Marshall

To Jefferson City

Cooper County

Boonville

Howard County

Scale:
1 inch = Approx. 10 mi.

ix

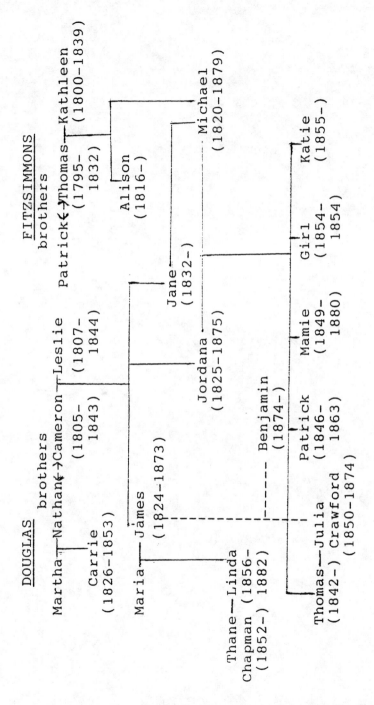

FITZSIMMONS
brothers

DOUGLAS
brothers

Patrick ← Thomas — Kathleen
(1795– (1800–1839)
1832)

Martha — Nathan → Cameron — Leslie
(1805– (1807–
1843) 1844)

Carrie
(1826–1853)

Alison
(1816–)

Michael
(1820–1879)

Maria — James
(1824–1873)

Jane
(1832–)

Jordana
(1825–1875)

Benjamin
(1874–)

Thane — Linda
Chapman (1856–)
(1852–) 1882)

Patrick
(1846–
1863)

Mamie
(1849–
1880)

Girl
(1854–
1854)

Katie
(1855–)

Thomas — Julia
(1842–) Crawford
(1850–1874)

xi

LEWIS

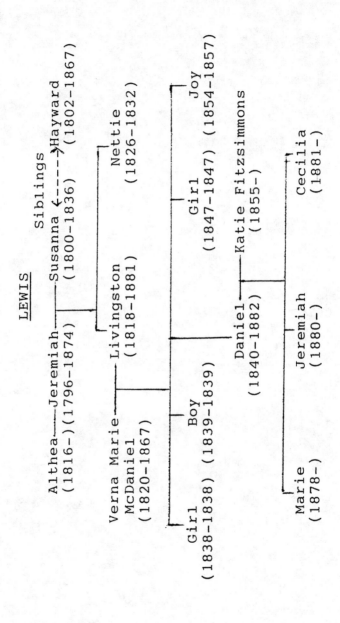

Siblings

Althea——Jeremiah——Susanna ⟵----⟶Hayward
(1816–) (1796–1874) (1800–1836) (1802–1867)

Nettie
(1826–1832)

Verna Marie——Livingston
McDaniel   (1818–1881)
(1820–1867)

Girl
(1847–1847)

Joy
(1854–1857)

Daniel——Katie Fitzsimmons
(1840–1882) (1855–)

Boy
(1839–1839)

Girl
(1838–1838)

Jeremiah
(1880–)

Cecilia
(1881–)

Marie
(1878–)

(Slaves)

DOUGLAS

FITZSIMMONS

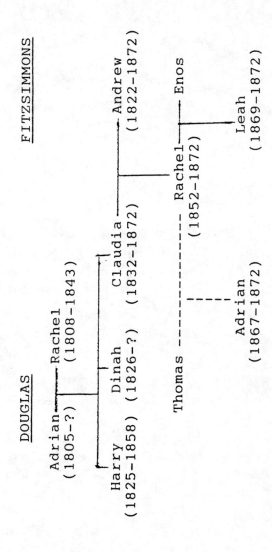

Adrian — Rachel
(1805–?)   (1808–1843)

Harry   Dinah   Claudia — Andrew
(1825–1858) (1826–?)   (1832–1872)   (1822–1872)

Thomas ------------ Rachel — Enos
                    (1852–1872)

Adrian   Leah
(1867–1872)   (1869–1872)

"Man is the measure of all things."
    – Protagoras (5th century B.C.)

"For thou hast made him a little lower than the angels, and hast crowned him with glory and honour."
    – Psalm 8:5 (KJV)

*"Like a windstorm
Punishing the oak trees,
Love shakes my heart."*
    *– Sappho
(translated by Willis Barnstone,
William E. McCulloh)*

*" 'Tis better to love and lose
Than never to love at all."*
    *– Alfred, Lord Tennyson
(paraphrase)*

PROLOGUE
MAY 12, 1861

TO WAR

*"The one who goes is happier
than those he leaves behind."*

— *Edward Pollock
The Parting Hour*

Prologue

He was leavin. Her Thomas was leavin Brownsville over some crazy notion of savin Missouri, an she didn't want him to go. Yet, she was powerless to stop him. Determined, he was. Why, ever since he'd busted into her kitchen yesterday mornin she'd knowed he was goin. Her son was goin to war.

Attempting to maintain a sense of normalcy at the breakfast table, Jordana Fitzsimmons took a spoonful of sorghum and mush. The mixture stuck in her throat. She pushed the bowl away in disgust.

He was risin now, all five feet eight inches of him, in his eagerness to be off. The others rose too: Michael, Patrick, Mamie, Katie, and Jane. And as Jordana pushed back her own chair, she knew she couldn't hold him no longer. Them icy fingers thet had touched her yesterday was feelin her heart again. Fur Thomas was ever bit as excited now as he was then.

"Guess what's the latest news at the mill?" he'd panted as he rushed into her kitchen.

Turning from the work table where she rolled pie crust, Jordana had asked coolly, "Ain't the smithy got no news this mornin?"

"Aw, My Ma, you know—"

"I know your Pa has need of you next door. You said you'd work hard; no more fiddlin round."

"I know, but—"

"But what?"

"I jist plumb furgot, I reckon. Anyways, there really is excitin news this mornin. About Camp Jackson."

"Camp Jackson?"

"You know—thet camp over there by St. Louis. Anyways, our militia was doin maneuvers over there, mindin their own business like, when this here feller, Lyon, attacks them. I mean to tell you they took our Missourians prisoners. Like common criminals, they did. An over twenty folks was killed. Women an youngins, even." He paused, drawing himself up straighter.

"So? What's thet got to do with us?"

"Why, everything. Look, My Ma, this can git serious like. Missouri can't be pushed around jist cause some feller thinks we're wrong. Thet's why Wade an me is goin over to Marshall to join—"

"No!" Jordana jabbed a top crust so hard she tore a hole in it.

"But, My Ma, Wade's set to go within the hour. An I'm goin—"

"Confound it, I said no." She turned then and waved a floury fork in his direction. "You're jist a boy yet. An you're needed here."

"I'm most nineteen," Thomas defended. "Anyways, My Pa's got Andrew an Patrick—"

"But they ain't you."

"Reckon not. But look, My Ma, a whole passel of folks is goin."

"An jist who is these folks?"

"Well, Uriah Martin fur one."

"Okay, Uriah an Wade an you. Now, who else?"

"No one fur certain." Thomas shifted uneasily. "Though lots of fellers is thinkin on it."

"What about Daniel?"

"Daniel Lewis? How should I know? He don't while away his time at the mill. Anyways, he purt near has to stay home an help his Pa make furniture. Or else care fur his Ma."

"Well, from all I hear his Ma could use the care, thet's fur certain. An, as fur helpin his Pa—why, I've a mind to trot you next door an hang an apron on you myself. Leastwise then maybe you'd furgit this notion of joinin up."

But Thomas didn't forget. And when Michael took his side, Jordana knew her cause was lost.

"Aye, Colleen, me lad's purt nigh a man, mind. I reckon he can choose fur himself."

An so this mornin her son was leavin.

"Well, I'd best git my gear," Thomas said, then strode with a cocky air into the dining room.

Even before he returned, Jordana knew what he'd gone for. The Kentucky Rifle. He'd take it an thet powder horn from the mantle not knowin thet she felt good an bad both at seein the thing.

xxiii

The instant Thomas re–entered the kitchen, fourteen–year-old Patrick lunged for him. "Hey, you can't take thet!" My Ma said Uncle James left it fur *us*."

"Well, I reckon us is me today. Cause this fightin is important like. See?"

But Patrick didn't see. He grabbed the long barrel and attempted to wrest it from his brother.

"Why, you little whippersnapper!" Thomas reared back for a well–aimed punch, then stopped. For a burly hand had grabbed his fist. A matching hand clinched Patrick's arm.

"Aye, Lads, thet's enough now. Thomas is goin to fight, to be sure. He can have the gun."

In the silence which followed Michael's pronouncement, Jordana sighed. It was jist as well, she reckoned. Though thet gun stood fur her early Kentucky home an her beloved brother James, it mostly reminded her of her pa, Cameron Douglas. The mere thought of him made her shiver. An thet gun her son insisted on totin had first been his. James had only come into it upon Pa's death. An James had given it to her when he took off fur gold country in '49. He never said why he wanted to give it up an she never asked.

"Well, I'd best russle up some grub fur you." Jordana turned to where a bandanna already lay on the work table. The door opened then and someone entered. Jordana knew even before she heard the usual, "Mornin", that it was Claudia coming to clear up.

"Good mornin." As usual it was Jane who returned the slave's greeting. What in the world her sister saw in thet scrawny nigger Jordana jist couldn't figure out. Unless maybe she felt other than human herself with thet birthmark on her face an all.

"Oh boy, fried apple pies!" Patrick was beside his Ma in an instant reaching a freckled hand for the half–moon confection.

"No." Jordana smacked his hand. "Them is fur Thomas."

Abashed, Patrick retreated to a split–bottom chair. "It ain't fair," he whined. "Mamie's got one."

Jordana turned then to shake a finger at her twelve–year-old daughter who was already licking the sugar from a snatched pie.

"Confound you, Youngin. I wanted thet fur Thomas."

But Mamie continued licking the precious white sugar, her cool green eyes daring her ma to take the sweet from her.

Turning back to the work table, Jordana sighed. Thet Mamie was gittin too big fur her britches. Still, she was a purty girl with thet reddish hair an all. She'd do all right.

Moments later Jordana knotted the red bandanna. "There." And she handed the parcel to Thomas.

But Patrick reached it first. "It's mine," he declared. "Thomas gits the gun, I git the grub. I'm goin too."

"No!" Jordana snatched the bundle and shoved Patrick back into his chair. "*You* ain't goin off to no war."

"But My Ma, I'm most fifteen."

"Well, fifteen ain't eighteen an you ain't goin."

Even as she opposed her second son, Jordana felt again those frosty fingers pressing her heart. She was scared. Scared fur Patrick. Even more than fur Thomas. Why, ever since he was born she'd been scared. Course on thet warm day in June of '46 she'd been scared of only one thing— her or thet new baby dyin. When they lived, she'd felt safe, fur awhile. Until Michael said it was on thet very mornin thet men from all over Saline County had met in Marshall. Goin to fight the Mexicans, they was. An they'd come back too. Ever one of them. Still, Jordana was scared. It seemed an omen thet her sandy–haired boy would die at war. But not in this war, he wouldn't. *She'd* see to thet.

"Aye, Lad, your Ma's right, to be sure."

"I should of knowed it'd be thet away." Patrick's normally soft voice grew hard. "Thomas gits everything around here. No one cares a whit about me."

For a moment the only sound was that of Claudia scraping leftovers into the slop bucket behind the stove. Then a tiny voice spoke.

"I like you, Patrick. Really an truly I do." And Katie, all the love of her six–year–old soul reflected in her blue-gray eyes, patted her brother's arm.

But Patrick was in no mood for sympathy. "Leave me alone. You're jist a kid, anyways." With that, he shoved Katie aside, stomped across the room and jerked open the door to the stairway.

As the door slammed and angry footsteps receded, Mamie jumped to her feet. "Oh fur heaven sakes, now look what you've done! You're a bunch of meanies. All of you." And she bounded across the room to follow her brother, a half eaten pie still in hand.

As the door slammed a second time a third pair of footsteps sounded. Katie, her rag doll, Molly, dangling by one arm, scampered across the room to press her face in the frills of Aunt Jane's apron.

"Don't cry, Child. Why land sakes, they meant no harm." And Jane patted Katie's brunette braids.

Once again silence dominated the room, broken only by Claudia as she poured scalding water into a dish pan.

It was Thomas who broke the spell. "Well, reckon I'd best git goin. Thanks fur the grub, My Ma."

Jordana touched an apron corner to her eyes then as Thomas grabbed a worn cape from the hook above the woodbox. Her son was leavin.

Outside, the balmy breeze failed to warm Jordana's spirits. It didn't seem right somehow fur thet wind to blow. It didn't seem right fur them apple trees to bloom. It didn't seem right fur them violets to poke their heads up by thet split–rail fence. It didn't seem right fur them hens to cluck this mornin. None of it was right. Fur them things was alive. An thet first youngin to come alive from inside her was goin away. To fight, an maim an maybe die. Jordana shivered. It was like losin cousin Carrie all over again.

Michael and Thomas stepped from the porch, then walked down the path and through the opening in the fence to the dirt road. Andrew, Claudia's husband, stood beside the buggy chewing a wad of tobacco as he loosely held the reins to Old Red, the bay Morgan.

"Aye, Lad, take care, mind." Michael reached a burly hand to tousle his son's hair, then turned aside.

Thomas' lips curved into a smile then as he tossed his cape and food parcel onto the seat of the buggy. Then with rifle in hand, he climbed in himself. Andrew mounted to the driver's seat, flicked the reins and settled back as Old Red trotted toward the corner.

As the buggy turned east onto Main Street, Thomas looked back and waved. And everyone at home waved in return. Everyone, that is, but Katie. She stood in the kitchen doorway clutching Molly to her heart. And her tiny chin quivered as two giant tears slid silently down her cheeks.

PART I
1865-1868

AFTERMATH

"The day goes by like a shadow o'er the heart,
with sorrow where all was delight..."
— Stephen C. Foster
My Old Kentucky Home

Chapter 1

It was a Sunday afternoon in August, 1865. Thomas, his left ankle resting on his right knee, sat on the log bench beneath the old oak tree facing West Street. The corners of his lips turned downward as he puffed on a homemade corncob pipe. He'd turned twenty–three the week before an he felt plumb old. Old an battered an hot. Taking a blue bandanna from his left trouser pocket, he mopped his forehead. It was a scorcher, thet was fur certain. Not as blisterin' as the summer of '61 though. Why, he'd darn near suffocated on thet train ride from Sedalia to Jefferson City.

Still, the excitement they'd had at Boonville most made him furgit the heat. Fur it was at Boonville thet he an Wade had finally seen thet rascal, Lyon. He was a scoundrel all right. Why, he an them Feds had chased the State Guards plumb into a wheat field.

Course at first they'd fought hard. Missouri was a state worth fightin fur. But when them nine pounders started explodin, a feller got kinda confused like. Confused an scared. Before long even old Marmaduke seen they hadn't a chance. He'd signaled fur retreat. They'd retreated all right. Why, Thomas had never run so fast in all his born days. Wade too, had skedaddled like his pants was on fire.

An so they lost. "The Boonville Races" them Feds had sneeringly called it. As though the State Guards was cowards.

Footsteps on the back porch pulled Thomas to the present. It was Rachel, totin a bucket. Thomas' eyes followed the dark figure as she stepped into the yard. When she disappeared behind the tree trunk, he edged toward the right end of the bench for a better view. Tall, like her father, Andrew, Rachel carried herself with grace, her bare brown feet skimming swiftly across the ground. Stopping beside the well, she re-

3

moved the lid, then lowered her bucket.

Thomas planted both feet on the ground, then leaned forward, his thin lips curving into a smile. My but thet youngin was gettin to be plumb purty. Purt near as purty as her grandma, thet first Rachel, had been, accordin to Aunt Jane.

Rachel rose then, replaced the wooden lid over the well, and lifted the bucket. As she strode back across the yard Thomas shifted toward the left end of the bench. She was a dandy woman all right, with them long limbs, high breasts an rounded haunches. Why, it was enough to drive a man plumb crazy. He sighed as she disappeared through the kitchen doorway.

Crossing his legs again, Thomas reminded himself that Rachel was no longer a slave. Free she was, like her parents. Yet, fur all thet they'd remained loyal to his family. Course My Pa never had seen Andrew as a slave. Still, it seemed a shame to pay niggers fur workin. What had Missourians fought fur, anyways?

Even now, Thomas could smell the stench of fallen soldiers on that blistering August morning at Wilson's Creek. All around them men were being slaughtered. But he an Wade jist laughed. They reckoned them Feds was goin to lose this time. Leastwise they figured to see thet bastard, Lyon, get his comeuppance. He did too. An they'd whooped like crazy when thet sharpshooter brought him down. Satisfyin it was. Jist plumb satisfyin.

But death is no respecter of persons. Moments after General Lyon breathed his last, Wade took a musket ball in the arm. And even as he waved away Thomas' concern, a bullet slammed into his temple.

The battle was over by noon, the Southern boys the winners. But few of them had felt victorious when they were left with the gruesome task of burying over five hundred corpses. Mechanically, Thomas had spaded earth and kicked remains into trenches. Federals and State Guards alike were treated as so much garbage. Except fur Wade. Angrily, Thomas had shoved a fellow Missourian aside when he had aimed a giant boot at Wade's body.

"I reckon this here feller needs fixin like," he'd growled. Then kneeling, he'd removed the bandanna from his own sweaty head and tied it around his friend's bloody one. Awkwardly, he patted sticky clumps of dun–colored hair. Gently, he lowered the mutilated body into the ground.

He was shoveling earth over the body when he realized the futility of what he'd done. Wade was dead. His best friend had hightailed it straight out of life. An all the carin in the world wouldn't make a lick of difference. Made a feller choke up like, seein the ends of thet red bandanna disappear neath the sod of Bloody Hill.

Again the sound of footsteps on the back porch drew Thomas from his reverie. It was Katie. She smiled as she hurried toward the bench, her ribboned braids bobbing. Seating herself, she smoothed her gingham skirt, then reached for his left hand. Thomas jerked it away.

Noting the way she quickly folded her arms across her chest, Thomas felt mean. Jist plumb mean. But he couldn't help it. He wasn't goin to buddy up to Katie even if she was a good youngin. Still, he didn't like seein thet chin quiver. Course Katie was lookin fur somethin to do, a feller could see thet. If it wasn't Sunday she'd be stitchin thet little cloth thing Aunt Jane helped her with. Thomas' lips curved upward at the thought. Katie wasn't no good at sewin, thet was fur certain. It was them letters she loved. Letters an words an verses. Katie sure did love them verses. Most as much as she loved him, he reckoned.

Crossing his legs again, Thomas recalled that October day in '61 when he had stumbled onto the back porch and into the kitchen. Katie had seen him first.

"Thomas!" she'd squealed, jerking on the tattered cape which covered his gaunt frame. When the cape slithered to the floor, Katie screamed.

"Oh my goodness! Why, where's your other arm, anyways?"

"Blown to bits near the Anderson House in Lexington," he'd spat. "An thet Kentucky Rifle too."

Katie had bit her lip then, her tiny chin quivering. But eventually she'd come around. Fur it was Katie thet carried away them putrid rags when Aunt Jane changed the poultice on his stump. An it was Katie who'd fed him broth an held his left hand. But Katie had disappeared when it was time to lay out Patrick.

Thomas sighed, planted both feet on the ground and stared at the split–rail fence. It was plumb crazy what had happened. Jist plumb crazy. Why, Patrick had never even left home. Course he'd bellyached about not gittin to fight. He'd smash them Feds to a pulp when he was eighteen, he would. Only the Feds got him first.

It was My Pa they'd come fur, thet spring of '63. Tied him up like a criminal, they did. Jist cause he refused Governor Gamble's order to join up with the Union. They'd only jist got him into their wagon when a shot was heard.

Thomas knew without looking that Patrick had the illegal shotgun. But before he could reach his brother, a Federal returned the fire. Patrick had died instantly from a gaping wound in his chest. Even so, the Feds weren't finished. They confiscated the shot gun, seized the buggy and Old Red, and cleaned out the root cellar. Inside, they smashed My Pa's rocker and carved "Union" on the writing table in the parlor.

By the time they pulled away, Thomas was seething. Damn them Feds, anyways. What right did they have to tear up a feller's home an hurt his family? He'd git him a Navy Colt .36 he would, an blow the brains out of any Fed who came near him again.

"Hi."

Thomas started at Katie's greeting. She was smiling and waving at a wagon which creaked by on its way south.

It was Mr. Crawford an Julia—Wade's family. Thomas felt plumb awful watchin them. Fur Julia looked purt near like her brother. Course her hair was gold an all, but thet slim nose an them high cheek bones was Wade's.

Raising his left sleeve to his eyes, Thomas nonetheless summoned a smile in answer to Mr. Crawford's wave. Real friendly, he was. Why, he'd been to see Thomas right often thet first year after Wilson's Creek. A widower, he seemed lonely like an wantin to talk of Wade. But Thomas hadn't talked much. What was the use in talkin, anyways? Wade was dead. Buried. Gone. And with him had gone a piece of Thomas' heart.

"I saw them at church this mornin." It was Katie again, talkin about the Crawfords.

Course she'd seen them. The Crawford's was church goin folks. Everybody knowed thet. Anyways, so was his family. Except fur himself an My Pa. Course Mamie never went jist cause she was religious, Thomas was certain of thet. Most likely she had in mind to see thet Daniel Lewis, his shop bein next door to the church an all.

At the thought of Daniel, Thomas' lips turned downward. Now there was a Fed fur you. Story was he'd fought in Arkansas an the battle at Westport. Well, Thomas was plannin a little battle of his own. Sometime ago he'd placed an order with the Lewises. CSA, thet's what he'd ordered. Engraved on maple. The elder Lewis hadn't said a word. He'd simply nodded, bitin hard on thet cigar of his. But Daniel wouldn't be so nonchalant, Thomas reckoned. An it was Daniel he intended to see tomorrow.

❖   ❖   ❖

Daniel was alone when Thomas entered the cabinet shop the next morning. Looking up from the table leg he was sanding, the younger Lewis spoke matter-of-factly.

"You've come for your plaque."

"You're damn right I have." His legs straight as sticks, Thomas glared at his enemy. "An it had best be ready."

"It is." Daniel laid the oak leg on the work bench and steadied it with a planer. Then slowly he rose from the three–legged stool. Pulling a rag from his trouser pocket, he methodically wiped his hands. Slender hands these were, with long, delicate fingers and short, rounded nails.

Impatient, Thomas' lips formed a taut line. But Daniel never hurried. When at length he'd finished, he returned the rag to his pocket and strode toward the payment counter. And if he heard the moaning which drifted from the living quarters above, he gave no sign.

Reaching beneath the counter, he pulled out the plaque and a clean cloth. Carefully, he wiped the wood free of dust, then held it up for Thomas' inspection.

The oval–shaped maple glowed from its polishing. A grooved border enhanced the CSA which stood a good half inch from the muted background.

"Dandy. Jist plumb dandy," Thomas spat, continuing to glare at Daniel.

But the gray eyes which met his were void of emotion.

"Your father can make a set of new shoes for Boots or—"

"I'm payin cash. Real money." And Thomas slapped a Missouri three dollar bill on the counter.

For a second Daniel simply stared at the bill while the face of former Governor Jackson stared back at him. Then calmly, he reached below the counter.

Thomas shifted warily fingering the butt of his Colt .36 which protruded from the band of his trousers, barely concealed by his worn vest. Let him try an pull somethin, the scoundrel. Jist let him try, an I'll blast half thet face away, beard an all.

But Daniel merely placed a used cigar box atop the counter. Opening it, he carefully put the bill inside, then slipped it back beneath the counter. He wrapped the plaque in a soft cloth then and handed it to Thomas.

"Thank you," he said. "Please trade with us again sometime."

Thomas bristled. "Now, jist a minute. Who do you think you are anyways, actin so high an mighty? I'll not trade with you or any other damn Fed if I can help it."

But the eyes which met his were as vacant as before.

❖ ❖ ❖

It was after supper and once again Thomas sat on the log bench beneath the oak tree. Whatever ailed thet Daniel Lewis, anyways? Why, in all his born days he'd never met a feller the likes of him. Jist plumb—

"Aye, Lad, it's a fine evenin, to be sure."

Thomas started as a burly hand touched his shoulder. My Pa must be thinkin serious like, he reckoned. Why else would he mosey beyond the back porch after supper?

"Aye, Lad, I reckon you're feelin right bad about now." Michael seated himself beside his son. "Can't say as I blame you, mind. Missouri lost any way you look at it."

"You're damn right we did. An it ain't fair."

"Aye, Lad, thet it ain't. Still an all, the War is done. We can't keep fightin."

"Oh yes, we can." Thomas stood then and glared down at his pa. "Anyways, the War ain't over yet fur me."

"Aye, Lad, I know you're a mite upset. An thet's natural enough, I reckon, seein as how you lost your best friend an all. Still, I'm thinkin we'd best go on. Put it behind us like."

"Well, I won't!"

"Aye, Lad, I ain't aimin to change you mind. But thet there plaque over the mantle—it's got to go."

For a second Thomas glared defiantly at his pa. But the steel in those usually kind eyes demanded obedience.

Ten minutes later he stood in his upstairs bedroom, plaque in hand, wishing he lived in a cooler place. It was plumb stiflin up here. Reminded him of thet Anderson House in September of '61. Only now it was August of '65. An the War was over.

"Like Hell it is," he muttered. Then without even bothering to remove his boots, he stood on his bed and yanked down the Bible verse he'd printed years ago. "Thou shalt not kill" was replaced by CSA.

Across the room, he studied the maple plaque with pride. It looked plumb good hangin there. Missouri an CSA—they belonged together. Anyways, fur him they did. Fact was, thet Stars an Bars belonged there too. Only he didn't have one. Course he might git someone to make him one. Aunt Jane would do a dandy job. Still, she'd probably take on about the War bein over like My Pa did. My Ma wasn't worth thinkin on. Why, she couldn't stitch a shirt thet buttoned straight. Still, there must be someone—

Thomas wiped his sweaty forehead with a blue bandanna. As he slipped it back into his pocket, he remembered a red one. A red bandanna disappearin neath clods of dirt. Wade. Jist thinkin on him made a feller git all choked up like. Still, Wade loved Missouri. Fact was, if he was here he'd find a way to git thet Stars an Bars. Even if it meant askin Julia. Julia? Course she was the one to ask. It was jist plumb dumb of him not to think on her before. An she'd do it, he reckoned, fur Wade.

Smiling, Thomas turned and clattered down the stairs.

Chapter 2

Scarlet and gold leaves crunched beneath their feet as Jane and Katie stepped along Main Street. Jane breathed deeply, inhaling the crisp autumn air along with the tangy scent of apples. My but thet fruit in her basket looked invitin. Not as invitin as a cup of strong tea though.

Land sakes, how long had it been since she'd had real tea, anyways? Before the War, she reckoned. Course there'd been sassafras tea aplenty. But thet didn't count. Why, thet bark stuff was downright weak compared to the stout brew Claudia made. An tonight she'd have Claudia fix her some. Course Jordana wouldn't take kindly to thet. Fact was, her sister didn't take kindly to anyone amessin about in her kitchen. (Except fur clearin up, of course. Jordana never tidied up afterward.) She wouldn't like it either when Jane invited Claudia to sip tea with her. But Jane didn't much care what Jordana thought. She was jist a stick–in–the–mud, anyways. Besides, Claudia was her friend.

Shifting her basket to her left arm, Jane frowned. She reckoned she'd never furgit thet day the Douglas family left their farm in Kentucky. Scared she was, even if she was a big girl of five. An Claudia too. Why, they'd clung to each other like they was adrownin. But James wasn't scared. Fact was, he seemed downright happy like, as he rode his horse beside the wagon. Showed off he did, alaughin an ateasin.

But he wasn't laughin thet day two years later when he found Pa in the hemp field. Dead, he was. Murdered, James had said. An right quick like he sold off Adrian, Claudia's coal–black pa. Claudia had shook fur hours thet day. And Jane had shook too. Later though, Jane commenced to wondering. Had Adrian *really* killed Pa? Or had it been Harry, Claudia's older brother?

Poor Harry. Too bad thet mob strung him up before they could even try him. Course he wasn't a Douglas by then. Thet rape happened years later, after James had sold the farm an run off to find gold.

An James' leavin hadn't bothered her one bit. Why land sakes, she never missed him. Leastwis not like Jordana did. It was Robert, Jane missed. Robert Saylor, James' best friend. Even now, purt near fifteen years later, her heart beat faster jist thinkin on him. Tall, lanky an shy, he was. Still an all, he *had* noticed her. More than once them dark eyes had caused her right cheek to color up as red as her left one. Fact was, she had hoped—

"Good morning, Miss Douglas, Miss Katie," a kind, if emotionless voice interrupted Jane's thoughts. It was Daniel Lewis of course, atippin his stovepipe hat an agoin on. Jane sighed, wishin he'd stop an talk sometimes. Still an all, you couldn't blame him none. Why accordin to town gossip, his ma was a mite touched in the head. Downright crazy, some said.

At the corner of Main and Spring Streets, Jane put down her basket of apples and took the bag of pecans from Katie. "Go on in there now an see if we got some mail. An don't dilly dally atalkin to Bonnie."

"I won't." And Katie skipped into Chapman's Dry Goods, the tips of her braids bouncing beneath her knitted cap.

As Katie disappeared from view, Jane smiled. My but thet child an Bonnie did git along. Thet second boy, Thane, was nice enough too, even if he was a mite shy. Too bad their pa had got killed. But land sakes, even if they was Feds, Jane felt sorry fur them. Course she didn't cotton to thet young Will arunnin the store these days. Awful uppity, he was. Still an all, she reckoned Minnie couldn't mind the store by herself.

"Drat it all, no mail. An Bonnie wasn't there either." Katie pouted as she took her bag back from Jane. "An I wanted to see her somethin awful like. Really an truly I did."

"Why land sakes, Child, don't carry on so. You'll see her again soon. But right now we'd best git along to Crawford's." And Jane, picking up her basket, strode swiftly down Spring Street.

Crawford's Grocery seemed almost quiet when Jane and Katie entered. Only a few men lounged by the pot–bellied stove. And Jane ignored these as she strode toward the counter to deposit her basket. Katie placed her pecans on the counter too, then turned toward the candy jars.

"Good mornin, Miss Douglas. What can I git fur you today?" Dudley

Crawford cleared his throat as he approached the counter.

"Well, let's see now, I'll have two pounds of oatmeal, an ounce of cinnamon, a half pound each of coffee an tea an a quarter pound of sugar. Oh, an a licorice fur Katie."

"Fur me? Oh my goodness. Why thanks, Aunt Jane. I'll love you fur ever an ever. Really an truly I will." Katie beamed as she twirled on one foot, her long arms extended.

Jane smiled then, thankin the good Lord thet the child was happy. She frowned though, when snatches of the conversation by the stove reached her ears.

"Say, y'all hear about thet there raid on Chapman's place last night?"

"Yep. Serves em right too." Uriah Martin spoke coldly.

"Sure does. Did the boys take anything much?"

"Naw." This from Tevis McKinley as he shot a stream of tobacco juice toward the sand around the stove. "Jist a couple of blankets an some grub. Thet young Will was too quick fur em."

"A chip off the old block, eh?"

"Reckon so. Course thet little gal is right spunky too—"

Jane, from her place beside the counter, fumed. Land sakes, couldn't them men see they was ascarin poor Katie? Didn't they know Bonnie was her best friend? Why, the child was ahuggin herself like she was afreezin. An thet little chin was aquiverin too. Fact was, if thet Uriah an Tevis wasn't such good buddies to Thomas, she jist might march right over there an give them both a tongue lashin.

"Speakin of the enemy, here comes dumb–bell Fudd."

The words were barely spoken when a wizened old man stepped into the store. Closing the door carefully behind him, he tottered toward the stove.

"Mornin," he nodded toward the party, his head continuing to shake. "A mite chilly out there," he offered.

"So tis."

The group grew silent then, except for Tevis who aimed a stream of tobacco juice at Harvey Fudd's boots. It missed by inches.

The old man turned away then, his face crimson, his head still shaking. Then spotting Jane and Katie, he smiled.

"Mornin, Miss Jane, Miss Katie."

"Good mornin," Jane smiled in return. "Fact is, it does seem down-right chilly out there."

At this, Mr. Fudd beamed, then turned toward the candy jars.

"Julia!" Mr. Crawford called his daughter who was stocking shelves toward the back.

"Yes, Papa." Julia descended the ladder and hurried toward the front. Then seeing Mr. Fudd, she slowed her pace. Her skirts barely brushed the wood floor as she reluctantly slipped behind the counter.

"What'll it be today?" she asked resignedly.

"Well, I've got these here apples an some feathers." He placed two knarled winesaps on the counter, then dug into his trouser pockets for what were obviously sparrow feathers.

"Sure." But Julia ignored the offerings.

"An I want some of thet there candy." He touched a dirty finger to the jar of peppermint sticks.

Julia removed the lid, extracted a stick and shoved it toward the old man.

"Huge sale there, Miss Crawford."

As the men beside the stove guffawed, Julia beat a hasty retreat to her ladder.

Mr. Fudd, his head shaking more than ever, stuck the candy between his toothless gums and sucked noisily. Already saliva was seeping from the corners of his mouth. He turned again toward the party by the stove.

Mr. Crawford cleared his throat. "Mr. Fudd, uh—" he coughed lightly, then tried again. "Mr. Fudd, I think you'd best move along now."

For a moment Harvey Fudd's head ceased shaking as he stared at the store owner, a look of pain crossing his face. Then sucking the peppermint with renewed vigor, he slowly made his way to the door.

Jane's heart went with him. Why land sakes, even if he was a Fed, he was a person. What was the matter with folks, anyways?

"Them men was jist plain mean, wasn't they, Aunt Jane?" Katie asked as minutes later she and Jane left the store.

"No, Child. Jist a mite unkind, thet's all." Still, Jane wished them men had been nicer. After all, Mr. Fudd was worth carin fur jist like other folks. Like Katie here, or Claudia.

At the thought of her friend, Jane stepped lighter. Fur tonight she an Claudia would sit an sip real tea. An she reckoned if she tried hard enough she jist might git Claudia to talkin.

Chapter 3

The door closed heavily as Michael Fitzsimmons left the cabinet shop. Inside, Livingston Lewis slid the order for a new rocker into a cigar box, then returned to the finishing table. He needed to finish staining that washstand before closing time.

Puffing on his Havana, he picked up a soft cloth and, rubbing mahogany stain into the finely sanded pine, allowed his thoughts to follow the man who'd just left. Michael Fitzsimmons was a fine man. A mighty fine man. Too bad he'd been conscripted by the Union. But then so had lots of other men. In a way Livingston admired them. It couldn't be easy, fighting for a cause you didn't believe in. Even so, Michael had not allowed the injustice to embitter him. He'd returned home and continued loving people just as he always had. For Michael loved everyone, even his freed–man, Andrew.

At the thought of the ex–slave, Livingston bit down on his long cigar. Lord, he hated darkies. Had ever since he was a four–year–old boy back in Harrisonburg, Virginia. Ah, but he'd felt proud that day. Mighty proud. For Father was taking him to have his first hair cut. He'd done fine too, sitting very still while the old darkie clipped his thick hair. Then it was Father's turn. Livingston had been fascinated when the old man laid his father back and lathered up his face. He'd been a bit scared though when he saw that razor stropped. And that fear turned to outright terror when the old darkie nicked his father's face.

His father was dying. He knew it. For a crimson ribbon trickled across the snowy lather and down those long, dark fingers. Any minute now his father would stop breathing. Instead, he'd laughed. *Laughed*, while Livingston stood rigid with fear. And then Livingston had cried. Cried like

14

he never had before. Father was safe. But Father was angry too. He'd scolded him afterward for being a baby, like Nettie.

Well, scolding or no, from that day on Livingston had avoided darkies. And across the years his fear had changed first to contempt, then to outright hatred. He despised those folks for allowing themselves to be treated like animals. Didn't they have any sense of dignity at all? Evidently not, for it had taken a white President to free them. And now a white Congress was trying to make them citizens. Incredible. Let them earn their own way.

Tapping ashes into the sand about the pot–bellied stove, Livingston pulled out his watch. 5:45. He might as well start cleaning up, he supposed. He did wish though, that Daniel would get back with that load of wood. It had looked like rain all afternoon and that March wind was rising. Of course Daniel was always careful. Even so—

Returning the jar of stain to its place on the shelf, Livingston took down the turpentine and began to clean his hands. Puffing easily on his Havana, he recalled how Uncle Hayward always teased him for taking such pains in cleaning up. "You wipe them fingers like they was spun glass," he'd said. Yet, despite his joshing, Livingston had liked the older man. Even so, he couldn't go along with the idea that George Washington's descendant was a disgrace simply because he'd joined the Secessionists. But Uncle Hayward did. He'd been jubilant too, when John Augustine Washington III was killed. And even more thrilled when Hampshire County became part of that new state, West Virginia. Maybe it was because of Uncle Hayward that Daniel had decided to fight for the Union. The boy had certainly idolized him, back in Romney.

But Livingston wasn't really a Union man. Maybe that was because his roots were in Harrisonburg rather than Romney. Virginia was his home. And when he'd heard how General Sheridan's men had ravaged that lush Shenandoah Valley, he had bled a little inside.

Ah yes, he was glad, more glad than he could say, that he hadn't been there to witness the destruction. His father's account had been real enough. And full of heartbreak. For Father was a Union man. A strong Union man. And his opposition to slavery had cost him dearly. For Jeremiah Lewis had been barred from the church pulpit where he had served so long and faithfully. He was a broken man, a mighty broken man by the time the War was over.

Yet, despite his father's setbacks, Livingston had no intention of going to see him. For Father hated him. He knew it. And though he'd always suspected it, he'd known for sure the day his little sister, Nettie, was killed. For his father had blamed him. *Him*, Livingston, who loved Nettie so much. He'd loved her as though she was part of himself, letting her tag along when he went out on errands or simply to play.

Biting his Havana, Livingston groaned as he recalled how negligent he'd been that afternoon in the fall of 1828. But he and Gale had got to playing. And he was having such fun chasing his friend that he forgot he was supposed to buy yeast for his mother. And he forgot to watch out for Nettie. Even so, how was he to know the farmers would choose that day to drive their cattle south? Then suddenly the cattle were out of control, stampeding through the square.

It was then Livingston remembered Nettie. Where was she? Frantic, he'd searched beneath broken porch railings, toppled bricks and scattered leaves. At last he'd found her near the Court House. Dead.

And so his father had beat him. Smack, slap, slam, went the razor strop. Whack, whip, wham! It sliced again, cutting his legs and buttocks. Holding himself as rigid as possible and trying not to cry, Livingston felt he would die if it didn't end soon. And then it did. For his mother had screamed for Father to stop. Nevertheless, the damage was done. For ten–year–old Livingston vowed never to forgive his father. He never forgave himself either for neglecting Nettie. Or for being so sentimental as to love her in the first place.

Laying aside his cleaning rag, Livingston crossed the room to the payment counter. There he carefully reviewed the day's transactions. Everything seemed in order. He closed the ledger then, latched the front door and snuffed out the lamps. Picking up a lantern, he trudged up the stairs.

At the top of the stairway, Livingston opened a door and entered his sitting room. Lighting a lamp, he studied Verna Marie. Ah, but he'd be glad, more glad than he could say, if only she'd get well again. Yet, she sat as always in the overstuffed chair by the window, staring down at Bridge Street.

Livingston touched her then, gently on the shoulder. She responded as usual, whimpering and turning her heavy face away from him. Biting on his Havana, Livingston stooped to rearrange the quilt about her thick ankles, recalling as he did so how slim those limbs used to be.

It was in the spring of 1836 that he had met her, at a hardware store in Romney. He was attracted to her from the start, for she was a lovely young lady. Mighty lovely. Petite, with a tiny waist and small breasts, she aroused his protective instincts. And from her tear–filled eyes it appeared she would need protection.

"Her Daddy just died a month ago," Uncle Hayward explained. "And she's not strong like her mother."

Having recently lost his own mother, Livingston understood how bereft Verna Marie must feel. Even so, he wanted to get on with life. He wanted to make Verna Marie happy as well as protect her. And apparently he succeeded. For within a matter of weeks she was smiling as she fluttered about the store. A year later they were married.

Standing, Livingston tossed the butt of his Havana into the pot–bellied stove and reached for another one. Clipping the end and lighting it, he sighed. Ah, but Verna Marie's happiness had been short–lived. For the following year she'd given birth to a tiny baby girl. Stillborn. And Verna Marie had wept. She'd wept for months. Finally though, Livingston had convinced her to go on.

Heavier, but still lovely, Verna Marie had gravitated back into society. Then in 1839 a son was born. He too, failed to live. But this time, when they buried the boy beside his sister, Verna Marie didn't weep. Instead, she drew into herself, forming a tight knot inside an increasingly heavy body. Ah, but Livingston had been glad, more glad than he could say, when in the summer of 1840 another son was born. Daniel.

From the first, Livingston loved him. For he was a good boy. A mighty good boy. But if Livingston loved him, Verna Marie positively doted on him, the cherub sweetness of his baby face reflected in her own plump one.

For seven years Daniel was the center of his mother's universe. And then another girl was born. And died. Again, Verna Marie withdrew. From her mother, her friends, Livingston, even Daniel. Thus it was for his son that Livingston decided to move the family. He would do anything to ensure the boy's happiness. They would travel to Indiana, Illinois, Kentucky, Missouri—anywhere so long as it was away from Virginia.

Had the move to Brownsville been a mistake? Puffing on his cigar, Livingston sighed. He couldn't be sure. For Brownsville was a far cry from Romney. Even so, once they were settled in, Verna Marie seemed happy. Though she'd gained still more weight, she seemed content enough with her church and new friends. And Daniel, of course.

And then in '54 another girl was born. When she lived, they named her Joy. For they loved her. Yet, even as Livingston adored his daughter, he ached for his son. Daniel had been replaced in his mother's affections. A gangling teenager now, he couldn't possibly compete with a plump, rosy–

cheeked infant.

Biting on his Havana, Livingston recalled the perpetual hurt in his son's eyes as Verna Marie lavished her love on Joy. It was then that he decided to take Daniel into his shop. Ah, and he'd been glad, more glad than he could say, when Daniel fell in love with woodworking. And he was good. Mighty good. Those long fingers of his caressed a piece of wood like it was the most precious thing on earth. And the warmth of the wood seemed to seep into the boy, making him almost happy.

Over the next three years Daniel seemed to forget that Joy had taken his mother's affections . He loved his little sister. And Joy loved him. Big brother gradually became as important as Mama. That's why one morning she followed him down to the shop.

Clinching his Havana between his tobacco–stained teeth, Livingston admitted that he had been negligent that day. He should have sent her back upstairs. But he hadn't. For Joy was a beautiful child. Mighty beautiful. Her brunette curls and lively chatter reminded him so much of his own sister, Nettie, that he liked having her around.

He was busy with a customer and Daniel was planing a spindle when it happened. A choking sound. By the time he realized it was Joy, Daniel had dropped the plane and flung his sister over his lap. He'd beat her on the back then. Hard. But still she choked—on the sawdust she'd tried to eat.

With the death of Joy, Verna Marie turned inward again. She seemed oblivious to those about her as she plodded through the days. But the nights were worse. Lord, how many times had Livingston awakened to find his wife gone? How many times had he traipsed to the cemetery to find her there, staring silently at Joy's grave?

It was in the spring of 1858 that Verna Marie had been permanently changed. Once again, Livingston had awakened in the middle of the night to find her gone. And he was tired that night. Mighty tired. Even so, he hauled himself out of bed and pulled on his trousers. He even took time to light a new Havana before picking up the lantern and going out. But that night she wasn't at the cemetery. Worried, Livingston had called her name softly as he paced among the tombstones. But there had been no answer. He'd searched for her then, on Patrick Street, Brown, Bridge and even Main Street. To no avail.

Lord, but he was worried when he arrived back home. Mighty worried. And then there'd come a banging on the shop door. Livingston had hurried down to find an unconscious Verna Marie in Will Chapman's arms.

"She's been hurt," his friend said. "We heard her out in front of the house. Wife made me bring her in." He glanced away from Livingston then. "I seen a nigger buck runnin away. Couldn't tell whose."

Remembering, Livingston chomped down on his Havana with such force, he bit it in two. Picking up the burned end from the carpet, he flung it into the stove. Lord, he'd been angry that night. Mighty angry. For the rips in Verna Marie's waist and the blood on her skirts told the story. She'd been raped. A darkie had defiled his wife.

It was several weeks before they found the culprit, a buck named Harry who'd escaped from the old Douglas farm east of town. By June he and two other slaves had been arraigned and were awaiting trial. When Livingston got word, he saddled Boots and set out for Marshall. He arrived at the jail just in time to see the prisoners being dragged out by a mob. Lord, it felt good to see that Harry strung up. Mighty good. Livingston had stood, lightly puffing on his Havana, and smiled as Harry struggled before breathing his last.

But Harry's hanging hadn't helped Verna Marie. She remained in a stupor. Hour after hour, day after day, she sat by the window, staring into space, never acknowledging her husband or son.

Ah well, maybe someday she'd be better. Livingston sighed as he trudged into the kitchen. In the meantime, he wished Daniel would get home. He was worried about that boy. Mighty worried. Every since the War he'd pulled into himself, staring vacantly at the world. It seemed as though part of him had died somewhere. Livingston would give anything to help his son. But Daniel had shut him out.

Biting his Havana, Livingston added wood to the kitchen stove, then took out a skillet for frying ham. He was mixing up a batch of biscuits when a crash caused him to jump. A crash, then the sound of splintering glass. Wiping his hands on a towel, he hurried to open the sitting room door. It happened again then. And again. And again. Biting his cigar, Livingston sighed. Lord, they'd finally got him too.

He had started down the stairs when Verna Marie began whining. "No," she begged. "Please, oh please, leave me alone."

Instantly, Livingston turned and strode back up the stairs. By the time he reached his wife she was shouting and flailing the air. Firmly, Livingston grasped the heavy hands.

"No," she screamed. "Leave me alone."

Removing his Havana, Livingston knelt before her, speaking gently. "It's all right, Dear. Everything's fine now. You're safe with me,

Livingston. I won't let anyone hurt you."

"Daddy?" The pudgy face lighted. "Daddy, is that you?"

"Yes," Livingston choked. "Yes, Dear, it's Daddy."

Verna Marie quieted then and closed her eyes. Moments later she slept.

With unsteady hands, Livingston drew the quilt more firmly about his wife then reached for his Havana. Biting on the cigar, he quietly made his way downstairs. Lord only knew what he'd find there.

It was dark when Daniel returned. Inside the barn, he unhitched the gray and the black, rubbed them down, then measured out oats. He moved to Boots' stall and gave the chestnut an apple, patting him as he ate. God, it felt good to rest a minute. He'd leave the unloading for morning.

He'd just closed the barn door when several figures came flying around the corner. "Out of the way, you damn Fed!" And a body plowed into him, knocking him to the ground.

Dazed, Daniel sat for a moment trying to collect himself. Thomas Fitzsimmons he'd recognized. The rest he didn't know. He only hoped they weren't harassing Union families again. Ah well, what was it to him? He rose then, dusted off his trousers and collected his lantern.

Turning the corner, he stopped. Shards of glass glistened on the packed ground. Stepping carefully, Daniel made his way to a window. Through jagged holes his saw his father taking inventory.

"Father?"

"That you, Daniel?"

"Of course. Let me in."

Inside, Daniel saw glass everywhere. Nothing else appeared damaged though. Even so, to replace all those window panes—

"Well, I hope you're planning to pay for this."

The contempt in his father's voice jarred Daniel. "I don't understand."

"Sure you do. You know this is Secesh doing. Now, didn't you fight for the Union?"

Mystified by his father's attitude, Daniel turned away. Of course he had fought for the Union. He believed in it, pure and simple. Didn't his father believe too? His Uncle Hayward certainly did. Ah well, what difference did it make now? The War was over.

Silently, Daniel walked to the back room and picked up a broom. Returning to the front of the shop, he mechanically began sweeping up glass.

Chapter 4

A mild May breeze stirred the muslin curtains as Thomas stood before his cracked bedroom mirror struggling to tie a cravat. Darn thet thing, anyways. He reckoned he'd jist lap it over like, an let it go at thet. Anyways, Julia was bound to like his pin–striped trousers, even if they was a mite worn. An she must like him too, seein as how she let him come courtin. Course she did have a dandy eye fur detail—

Thomas paused then and glanced across the room to where the Stars and Bars was draped above the head of his bed. It made a feller feel plumb proud to see thet hangin there. Why, Julia had sewed them crimson an white bars an them seven white stars to look purt near as good as the one they'd raised at Lexington.

Course he hadn't seen it himself. He'd been lyin in thet stiflin third floor of the Anderson House moanin with a fever an the loss of his arm. But he'd heard about it sure enough. He'd heard thet Governor Jackson gave Mulligan an his damn Feds a dandy little speech, all about the State Guards carin fur their own. Most made a feller feel plumb proud jist bein a part of it. An now, purt near five years later, he still felt proud. His cravat fixed to the best of his ability, Thomas reached for his worn vest. Slipping his stump through the right arm hole, he almost wished he'd decided to go with the boys this evening. Sounded excitin like, them pranks Uriah aimed to pull on Fed stores.

At the thought of Uriah Martin, Thomas' lips curved upward. It made a feller feel plumb important havin him fur a friend. Course they'd knowed each other before the War, Uriah bein the miller's son an all. Still, in them days Wade—

Wade. Thomas' lips straightened to a taut line. Damn him. Why had

21

he gone an got himself killed fur, anyways? It jist didn't seem right, the gang meetin without him. Take this here Honest Men's League now. Wade would have laughed at thet fur certain. "They ain't no honest Feds," he'd say. An the rest would agree. Why, no feller in this here town or any other could stop Missouri boys from doin what they'd a mind to do.

Thomas' lips curved upward again as he recalled the previous evening. They'd met after dark at the mill, him an Uriah an Tevis an Melvin, Uriah bein sure his Pa was done fur the day. Wonderin, they'd gone on fur a time about how folks was gittin arrested fur hasslin Feds.

Then Tevis, mischievous like, had drawled. "Aw, thet marshal ain't goin to bother the likes of us. Fact is, I jist feel like singin. How's about old 'Joe Stiner'?"

They'd laid into it then, all of them stompin the wood floor an shakin fists at imaginary Feds.

> *My name is Joe Stiner*
> *I come from Amsterdam;*
> *I am a full–blooded Dutch man*
> *From that there is no sham...*
> *One day as I was drinking*
> *Mine glass of lager beer,*
> *And thinking of no danger*
> *In this great country here,*
> *They all cries out "This Union,"*
> *"This Union!" very loud.*
> *And they makes us walk together*
> *In one very big Dutch crowd.*
> *Now they say we got to fight*
> *This Union for to save,*
> *Mine God and Himmel did I think*
> *Such a country we should have...*
> *They say that Price has got*
> *Most all his secessionists*
> *Camped way down on Crane creek*
> *'Twas in a pretty fix.*
> *And so we goes down there*
> *Within about four miles,*
> *When our batteries they did crack*
> *And our rifles they did play.*
> *What I seen there*

> *I never shall forget,*
> *Seemed like the ground was all alive*
> *With secessionists.*
> *Their blamed old rifles shot so true,*
> *I can not tell you why.*
> *They strike us in our stomachs*
> *And they hit us in our eyes.*
> *They kills our General Lyon*
> *And they makes our Siegel run*
> *Solomon hid in the college,*
> *I tell you it was no fun.*
> *They kills our men, they took our guns,*
> *They knocked us into fits.*
> *And many a prisoner, too, they took*
> *But I gets up and gets—*[1]

At this point, Melvin had whipped out his pistol and shot a hole through the window glass. Instantly, the other three had drawn their own weapons.

"What you see out there Old Boy?" Uriah had asked, his steel eyes fastened on Melvin.

"Shadders. Must be some critter sneakin around like. Up to no good, I figure."

"Well, we'd best look around then." And Uriah had led the way down the stairs and outside. Fur nearly half an hour they'd looked, checkin tall grass, wadin in the creek, even climbin on the wheel. An they hadn't found a thing. Back inside, Tevis grinned. "What'd I tell you? They ain't fixin to cart us off to no jail. Come on, let's git back to singin." And he started off again.

> *Now I am in Springfield,*
> *My legs were almost broke,*
> *And for the want of lager beer*
> *I was so nearly choked.*
> *This blamed old secessionist country,*
> *Will never do for me,*
> *I vamish runs, I gets away,*
> *For the city of St. Louis.*
> *When I gets there*
> *May I be roasted done,*
> *If ever I shoot secessionist again*

For money, love or fun...[2]

Thomas found himself humming that same ballad as he slipped on his tattered coat. Turning to the mirror, he surveyed himself one last time. Patting his brunette waves into place, he smiled. Looked right smart he did, even if one sleeve was pinned up like. Picking up his pipe then, he dropped it into his pocket and strode toward the stairs.

In the Crawford's parlor, Thomas shifted nervously. Aside from bein too warm, the ghost of Wade made him feel uneasy like. A feller could go plumb crazy rememberin them darin dark eyes an thet impish smile. Course Wade had never set much store by Julia. Still, she was his sister. After all—

Thomas' thoughts were interrupted by the sound of Mr. Crawford clearing his throat. "Well, Son, how's the blacksmith business these days?"

"Well, uh—" Darn it, anyways. Why did everyone have the idea he took to the smithy? Jist cause My Pa was a blacksmith didn't mean he aimed to be one. Why, he never even bothered with the place cept to make bullets.

"Uh—fact is, Mr. Crain had several horses shod last week. Purt near six of them, I reckon."

"I see." Mr. Crawford pressed a foot to the floor and his rocker moved gently.

Thomas reached into his pocket then and removed his pipe and tobacco. Once he'd finally managed to get it filled and lit he felt better. Turning to Julia, who sat on his left, he asked, "How's things goin at the store?"

"Fine," she said, keeping her eyes on the embroidery hoop in her lap. "Leastwise they would be if it wasn't fur thet dumb Harvey Fudd."

Mr. Crawford coughed nervously. "Can't say but what I agree with you there. Course I like him well enough an all. Still, he is a Fed—"

As the older man pressed the floor to move his rocker again, Thomas relaxed. Crossing his legs, he studied the woman beside him. My but she was purty. Them delicate hands an slender waist an shapely breasts made him feel all crazy like. Why, a feller could purt near find Wade in them violet eyes, he reckoned.

"What's your Pa think of them niggers bein made citizens like the rest of us?" Again, Mr. Crawford's nervous cough demanded Thomas' attention.

"Well, My Pa now, he takes to the idea."

"I see."

"Course it makes a feller kind of uneasy like, havin them about an all."

"Yes. Well, I can't say but what I agree with you there," Mr. Crawford cleared his throat. "It does kind of make a man wonder what you young fellers fought fur."

Wade.

The name hung unspoken in the air. Placing both feet on the floor, Thomas turned to Julia. What was she thinkin on, anyways? Did she miss her brother?

Julia looked up then, her dark eyes filled with apprehension. It was all Thomas could do to keep from touching her. My but a feller could go plumb silly, lookin at her this way. Fact was, with them fine lips she—

"Julia, Dear, how about some music?"

"Yes, Papa." Julia smiled then as she laid aside her pillow case and advanced to the old Broadwood piano. Seating herself on the stool, she began to play and sing.

> *A walking and a talking and a walking goes I*
> *To meet my dear lover in the meadows fair by,*
> *A walking and a talking is all my delight*
> *I can walk with my sweetheart from morning till night.*[3]

A smile curving his lips, Thomas tapped his foot in time to the music. My but them words made a feller feel fine.

> *Meeting is a pleasure but parting is a grief,*
> *And an uncontent lover is worse than a thief.*
> *For a thief can but rob you and take what you have*
> *But an uncontent lover will bring you to your grave.* [4]

Thomas frowned. Why did she have to sing thet verse fur, anyways? It made a feller feel all sad like. Course it was only a ballad. Still, he felt a mite better when she was done.

And he felt better yet when, half an hour later, Julia handed him a cup of tea. And smiled. Quickly, he set his cup and saucer aside and reached for her hand. Then just as quickly he drew back. My but he'd purt near furgot thet her Pa was watchin. Still, thet smile made a feller feel plumb good. An someday Julia would be his fur the askin. Until then he'd jist have to be acceptin like, he reckoned.

But bein acceptin like wasn't what Thomas wanted. He wanted Julia. Now. He needed her somethin awful like. Fact was, he plumb ached to feel the woman of her. He reckoned if he could have her he could git goin again an furgit thet other Crawford. The one thet slept neath the sod of Bloody Hill. Lifting his left hand, Thomas brushed his coat sleeve across his eyes. Darn it all, anyways. Why did it have to hurt so bad fur? Why?

At home, he decided against going inside. What was the use, anyways? A feller could go crazy like, tossin an turnin on thet hot straw tick. Outside was better. A feller could breathe like out here.

Cutting across the back of the lot, Thomas strolled past the root cellar, the apple trees and the woodshed. Rounding the corner of the house, he stopped outside the kitchen window, beneath the cherry tree.

Solemnly, he reached up and snapped off the tip of a branch. In the dappled moonlight, he could see the pointed, stiff leaves and the small, hard fruit. Curling his fingers about the greenery, he sighed. Growin things. Food fur the family. Thet's what he wanted to do. My Pa would work in thet smithy until his dyin day, he reckoned. But Thomas wouldn't. *He* would care fur the land. He would love this here spot of Missouri like it was his very own. Anyways, it would be someday. An then Julia—

C–r–e–a–k. The sound of an outhouse door being opened caught Thomas' attention. He knew in an instant it wasn't the one used by the family but the one behind the blacksmith shop. Letting the twig fall from his fingers, he watched as a tall, lithe figure emerged into the moonlight. Rachel.

The outline of rounded breasts and curving haunches was more than Thomas could bear. Breathing heavily, he jerked off his cravat. Then silently he stalked the length of the garden. And just as Rachel reached the corner of the building, he pounced. Stuffing the cravat into her mouth, he shoved her to the ground, his knee coming down on the back of her neck. For one brief second he wished for his Colt .36. But it was in his chest of drawers, upstairs. Well, never mind thet. He'd git what he wanted without it.

"Hold still, you damn nigger. An don't take on screamin an cryin. Why, fur two cents I'd kill the likes of you."

But Rachel, like her mother, suffered in silence.

Awkwardly, Thomas unbuttoned his trousers, then kicked the girl onto her back. My but she was purty. Yet, even as he yanked her shift up to reveal chocolate thighs, his heart returned to a stifling August morning. Muskets fired; cannons roared; commanders barked; horses screamed; wounded shrieked; dying—

Damn. Damn. Damn. Why did Wade have to die fur, anyways? Why?

Chapter 5

Somberly, Jane stared out the dining room window. Downright hot it was. Too hot fur sittin inside an arockin. Still an all, she didn't aim to carry on before half the neighborhood. Fur Claudia was aleavin. Claudia an Andrew an Rachel were amovin. An she couldn't bear it.

Land sakes, she never dreamed such a thing could happen. Course she'd knowed somethin was wrong when last evenin at supper Michael didn't eat. Picked at his food he did, till Jordana got miffed.

"Confound it, Michael. I fixed them taters special jist fur you. What's the matter with them, anyways?"

"Aye, Colleen, the taters is fine. It's me Andrew I'm thinkin on."

"Andrew?" Jane had looked up from her plate of cornbread and pork.

"Aye, Lass. He's leavin."

"Aleavin? What do you mean, aleavin?"

"Movin. Goin to the north part of town. Says he's goin to build a cabin an set up his own smithy. A gamble, to be sure. But meself, I can't talk him out of it."

"Why?" Jane had forgotten her own supper by then.

"Aye, Lass, I don't know. Anyways, they're fixin on stayin, I reckon. Plannin on startin their own church even."

At this, Jane winced. Why land sakes, it wouldn't be Sunday without Rachel an Claudia ajoinin them fur church. Why, she'd be downright lost without her friend asingin along back there in thet balcony. Thankin the good Lord fur blessins jist wouldn't be the same no more. Not with Claudia aleavin.

Still an all, she'd amade do if Claudia had atold her. Why land sakes, they was *friends*. But Claudia hadn't said a word. Downright cold she was, as she tidied up thet kitchen after supper. Hurtin too, most likely. Fur she'd pressed them lips together till they purt near bled. Fact was, she acted jist like she'd done all them years ago when James had raped her. Only then she'd let Jane hold her. This time she hadn't. Why land sakes, she didn't even have the gumption to say good–by.

Laying a hand over the birthmark on her left cheek, Jane sighed. Somethin was wrong. Jist plain wrong. Her best friend was aleavin an she didn't even know why. An Michael? How did he feel, anyways? Why, he must be ahurtin to beat the band out there ahelpin to load thet wagon. Fur Andrew had been his friend fur years. Why land sakes, purt near every story he ever told bout thet "wee little family in the wee little house in a wee little town in Tennessee" included Andrew. "We was wee little lads when Me Uncle gave him to me," he'd say.

An now Andrew was aleavin. Andrew an Claudia an Rachel. Jane wondered how the girl felt about it all. Course she hadn't been about much lately. Feelin poorly like Claudia had said, as she toted water fur her. Fact was, she looked downright peaked as she stood beside thet wagon. Upset too. Not as upset as Claudia though. Or Andrew. Why land sakes, Andrew seemed downright mad. Why, he chomped thet wad of tobacco like it might up an run off if he stopped fur a minute.

Course things could be worse, she reckoned. Claudia could be amovin way off somewheres like other freed slaves had done. Still an all, Jane wasn't too sure about goin avisitin. Fact was, Claudia had flat out given her the cold shoulder jist fur mentionin it.

The rocker creaked then as Jane leaned closer to the window. Land sakes, after all them years of sharin hard times it *couldn't* be endin like this.

But it is. For now the wagon is loaded and Andrew is helping Rachel and Claudia onto the high board seat. He takes his place beside them then and lays the whip to an old gray mare. The horse strains and the wagon begins to move. Michael waves, calling, "Aye, friends, good luck to you now." But the rigid forms on the wagon don't acknowledge the send off. The wagon creaks forward, its wooden spokes rolling slowly past the window of the plank house facing Main Street.

Inside, Jane ceases rocking. Staring after the disappearing wagon, she recalls the words of an old song folks used to sing back in Kentucky.

Oh my darling Nellie Gray,
They have taken you away,
And I'll never see my darling anymore.
I'm sitting by the river,

And I'm watching all the day,
For you've gone from my old Kentucky shore.[1]

Course them words was put down years ago when white folks traded slaves purt near as much as they traded livestock. An them days is past. Still an all, Claudia is aleavin. Her best friend is amovin off. An who knows when Jane is apt to see her again?

Chapter 6

Grunting, Jordana yanked the rope tied to the brimming bucket, then sat back on her knees, her arms aching. My but thet thing was heavy. Purt nigh as heavy as an armload of wood, she reckoned. Still, she'd best git busy; them dishes wouldn't do themselves. Reluctantly, she leaned once more over the well. When the bucket was nearly to the top, she gave a final heave and pulled it to the surface.

Setting the pail on the wooden platform, Jordana sighed. My but it was hot. Still early mornin it was, an she was sweatin already. Wiping her face on her apron, she carefully placed the wooden cover over the well and began working at the knot on the rope. Ten minutes later the handle was free. Lifting the bucket, she set off for the kitchen, slopping water with every step.

Confound them niggers! Why did they have to leave fur, anyways? Here it was still early an she was plumb tuckered out already. Course Katie would help with the tidyin up. But Jane wouldn't, thet was fur certain. Why, whatever ailed her sister, anyways? Sittin in her chair she was, jist starin at her sewin like it wasn't even there. An her hair. My but it was a mess, all comin lose in back an fallin round her face like. An all because of them niggers. Why in the world she took on so over their leavin Jordana jist couldn't figure out. Course Jane always had stuck up fur folks thet wasn't no good. Still—

On the porch, Jordana plunked down the bucket and plopped into a cane–bottom chair. She had need of rest. After all, there was jist so much a body could do. But she'd only begun to relax when Mamie appeared. Dressed in a clean calico, she obviously planned to go visiting.

"Ain't it a mite early fur gaddin about?" Jordana asked coolly, eyeing her oldest daughter.

"I'm goin to fetch the mail."

"In your next best dress?"

But Mamie never answered. Ignoring her mother, she padded across the porch and down the path, her full skirt swaying.

"Confound you, Girl, if you're thinkin on turnin thet Daniel Lewis' head, then you've got another thought comin. Cause he ain't about to take up with the likes of you." Jordana had risen now and was shaking a finger at the retreating figure.

Slowly, her demeanor registering disdain, Mamie turned around. Leaning a slender arm on the fence rail, she studied her ma through cool, green eyes. "I'll buy you some horehound drops," she purred. And with that, she picked up her skirts and slinked across the road.

Sighing, Jordana dropped back into her chair. Thet girl. Where had she got thet crazy notion of wantin Daniel Lewis' attention, anyways? Didn't she remember he was a Fed? An Mamie hated Feds. Why, ever since Patrick's death—

Patrick. Despite the warm weather, Jordana shivered. Course she'd knowed from the start thet thet War was no good. Hadn't Thomas come home all tore up like? Confound them Feds! Why had they come fur Michael, anyways? Couldn't they see he wasn't the fightin kind? An Patrick. Couldn't they see thet *he* was jist a boy? Couldn't they see thet she had need of him?

But the Federals hadn't considered what anyone needed that day. They'd simply taken: Jordana's husband, her foodstuffs and her son. And it was the loss of the son that had hurt the most. For even now, over three years later, cool fingers brushed her heart when she thought of Patrick. Jist plumb awful he'd looked thet day, lyin on her bed an bleedin. Dead, he was. An she was powerless to bring him back. Her sandy–haired, freckle–faced, adventure–lovin son was gone. Furever. Shiverin, she'd climbed them stairs an crawled into Jane's bed. An still she shook. Cold, she was. Too cold to move. Too cold to attend the funeral, thet was fur certain. Why, she reckoned it'd be weeks before she'd feel warm again. And so it had been. Weeks and months. And then a year had passed. An entire year it took for Jordana to decide she was able to work again.

Thinking of work, Jordana sighed. She'd best git busy, she reckoned. Katie'd be needin thet water fur washin dishes an scrubbin the floor. Rising, she reached for the bucket. But just then a hen fluttered by, clucking as she went. Confound thet critter. Them hens was supposed to be penned up. After all, this wasn't the farm.

Turning to step off the porch, Jordana's foot caught the bucket. Grabbing the support post, she managed to remain upright. But the bucket toppled.

As she watched the precious liquid flow from the wooden bucket, streaming across the plank floor and dripping over the sides, Jordana sighed. Confound thet thing! Now she'd have to catch thet hen, pen her up *an* tote another bucket of water.

Twenty minutes later, a disgruntled Jordana lifted a second bucket of water from the well. Setting off for the kitchen again, she allowed her mind to recall another wooden bucket and another source of water.

It seemed so long ago now, Kentucky an thet summer of 1833. She wasn't but eight thet year when she first discovered the Big Spring. It was a Saturday an her family had gone to visit kinfolks in Glasgow. After dinner, Uncle Nathan asked cousin Carrie to fetch some fresh water.

Carrie had turned to her then. "Want to go along?" she'd asked.

Jordana nodded. Course she wanted to go. After all, she'd a mind to have fun with Carrie. An they did too, laughin an playin so much thet it wasn't no time till they got to thet spring. An then there it was—water galore comin right out of thet bluff an fallin down like to make a purty little pool.

Carrie had dropped her bucket then an dipped a tin cup into the pool. Jordana followed with a cup of her own, wonderin if the stuff was as good as Carrie seemed to think. It was. Smackin her lips, she'd guzzled thet sparklin water, then dipped her cup again fur more. An more. An more. Wonderful, it was. The most wonderful water in the whole world.

The cousins played then, tossing water on each other, squealing at the delicious, cool feeling. Thet feelin stayed too, as they meandered back to Carrie's house, totin the bucket between them. Plumb light thet bucket was, not heavy like this one she hauled from the well. Course Carrie had been there then. Carrie, with thet long flaxen hair blowin round her face. Carrie, who liked to run an dance an giggle. Carrie, who'd loved her like a sister.

Oh, Carrie. Shivering, Jordana plodded toward the back porch. She stopped for a moment, recalling the day Pa had announced they were moving.

"You mean leave Kentucky?" She'd stared at him, chilled to the bone. "Thet's what I said."

Jordana had turned away then, knowin thet it was so. Knowin thet she was powerless to change Pa's mind. But she hadn't liked it, thet was fur certain. An so she'd defied her Pa. It was their last visit to Glasgow before movin to Missouri an Pa had said they mustn't linger visitin. But she an Carrie took off fur the Spring, anyways. Freezin it was, thet cup of water she drank thet mornin in March. Freezin, but wonderful. She'd drunk till she couldn't hold no more, then shivered all the way back to Carrie's house.

She'd warmed up right quick like, though, when Pa got hold of her. He'd jerked off his belt an whipped her somethin awful. She'd cried then, wipin her eyes with her dress tail. Confound it, why did Pa have to be so mean fur, anyways? Couldn't he see thet she was hurtin? An James. How *could* he be so acceptin like? Why, he was actin plumb silly beggin to drive an all. Anyways, she wished he'd sit by her. Maybe then she'd stop shiverin. Course she wouldn't let no nigger hug her, thet was fur certain. Jane was plumb stupid to hang onto Claudia thet way. After all, them niggers wasn't actin right. Why, they was starrin ahead like nothin in the world was wrong.

But everything was wrong. They was leavin Kentucky, the Big Spring an Carrie. Confound it all, anyways. It wasn't right to leave thet way. After all, there wasn't no kinfolks in Missouri. Course she an Carrie could write letters, she reckoned.

And they did. For twenty years they exchanged greetings every month or so. Then suddenly, Carrie's letters had stopped. And Jordana didn't know why. Until she received a note from Uncle Nathan. Carrie'd died, he said, in the cholera epidemic of 1853.

Jordana set her bucket of well water on the back porch and wiped her face with her apron. Confound it all, things jist wasn't fair. Why, she'd loved Carrie. An Patrick. An she'd lost them both.

Trembling, Jordana lifted the bucket again, an sighed. Here it was nigh midmornin an she still had the breakfast dishes an sweepin up to do. Still, things wouldn't seem near so bad, she reckoned, if only Carrie was here.

Chapter 7

It was hot in the upstairs bedroom. Hot and close as Katie struggled to help Mamie make their bed.

"Oh fur heaven sakes, Katie, jist yank up thet sheet an let it go. Why bother with tuckin it all in like? No one's goin to see it, anyways." With that, Mamie flung her feather pillow onto the bed and flounced from the room.

Staring after her sister, Katie dug both fists into her waist and sighed. Drat it all, why did Mamie have to be so bossy fur, anyways? Jist cause she was purt nigh grown up didn't mean she could treat Katie like some youngin thet didn't know nothin.

Turning back to the bed, Katie pulled her side of the sheet up, smoothing out the wrinkles and tucking the ends beneath the straw tick the way Aunt Jane had showed her. Plumping her own pillow, she nodded. There. Mamie could leave her side all frumpy if she'd a mind to, but Katie wouldn't.

Crossing to the chest of drawers, Katie lifted the lid from her K box. Gently, she removed two red ribbons. Then looking into the oblong mirror, she carefully tied one on each of her long, brunette braids. She'd just finished when Mamie sauntered in.

"My Ma says you'd best hurry up. She needs you to dry dishes."

Incensed, Katie turned her back on her sister and began straightening things on the chest. Drat it all, she was at it again. Bossin her around—

"My but them is purty ribbons," Mamie purred as she sidled across the room to stand by Katie. "Most nice enough fur church goin or fur school."

At the mention of school, Katie's chin trembled. She loved school. Really an truly she did. An even if she couldn't go no more she could pretend, couldn't she?

"An I spect My Ma wants them kept fur such." With that Mamie deftly removed both ribbons. By the time Katie realized what had happened Mamie was across the room and disappearing through the doorway.

"Give me my ribbons!" Katie cried, advancing toward her svelte sister.

"Now, Katie, don't take on so. It ain't lady like." And Mamie slinked from the room.

Katie had a mind to chase after her, but she didn't. It wouldn't do no good, anyways. Once Mamie reached the kitchen My Ma would take up fur her.

Sighing, Katie turned back to her room. It wasn't fair fur Mamie to be so mean. Really an truly it wasn't. Crossing to the window, she knelt before it, studying the maple tree across Main Street. As always, the gentle sway of them huge limbs made her feel lots better. Why my goodness, if it wasn't fur thet tree over there she'd be purt nigh done in by now.

Fact was, she'd come here thet day Thomas had got home from fightin. Her chin trembled as she remembered how awful he'd looked. Thin he was, like a broom straw. An thet rag on his stump. Why, it stunk somethin awful. Still, she'd held out her arms to him. After all, he was Thomas an she loved him. Really an truly she did. But Thomas had pulled himself away from her, like she was poison or somethin. An she couldn't stand it. Fur Thomas didn't love her no more. An so she'd sat before this very window an hugged herself an cried. Drat it all, how come he'd took to thet dumb War fur, anyways?

Thet War was nothin but trouble. An the worst part was thet spring of 1863. Fur it was then thet them awful Feds had come fur My Pa. An Katie'd purt nigh come apart, her heart bein tore in little pieces like, when they'd tied My Pa up. Why my goodness, thet wasn't right. Really an truly it wasn't. Cause My Pa was the one thet told her stories. Rode her on his knee he did, tellin all about Tennessee. An every now an again he'd go over her favorite, thet one about "A wee little lad, whose wee little Dad gave him a wee little coin fur a wee little stage ride." Only now there wouldn't be no more stories. Cause they was takin My Pa away. But not before they'd shot Patrick.

Patrick. Katie wrapped her arms about herself, her chin trembling. My goodness, but she had loved him. Really an truly she had, even if he did like Mamie best. Cause Patrick was always so eager like. Why, he'd run off after Thomas an Wade when they went gaddin about. Or he'd hurry off to help My Pa soon as breakfast was over. Always in a hurry, he'd grab the first piece of cornbread or the first handful of fresh cherries, then share some with Mamie. Always together, he an Mamie was. Why my goodness, them two would swap stories an laugh till their sides ached. An then them dumb Feds had stopped it all by shootin him.

Katie felt it was her own heart bleedin thet day when she saw him lyin there on thet bed. Pale, he was. Why, them freckles looked like dots on a newly washed tea towel. An how still. My goodness, but he'd laid so still. And Katie had wept.

Later, she'd knelt before this window, hugging herself and rocking back and forth. My Pa an Patrick was gone. She'd purt nigh come all apart thet day. Till she saw them leaves across the way. Pale green they was, an brushin thet blue sky like they was paintin a picture. Katie had stretched her arms then, as though to embrace the beauty before her. And gradually, she'd ceased weeping.

Course she'd longed fur My Pa now an again. Every day fur purt nigh two years she'd missed him. An then he'd come home. He'd stood in the kitchen lookin gaunt an old an sad. So sad thet Katie wanted to rush right up to him an grab his hand. But she didn't. Why my goodness, how did she know thet War was over with, anyways? Them dumb Feds jist might come back an shoot My Pa same as they had Patrick. No, she'd jist stay clear of My Pa. Thet way she wouldn't come all apart like, when he went away again.

And so, even though she ached for My Pa to love her, Katie remained aloof. Hurried off like she did, ever time he got set fur story tellin. An then one day after what seemed like furever, My Pa had followed her to this very room after dinner.

"Aye, Lass, I reckon you're hurtin right bad jist now. So, I'm thinkin maybe you can use this. Fur your purties like." And he handed her a small, oblong box. Metal it was, with tiny legs, an a big K etched on the lid. Course My Pa had made it. Fur her. An she couldn't think of nothin to say. So she sat quiet like when My Pa turned away. But her chin trembled when she saw them big shoulders heavin as he left the room.

Setting the box on her chest of drawers, Katie knelt before the window and wrapped her arms about herself. Rainin it was, with big drops drummin on the glass. Yet them giant limbs across the way seemed to enjoy it like. Why my goodness, they jist stretched wide as could be, catchin purt nigh every drop. An them drops turned all sparkley like when the sun finally peeked out.

An then she heard it. Thet faint voice callin her to reach out like, an love folks. To open her heart like an let My Pa in. Fur a long time she'd stayed still, watchin them rain–drenched leaves across the way—an ponderin. Then slowly, she'd stretched her arms an smiled.

My Pa had hugged her real fierce like. "Aye, Lass, I've missed you, to be sure." He'd patted her head then an started off on another story about the wee little family who lived in a wee little house, in a wee little town in Tennessee." And Katie had listened, her heart brimming with joy.

Her an My Pa was friends all right. All the same, even he couldn't keep Andrew's family from movin off like. An he daren't cross My Ma when she said Katie'd have to quit school an help out at home..

An thet hurt. Fur Katie loved school. Really an truly she did. Course she'd only jist gone thet summer of '61 an part of '62. An last summer. All the same, she'd loved ever minute of it. Well, not *ever* minute. Cause she didn't take much to cipherin. All them numbers made her go real dizzy like. No, it was them letters thet she loved. An them purty sounds they made all wrote up into words. They made her feel jist plain happy inside. Like thet verse about the blacksmith.

> *Under a spreading chestnut–tree*
> *The village smithy stands;*
> *The smith, a mighty man is he,*
> *With large and sinewy hands;*
> *And the muscles of his brawny arm*
> *Are strong as iron bands.*
> *His hair is crisp, and black, and long,*
> *His face is like the tan;*
> *His brow is wet with honest sweat,*
> *He earns whate'er he can,*
> *And looks the whole world in the face,*
> *For he owes not any man.*
> *Week in, week out, from morn till night,*
> *You can hear his bellows blow;*
> *You can hear him swing his heavy sledge,*
> *With measured beat and slow,*
> *Like a sexton ringing the village bell,*
> *When the evening sun is low....*[1]

Course My Pa didn't look jist like thet. But she could pretend, couldn't she? Only pretendin did have limits. Fur it wasn't the same as readin them words straight from a book. Katie sighed. Cupping her chin in her hands and planting her elbows on the window sill, she wished, not for the first time, thet Bonnie was her sister. Why my goodness, Bonnie was jist plain lucky. Cause she got to go to school. In grade six, she was. Readin an learnin all them fine stories an verses. The Chapman's had books at home too. Lots of them, Bonnie said. But Katie's family didn't. The only book Katie knew of was the family Bible which sat on the writin table in the parlor. Course My Ma wouldn't let anyone inside thet room, cept fur company. Sometimes though, Katie would sneak in an try to read some. With Aunt Jane's help she got on well enough. Them Psalms was her favorite. Specially number one hundred. Why my goodness, it made her feel so warm an glad like thet she'd learned it right off.

> *Make a joyful noise unto the Lord, all ye lands.*
> *Serve the Lord with gladness: come before his*
> *   presence with singing.*
> *Know ye that the Lord he is God: it is he that*
> *   hath made us, and not we ourselves; we are his*
> *   people, and the sheep of his pasture.*
> *Enter into his gates with thanksgiving—* [2]

"Katie."

It was My Ma remindin her of them dishes. She'd dallied long enough.

"Comin," Katie called, scrambling to her feet. As she hurried toward the door, she spied the metal chamber pot beside the bed. Thet Mamie! Drat it all, she'd furgot to empty it again. Reluctantly, Katie took hold of the handle.

"Katie!" It was My Ma again, angry this time.

Hurrying, Katie whisked through Thomas' room and started down the stairs, the pot banging beside her. She was on the next to the last step when her bare feet slipped.

Bang. Bang. Bang. The pot rolled to a stop beside the door.

"Katie, you'd best not be playin round up there." My Ma jerked open the door to find Katie sitting in a puddle of urine.

"Confound you, Girl, can't you be more careful like?" And My Ma hurried off. She returned in seconds with a handful of rags. Thrusting them at Katie, she scolded. "You'd best clean this mess up, then git busy dryin them dishes. An change thet dress too."

Twenty minutes later, Katie stood, with tea towel in hand, staring out the window at the cherry tree. Drat it all, anyways. Why did she always have to git bawled out? What about Mamie? Hadn't she left thet pot unemptied? An snatched her ribbons too. Jamming a fist into her side, Katie glowered. It was unfair, thet's what it was. Jist plain old unfair.

❖   ❖   ❖

By the early morning light Katie pulled on her dress and braided her hair, careful to stay out of Mamie's way. Cause Mamie didn't take to folks botherin her when she was dressin. Specially when she fixed thet auburn hair of hers. Why my goodness, she brushed thet long stuff fur hours ever mornin an ever evenin. An she was jist gettin started fur now.

Downstairs, Katie went immediately to the cookstove. Stooping, she pulled out the pan of ashes. She was halfway across the room when sunlight spilled across her path. Ordinarily Katie loved those first rays of warmth. But this morning she frowned. Somethin was wrong. Fur them lemon rays was hittin on somethin red like among them ashes. Puzzled, Katie poked a finger among the cold embers. What was thet, anyways? An then, as she noted the tip of her brown braids flung forward across her shoulder, she knew. Thet Mamie! Drat it all, how *could* she be so mean?

Clutching the pan to her chest and biting her lip to control her trembling chin, Katie continued toward the doorway.

"Aye, Lass, what's troublin you like this mornin?" It was My Pa, entering the kitchen from his and My Ma's bedroom.

"Nothin." Katie stared straight ahead.

"You bein sure?" And he patted her head gently.

Katie nodded. Her chin ceased trembling then and she held the pan more loosely. Why my goodness, what did it matter fur, anyways? My Pa loved her. Really an truly he did. An thet was all thet counted.

Chapter 8

She was dead. He knew it the moment he awoke and felt the stiff body beside him. Verna Marie, that petite, winsome, beautiful woman of his dreams was really gone.

Pushing aside a comforter, Livingston Lewis stepped onto the flowered carpet, then thrust his feet into wool slippers. Sighing, he reached for his dressing gown. He'd have to tell Daniel, of course. Then have someone lay her out. Minnie Chapman? Maybe. Come to think of it, she'd been the only woman in town to ask after Verna Marie since that dreadful night when the darkie—

Livingston shivered as he lighted the lamp. Lord, it was cold. Mighty cold. But then what could one expect? It was February, after all, not summer time. Snipping the end off a Havana and lighting it, he felt somewhat better. Still, that form on the bed disturbed him. He was sad, more sad than he could say, that life had been too much for Verna Marie.

Studying the puffy face reposed upon the pillow, he recalled the heart-shaped one that had first captured him. Surrounded by lustrous brunette hair, and accented with misty brown eyes and dewy pink lips, he had thought it the most beautiful face in all the world.

Biting his Havana, Livingston turned away from the bed. He'd make the casket himself, from maple wood. Maple was fine for caskets. Mighty fine. Once it was stained a warm brown, he'd feel better about laying Verna Marie to rest.

Most of a new cigar dropped to the floor, its lighted end flickering against the patterned carpet. Lord, he'd bit the thing in two. Stooping, he wrapped his fingers about the khaki band, then strode into the sitting room. Opening the door to the pot–bellied stove, he flung the cigar inside then

---

spat out the stub. Clanging the door shut, he pressed his lips together and groaned. He'd care for the fire later. Just now he must awaken Daniel.

❖　　❖　　❖

A north wind whipped through the cemetery, tearing at Daniel's lank frame. Drawing the collar of his greatcoat more firmly about his bearded face, he looked across the mound of dirt to where his father stood.

Poor man. The wind was whipping him too, ruffling his salt and pepper hair and scattering the ashes from his ever-present Havana. Daniel sighed. Did this man who clamped that cigar between his teeth really care for the woman whose remains lay in the casket? Ah well, who could know? His father was a closed man, pure and simple.

His stovepipe hat in his gloved right hand and his left hand hanging limply at his side, Daniel turned his attention to the open grave. And saw nothing. For the woman being interred there was a stranger. The truth was, *his* mother had died the day his baby sister, Joy, was born. He'd mourned then. There was no reason to mourn now.

Let not your heart be troubled: ye believe in
God, believe also in me...[1]

The perfunctory words of the minister merely accentuated the void in Daniel's soul. God? There was no such person. And personally, he didn't see any reason for this kind of service. Yet, his father had insisted on having a minister. Why? Because his own father had been one?

Daniel toyed with the brim of his hat. Why had his father never told him of his grandfather? Did he think his great-uncle Hayward's yarns were enough? Ah well, that was all in the past. It was over, pure and simple. There was no point in dwelling on it now. Or God either. His mother was dead. That was all.

The minister's remarks concluded, Minnie Chapman began to sing.

There's a land that is fairer than day
And by faith we can see it afar...[2]

Bonnie joined her mother, then the minister and Livingston chimed in. Only Daniel remained silent. What was the use of singing? His mother was dead. Nothing changed that.

The singing finished, the Chapmans and the minister shook hands with the Lewis men and left.

Without a word, Daniel settled his hat over his wind blown hair and reached for a shovel. Working with his father, he mechanically tossed dirt onto the maple box, careful not to notice the frozen mound beside it. No use thinking of Joy. She'd been gone for ten years.

The dirt is mounding up now. A couple more shovels full and they are through. Relieved, Daniel takes the second shovel from his father. He watches then, as though from a distance, as his father places a cedar bough on the fresh turned earth.

Ah, so he does care. But caring hasn't done him much good, has it? Because in the end, he'd lost her.

Hoisting the shovels to his shoulders, Daniel turns toward Locust Street. And as he strides into the biting wind, he feels like a hollow shell. Empty and alone.

Chapter 9

A balmy March breeze stirred the stray curls framing Jordana's face as she mixed up a batch of cornbread for dinner. She smiled. Thet warm air an the smell of them beans an taters cookin made her feel almost happy like.

Pausing, she glanced out the window. Through swaying cherry branches she could see Thomas plowing the garden, his right sleeve tucked neatly about his stub. My but she was proud of thet boy. Why, she felt plumb warm all over jist watchin him stride along behind thet Morgan, his dark hair lookin almost russet like beneath the mornin sun. He'd do all right, she reckoned. Leastwise he had so far. Now, if only Carrie—Jordana shivered. Course Carrie couldn't never see Thomas. Where did she ever git thet crazy notion from, anyways?

Sighing, Jordana crossed the room to the cookstove. Taking a cast–iron skillet, she spooned lard into it and set it on a front burner. Then returning to the work table, she set about putting away the flour and cornmeal. My but she missed thet Claudia. Havin to cook *an* clear up was jist about more than a body could do. Course there wasn't much money fur servants now, anyways. Why, ever since thet new smithy on Main Street went in, Michael's trade had dropped way off like. Still, she reckoned things wasn't too bad. Leastwise now she didn't have to git onto Thomas fur not helpin his Pa.

Glancing out the window again, Jordana sighed. Thet Thomas. Why was he stoppin fur, anyways? Why, she'd a mind to trot right out there an put his hand back on thet plow herself. For Thomas was standing at the end of the row staring down toward the mill and Davis Creek.

Thet mill. Confound thet place. An if Thomas thought he was goin to fiddle round down there today he had another thought commin. Cause she wouldn't stand fur it. After all, taters an corn didn't grow by themselves, so he'd best git at thet plowin.

Just then, as though he could hear his Ma, Thomas lifted his hand and waved at a figure standing in the open door of the mill. And as the figure returned the greeting, Thomas turned back to his plowing. Picking up the reins, he shouted to the Morgan.

Relieved, Jordana watched as steel blades slowly turned up new earth. Thomas was workin again. An she was right glad. Fur she—

The smell of burning grease brought Jordana around with a start. Thet skillet. Confound thet thing. Now thet lard was hissin an poppin an smoke was goin everywheres. Rushing to the stove, she grabbed the black iron handle.

"Ouch!" She dropped the skillet back to the stove, and shook her burned hand. Confound it, thet hurt. Snatching up the nearby can of lard she smeared it on her fingers and palm, then wrapped her hand in a tea towel. Her hand throbbing, she glared at the skillet which still sat on the stove, grease sputtering, smoke rising. Confound it, she felt like bawlin. Lifting a corner of her apron to her eyes, Jordana sighed. Why did life have to be such a trial fur, anyways?

After supper Jane lit a lamp and settled in the sewing rocker next to the fireplace in the dining room. My but thet fire felt good. Even if it was warm like durin the daytime them nights was cool.

Reaching for her sewing basket, Jane took out the waist she was making for Mamie and threaded her needle. She'd taken only a few stitches when Michael entered the room. He sank into the rocker on the opposite side of the fireplace and sighed. He didn't say anything though, just sat with his huge hands laced across his firm belly, his eyes half closed.

Watching him, Jane sighed. Michael was fine an all, but land sakes, she wanted a man of her own. Fact was, she purt near ached fur a husband to love. One thet would think her downright purty, in spite of thet awful birthmark on her face. A kind man, she wanted. A man like Robert Saylor.

Just the thought of her brother's friend caused Jane's heart to beat faster. Robert. My but she wished he'd astayed in Missouri stead of traipsin off to California with James. Why land sakes, if he had they might abeen married up by now. Stead, here she set, a spinster, stitchin up clothes fur her niece. Course there was a chance James an Robert might come back sometime. Still an all, James seemed real settled like out there. He'd married up with a Spanish girl, even. Accordin to Jordana, thet was. She was the one thet got James' letters, such as they was.

"Aye, Lass, I reckon thet shirt thing you're makin is fur Mamie."

Michael's observation so startled Jane that she stuck her finger. Dabbing it with a scrap of material, she glared at him. "Land sakes, you scared the daylights out of me. Course this is fur Mamie. A new waist fur church goin. An speakin of church, I jist might stitch you up a new shirt if you'd go along."

"Aye, Lass, I reckon you would. But you know I don't take to church goin. Me Mom did enough of thet to last me an Me Dad a lifetime. Said she was chosen by God to be the elect, mind. But meself now, I always thought folks'd be best off if they jist lived like the Good Book says. Seems like lovin folks is most like God. Course Me Mamie now, I've a mind she's not thinkin much about God, even at church."

Jane frowned. Course Michael was right. Why land sakes, jist last Sunday Mamie'd come out of church an looked right up at the Lewis' livin quarters. An waved she had, real bold like. Served her right when Daniel ignored her. Still an all—

"Aye, Lass, our Mamie's wastin her time, to be sure. Not gettin no younger, either."

Jane nodded. Course Mamie wasn't gettin younger. Still an all, her eighteen years made Jane feel downright old. Why land sakes, she was all of thirty five, an still alookin fur a husband. Taking in a tuck, Jane sighed. My but it must be nice havin youngins of your own. Take Katie now, she sure was a sweet child. Child? Katie wasn't no child. Why land sakes, thet youngin was agrowin to beat the band. Astretchin up she was, an afillin out. Fact was, she had more bosom already then Mamie would ever have. Still an all, Katie didn't flaunt herself. Why land sakes, thet child cared a sight more fur others than fur herself. Leastwise most times. Course she'd been a mite slow about lovin her Pa after thet War. But thank the good Lord, she'd finally come around.

Laying down her needle, Jane touched the birthmark on her face, then tucked a strand of hair into place. My but she hoped Katie never lost a friend the way she'd lost Claudia. It hurt too much. Why land sakes, she'd moped about fur weeks awishin Claudia'd come back. But she hadn't. Fact was, things was changed furever. Fur Claudia lived in a different world now. Still an all, Jane jist might mosey over to see her one of these days. In the meantime—

The sound of footsteps caused Jane to look up. Must be Thomas.

Maybe he'd come in the dinin room an sit fur a spell stead of goin off like. But he didn't. He just told Jordana "bye" and went out the kitchen door.

"Land sakes, thet Thomas sure goes out aplenty these days."

Michael nodded, his thick shoulders arching, then settling down again. "Aye, Lass, I worry about Me Lad, to be sure."

Thomas sat on the edge of his bed, his left ankle resting on his right knee, staring into the semidarkness of the room. The corners of his lips turned downward as he puffed on his corncob pipe. He felt whipped. Whipped, beaten and abandoned.

Uncrossing his legs, Thomas planted both feet on the wood floor, and studied the Colt .36 which lay on his chest of drawers beside the coal oil lamp. He'd come damn near hurtin somebody with thet thing this evenin. An it was Uriah he'd shot at. Uriah, who was his friend. Uriah, who pulled off more dandy pranks than a feller could shake a stick at. Uriah, who'd called him a coward. A coward! Why, in all his born days he'd never been called no coward. Anyways, if anyone was a coward it was Uriah himself. Fact was, if thet rascal was so darn brave he would've planned thet robbery fur in the daytime, the way them James Boys did. Instead, he'd planned it secret like, fur after dark.

They'd all met at the mill as usual: himself, Uriah, Tevis an Melvin. Uriah'd given them last minute instructions, then they'd gone separate ways, meetin at the bank on Lexington.

From the beginnin, things was wrong. Tevis had such trouble pickin the lock thet Uriah got mad. By the flickering light of his lantern, Thomas had seen the leader's jaw harden and his eyes become points of steel. And then without warning, the lantern had gone out.

"Darn it all, anyways."

"Shut up." It was Melvin, slappin a hand over his mouth. "There's someone inside."

He saw it then, the glow of a lamp through the front window.

"What'll we do now, Boss?" This from Tevis, who chewed his tobacco with vigor.

"Wait fur a bit. Then Melvin'll go in an take care of thet clerk. The rest'll be easy."

Seconds later, Thomas heard footsteps. "Pst. Somebody's comin, down Spring Street."

Instantly, the four of them had flattened themselves against the brick wall. And waited. They didn't have to wait long. Within minutes a man stopped at the corner, a lantern dangling at his side. Harvey Fudd. Why, Thomas would've knowed thet wiry frame anywheres. The boys held their breath. Then sighed in relief as Mr. Fudd crossed the street and stopped before Crawford's Grocery.

"What's thet fool adoin?" Uriah asked as the old man lifted his lantern to the store window.

"Probably jist needs to look at them there peppermint sticks." Tevis spat a stream of tobacco toward the street.

They all laughed then. A bit too loud.

"Hey," a voice called from across the street. "What you guys doin over theres?"

"Damn!"

"Shut up." Again, Melvin clapped his hand over Thomas' mouth.

"But thet old man—"

"I *said*, shut up." A gun rested against his ribs.

"Never mind." Uriah shoved Melvin's arm aside. "Git yourself ready to go in."

Melvin obliged, his hand groping for the doorknob. He was turning it when a voice called again. This time from the middle of the street.

"Hey, what you guys adoin?" And Harvey Fudd waved his lantern. For an answer, Melvin whirled and fired his pistol. The lantern went out.

"Hey, what'd you do thet fur?"

Melvin whirled again, but Uriah knocked the gun from his hand. "Furgit thet old fool," he snarled. "He can't see now, anyways."

Melvin had just retrieved his gun when a light shone through the window.

"He's spotted us," Tevis hissed.

"Naw, he ain't. Go on in, Melvin."

"Hey, you guys—" It was Harvey Fudd again. Only a few feet away this time.

"I'm skedaddlin out of here." And Tevis darted off.

"Why, thet coward—"

The light behind the window intensified.

"Hey, you guys—"

"I'm hightailin it too." Thomas turned then and sprinted for Spring Street.

"Hey you, git back here!" Uriah bellowed. "Jist cause thet Wade Crawford was a coward don't give—"

Bang!

Whop. Thomas hit the dirt with a thud. Damn, but he'd got too much powder in thet gun. An it hadn't made a lick of difference either. Fur Uriah was still yellin like he'd never been touched.

"You sonofabitch. Cowar–r–rd!"

Bang! This time the bullet whizzed by Thomas. Startled, he'd scrambled to his feet and rounded the corner. An he hadn't stopped runnin till he reached Main Street. But fur all thet, he wasn't no coward. Fact was, him an Wade'd shot them Feds—

Wade. Damn it all, why *couldn't* he furgit thet feller, anyways? Lifting his left arm, Thomas wiped his sleeve across his eyes. Rising, he studied the Stars and Bars which hung above his bed. And the CSA. Wade had died fur Missouri. An he'd lost an arm. They wasn't cowards, neither one of them.

His legs straight as sticks, Thomas glared at the flag. Next time, he'd show thet scoundrel Uriah jist what a real soldier was. He'd stay right there an lay into them Feds till they begged him to stop. Then they'd see who was cowards. Feeling better now, Thomas put away his gun, blew out the lamp and went to bed.

Chapter 10

Standing before the chest of drawers in her bedroom, Katie fingers the lumpy blue mittens and sighs. Drat it all, tomorrow is Christmas an she don't have a nice gift fur Bonnie. Jist them mittens—thet's all. An they're ugly. Really an truly they are.

Katie's chin trembles as she recalls the hours she labored with knitting needles and yarn. Hours an hours she worked an them things is still ugly. Biting her lip, she rolls the bulky mittens in heavy brown paper. Now, fur some string. She rummages through her drawers, looking for a length of yarn. Only there ain't any. Drat it all, anyways. Why, Bonnie won't have nothin if she can't make a bow.

With that, Katie slams the last drawer shut and stares into the mirror, her arms crossed over her developing breasts. And the sight of her plain braids gives her an idea. Slowly, she unfolds her arms and extends a hand to her K box. Gingerly, she removes the lid.

Yellow ribbons. Two bright satiny lengths to tie about her braids. Well, from now on, one will jist have to do.

Pulling a lemon length from the box, Katie carefully wraps it about the brown paper and ties it in a simple bow. There. It's purty now. Really an truly it is. Purty enough fur her best friend.

❖   ❖   ❖

Daniel Lewis pulled up the collar of his great coat as he emerged from the cabinet shop. God, it was cold. And with the wind whipping like it was, that snow could drift in no time. Ah well, what did he care? A box of cigars for his father and Christmas would be over.

Crossing Main Street, Daniel wondered what it would be like to have a family gathering at Yuletide. The last time he remembered any sort of

49

gaiety was when his sister, Joy, was living. In years since, Christmas had meant helping his father move his mother's body from her chair in the sitting room to the one in the kitchen and back again. That and rereading his great–uncle's latest letter. Each year those things had seemed trivial. Now, even they were gone. For his mother lay beneath the frozen earth on Locust Street and his Uncle Hayward rested in Indian Mound Cemetery outside Romney, West Virginia. That left his grandfather the only living relative. And for all his father spoke of him, he too might as well be dead.

Daniel sighed. Ah well, if he wanted a family he ought to get married and have one of his own, he supposed. Only he didn't want to marry. At least not right now. At twenty seven he was mature enough, of course. The truth was, his father thought he should have married several years ago. But Daniel was particular. When he married it would be for life. And he simply didn't know any woman he would want to spend that much time with. He did think Mamie Fitzsimmons was pretty. And she was obviously attracted to him. But court her? That could lead to love. And Daniel had no room for that.

Chapman's Dry Goods was a busy place this morning. Daniel decided to get the cigars first, then check the mail.

"Can—can I help you?" It was Thane, the Chapman's younger son. At fourteen, he was small for his age and obviously self conscious around adults.

"I suppose so. I want a box of Havanas, pure and simple."

"Fur—fur your Pa?"

Daniel nodded.

"All right. Let's see, we've got several kinds of designs on the lids. Would you like to look—"

Daniel held up his hand. "Any box will do. The truth is, he probably won't notice anything but the cigars anyway."

Nonplused, Thane stared down at his hands. "Well gosh, I jist don't know. Course— Well all right, I'll git you one." Thane turned to the shelves behind him and took down the nearest box. Handing it across the counter to Daniel, he said, "You can jist put thet on our bill at your shop. Some—someday, we'll git thet hall tree paid fur."

"No hurry." Daniel slipped the box beneath his arm and turned from the counter. As he did so, a gust of cold air drew his attention to the door. Katie Fitzsimmons stepped inside.

"Hello, Katie," Thane ventured, then turned quickly to rearrange dishes on a shelf, his pale face flushing.

"Oh, hello," Katie puffed as she hurried on toward the post office.

Daniel followed slowly, his boots faintly tapping the wooden floor. At the post office he stopped several feet from Katie. His stovepipe hat in his hands, he noted how much she'd grown since he'd last seen her. The top of her head must reach to his chest by now. And through her worn gray cape he could see the outline of budding breasts.

Chagrined, Daniel toyed with the brim of his hat and shifted his attention to the girl's face. Her hood thrown back, he noted a creamy complexion and eyes which were wide and dark. Eyes which seemed like dense smoke as she slid a small package beneath the grille to Bonnie.

"Oh, Katie!" Bonnie squealed as she pulled at the yellow bow. "It's your hair ribbon, ain't it?"

At Katie's nod, Bonnie flapped the ribbon about, then tied it around her own chestnut curls. "There." She patted the bow, then turned her attention to the package. Unwrapping it, she gasped. "Oh, Katie, jist what I wanted. An blue to go with my new cape." Thrusting her hands into the lumpy mittens, she thumped them together.

"My goodness, you mean you really like them?"

"Course I like them. You made them, didn't you?"

At Katie's nod, Bonnie grinned. "Then I'll wear them furever." With that, she thumped her hands together again. Then stopped, her eyes resting on Daniel. "Oh my, I'd best quit playin an git busy. Mr. Daniel's needin his mail."

"No hurry, Miss Chapman."

"All right then. I'll be with you in a minute." Hurriedly, Bonnie took off the mittens and laid them aside. Leaning toward the grille, she whispered to Katie. "I've got somethin fur you too."

Seconds later, she slid a slim volume toward her friend. "Merry Christmas, Katie."

Her hands trembling, Katie reached for the book. "Oh my goodness, a book of them verses. I—I don't know what to say."

"Why fur cryin out loud, you said it already." And Bonnie patted the lumpy mittens.

Katie turned to go then and as she moved past Daniel he noted the expression on her face. Pleasure, pure pleasure, was registered in a broad smile and eyes that shone like sapphires as she lovingly patted her book.

Chapter 11

Jonquil rays of sunlight streamed through the open doorway as Jordana poured herself and Thomas a second cup of coffee. Returning the pot to the stove, she reseated herself at the table, frowning at Michael. Confound thet man. How could he set there stirrin whiskey in his tea, like this was jist any old mornin? How could he eat corn cakes an sorghum an side meat like nothin in the world was wrong? Couldn't he see what them flowers was doin to her? Didn't he care?

Staring at the bouquet of red and white peonies in the center of the table, Jordana felt those familiar fingers, coolly stroking her heart. Earlier, she'd purt nigh froze when Jane brought them things inside sayin, "Why land sakes, ain't them purty? Fact is, they're so purty I aim to put them on Patrick's grave."

But Jordana didn't want to put flowers on her son's grave. She didn't even want to *see* his grave. Confound it, why did she have to hurt so much fur, anyways? Why couldn't she jist furgit Patrick easy like?

Shivering, Jordana sipped her coffee, peering over the marbled cup's rim at her oldest daughter. And smiled. My but thet youngin was bein helpful this mornin. It warmed her right up jist watchin Mamie work. Why, already she'd fried corncakes, brewed coffee an turned over them plates. An now she was pourin Jane a third cup of tea.

Mamie set down the tea pot then, laid the strainer on a saucer and carried the cup around the table. Turning her back briefly, she set the full cup before her aunt, then proceeded to gather up the dirty dishes.

Smiling her thanks, Jane lifted the cup to her mouth, then plunked it down again. "Why land sakes, there's somethin afloatin on top this tea. An it looks like—like spit."

For a moment no one spoke. Then Mamie turned from the work table where she was pouring water into the dish pan, her willowy body rigid with contempt.

"Serves you right, you old meanie. Pickin them flowers fur Pat— Patrick like they was goin to make everything okay. Well, they ain't. He's dead, fur heaven sakes. An it's your fault. Cause if you'd cared a whit–"

"Aye, Lass, thet's enough now. We all miss Patrick, to be sure." Michael's thick shoulders rose, then settled down again. "Pour out thet bad tea now, an git your aunt some fresh."

For a second Mamie looked as though she'd defy My Pa. Then abruptly she dried her hands on a tea towel and stalked to the table. Picking up the cup, she carried it to the slop bucket behind the stove and emptied it. Returning to the table, she poured more tea and carried it to Jane. That done, she glared at each of them in turn, her green eyes icy with suppressed rage.

"There. I hope you're happy now. Cause I hate you. All of you." With that, Mamie darted toward the door and outside.

Jordana sighed, then rose and began to clear up. All too soon them dishes was done an Michael was reachin fur her hand.

"Aye, Colleen, the mornin's fair, to be sure. Me Lad's fine."

But Patrick wasn't fine. He'd been shot—killed by them awful Feds. Confound it, why couldn't she furgit thet horrid day? Why couldn't she furgit thet pale face, bloody shirt an lifeless form? Why couldn't she furgit—

As though hearing her thoughts, Michael leaned over and kissed her softly. "Aye, Colleen, Me Lad's gone, to be sure. An I reckon you're hurtin right bad, mind. Still, I'm thinkin it's best fur us to remember them good things, them thet was extra special like."

Incensed, Jordana pulled away. Confound Michael. Didn't he know she was tryin? Couldn't he see thet memories, even good ones, wasn't no good? Thet thinkin on thet sandy–haired, freckled–faced, laughin boy gave her chills?

Ignoring Michael's outstretched arm, Jordana stumbled toward the doorway. And she had one foot on the outside step when her eyes fell on the water bucket sitting on the washstand. She would have fallen then if Michael hadn't caught her. But Jordana didn't see Michael. Instead, she saw a small girl, her flaxen hair whipping about her pixie face as she swung an empty bucket on her way to the Big Spring. Carrie. Oh, my purty, darlin Carrie. Why did we ever have to say good–by fur, anyways?

It was Michael then who dried her tears, his own shoulders heaving.

❖ ❖ ❖

Silence pervaded the atmosphere in the Lewis Cabinet Shop on the morning of May 30, 1868. Silence save for the sound of sandpaper as Daniel smoothed a chair spindle. Though business was normally brisk, today only a few customers had been in. Everyone it seemed, was headed for the cemetery.

Puffing on his Havana, Livingston glanced from the table he was staining to the windows fronting Main Street. A lot of people had gone by this morning. A lot of people. For Union and Secesh alike were taking flowers to decorate the graves of their War dead.

Biting down on his cigar, Livingston sighed. What did a man do when his dead was among the living? There were times when he was sure, more sure than he could say, that the Secesh had killed his Daniel. There were times when it seemed his son's soul had expired, leaving the mere shell of his body to carry on. There were times when he was certain the real Daniel had ceased to exist.

Like now. From all appearances the younger man, bending his bearded face over the woodwork, was as alive as a man could be. Yet, when that man looked up those gray eyes were vacant. And those slender fingers caressing that spindle of pine were no longer seen curling into a fist at the feel of anger. It was a mere frame which worked across the room. It wasn't his son, Daniel, at all.

Clenching his Havana between his tobacco–stained teeth, Livingston groaned. Lord, what he wouldn't do to see his son whole again.

Several minutes passed before Livingston looked up again. This time an entire family passed before the windows. The Fitzsimmons. The older boy, Thomas, strode ahead of the others, marching with such precision that, despite the loss of his arm, he seemed ready for combat. And, if the town gossips were to be believed, he'd been involved in several bush-whacking activities of late. That was too bad. For his father, Michael, was a fine man. A mighty fine man.

But the Michael who followed his son this morning, looked spent. His burly shoulders rose and fell as he gripped his wife's arm. And his wife kept using her free hand to dab at her eyes. Livingston was sad, as sad as he knew how to be, for the tragedy which had taken the Fitzsimmons boy. Still, their loss was no more than so many others.

Yet, that youngest Fitzsimmons girl looked like she'd lost the whole world. With braids pinned in a crown about her head, she stared in front of her, her round chin quivering. And a man would think it was freezing outside the way she pressed her arms about herself. It was as if she was shutting out everything and everybody. She even seemed oblivious to her aunt who strode beside her. And Jane Douglas had that no–nonsense look on her birthmarked face as she carried a bright bouquet of flowers.

Puffing his Havana, Livingston waited for the older girl to appear. She didn't. With a sigh of relief, he returned to his work. That Mamie was a sly one. Mighty sly. She might even be pretty if a man liked the sleek, lean type. But Livingston didn't trust her. Lord, he was uneasy when she paced before the shop. She wasn't right for Daniel. Not right at all.

Livingston had been engrossed in his work for some time when he became aware of another figure passing his windows. This time, it was a spindly old man moseying along, his head wobbling as he sniffed the bouquet in his hand.

Bouquet? Livingston chuckled. For the assortment of grasses and weeds held in the knobby hand was a far cry from flowers. But then what did Harvey Fudd know of flowers? For that matter, why was he going to the cemetery anyway? He'd lost no family in the Secesh Army. Or the Union Troops either. Ah well, it takes all kinds to make a world.

Still chuckling, Livingston returned to his work.

Chapter 12

Large raindrops dripped from the brim of his soft hat as Thomas rapped on the Crawford's front door. He shivered, wishing the rain would stop. His hand was raised for a second knock when the door opened.

"Good evening," Julia beckoned him inside with a slim hand.

Thomas picked up his lantern and stepped over the threshold, glad to be in from the cold. The heat comin from thet pot–bellied stove made a feller feel all cozy like. Extinguishing his lantern, Thomas handed his hat and cloak to Julia. He stepped toward the parlor then, half expecting to see Wade.

But of course it was Julia who led him into the room. Seating herself on the sofa, she took up her embroidery. "Papa will be along shortly," she said.

Thomas nodded, feeling foolish. What was he supposed to say, anyways? Course he was attracted to Julia, thinkin on marrin her even. But fur all thet, he didn't really know her. Wade had been his friend.

"Damn!" Thomas swore softly as he flung a glowing match into the stove. What was the matter with him, anyways? Couldn't he even court without thinkin on Wade?

Puffing on his corncob pipe, Thomas walked stiffly to the sofa and seated himself beside Julia. "Cold evenin out there," he ventured.

"It is a bit chilly," Julia conceded, her blonde head bent over her work. "Still an all, the rain is nice."

"Sure enough is. Them farmers need it somethin awful." His legs crossed, Thomas slipped his arm along the back of the sofa, his fingers barely touching Julia's shoulder.

Julia stiffened, then leaned toward the lamp, seeming to study the intricate pattern on the pillowcase in her hand.

"Somethin the matter?"

"No."

"Then move closer like. I—"

"Well, Son, good evenin. I didn't know you were here already." Mr. Crawford cleared his throat as he entered the room.

Instantly, Thomas removed his arm from about Julia and rose to his feet. "Evenin, Mr. Crawford."

The older man nodded, then settled into his rocking chair.

Thomas sat back down on the sofa, a little farther from Julia this time. His lips in a straight line, he studied the man across the room. Noting his heavy frame and balding head, Thomas thought, not for the first time, how different Mr. Crawford was from his son. Fur Wade was thinner. Taller too. An he had lots of dun–colored hair. But Wade differed in more than jist looks. Fact was, thet boy was so cheerful like it made a feller feel plumb good jist bein around him. He was darin too. Like thet time—

"Anyhow, business ain't much good these days." Mr. Crawford's voice sliced through the picture in Thomas' mind, pulling the corners of his mouth downward.

"You not agreein, Son?" Mr. Crawford coughed lightly.

Thomas started. Then placing both feet on the floor, he spoke matter–of–factly. "Course I agree, Sir. Business ain't no good anywheres jist now. Not even at the smithy. Fact is, it's enough to make a feller git all worried like."

"Can't say but what I agree with you there." The older man shook his head, then pressed his foot to the floor.

Watching Mr. Crawford rock, Thomas tried to think of something to say. But the other man spoke first.

"Who's goin to be our next President, Son?"

"Seymour, I reckon. Leastwise I hope so. I ain't votin fur thet butcher, Grant, thet's fur certain. Why, I mean to tell you it could git real serious like, if he gits to runnin things."

Mr. Crawford nodded. "Can't say but what I agree with you there. Why, he'd like as not start thet War all over again, jist so he could win a battle."

The mention of battle caused Thomas' mouth to turn downward again. Damn! Why *couldn't* he furgit thet fight at Wilson's Creek an—

"You know course thet some states is thinkin of lettin niggers vote?"

"Vote'?" Thomas leaned forward, his legs rigid. "Why, thet's plumb crazy. Them niggers don't know nothin. Why, they ain't even got sense enough to come in out of the rain."

"Can't say but what I agree with you there. I jist hope Phelps gits to be governor. Thet Fletcher ain't no good."

Thomas nodded, his lips taut. Thet Governor Fletcher was a bastard, all right. Why, he'd purt near ruined the gang by sendin troops to put down "bushwhacking". But Uriah had jist told the fellers to lay low fur a spell. Afterwards they'd started harassin them Feds all over again. Easy like, of course.

"Well, Son, what you think of thet new Ku Klux Klan?"

Thomas started. Why, jist yesterday Uriah had been speakin on thet very thing. Wanted the boys to think on it like. Course Melvin took to the idea right off. But him an Tevis wasn't sure.

"Fact is, Sir, I don't know much about this here Klan."

"Well, most I hear is from them stove–huddlin gossipers. They have it thet the Klan's tearin up over in Lafayette County."

"Sounds serious like."

Mr. Crawford nodded. "Myself now, I don't want no run–ins with the law. Them Feds purt nigh ruined me durin thet blasted War."

Thomas nodded, his lips taut. He remembered how them darn Feds had cleaned out every business in town run by State folks. Only Mr. Crawford's advanced age had kept him from bein carted off like My Pa.

"Well, Son, speakin of counties, I hear Lafayette an Pettis is tryin to git a railroad goin. Maybe it'll come through here."

"It'd be good fur business like." Thomas agreed. "Jist so it's better than thet thing me an Wade rode on from Sedalia to Jefferson City. Why, I mean to tell you we like to suffocated thet day."

Mr. Crawford grew quiet then, just rocked like an old man, back and forth, back and forth. After awhile he cleared his throat. "Julia, Dear, how about a cup of tea."

"Yes, Papa." Julia laid aside her embroidery work and left the room.

Impatiently, Thomas waited for his tea. Course he'd rather have coffee. Still, he was right thirsty this evenin. An Julia did make some dandy molasses cookies.

But this time there were no cookies. Julia merely poured tea into a porcelain cup and set it on a nearby table. Before Thomas could even thank her, she swished across the room to her pa.

When she settled back on the sofa again, Thomas noticed for the first time a few tiny patches on her calico dress. Business must be off more than he thought. Course there wasn't much he could do to fix things. Not now, anyways.

Draining his cup, he set it back on its saucer and took up his pipe. Tapping the ashes into the cup, he slipped the pipe into his pocket. Standing, he looked down at Julia.

"Thanks fur the tea. I'd best mosey along home now."

"Come again, Son," Mr. Crawford lifted a hand in farewell.

"I'll do thet."

Thomas sauntered to the dining room then, where Julia held his cloak and hat. He didn't take them immediately, however. Instead, he slipped his arm about Julia's waist. As he drew her toward him, Julia placed a hand on his chest.

"Thomas, please—"

Thomas stood still, his legs straight as sticks. "You don't care fur me." It was a statement.

I don't know." Julia blinked, then turned her blonde head away from him.

"Well, you'd best think on it, cause I aim to marry you someday." With that, Thomas donned his wraps, lighted his lantern and went out.

❖   ❖   ❖

November 3, 1868, dawned cool and damp. As Thomas and Michael strode down Main Street toward Chapman's Dry Goods, Thomas found himself wishing the polling place was somewhere else. It made a feller feel plumb uneasy like goin to a Federal store. Fact was, he hadn't set foot inside one since he'd got thet CSA from Daniel Lewis. Still, today was different. Today was election day. An he meant to vote all them dang Republicans out of office.

Passing the Christian Church, Thomas recalled hearin thet a new bunch was meetin in town. Presbyterians, they was. An thet seemed jist plumb stupid to him. Why, what did Brownsville need another church fur, anyways? The one they had was plenty good fur such as went.

At the corner, the Fitzsimmons men crossed Bridge Street, then Main. They were halfway across the damp earth road when Thomas realized something was wrong. Why, Alastair Godwin had Mr. Crawford by the arm an was pullin him away from the store. An since Mr. Godwin was one of them Honest Men folks, this could spell trouble like.

Thomas and Michael hurried toward the store.

"Aye, friend, what's the trouble here?"

"Nothin's the trouble. This here Secesh jist aims to vote, thet's all."

"Aye, I reckon so. An me too, mind."

"Well, you ain't goin to, an neither is he." And Mr. Godwin tightened his grip on Mr. Crawford's arm.

At this, Thomas stepped forward, his legs stiff as boards. "Now, wait jist a minute. This here man runs a store in town an he can vote if he's a mind to. An so can we."

"Not in Saline County, you can't."

"Course we can. What you tryin to pull anyways, you damn Fed?"

"Nothin, you dirty Secesh."

"Why, you lousy bastard." With that Thomas reared back and prepared to punch Mr. Godwin.

A burly hand grasped his wrist. "Aye, Lad, thet's enough now."

For a second Thomas simply glared at My Pa. Then reluctantly, he lowered his arm. Damn, but he wished he'd brought along his Colt .36. Still, he aimed to vote. An if thet took fightin like—

Striding to Mr. Crawford, Thomas shoved him toward the door. "Go on in there now, an vote."

But to Thomas' surprise, Mr. Crawford turned away. "No, Son, I ain't one fur makin trouble."

"Course not. But you got this comin to you."

"Can't say but what I agree with you there. Still, I'd best git on back to my store."

"Now, there's a good man fur you." Alastair Godwin smirked as Mr. Crawford walked away. "An you two can jist run right along behind him."

"Listen here, Godwin, you can't do this. Why, My Pa an me—"

"Alastair, what's goin on out here?"

Thomas started as a huge man appeared in the doorway and slowly stepped outside.

"Oh, it's jist them Fitzsimmons, Mack. They're—"

"Aye, Sir, I'm Michael. An I fought fur the Union, to be sure."

Godwin snorted. "Conscripted, he was. They're Secesh, both of them."

"Then you'd both best mosey along home."

For a second Thomas hesitated, his mouth dry with fear. In all his born days he'd never seen a man as tall or as muscular as this one. Why, them upper arms of his were purt near as thick as his own thighs. Still, he was a Missourian. He'd fought fur her an he'd dang well vote fur her.

His lips taut, Thomas glared up at the man called Mack. "An jist who do you think you are, anyways, tellin us what to do?"

"I'm from the Sheriff's office in Marshall. Sent here to keep order. So like I said, you'd best git along home."

"Aye, Sir, but—"

"Listen, Fitzsimmons, unless you want trouble you'd best leave." It was Godwin again, angry this time.

Michael turned away. But Thomas refused. "I ain't leavin. I came here to vote an I aim to do jist thet." Defiantly, he attempted to pass Mack.

The next thing Thomas knew his left wrist was bound and he was being dragged across the dirt toward the hitching post. Angrily, he kicked at Mack, barely missing his shin. But he swore, howling with pain, when a jerk on the rope nearly tore his arm from its socket.

"Listen, Secesh, if you don't want this arm to go the way of thet other one, you'd best not strike at me again." With that, Mack tied the other end of the rope to the hitching post.

Seething, Thomas dug his heels into the soft earth. A hand gripped his shoulder.

"Aye, Lad, I reckon you're hurtin right bad like. But thet War is over an past. I'm thinkin we'd best stop fightin."

"Well, I won't! An if you do, then you're jist as bad as them damn Feds."

Slowly, Michael withdrew his hand and turned away. Putting one foot before the other, he trudged across the street, his thick shoulders heaving.

Watching My Pa go, Thomas legs stiffened. Damn, but he was mad. Mad at My Pa, mad at Mr. Crawford, mad at them stinkin Feds. An he was mad as hell at Wade. Bending over, Thomas brushed his eyes across the rope that bound his left wrist to the post.

Chapter 13

Light snow was falling that December morning when Daniel Lewis entered Crawford's Grocery. He'd come for a Christmas ham. Personally, he didn't think one necessary since he and his father would be the only ones to eat it. But Livingston had insisted.

"Why, Son, we always had ham for Christmas dinner when I was growing up. And it was a fine meal. A mighty fine meal. Why, with sweet potatoes, biscuits and red–eye gravy, it was food fit for a king. Of course the ham and potatoes were usually gifts from parishioners. But we enjoyed them just the same. Now, I admit that Missouri is a far cry from Virginia. Still, Missouri ham is better than none."

Inside the store, Daniel removed his stovepipe hat. Striding to the counter, he stopped. Something was wrong. For the old man standing before the candy jars was definitely upset.

"No. Papa said not to take no more nuts." Julia Crawford blinked, then turned away from the customer.

But the old man wasn't easily dismissed. "Please? They're all dried out an everything." And he held out a handful of black walnuts.

"Please, oh purty please." Snickers accompanied the echo from beside the stove.

Glancing around, Daniel identified the taunter as Tevis McKinley. Secesh, of course. The rest were too, even Miss Crawford.

"No. I already told you, I ain't takin no nuts."

"But, Miss Crawford, jist look. They're real nice. Big too." And he placed the walnuts on the counter for her inspection .

At this, Julia snapped. "Look, Mr. Fudd, I don't need no nuts an you don't need no peppermint sticks." With that she gave a flip of her slim hand, sending the nuts flying.

For a second Harvey Fudd looked stunned. Then, his face flushing, he bent to gather the scattered walnuts.

"Good nough fur you, Fed," called a voice from beside the stove.

The contempt emanating from the group around the stove slashed Daniel's indifference. His fingers curled around the brim of his hat; a tightness filled his chest. Who did those men think they were, treating an old man like that? He was every bit as good as any of them. Maybe better.

Without stopping to realize what he was doing, Daniel removed his right glove, unbuttoned his great coat and withdrew his coin purse from a trouser pocket. Opening it, he extracted a nickel. Flinging the coin onto the counter, he snapped.

"Give Mr. Fudd a dozen of those peppermint sticks."

"But Papa said—"

"You heard me." Daniel tapped his fingers against his thigh.

"Oh. Why yes, of course." Julia blinked, then opened a jar and counted out twelve sticks. Shoving them toward Mr. Fudd, she snatched the nickel as though she feared he'd take it too.

But Harvey Fudd had eyes only for the candy. His face glowing, he pocketed his nuts, then selected a stick. Sucking noisily, he gathered the others into his wizened hands. Turning to Daniel, he smiled.

"Thank—thank you, Mr. Lewis, Sir."

"You're welcome. Enjoy those now."

But as Harvey stood sucking his candy, a voice taunted, "Here, Fed, you missed one of your nuts." And before Harvey could move aside a walnut smacked his cheek.

"Hey, what'd you do thet fur?" Harvey's hand flew to his face. Upon discovering he wasn't hurt, he bent to search for the missing nut.

"Mr. Fudd."

At the sound of Daniel's voice, Harvey looked up.

"I know you want that walnut real bad. But personally, I think you'd best go now." And laying a hand on his arm, Daniel gently steered Harvey Fudd toward the door.

The old man gone, Daniel stalked back toward the counter. Stooping, he picked up the stray walnut, his fingers closing over it. Then turning toward the men by the stove, he spoke contemptuously. "You boys really think you're a brave bunch, don't you? Well let me tell you right now, you're nothing but cowards. Every last one of you. For only cowards pick on the elderly." With that, he hauled back and hurled the walnut in their direction. It hit the pot–bellied stove, shattering into a hundred fragments.

Daniel took his time then, buttoning his coat and pulling on his gloves. Then tipping his hat to Julia, he spoke curtly, "Good day, Miss Crawford." With that he stalked to the door and went out, minus the ham he'd come for.

❖   ❖   ❖

Inside his own sitting room, Daniel flings his stovepipe hat and his leather gloves toward the small writing table. Then ripping off his great coat, he hurls it in the direction of the sofa. Standing before the window, he stares down at Bridge Street, his fists clenched by his sides. Snow continues to fall, filling in the tracks of those who walk below. But Daniel doesn't see them. He sees only Harvey Fudd. A wiry old man who wouldn't hurt a flea. A sensitive soul whose crimson face reflects a wounded spirit. A kind man who wants nothing more than a peppermint stick and acceptance.

Turning from the window, Daniel winces at the constriction in his chest. God, but he's done it again. Allowed another human being inside the sanctuary of his heart. And it hurts, pure and simple.

Overcome by emotion Daniel sinks into the chair by the window. For many moments he sits, staring at his hands. Hands that had once reached for his mother. Hands that now revel in the smooth texture of wood. Hands he had thought destined for nothing but good. Then suddenly, he's hiding his face in those hands, allowing tears to trickle between his long fingers, dripping onto the carpet.

And so for the first time since Marks' Mills, Daniel Lewis gives himself to weeping.

PART II
1869-1871

PROGRESS

"...it was the spring of hope..."
— *Charles Dickens*
A Tale of Two Cities

Chapter 14

March roared in like a lion in 1869. And this morning it was cold. Bitterly cold. But inside the Lewis Cabinet Shop, Livingston sweat as he worked. For the whipping winds outside couldn't compete with the snapping flames inside the pot–bellied stove. The place was a virtual oven. And now, Mr. Fudd was reaching for yet another stick of wood.

"Mr. Fudd, *please!*" Livingston removed his Havana as he spoke. "We don't need any more heat."

Evidently he'd spoken more sharply than he'd intended, for Harvey Fudd stopped, his face turning crimson. "I—I'm sorry, Mr. Lewis, sir. I'll put it back." And he carefully laid the kindling in the woodbox while continuing to suck a peppermint stick.

"That's all right," Livingston said, then returned to his Havana and a chair leg he was grooving.

"Say, Harvey, I've got a job for you over here." It was Daniel's voice, reassuring, yet commanding respect. "Take this rag and clean all the stain out."

"Oh yes, Mr. Daniel, sir, I will."

Livingston smiled then in spite of himself. Of course Daniel didn't need a clean rag; he'd only begun to stain that chair seat. Come to think of it, Daniel used a lot of things he didn't need these days. Ah well, what was a little stain or turpentine if it made his son happy? And he was glad, more glad than he could say, to have the old Daniel back.

It had all started last Christmas when Daniel invited the old man for dinner. Skeptical, he'd given consent. Then wished he hadn't. For Mr. Fudd's manners were appalling. He smacked his lips, mushed sweet potatoes and stewed apples between toothless gums and licked ham grease from his fingers. And at the close of the meal, he'd belched. Loud. To Livingston it was the epitome of rudeness. For despite the fact his father had been but a poor preacher, the Lewis children had been taught good manners.

He had to admit though, that despite his initial dislike of the old man, he'd done well to accept him. For Daniel liked him. Kind, sympathetic Daniel had become attached to this eccentric, uncouth man. And Livingston would tolerate anything for the sake of his son.

He'd been surprised though, at Daniel's proposal on Christmas evening. It was near bedtime and he'd sat in the overstuffed chair reading, when his son broke into his thoughts.

"I've decided to ask Harvey to help out in the shop."

Livingston had gaped then, nearly losing his Havana. But Daniel had held up a smooth hand. "I'll see he does no harm."

Thus the following Monday, Mr. Fudd had arrived early, ready for work. Hurrying to the stove, he removed the box of ashes and carried them to the dirt path in front of the store. Then quickly, he laid a fire. In no time the room was comfortably warm. And so a pattern was established. Mr. Fudd kept the shop warm and swept up while Livingston and Daniel worked.

By Saturday noon, Livingston had to admit Mr. Fudd was indeed a help. As the old man put on his coat to leave that day, Daniel motioned him to wait. Slipping behind the small counter, he pulled out an old cigar box. Extracting two greenbacks, he handed them to Mr. Fudd.

The old man simply stared at the money, his head shaking. "Why, Mr. Daniel, sir, what's thet fur?"

"It's your pay, Harvey."

"Oh no, I can't take thet. Why, I—I'm jist a foolish old man." He paused then and looked straight at Daniel. "I work fur love." And he tapped his thin chest.

Daniel smiled then, a quiet smile which traveled from his sensitive mouth, to his kind eyes, to his gentle hands. Considerately, he replaced the money in the box. "All right, Friend, you work for love. And Harvey— you're a good man."

The following Monday Mr. Fudd arrived early as before. As before, he had the shop warm within minutes. Once the fire was going, Daniel stopped sanding long enough to hand a new cigar box to his helper.

"Why, Mr. Daniel, sir, what's this fur?"

"It's for you. And when that's gone, there'll be more."

Mr. Fudd touched the box reverently, his head shaking. "Mine?"

Daniel nodded.

The old man lifted the lid then and let out a cry of joy. For inside were peppermint sticks. Lots and lots of peppermint sticks. Lots of colors too: yellow, green, blue, pink, and of course the inevitable red.

"Why, thank—thank you, Mr. Daniel, sir." And he placed a yellow stick between his gums.

"It's all right, Harvey. You've earned it by keeping the fire going and everything."

"Oh my, the fire." Setting his box aside, the old man hurried to add more wood to the already blazing fire. And every workday since, the shop had been unbearably hot.

Ah well, Livingston thought as he rolled up his sleeves another notch, it's worth a little heat to see my Daniel so happy.

Daniel smiled. For despite the cold rain spattering his bedroom window, he felt wonderful. So warm, so full, so alive. He felt as though he had emerged from a shell of loneliness into a world filled with love.

Lacing his fingers loosely behind his head, Daniel breathed in contentment and closed his eyes. Sleep came so much easier these days. Indeed everything was easier: walking, talking, eating, even working. And it was all because of Harvey Fudd.

Loving another person had never come easy for Daniel. For though his heart craved that special closeness that comes from sharing one's self, his vulnerable nature made him reluctant to reach out. He feared rejection, pure and simple. And the inevitable pain which followed. It didn't seem right that he should suffer when all he did was care for others. Even so, it happened.

The earliest object of his affection had been his mother. His childish heart had opened like a flower beneath the sunlight of her smiles. He'd been nurtured when those gentle fingers touched his charcoal hair or caressed his dimpled elbows. Even as he emerged from childhood to puberty, that affection continued. She no longer touched him, of course, but she baked his favorite gingerbread and stitched his shirts with extra care. In return, he loved her completely.

Then abruptly, his whole world changed. For his mother found a new person to love—his baby sister, Joy. After that, there was no more gingerbread or special shirts. There was only an emptiness inside himself. A void suffused with loneliness. And that loneliness prevailed, even when he worked in the shop with his father. The only thing he'd felt those days was the smoothness of wood beneath his fingers. Though it was an inadequate substitute for love, he made it suffice. For he vowed he'd never care again. Ever.

But he did. For as his baby sister emerged into childhood, she reached for his heart. He tried to distance himself, but her bubbly spirit and brunette curls were ever there, begging him to care. And so he did. He'd let her ride on his shoulders when he went for the mail. He'd bought her horehound drops and licorice whips. Thus by the time Joy was three, Daniel loved her, pure and simple. And then in a matter of seconds, she'd choked to death on sawdust.

Daniel sighed and opened his eyes. Gazing through the darkness at his rain–spattered window, he realized he still loved that little girl. Part of him always would, he supposed. For Joy had filled him with laughter and hope.

Yet the pain that had followed his sister's death had been more than he could stand. And so once again, he'd closed his heart to love. It simply wasn't worth the risk.

But then came War. And once again his world was flipped upside down. He hated the thought of war ,pure and simple. His sensitive nature simply couldn't fathom the idea of killing. This being so, he delayed enlisting as long as possible, hoping the hostilities would blow over. But such was not to be. When conditions continued to worsen, he knew he'd have to go. If nothing else, he must be assured that he and his father could continue their business unmolested.

And so the morning of October 12, 1863, found Daniel marching behind Union General Brown as they pursued Secessionist Shelby from Boonville to Marshall. Concentrating on the beauty of the day, he answered politely the questions of a fellow soldier, Russell Long. Russell, a Marshall boy himself, was anxious to stop the Secesh before they reached his home. By afternoon Russell's concern for his family was causing Daniel pain. He clenched his fist at the thought of his companion's widowed mother and younger siblings being routed from their humble home.

More convinced than ever that killing was wrong, Daniel trod the dirt road in silence. Then toward evening, as they neared the town of Salt Fork, Brown ordered his men to fire six pounders into Shelby's rear guard. When a Secesh was killed outright, Daniel's fingers automatically clenched into a fist. And when Shelby's men retaliated, severing a fellow Yank's legs, a band tightened about Daniel's chest until he could scarcely breathe.

That night, as he shared Russell's jug of corn liquor, Daniel tried to put the events of the evening behind him. But couldn't. Killing was senseless, pure and simple. Already he was wishing he hadn't signed up. Even so, he was pleased when the following day, they routed Shelby, preventing him from taking Marshall.

But the battle over Marshall seemed child's play compared to the ordeals which followed. For the spring of 1864 found Union troops deep in Arkansas, heading for Louisiana. After a fierce battle they took the town of Camden, about a hundred miles south of Little Rock. But victory was short–lived. With Secesh armies threatening and supplies running low, General Steele sent a wagon train to Pine Bluff for provisions. Russell was among those selected for the trip. As the wagons set off, Russell waved to Daniel, a smile on his young, lean face. For, once assured his family was protected by Union troops, Russell had become enthused about the War. But not Daniel. He didn't suppose he could ever feel good about fighting. And now, as he gazed after the retreating wagons, he wished he was going too. At least there he'd have a friend. Ah well, Russell would return within the week.

Only he didn't. At a place called Marks' Mills Secesh captured the train of provisions. And they wounded, captured, or killed most of the Union men.

Daniel, upon hearing that his friend was dead, wept. Giant tears slipped between his fingers as he sat, face in hands, before the camp fire. God, he hated war! He hated fighting, he hated killing, and yes, he hated life itself. For life was a cruel taskmaster, snatching from him yet another person he had dared to care for.

Angrily, Daniel stalked along with the remaining troops as they retreated to Little Rock. But even retreat wasn't easy. At a place called Jenkins' Ferry, they had to ford the Saline River. All night they worked, struggling in the rain, trying to get their wagons and artillery across. Dawn came, and still they struggled. And then when it seemed nothing could be worse than the fog or mud, the Secesh attacked.

It was then that Daniel learned to kill. Still grieving for Russell, when he saw a musket barrel aimed at him, he didn't think twice; he simply shoved his bayonet into the Secesh's belly. Jerking it free, he slashed at another and another and still another. By afternoon Daniel had lost count of the enemy he'd slain. Yet, he felt no shame. And the truth was, he felt no excitement either. Not even when the battle turned in their favor.

That night he sat beside the campfire, whittling a stick he'd found.

Refusing both food and liquor, he concentrated wholly on the wood in his hands, savagely slicing it with his knife.

"Young man."

Daniel looked up to see a major at his side. Standing, he saluted.

The officer waved him at ease. "We need a fellow like yourself." He nodded toward the knife and mutilated stick. "Follow me."

Daniel hesitated. Then strapping on his gear, he strode after the major. They halted outside a tent.

"Inside." The major nodded, lifting the flap.

Daniel stepped inside.

"Boy am I glad to see you." A doctor, his apron smeared with crimson, shoved a bloody knife into his hands. "We're the medical team," he explained. Then, sensing Daniel's hesitation, he snapped. "Get busy."

That night eclipsed any suffering Daniel had ever known. His hands, so used to the warm, satiny feel of wood, were forced to press cold, clammy skin. He tried to distance himself from the gangrenous limbs on the table and his own bloody appendages. But soon it all ran together: the writhing body before him, his own exhausted frame, and the instrument in his hands. It was butchery, pure and simple. His mind scarcely registered the screams about him as deftly he cut away skin and tissue, then severed limbs with a blood streaked saw.

After an eternity, morning came and Daniel emerged from the tent. The atmosphere had cleared. But Daniel's brain remained enshrouded in fog. Mechanically, he doused his uniform in the river to rid it of blood and waste. Mechanically, he washed his hands. Mechanically, he collected his gear in preparation for the resumed march to Little Rock.

From that day on he moved through life, a mere form. The remaining events of the War and of those first years back at home failed to penetrate that rigid exterior, failed to touch the aching loneliness inside him.

And then on a cold day last December, he'd seen an eccentric old man being ridiculed. And the simple childlike innocence of that wiry being had poked a hole in his armor.

Smiling in the darkness, Daniel pondered the mystery. Why had love claimed him again in the form of a man he scarcely knew? What was there about love that could fill a man's being with peace and contentment? He didn't know . He only knew that he derived pleasure, pure pleasure, from something as simple as watching Harvey Fudd suck on a peppermint stick.

Chapter 15

It was after supper and the Fitzsimmons family sat around the kitchen table, basking in the lingering warmth from the cookstove. That is, they all sat except for Mamie. She stood, as she always did this time of evening, before the mirror over the washstand, brushing her long hair.

To Jane, who poured hot water over tea leaves, it seemed that Mamie was becoming increasingly self–centered. Downright hard to get along with, she was. Glancing at her niece's sleek mane, gleaming to an almost copper hue in the lamplight, Jane wondered if the prospects of being a spinster worried the girl. Course it was bound to. Some. Still an all, thet didn't give her no right to be so blamed impudent. Why land sakes, twenty wasn't *ancient*. Leastwise she wasn't thirty four an—

"Thet sure was good peach pie, My Ma. Really an truly it was." Katie licked her fork before accepting a cup of tea from Jane.

"Aye, Colleen, it was, to be sure," Michael agreed. "An I'm thinkin we'd best enjoy it, mind, cause there'll be no peaches this year. Thet last cold spell nipped them buds right good."

"Sure did," Thomas spoke from around his corncob pipe, as he watched Michael lace his tea with corn liquor. "But fur all thet, we'll have apples aplenty. An nothin in this world beats them fried apple pies."

"Well, I like peaches, anyways," Katie defended. "An cherries."

No one disputed her word. For the attention had returned to Thomas who was now sipping from the jug. To Jane it seemed he'd been adrinkin steady like fur several months now. Not thet he ever bothered anybody. Still an all, it did set a person to wonderin.

"Confound you, Son, stop guzzlin thet foul–smellin stuff." Jordana's voice was sharp as she waved a finger in Thomas' direction.

But Thomas paid her no mind. Tipping the stone jug, he took yet another swig.

"Confound it, Thomas, I said quit." And Jordana rounded the table, preparing to snatch the jug.

But Thomas saw her coming. Quickly, he lifted his left hand, suspending the jug above his head.

"Now, jist a minute, My Ma. I ain't takin orders like some slave. An I ain't no youngin neither. Fact is, I'm a growed up man an I can take a drink of this here corn liquor or anything else I've a mind to. So you'd jist damn well back off."

With that, Thomas tipped the jug and gulped its remaining contents. Then setting the stoneware firmly on the table, he picked up his pipe and crossed the room. But at the stairway door he turned, shifting his feet nervously. "Jist don't none of you tell Julia," he said.

"Confound thet boy," Jordana reiterated, as Thomas' footsteps echoed noisily on the stairs. Then turning to her husband, she accused, "Anyways, it's your fault fur lettin him have thet jug."

"Aye, Colleen, I know you're upset, to be sure. But Me Lad's a man now, like he said. He can drink if he's a mind to.

For a moment Jordana looked nonplused. Then dabbing at her eyes, she went on. "Anyways, Thomas used to be such a nice boy. He never had need of drink till thet awful election last fall. If you hadn't trotted off leavin him tied up that away—"

Oh my, here we go again, Jane frowned in dismay. Land sakes, couldn't Jordana ever leave the past alone? As fur Michael, Jane thanked the good Lord thet her brother–in–law took life in stride the way he did. Course he hurt aplenty, she knew thet. Still an all, he never upbraided his wife fur *her* outbursts.

"Aw, My Ma, don't take on so. It ain't My Pa thet's hurt Thomas. It's them God–awful Federals. " And Mamie shook her heavy hair back from her face.

"Aye, Lass, them Fed's is a nuisance, to be sure. Still, thet's no cause to disrespect your Maker."

"Anyways, if them Feds is so awful, how come you're so sweet on Daniel Lewis?" This from Katie who'd just finished her tea.

"Fur the same reason you're stuck on Thane Chapman, Miss Smarty."

"Drat it all, anyways. Who said—"

"Nobody *said* anything. But I got eyes, ain't I? Anyways, Daniel's different. Why he's a real man, not jist some youngin." And Mamie resumed her brushing.

"He's different all right," Katie snapped. "Purt nigh crazy from all I hear."

"Aye, Lass, he was to be sure." Michael placed his empty cup on his plate and shoved the plate aside. "But he's right normal now. Meself, I'm thinkin thet wee little man's what's makin things special like."

"Course he is," Jane said. "Why, I always did think thet Harvey Fudd was downright nice if folks would jist give him a chance."

"An Daniel's been the one to do it. So there." Mamie spat as she turned back to the mirror.

Jane winced. Land sakes, she did wish Mamie wouldn't act so high an mighty with Katie. Still an all, she agreed thet Daniel Lewis was a good man. Why land sakes, if it wasn't fur thet stovepipe hat he might have been Robert Saylor back in '49. Both of them was tall, had thick beards an charcoal hair. Both had gentle hands too. She'd felt Robert's hands on her shoulders more than once in them days. Course she'd been but a girl then, only fourteen or so, about Katie's age. Still an all, she'd felt love. An thet love fur Robert persisted despite the fact he ran off with James to California.

"Aye, Lass, you're right purty when you smile like thet." Michael's voice punctured her daydream of Robert.

Embarrassed, Jane stammered. "Why land sakes, I—I didn't even know I was asmilin."

"Aye, Lass, you was, to be sure." And Michael smiled at her.

Jane touched the fiery brand on her face then and smiled even broader. Michael thought she was downright purty. Leastwise he'd said so. An thet gleam in them hazel eyes told her he meant it.

It was raining and Thomas was glad. Glad fur an excuse to git out of the garden an mosey on down to Crawford's store. Course he wouldn't be buyin much—jist some tobacco or coffee. Fact was, it was Julia he was goin to see. Cause he hadn't seen much of her since last fall. Jist thinkin on thet was enough to make a feller feel plumb miserable. Fur Julia had jist blinked at him an closed the door in his face when he went callin. But Thomas wasn't leavin. Leastwise not till he knowed why she was behavin this way. And so he'd shoved the door back open. Then planting both feet firmly on the threshold, he glared at her.

"Now, wait jist a minute. You know I aim to marry you. So why can't you be nice like, an let me in?"

At this Julia snapped. "No," she said, "I won't. Cause you ain't welcome here no more. Not after the way you got Papa in trouble with them Feds. So please, jist go away. Find some other gal to bother."

Thomas had purt near shoved her aside an entered anyway, then thought better of it. A feller could git into trouble with her Papa if he didn't go easy like. And Thomas didn't want to alienate Wade's Pa any more than he already had. He owed his friend thet much.

And so despite the fact he needed her somethin awful, Thomas had stayed away from Julia's house. He thought once of goin to church jist to see her, but decided against thet. A feller couldn't be expected to change his *whole* life fur a gal. Why, already he'd quit the gang because of her. He couldn't chance pullin off more shenanigans an havin Julia or her Pa find out. Anyways, he was sick an tired of Uriah Martin bossin him around. An he'd told him so.

Uriah had responded with a hardened jaw and eyes that were points of steel. "Why, you coward," he snarled.

"Now, jist a minute," Thomas, his legs straight as sticks, glared back at his friend. "I ain't quittin on Missouri jist cause I'm leavin this here gang. Why, a feller would have to be plumb crazy to do thet."

"Then you're crazy *an* a quitter. An I don't take to quitters, see?" And he'd spit in Thomas' face.

At that Thomas had pulled his Colt .36, but Uriah had merely laughed, a blood–curdling, bone–chilling laugh. "Go ahead, coward. Murder me an see what thet gits you."

In all his born days Thomas had never been so angry, or so ashamed. He'd have killed Uriah on the spot but fur Julia. It was plumb stupid of him to let Uriah laugh, then walk away. But he had to. Fur if Julia ever caught wind he'd pulled off a murder, she'd never consent to marry him. An he'd lose his last link with Wade.

Thomas sighed as he shoved open the door to Crawford's store, then brightened when a man beside the stove lifted a hand in greeting. Tevis McKinley. Good old Tevis. Fur despite every thing thet had happened, Tevis was still his friend.

Crossing the room, Thomas removed his cloak, checked the left pocket, then hung it on the back of a chair and sat down. Glancing about, he saw Julia grinding coffee for Mrs. Simms. If she noticed his smile, she didn't let on. Disappointed, Thomas gave his attention to relighting his pipe.

"Mighty wet out there," Tevis observed as Thomas tamped out damp tobacco.

Thomas nodded. "Makes a feller wonder if spring's ever comin."

"Sure does. Wonder if it'll be dry enough to start work on thet Lexington an St. Louis line purty soon?"

"Down Sedalia way?"

"Yep. Thet track's goin to go right through Hughesville, Houstonia an then us."

"How long you reckon it'll take to lay all the way to Lexington?"

"Hard to say. Three years maybe. Leastwise thet's what they're asayin."

"Thet sure sounds dandy. Bound to change a lot of things around here."

"Can't say but what I agree with you there," Mr. Crawford spoke from behind the scales where he weighed flour. "Thet railroad is goin to run right behind this here store. There you are, Mable." He smiled as he handed Mrs. Ponder a bag of flour.

"Thet will change a thing or two, won't it?" Thomas observed as he sat with his left ankle resting on his right knee.

Tevis nodded. "Other things are changin too."

"How's thet?"

"Well they're asayin a Colonel Walton from Lexington is goin to fix up them springs south of town."

"The ones owned by Dr. Yantis?"

"Yep. Plans on makin some kind of health spa. Leastwise thet's my understandin."

"A health spa?" For the first time Julia spoke, her heart–shaped face alight with pleasure. "Here? In Brownsville?"

Tevis nodded. "Thet's what they're asayin, anyways."

"A health spa," Julia mused. "Jist think, Papa, maybe we could git some of thet spring water. Thet would make such lovely tea."

"Can't say but what I agree with you there," Mr. Crawford smiled. "Spring water can taste mighty good."

"Reckon so. Leastwise My Ma has talked of spring water fur years," Thomas offered, his heart pounding at the look of pleasure in Julia's violet eyes. "Course thet spring she remembers was back there in Kentucky."

"Well, this here's bound to be better than thet. Fur it tastes real sweet like. Leastwise thet's what folks is asayin."

Thomas nodded. Then reaching into his cloak pocket, he pulled out a small cloth–wrapped bundle. Rising, he strode to the counter.

"Speakin on things sweet," he said, "this here's a sweet fur the purtiest gal I know." And he handed Julia a warm, fried apple pie.

Chapter 16

The first Sunday in June was gorgeous. The twittering of birds, the scent of roses, the warmth of sunshine made Katie want to rush outdoors, twirl about in her new dress and stretch her arms toward the sky. Instead, she sat dutifully in church, sandwiched between My Ma and Aunt Jane. Only one thing made it bearable to be inside a stuffy churchhouse on a brilliant day like this—them hymns. Why my goodness, them words jist made her feel all special like inside. Warm they was, an soothin. An if she closed her eyes, she could pretend she was right up there next to God himself.

> *Sweet hour of prayer, sweet hour of prayer,*
> *That calls me from a world of care,*
> *And bids me at my Father's throne,*
> *Make all my wants and wishes known!*[1]

Opening her eyes, Katie noted that My Ma wasn't singing. Course she rarely did. Leastwise she hadn't since thet dumb War took Patrick away. Still, Katie wished she'd do somethin besides wipe her eyes with thet handkerchief. Why my goodness, My Ma could smile purtier than anybody if she'd a mind to. Katie sighed. She loved My Ma. Really an truly she did. Still, she jist couldn't stand it, watchin her take on so. Why, ever now an again she jist wanted to take her in hand an tell her to stop actin so gloomy like. Course she didn't. But she wanted to, anyways. Jist like she wanted to light into Mamie fur bein such a brat.

Glancing beyond My Ma, Katie saw that her sister wasn't singing either. An she knowed right off like it was cause of Daniel Lewis. Why my goodness, it was jist plain silly the way Mamie shifted her eyes, searchin across the aisle fur Daniel. Course he wasn't there. She should have knowed he wouldn't be. Still, there was no accountin fur the dumb things her sister did.

Sighing, Katie turned back to Aunt Jane. And smiled. Fur Aunt Jane was singin all right. Loud enough fur all the rest of them put together. An thet glow on her face made her seem almost purty like, in spite of thet ugly birthmark. Course Aunt Jane didn't *always* sing like thet. Why my goodness, she'd purt nigh stopped bein happy altogether after them slaves moved off. Sad, she'd been. Really an truly sad. But thet was past now. Today she radiated contentment.

> In seasons of distress and grief,
> My soul has often found relief,
> And oft escaped the tempter's snare
> By thy return, sweet hour of prayer.[2]

It was during the sermon that Katie began to fidget. Now, *she* was the one glancing across the aisle toward the men. An not jist at any man either, but Thane Chapman. Course she knowed she was bein silly fur noticin him this way. But drat it all, she couldn't help it. Fur Thane wasn't a skinny youngin no more. Growed up he was, with broad shoulders thet narrowed to a trim waist an slim hips. An thet mustache! Chestnut it was, like them waves on his head. But his eyes were what Katie noticed most. Big an blue, they was. More blue even than Bonnie's. And when they turned toward her, Katie grew positively giddy with excitement.

But since those eyes were presently focused on the preacher, Katie let her glance fall on a second young man seated next to Thane. Randall Dalton. Why my goodness, how come he showed up this mornin, anyways? Why, she reckoned he hadn't been to church since before his grandma passed away last year. It jist didn't make no sense at all.

She let her glance shift then to the ladies' side of the aisle. Her eyes came to rest on a cascade of chestnut curls spilling gently over shoulders clad in violet satin. She did hope she an Bonnie could find time fur visitin after service. Why my goodness, they hadn't seen each other fur ages. Leastwise not since midweek. An thet was only when Katie called fur the mail.

And so as the congregation spilled out of the church near midday, Katie loitered on the grass instead of walking on home with her family. Within minutes, Bonnie was at her side.

"Oh, Katie, you're so purty!" Bonnie burst out as she fingered the pink upper skirt of Katie's dress. "An where'd you git thet dainty parasol, anyways?"

"Aunt Jane stitched it up fur me. Made the bow too." And Katie patted the poplin bow which nestled atop her upswept hair.

"Well, she really did a right nice job, thet's fur sure. I'll bet Thane thinks so too. He's standin right over there." And Bonnie pointed to a group of young men who lingered, only yards from themselves.

"Oh my goodness," Katie whispered, her head spinning with pleasure.

But it was Randall Dalton, rather than Thane, who broke away from the group.

"Nice day, Miss Chapman, Miss Fitzsimmons." He tipped his hat and smiled at Bonnie. "Miss Chapman, your mother gives her permission for me to see you home. If you're willing, of course."

"Oh my gracious," Bonnie's hand flew to her throat. "Why, yes. Yes, of course I'm willin." And she took his proffered arm. "Bye, Katie." She blew her friend a kiss then, her eyes shining.

Watching Bonnie leave on the arm of handsome Randall Dalton, Katie's thoughts returned to Thane. Glancing about, she saw him, alone now, his head bent, his hands inside his trouser pockets as he traced a figure in the dust with the toe of his boot.

As though aware of her scrutiny, Thane looked up. "Katie?"

Katie nodded, unable to speak for the pleasure welling within her.

Thane advanced toward her then, his normally pale face flushing. "I— I wondered— Thet is— Oh gosh, Katie, will you let me walk you home?"

"Oh my goodness, yes." And without thinking, Katie held out her right hand.

Thane smiled then, a shy, lopsided grin, as he took her small hand into his own larger, firmer one.

Silently, they strolled along Main Street, Katie acutely conscious of the man beside her.

"Nice day, ain't it?" Thane offered.

"Sure is," Katie agreed. "I like the sound of them birds best. Cardinals are the purtiest, don't you think?"

Thane nodded. "Cept fur you. You're *real* purty."

"Oh my goodness. Why, thank you."

At Katie's words, Thane blushed again, the color stealing all the way from his white collar to his chestnut hair. Then abruptly, he dropped her hand. After that neither of them spoke again until they reached the Fitzsimmons' back porch.

Thane turned to Katie then, his blue eyes level with her forehead. "Katie, I—I know you're Bonnie's best friend an all. An thet ain't bad. In fact, it's good. Real good. It's jist thet I wonder— Thet is— Oh gosh, Katie, what I mean to say is would you walk with me again next Sunday? Even if Randall don't take to my sister?"

"Oh my goodness, yes. Yes, of course I will."

"Thanks." And before Katie could say another word, Thane had turned and was hurrying down the path and across West Street.

Striding home from church, Jordana ignored her sister's comments on the morning service, letting her mind rush ahead to dinner preparations. Let's see now, thet pork an taters would be done. All she need do was wilt the lettuce (assumin thet Thomas remembered to pick it), slice the bread, an cut the pie. Course she knowed Thomas liked his apple pie fried. Still, there was jist so much a body could do, it bein the Sabbath an all.

Entering the kitchen, Jordana stopped short. Instead of fiddlin round like he usually did on Sundays, Michael was workin. He'd turned over them plates an cups an was removin the tea towel thet covered the butter an such. Why, whatever ailed the man, anyways?

"Aye, Colleen," Michael laid the towel on the work table and advanced to meet her. "It's a lovely day, to be sure."

"Thet's fur certain," Jordana snapped. "But confound you, what's the meanin of this?" She gestured toward the table.

"Aye, Colleen, I know you're wonderin, mind. But meself, I'm thinkin you'll like what I've got fur you." And taking up the Bellflower pitcher, Michael poured a glass of water and handed it to his wife.

Jordana simply stared at it.

"Aye, Colleen, it's spring water, to be sure."

"*Spring* water?"

"Aye. While you lasses was sittin in church this mornin, I hitched old Dobbin to the wagon and fetched several jugs of thet there Sweet Spring water."

"Spring water," Jordana repeated softly. "Spring water." Smiling, she lifted the glass and drank deeply, savoring the taste and the memory of a flaxen–haired girl dipping a tin cup into a pool of glistening water.

"My but thet was good." Jordana set her emptied glass on the table. Then picking up the nearly full pitcher, she carried it to the washstand. There, she placed her left hand in a basin and slowly poured the water over it. "Spring water." Soft tears slipped from her eyes and glided down her cheeks, falling gently into the smooth flow of clear water.

"Aye, Colleen, them is happy tears, to be sure." And a pair of burly hands caressed her shoulders, tenderly easing her against him.

For a moment Jordana relaxed, basking in the comfort of her husband's touch. Then remembering Patrick and Carrie, she felt again those cool fingers stroking her heart. Confound thet man, why couldn't he jist leave her alone?

She straightened then, and turning away from Michael, she marched across the room to the table. Pulling out a chair, she sat down.

"Let's eat," she said.

Chapter 17

Clip, clop. Clip, clop. The muted echo of old Dobbin's shoes mingled with the creak of wood as the Fitzsimmons' wagon rattled along the dusty street. It was August. And hot. So hot, in fact, that Jordana had nearly swooned as she walked home from church this mornin. She craved but one thing—a cup of thet cool, Sweet Spring water. Thus when she'd discovered only a spoonful of tepid liquid left from the week before, she'd grown angry.

"Confound you, Man, can't you see I have need of a cold drink?" And she shook her finger directly at Michael.

"Aye, Colleen, it's a hot one, to be sure. An I'm thinkin you might like to see them springs yourself. Have a special time like."

Jordana had hurried then to rustle up dinner, warm fingers caressing her spirit. My but she felt plumb good. After all, she wasn't used to gaddin about, specially on the Sabbath. A glimpse of them there springs was jist what she had need of.

And now, as the wagon turned from the dirt road and moved into the shelter of oak trees, Jordana felt almost happy.

"Aye, Colleen, they've been workin hard this week, to be sure. An I'm thinkin thet Pagoda is purt nigh the purtiest thing I ever seen."

"Thet's fur certain," Jordana agreed. For nestled among emerald oak leaves, the octagonal structure with its cupolaed roof and open sides looked cool and inviting. Glimpses of the gleaming Blackwater River beyond added to its enticement.

Oblivious to the outsiders strolling about, Jordana jumped from the wagon, sped across the rustic bridge and hurried into the Pagoda. At the far side she stopped, her hand on a wooden column, and stared below. And there, spurting from a pebble–lined basin, was the clearest water she had ever seen. With a cry of joy, Jordana raced down the broad, stone steps. Jerking off her calico bonnet, she flopped onto her stomach and drank greedily. Satisfied, she sat up, and cupping her hands, she caught the sparkling water and doused her face. My but thet felt good! Then giggling like a school girl, she pulled off her shoes and stockings. She wiggled her toes and laughed as the crystalline stream poured over her tired feet.

Gazing up through swaying branches to the patch of turquoise sky beyond, Jordana felt warm wings of contentment flutter about her heart. Gradually they stilled, allowing their comfortable beauty to seep into her spirit. My but this was a wonderful feelin. Purt nigh as good as what she'd knowed back there in Kentucky.

Course thet feelin wasn't so good when thet slave, Dinah, had been trotted off to the auction block in Glasgow. An what fur, Jordana couldn't figure out.

"Because," James had told her. "Jist because."

An then jist a few weeks later, *she* was leavin. The whole Douglas family was pullin up stakes an goin to Missouri. An despite her eleven years, Jordana cried, dabbin at her eyes with her dress tail. Awful it was, jist awful. After all, Kentucky was her home. Confound it, why did they have to leave fur, anyways?

"Because," James blurted, "the church session got wind of what Pa did to Dinah. He'll be barred from the fellowship in no time."

Still, Jordana hadn't understood. Why did everything have to be so complicated fur, anyways? Why, if it hadn't been fur Carrie, she'd have jist give up an died. But the memory of her flaxen–haired cousin and the marvelous taste of that Big Spring water had sustained her through the long, arduous trip to Missouri.

But movin to Missouri hadn't changed Pa one bit. Not long after they'd settled on a farm near Brownsville, Pa started fiddlin round with her, Jordana. His own daughter. Jordana winced to realize just how naive she'd been in those days. She'd eagerly followed him when he asked her to the barn to "help him". Course she had thought it a mite strange, him havin two slaves an all. Still, she'd be all right. This was her pa, after all. An she loved him.

The barn was empty when they entered. Empty an silent. There was only the smell of manure an dust an hay. An it was toward the hay thet Pa had shoved her.

"Take them drawers off," he'd ordered.

Mystified, Jordana had pulled her underdrawers down to her knees. Why was Pa unfastenin his trousers fur, anyways? An then he was rippin her drawers plumb off her.

Jordana dabbed at the tears in her eyes as she gazed at the bright August sky. Cool fingers threatened to invade the warm recesses of her heart. Trailing her hand in the stream of glistening water, she felt the stir of warmth again. An almost, she could furgit. Almost, she could furgit how glad she'd been thet day James found Pa dead in them hemp fields. Almost, she could furgit her vow never to trust another man.

But then there was Michael. Only sixteen she was when he proposed, an scared as a rabbit. Yet, she'd gone plumb silly an married him. After all, Michael was the kindest, most carin person in the world. An thet kindness brought with it warmth. She wondered though, as she had before, if he'd have married her had he knowed about Pa. Probably so. Fur Michael was different thet way. He didn't love you cause you was smart or purty or pure. He loved you cause he loved you. He didn't need no other reason.

"Colleen?" It was Michael, his hand on her shoulder.

Startled, Jordana looked up. Up beyond Michael to where a couple stood at the top of the steps. Well dressed they was, an waitin with tin cups in hand. Confound it, how long had they been gawkin at her, anyways? Jumping up, Jordana snatched her bonnet and shoes, and raced up the steps, leaving Michael to follow.

Panting, she plopped onto a seat in the Pagoda. Then pulling on her stockings, she studied the lady who waited at the top of the steps. Her wheat–colored hair was swept up in a neat roll beneath a broad, satin bow. And her powder–blue skirt rustled faintly in the breeze. Presently, her companion reappeared and offered her a tin cup. They smiled at each other, then touched their cups together and drank. Finished, they replaced their cups on the hooks extending from the ceiling and strolled off.

Jordana, her gray eyes following them, felt a twitch of envy. Then with a wave of her hand, she dismissed them. After all, they was nothin but city folks come fur a visit. An city folks was jist plumb silly, anyways.

Rising, Jordana walked to the steps and gazed once more at the spring below. Michael was down there now, fillin up his jugs. Fur her.

Suddenly, as she watched those burly shoulders bend over that spurting rush of water, Jordana had the urge to run down the steps, take that round chin in her hands and kiss her husband on the lips. But she didn't. Why, such a thing would be plumb stupid. Hadn't she loved before? Pa? Carrie? Patrick? No. She jist couldn't. A body could jist stand so much pain.

Back in the wagon, Jordana tied on her bonnet and gazed wistfully at the swaying oak branches which sheltered the Pagoda and that refreshing spring. Though she was plumb tuckered out now, she would come again. Despite them city folks and their highfalutin ways, she'd return. Fur today she'd experienced again thet delicious feel of spring water on her skin. Today, she'd pried from her soul feelins long repressed. Today, she'd finally come home. Fur today, she'd discovered a bit of Kentucky in the heart of Missouri.

Chapter 18

Jane was worried about Katie. Ever since this mornin she'd knowed thet child was sick. Why land sakes, she'd come to the breakfast table lookin white as a sheet. An ashakin too, like she was cold. Course purt near everbody was cold these days. Leastwise she was. After thet hot summer who'd have thought September would turn downright wintry? But Katie was more than a mite cold. And by midafternoon Jane's worst fears were confirmed. Katie had the ague.

Dispatching Thomas to the drugstore for quinine, Jane helped Katie undress and put her into her own bed. No use Mamie agittin sick too. Then filling a basin with tepid water and alcohol, she began bathing the girl's face.

"No!" Katie pushed her hand away. "Thet's too cold."

"I know, Child, but it's got to be done. Land sakes, we can't have you astayin sick this away."

But Katie, her eyes bright with fever, would not reason. "But, Aunt Jane, it's so cold. Really an truly it is."

"I know, Child, I know." And Jane continued sponging the thrashing figure until Thomas returned. Empty handed.

"What, no quinine? Land sakes, I need pills to git this child well. What's the matter with you, anyways?"

At this, Thomas pulled himself up, his legs straight as sticks. "Now, jist a minute, Aunt Jane. This here fever is spreadin everywheres. Serious like, it is. An them druggists is plumb out of pills. Why, in all my born days I never seen so many folks wantin help."

"Well, thank the good Lord fur whiskey, anyways." And Jane hurried down to the kitchen.

Seconds later she spooned the stout liquid between Katie's parched lips. But the fever remained unabated. Once, Katie thought Jane was Bonnie.

"Oh my goodness, you sure do look purty in thet blue dress. Does Thane think I'm purty? Course he does. Why, he said I looked jist plain silly wearin thet parasol fur a hat."

"Katie, Child, hush." And Jane began again to sponge the fevered body with water and alcohol.

"Is thet you, My Ma?"

"No, Child, it's me, Aunt Jane."

"Oh."

Wringing out a cloth for the hundredth time, Jane frowned. What was the matter with her sister, anyways? Why land sakes, she'd hardly poked her head in the door since Katie took sick. Course she never had cottoned to Katie much. Fact was, Jordana hadn't wanted no more youngins after Mamie. Then she'd had thet tiny girl, stillborn. An after thet, Katie.

Jane sighed, wondering just how long she could keep this up. And then twenty four hours after the fever had commenced, it broke.

"Aunt Jane?"

"Land sakes, Child, don't scare me thet away. Course, it's me." And leaning down, she kissed the cooled brow. "I'll fix you some warm broth now."

Half an hour later, Jane spooned the last of the broth into Katie's eager mouth.

"Um. Thet was good. Really an truly it was." And Katie stretched a trembling hand to touch her aunt's arm. Seconds later, she slept.

Empty bowl in hand, Jane tiptoed from the room and down the stairs. Land sakes, but she was tired. She'd jist put this dish on the table an plop into a rocker. But in the kitchen she found Jordana, pouring up another bowl of broth.

"Fur Michael," she explained.

"Land sakes, can't thet man come home fur his dinner?"

"Confound you, Jane, he's sick. Just plumb tuckered out, he is. You'd best see to him." And nodding toward the bedroom, she handed the bowl to Jane.

"Well, of all the blamed—" Jane stopped, knowing it was useless to complain. Ever since Patrick's death Jordana had avoided sick rooms like they was the plague.

At the bedroom door, she knocked. When Michael failed to answer, she peeked in. There he sat, shaking like a leaf, trying to unlace his boots.

Crossing to the bureau, Jane set down the bowl, then knelt before the bed.

"Land sakes, let me do this," she said, and quickly eased his feet from the heavy boots. Best leave his socks on, she decided. But he needed a night shirt. Unsure of where to look, she began poking among drawers. Land sakes, she hated nosin through other folks' things. Still an all, it couldn't be helped.

"Aye, Lass, in there." Michael pointed a shaky finger toward the left hand drawer on the bottom. He began fumbling with his shirt then, but in the end it was Jane who slipped on the night shirt and eased him into bed. She managed to get a little broth down him before he pushed her hand aside.

"Aye, Lass, thet's enough now."

A short time later, he threw off the covers. Jane, retrieving them, touched his flushed face. Land sakes, he was aburnin up with fever. Quickly, she ordered Thomas back to the drug store for more alcohol, then spooned whiskey into her patient's throat. By then Michael had thrown off the covers again. Pulling them back up, she sighed.

"Land sakes, Michael, you got to stay covered."

But he didn't. And when next she pulled them up, he grasped her arm. "Aye, Colleen, love me jist a little. Please?"

For once, Jane held her tongue. No use atryin to talk sense to a man beside himself with fever. Instead, she gave him another spoonful of whiskey and mixed water and alcohol in a basin. Land sakes, she did wish Thomas would hurry up. Why, this little dab of alcohol didn't amount to a hill of beans.

But when Thomas returned, he was empty handed as before. "There's more fever in this town than you can shake a stick at," he complained. "Makes a feller feel real helpless like. No alcohol or quinine either. Plumb sold out everywheres."

Jane stared at him, a frown creasing her brow. Then giving her nephew a gentle shove, she said, "Bring me a jug of thet corn liquor."

Now it was Thomas' turn to stare.

"Land sakes, I ain't aimin to *drink* it. Now, scat."

Seconds later, Thomas reappeared with the jug. Uncorking it, Jane poured a generous amount of the liquor into her basin half full of water.

"Aunt Jane, thet's jist plumb stupid. What you aimin to do, anyways?"

"*I'm* again to bathe your pa. An *you're* again to hold him still."

"Now, jist a minute, Aunt Jane. You know I can't—"

"Course you can. Now, git busy."

For hours they worked, Jane sponging the fevered face and limbs while Thomas literally leaned on his Pa to keep him quiet. And their persistence paid off. In the wee hours of the morning, the fever broke. Sweat poured down Michael's heavy frame, soaking the bed.

Jane's laugh was nearly hysterical. "Why land sakes, he's agoin to be all right after all." She swooned then, but grasped the bedpost to keep from falling.

"Thomas," she ordered. "Git your ma or Mamie to help change your pa. I got to rest fur a spell."

When Jane awoke, it was still dark. Sitting upright in her sewing rocker, she glanced about. By the glowing coals in the fireplace, she saw her sister sleeping in Michael's rocker. Michael. How was he? Land sakes, was no one awatchin him?

Rising, Jane lit a lamp, then hurried through the kitchen to the bedroom.

"Aye, Colleen, is thet you?"

"Land sakes, no. It's jist me." Jane crossed the room and set the lamp on the bureau . Then nearing the bed, she smiled at the big man lying there. "Well, you certainly look a mite better. You purt near scared us all to death there fur awhile."

"Aye, Lass, I am feelin better, to be sure."

"How about some broth?"

At his nod, Jane slipped into the kitchen. But minutes later when she returned, Michael was asleep.

Drawing the covers more firmly about his burly shoulders, she stooped to kiss a bristled cheek. Land sakes, she was glad he was amendin. Things would be down right awful around here without him.

❖   ❖   ❖

Katie opened her eyes to see sunlight streaming through the east window, dappling the plank floor with globs of gold. Stretching her arms, she decided to get up. She'd laid in Aunt Jane's bed long enough. Shoving aside the covers, she swung her bare feet onto the floor and stood up. And promptly sat down again. My goodness, but she was weak.

Chagrined at her own infirmity, Katie crawled back under the covers. Drat it all, why did she have to be sick fur, anyways? Right now she wanted to be out in thet sunshine somethin awful. Fact was, she reckoned she'd be willin to sweep the porch or gather the eggs, even. Anything to be outside.

Still, she could read. Why my goodness, she had thet new book of poems. The one Bonnie give her. Fur Bonnie had come to see her last evenin, bringin a dish of custard along with them poems.

My but thet custard tasted good. Katie had eaten two helpings while listening to her friend's chatter. Seated in the rocker, Bonnie had swayed as she spoke. "Ma's goin to make me stay home next week an pick apples. She says Thane can mind the post office jist as well as me. Nonsense. Anyways, I don't take to the idea of pickin an dryin apples. Course now, I'll pick some." She grinned. "Randall does love them apple dumplins. Purt near as much as grape pie."

"Oh my goodness, this sounds serious like."

"It is. He comes courtin twice a week now."

Katie was happy fur Bonnie. Really an truly she was. Nothin was too good fur her friend. And this morning, still thinking about Bonnie and Randall, Katie opened her new book of poems to one by Percy Bysshe Shelley.

> *The fountains mingle with the river,*
> *And the rivers with the ocean;*
> *The winds of heaven mix forever,*
> *With a sweet emotion;*
> *Nothing in the world is single;*
> *All things by a law divine*
> *In one another's being mingle:—*
> *Why not I with thine?*
> *See! the mountains kiss high heaven,*
> *And the waves clasp one another;*
> *No sister flower would be forgiven*
> *If it disdained its brother;*
> *And the sunlight clasps the earth,*
> *And the moonbeams kiss the sea:—*
> *What are all these kissings worth,*
> *If thou kiss not me?*[1]

Katie let the book fall from her hands with a sigh. Drat it all, when was Thane goin to kiss *her*, anyways? He liked her. Really an truly he did. But as fur kisses—

A knock on the door caused Katie to start. "Yes?"

"Can I come in?"

Oh my goodness, it was *Thane*! Closing her book, Katie ran her hands through her unbound hair and patted her cotton gown. "Yes, of course.

Please, come in."

Thane entered then, carrying a jar filled with goldenrod.

"Fur you." He extended them toward her, a blush stealing across his fine face.

Katie sniffed. "Oh my goodness. Why, thank you."

He smiled then, that lopsided grin that made Katie go all lightheaded.

"Nice day outside," Thane commented as he placed the bouquet on the bureau, then seated himself in the rocker.

"Sure is," Katie agreed. "An I'm feelin lots better. Really an truly I am."

"Gosh, Katie, thet's wonderful." Thane looked down at his boots then. "I—I heard you had a purty rough time of it there fur awhile."

Katie nodded, her large eyes blue in the morning light. "I'm better now, anyways. Course I'm bound to be, seein as how Aunt Jane hovers about me an all."

Thane laughed. "She sure was fussin at your pa when I came in. Said he had no business traipsin out to thet smithy so soon."

"Thet's My Pa all right. Jist plain stubborn when he's a mind to be. Still, he's purt nigh the best pa in the world." And Katie stretched her arms and smiled. Then frowned. Fur Thane was blinkin them blue eyes somethin fierce like. Drat it all, why had she said thet fur, anyways? Course Thane still missed his own pa now an again.

"I'm sorry, Thane. Really an truly I am."

"Thet's okay," he tried to smile. "Mostly by now I'm used to gittin on without him. I—I jist wish them Secesh hadn't killed him—thet's all." He stared at the floor again.

For several moments the only sounds were the rustling of tree leaves and the chirping of birds. Finally, Katie spoke.

"How's business at the store?"

"Not bad. Fact is, it's good. Real good. Course Will can be overbearin at times. He an my ma don't see eye to eye about runnin things. Myself, I'd do different from either one of them. But then it ain't really my affair." Looking up, he smiled. "Well, never mind thet. It's too purty a day to be all down–in–the–mouth."

At the mention of mouth, Katie touched her lips. My but she wanted him to kiss her.

He was risin now, walkin toward the bed. He knelt down then and looked Katie full in the face. Then flushing, he looked at the patchwork quilt. "Gosh, Katie, I—I'm so glad you're feelin better. Maybe now I can come courtin again."

At Katie's nod, he gave her that shy, lopsided grin. Then patting her hand, he rose. "I—I'll see you then."

And, before Katie could reply, he was gone.

Staring after him, Katie bit her lip to keep her chin from trembling. Drat it all, what was the matter with Thane, anyways? Why, the way he acted made her jist want to hate him. Really an truly it did. Only she couldn't. Cause she liked him too much fur thet.

Chapter 19

Lemon rays of April sunlight warmed Thomas' face as he strode swiftly down Main Street. He'd finished plantin the garden an hour early this mornin jist so he could have time to buy Julia a birthday present.

Jist thinkin on Julia made him step lighter. Why, it made a feller feel most happy like to be courtin again. Fact was, he hadn't touched thet liquor jug fur weeks now. Instead, he'd got drunk on visions of a heart–shaped face surrounded by clouds of honey–colored hair. An tonight he intended to kiss thet hair an them thin, sweet lips.

At Chapman's Dry Goods Thomas paused, shifting his weight from his right foot to his left, then back to his right again, his lips in a taut line. Damn, but he wished he didn't have to go in there an face thet Will Chapman. Made a feller feel a traitor like, givin business to them Feds. Still, he purt near had to if he wanted a gift fur Julia. An he wanted to please her somethin awful.

And he did. For that evening Julia gave a cry of delight when she saw the mirror and brush set.

"Oh, thank you," she said, her slim fingers caressing the gold–plated brush handle and the oval–shaped mirror.

"I'll keep this furever."

"Well, you'd better seein as how I got it special like." Thomas' lips barely turned upward as he settled himself on the sofa, expecting Julia to join him. Instead, she crossed the room and sat down on the piano stool.

"I promised Papa I'd play some tonight," she explained.

Disappointed, Thomas nonetheless enjoyed the sight of Wade's sister as she sat at the keyboard. Wisps the color of honey curled about her neck as they escaped from her upswept hair. Her slim back, clad in pink calico,

95

gave way to an even smaller waist. And the tip of a worn slipper peeped from beneath her full skirts as she pedaled the instrument.

She switched to another song then, a hymn he hadn't heard in years.

Jesus, lover of my soul,
Let me to Thy bosom fly.[1]

Thomas shifted his feet, wishing she'd go on to something else. Fur a song like thet made a feller feel most sad like. Leastwise it did him. Fur he used to believe thet stuff about God an love. Fact was, he used to sit in church an sing like all the rest, thinkin love was somethin special like. But it wasn't. Hadn't he loved Wade purt near as much as he loved himself?

For a moment the music, Mr. Crawford, even Julia fade from view. It is August, 1861. The afternoon sun beats unmercifully on the dark–haired Missourian as he gently ties a bandanna around the bloody head of his friend. Then tenderly, he lays the still form into a shallow grave and begins the gruesome task of filling the hole. Scoop a shovelful of dirt, toss it in. Scoop and toss. Scoop and toss. Until at last that slim body with its dun–colored hair is buried. Buried. Gone. Vanished. And the tall, dark–haired Missourian is left alone to curse and groan and anguish. All this fur love?

"No!"

He didn't realize he'd shouted until the music stopped and Julia and Mr. Crawford turned to stare at him.

"You all right, Son?"

"Course I'm all right." Thomas forced the ends of his lips upward as he nodded to the older man and Julia.

"Thet'll be enough piana playin fur tonight, Honey." And Mr. Crawford commenced rocking.

"Yes, Papa." Julia rose then and came to sit beside Thomas, though she never glanced at him as she took her embroidery work from a basket.

For a moment the only sounds were the creak of Mr. Crawford's rocker and that of Thomas' boots as he continued to move his feet uneasily on the carpet. Darn, but he was angry. Angry with Wade fur gettin himself killed. Angry with himself fur carin an fur lettin it show. Angry with Julia fur not lookin at him.

Finally, it was Mr. Crawford who broke the silence, chuckling softly.

"What's funny, Papa?"

"Oh, I was jist thinkin on thet picture I seen here awhile back in *Harper's Weekly*. A donkey they called it, only it looked more like a Missouri mule to me. Anyways, they're sayin thet dumb beast is a symbol fur them Democrats."

"Thet's silly," Julia said.

"Course it's silly," Thomas agreed. "Cause the Democrats is a heap better than them dang Republicans. I mean to tell you Missouri'd be a sight better off if we'd followed Gov. Jackson, an gone into the Confederacy." He paused, then added, "Leastwise thet's how it appears to me."

"Can't say but what I agree with you there, Son. Why, nowadays things is changin somethin awful. Take this here new amendment now. I reckon niggers is human an all thet. But as fur votin—" he shook his nearly bald head and pressed his foot to the floor. The rocker creaked in protest.

Thomas, his feet flat on the floor, removed his pipe from his mouth and spoke with restraint. "I agree, Mr. Crawford. Them niggers ain't got no business votin." He glanced at Julia then, and to his relief she lifted her lovely face and smiled at him.

For the rest of the evening Thomas basked in the glow of that one smile. He felt more hope than he had in a long time when he stood beside the dining room door ready to take his leave.

"Thanks again fur the gift."

"You're welcome." He reached out then and slipped his left arm about her waist. When she didn't resist, he brought his stump to her other shoulder in an attempt to bind her to him.

She stirred then and gently released herself. "Good night, Thomas," she said.

"Good night, Julia." Then swiftly he kissed her lips before he opened the door and went out.

She was agoin to see Claudia. Jane was agoin to visit her old friend an she didn't care whether folks approved or not. Why land sakes, if a freedman like Andrew could vote, then surely a white woman could visit a former slave if she'd a mind to.

And so on a cool April morning after the breakfast dishes were done, Jane set out for the north part of town. Dressed in a faded calico and wearing an ancient sun bonnet, she hurried along, a basket swinging on her arm. But by the time she passed the ponds, she was tired. Land sakes, she'd never walked this far before. Leastwise not in one stretch. Still an all, if she aimed to see Claudia—

When she spotted the African church house, Jane breathed a sigh of relief. Turning the corner, she saw a patch of spaded ground and a cow grazing nearby. She recognized the young woman dropping seeds as Rachel. No doubt thet tike trottin beside her was her youngin.

Heartened, Jane hurried toward the nearest shanty. She paused though, at the clanging sound of metal striking metal. Unable to resist a glimpse of Andrew, she peeked into the smithy. Immediately, a burly young buck suspended work and glared at her, a frown wrinkling his brow.

"What you want?"

"Land sakes, don't bite my head off. I only came to see Claudia."

At this, the second man straightened. Jane gasped. Land sakes, but Andrew looked old. Ancient he was, his grizzled gray hair rimmin a hard, seamed face. He spat tobacco juice before acknowledging her.

"She's inside," he jerked his head toward the living quarters.

"Thanks." Jane backed from the smithy and hurried up the footpath to the cabin door. Timidly, she knocked. Then louder.

She'd begun to wonder if anyone was home when the door opened a crack. It was Claudia ablinkin at her from the face of an old crone.

Jane blinked back, wanting to weep at the injustice of it all.

"Claudia?"

The wrinkled face nodded.

"I—I've come fur a visit. I've been downright lonesome these years without you. Can I come in?"

For several moments the sad eyes studied her, then slowly the door opened. Jane noticed then the baby in her friend's thin arms. Another of Rachel's, no doubt. She must be married to thet suspicious actin man aworkin out there with Andrew.

"Sit down," Claudia motioned to a hardback chair near the fireplace.

Jane removed her bonnet then and sat, dismayed at the dinginess of the one room home. For despite the flames flickering in the fireplace, she could barely make out Claudia as she rocked the baby.

"Thet your grandyoungin?

Claudia nodded. "This be Leah."

"Oh my, if only I'd aknowed, I could've made little Leah somethin. Anyways, I got this fur you." Jane pulled a long calico skirt from her basket.

Claudia merely continued rocking.

Jane tried again. "I got some tea too. Thought you might brew up some. Make it old times like."

Claudia said nothing. She merely continued to rock.

Exasperated, Jane tossed the skirt onto her friend's lap. "Land sakes, Claudia, what you bein such a stick–in–the–mud fur? This is me, Jane. Your childhood friend. Remember all them times we spent together?

Aleavin Kentucky behind, my ma adyin, then yours. But always we had each other. Leastwise it seemed so to me."

"We had bad times sure enough." Claudia rose, draped the skirt over the back of the rocker, then placed the little one on the dirt floor. She took up the tin of tea then and crossed to the log work table. Taking up a small pot, she sprinkled in tea, then ladled in cold water. Hanging it over the fireplace, she unwrapped corn bread. Cutting two wedges, she handed one to Jane.

"My but this is good." Jane spoke around her first bite.

Claudia said nothing, intent on feeding baby Leah a bit of her own bread.

"You attend church up the way?"

Claudia nodded.

"Land sakes, what I want to know is, are you adoin all right?"

Claudia's head snapped upright as though she'd been slapped. "What you mean all right? There be Claire an Lola over there, an Andrew an Rachel over here. Course I's all right."

Jane nodded, stung by Claudia's tone. Touching the birthmark on her cheek, she tried again. "Course you are. An we're fine too."

There was silence then. A silence that threatened to suffocate Jane. And then the door flew open and a child rushed in.

"Hey, Grammy, see what I got?" And he held out an earth worm.

"Thet's nice, Sweetling. Now go on out, an close thet door."

But the boy, noticing Jane, hesitated. "Hey, what you doin here?"

Jane never knew what she answered. Fur one good look at thet youngin told her everything. Thomas. Land sakes, thet boy belonged to Thomas. Course he was brown. Had kinky hair too. But the sunlight filtering into the room illuminated a face like her nephew. Thet broad forehead an taperin jaw, them thin lips an dimpled chin—

"This be Adrian. Named fur his great–grandpappy. Go on out now, an close the door."

The boy left then, banging the door behind him.

"Claudia?"

No reply.

"Land sakes, Claudia, I didn't know. But I'm sorry aplenty, now."

"No need bein sorry." Claudia rose and went to strain the tea, the baby clinging to her drooping skirt.

They drank their tea in silence. Then Jane rose to leave.

"I'd best get along now."

Claudia nodded.

"Land sakes, Claudia, I don't cotton to all this cold shoulder feelin. Can I come again, so we can talk like?"

"Reckon so." But she didn't stand up, or open the door for her friend.

Jane let herself out then, leaving a brooding Claudia to rock little Leah. She passed the shanties where most likely Lola and Claire lived, then left Claudia's world behind. By the time she was nearing home, Jane was angry. Land sakes, what had come over Thomas, anyways? An his ma an Michael, did they know? Well, she'd tell them a thing or two, she would. It was downright unfair what had happened. Why, who'd have thought Claudia'd be reduced to such poverty? Shameful, thet's what it was. An she'd a mind to have Michael make amends this very day.

But Jane's anger cooled when she saw Michael emerging from the smithy. Somehow, the sight of those broad shoulders, stooped from a morning's work, touched her heart. Michael was a good man. Anyways, it was Thomas—

"Aye, Lass, you been to town this mornin?"

The smile on Michael's face caused Jane to pause. Perhaps Claudia had understood the situation better than she did. "No need bein sorry," her friend had said. Fur some reason, "bein sorry" would purt near do Claudia in. An Jane loved Claudia. More than anything.

"Lass?"

"Oh my, I was wool gatherin jist now. But land sakes, course I been to town this mornin."

And grasping her empty basket, Jane hurried into the house.

Chapter 20

The afternoon sun blazed down upon Main Street where the Southern Route stage halted before the Central Hotel. Emerging from Chapman's Dry Goods, Daniel Lewis noted the number of passengers crammed into the coach. More tourists come to see the Springs, no doubt. He fingered his newly purchased brush absent-mindedly. It seemed to him that most folks coming to the resort were Secesh. But then of course, Brownsville was basically a secessionist town.

Crossing the street, Daniel noted the distinctive appearance of the first man off the coach. From his fine cowboy boots to his giant sombrero, he appeared Mexican. Yet, as he pushed back his hat, Daniel had the definite feeling he'd seen him somewhere before. Despite the leathery appearance of his face, those deepset eyes, full lips, and rounded chin looked familiar. Pausing, Daniel studied the young lady being helped down by the man. Of average height, she possessed a voluptuous figure over which she wore a peasant blouse and layered skirt. A crimson sash cinched her comely waist. Her olive skin and raven hair left no doubt about her heritage.

Daniel supposed some men might find her attractive. Personally, he preferred a woman who was less robust. One with a more refined nature, more delicate features. One like Mamie Fitzsimmons. In the first place, Mamie was taller, more stately. She sauntered like a lady, rather than skipping about. Her features were fine too. Her oval face with its slender nose and green eyes was beautiful, pure and simple. Her neck was slender too, and her hands. And her shiny, auburn hair, swept up in back, sat on her head like a crown. The truth was he found it a pleasure, pure pleasure, to watch her stroll by the shop. She—

God! Daniel's fingers tightened about the wooden brush handle. What

101

was he *doing*, thinking of Mamie this way? He had no right. Unless of course, he was looking for a wife. And he most definitely was not. Or was he?

Ah well, he had better things to do than stand around thinking about women. Like varnishing that walnut wardrobe, for instance. Or keeping Harvey Fudd in line. Hot as it was the old man had no doubt removed his straw hat to fan the elder Mr. Lewis. Last time he did that he'd scattered sawdust everywhere. Smiling, Daniel crossed Bridge Street. He supposed he'd better hurry on into the shop and rescue his father from the well–intentioned Mr. Fudd.

❖   ❖   ❖

It was hot. So hot that Thomas had escaped to the log bench beneath the oak tree. Course he should've been hoein corn, but sometimes a feller jist had to do somethin easy like. Like drinkin cold, Sweet Spring water on a sultry July afternoon.

Draining his cup, Thomas set it aside and lit his corncob pipe. Puffing gently, he leaned back against the tree trunk and closed his eyes. He'd evidently been dozing for some time when a deep voice shook him awake.

"Enjoyin your rest, Son?"

Thomas jerked himself upright, chagrined to be caught napping. Shuffling his feet in the dust, he studied the man before him. Who was he, anyways? Some highfalutin city slicker by the looks of them clothes an thet fine trunk. An thet beauty beside him—who was she? What did they want from him, anyways?

"Don't know me do you, Thomas?"

At the stranger's derisive tone, Thomas stiffened. "I jist might if you'd take thet monstrous hat off. Makes a feller feel uneasy like, when he can't see a man's face.

Laughing, the tall man pulled off his sombrero.

His lips in a taut line, Thomas studied the stranger. Darn, but he looked familiar. Fact was, he looked enough like My Ma to be—

Thomas' lips curved into a smile then as he stood and held out his left hand.

"Why furever more, you must be my Uncle James."

❖   ❖   ❖

From the beginning Katie loved her new cousin. Not only was Linda beautiful, she was helpful too. Why my goodness, she bustled about thet kitchen helpin to git supper on till Katie thought fur sure My Ma would holler in protest. But she didn't. Why, in her whole life Katie reckoned she'd never seen My Ma carry on this way. Why my goodness, she insisted they eat at the *dininroom* table, somethin they almost never did. An then she sent Thomas out to git beefsteak. After thet she brought out a lace tablecloth Katie'd never even seen before. An to top it all off, she got down her Chelsea Daisy dishes. Goodness, but they were gittin dolled–up this evenin.

Even so, Katie was happy. Fur her new cousin was somethin special like. Really an truly she was. An it was plain as day she liked all of them, even if she didn't speak English. Like now. For Linda was smiling as she talked rapidly, pointing to the food on her plate and looking about.

Uncle James laughed. "She wants to know where the chilies are."

"Chilies?" Jordana looked blank.

"Never mind, Sis." And turning to his daughter, James spoke rapidly in Spanish.

"*Si?*" Still smiling, Linda took up the pepper and ground it over her food until Katie, sitting beside her, sneezed.

"Enough." Uncle James took the grinder and set it down. But Linda merely smiled some more as she dug into her blackened food.

"Say, Uncle James, tell us about this here place called California," Thomas' lips curved upward as he spoke.

James paused then, took a fancy watch from his waistcoat pocket and smiled. "I don't reckon there's thet many hours left today."

"Aye, Brother, it's your story we've a mind to hear."

Re-pocketing his watch, James smiled at Michael. "Always did have you figured fur a right smart man. Mercy sakes, you had to be, to marry up with my sister." He laughed, then waved a ringed hand toward the rest of the family. "You're a mighty fine bunch too. So I know you'll like my story. Course as you know, I never did git rich off Sutter's gold, or anyone elses fur thet matter. Like to lost my shirt in fact. Then I joined up as a ranch hand an in no time I had my own spread. Raised horses—"

"Robert. What about Robert?" It was Jane, speaking in an unnaturally high voice.

"Robert? Oh, you mean Robert Saylor."

Jane nodded.

"Ah yes, my dear friend, Robert." James returned to his food, then waved his fork to everyone in general. "Let me tell you about old Robert. A good worker, he was. None better with horses. Worked fur me there fur awhile. Until I met Maria." James stopped, picked his teeth a moment, then went on. "Now, Maria was beautiful. Absolutely beautiful. Looked a lot like my *hija* here, only smaller." Again James paused, smiled at Linda, then continued. "Course I loved her. Unfortunately, Robert did too. He left the ranch soon after Maria an I was married."

"Where's he at now?" Again, Jane's voice sounded strained.

"Dead. Leastwise I heard he was. Killed a couple of years ago in a shootout in San Francisco. Over gamblin debts, I reckon."

Thomas asked more questions then and James went on talking. Only Katie seemed aware that Jane had ceased eating. Why my goodness, she sat there starin straight ahead an rubbin thet birthmark till it must be purt nigh sore.

"Aunt Jane?"

"Yes, Child."

"Are you feelin all right?"

Jane nodded.

"Really an truly?"

Jane nodded again.

But Katie wasn't convinced. Still, she hadn't much time to think about it, for once Linda finished eating, she rose from the table. Picking up her plate, she moved toward the kitchen.

"*Cáfe?*" she smiled.

"I'll get my own, thanks," Mamie snarled, shoving her cousin aside. But Linda ignored Mamie. Laughing, she brought in the coffee, while Katie poured the tea.

"My but Brownsville has changed since I left." It was James again, waving a spoon at everyone. "Meat market, bank, hotel—"

"Railroad's comin too," Thomas interjected. "Gradin was done last fall. You know they's already layin track down near Sedalia."

"Comin from the south, huh?"

Thomas nodded, his corncob pipe bobbing. "If they pull it off it'll come through Hughesville, Houstonia, Brownsville, Emma. On up to Lexington."

"Branch line?"

Again, Thomas nodded.

"Well, branch line or no, it's bound to be better than thet coach. Why mercy sakes, Hija an me practically bounced to pieces all the way from Independence."

"You must be plumb tuckered out then," Jordana said. "You'd best stay here fur the night."

"Oh, I plan to. Fact is, Hija an me figured on stayin fur some time. Fur a fee, thet is." And he reached for his coin purse.

"Aye, Brother, keep your money, mind." Michael shoved aside his empty dishes as he spoke.

James laughed then. "Like I said earlier, you're a mighty fine bunch. Course I plan on helpin out from time to time. But thanks, anyways."

"Thank *you*," Jordana said. "After all a body has need of kinfolks now an again."

"Oh my goodness, you're stayin," Katie beamed at Linda. "An you can share our room."

"Speak fur yourself, Miss Smarty," Mamie hissed.

"Land sakes, youngins, thet ain't no way to act. Why, there's room enough fur everybody. Mamie, you can come with me. Providin you behave yourself."

For a second, Katie stared at her aunt. "You mean it? Really an truly?"

"Course I do, Child."

"Oh, thet's wonderful! Now, you an me can be together." And Katie reached for her cousin's hand.

Perplexed, Linda turned to her father who spoke rapidly in Spanish. Turning back to Katie, she laughed. "*Si.*" Then quickly, she jumped from her chair and began stacking dishes.

Katie followed suit, feeling grown up all of a sudden. And Jordana, perfectly willing to let the girls work, turned her attention to James and Michael.

"I'm right glad you're here, James," she smiled up at him.

"Me too, Sis. I couldn't stand thet ranch once Maria passed on." He paused, drained his coffee cup, then spoke gently. "I miss gettin to see thet youngest boy of yours too."

At that, Jordana dabbed her eyes with the corner of her apron.

"Aye, Colleen, our Patrick's fine now, to be sure." And Michael laid a burly hand on her shoulder.

But it was to James Jordana turned for comfort.

❖　❖　❖

As she prepared for bed that night, Katie could scarcely contain her excitement. Twirling about, her arms extended, she felt positively giddy with pleasure. Linda was stayin. With her too. Right in this very room, she was.

Slipping into her cotton gown, Katie gaped at the array of clothes her cousin took from her trunk. Goodness, there was blouses, skirts an petticoats galore. Sashes an scarves too, in colors from chartreuse to vermilion. Katie felt purt nigh blinded by the array of garments Linda spread about the room.

And then this cousin was handing Katie a turquoise scarf.

"Fur you, *Si*?" she smiled.

" Fur me?"

"*Si*." Linda nodded, her black eyes snapping with excitement.

"Oh, thank you!" And Katie reached for her cousin.

But already Linda had turned to the chest of drawers and was brushing her wiry, dark hair. As Katie watched her cousin, she bit her lower lip. Drat it all, why couldn't she have gorgeous hair like thet instead of this straight brown stuff? Why was she so plain fur,anyways?

But plain or not, Katie couldn't resist her cousin's infectious laughter. Not even when Linda bounded onto the bed and stretched out on the side next to the window over the back porch. Katie's side.

Blowing out the lamp, Katie scampered across the room and crawled into bed on Mamie's side. She giggled then, when Linda tickled her chin with the ends of her hair. And laughed aloud as her cousin thumped the straw tick while rattling in Spanish. Finally though, Linda lay still, her soft breathing indicating she slept.

Katie smiled then as she fit the lumpy pillow to her head. Linda was wonderful. Really an truly she was. And she could hardly wait to show her off to Bonnie.

Chapter 21

Late afternoon sunlight cast an amber glow about Katie as she stood before her chest of drawers surveying herself in the mirror. Purt nigh purty, she was. Fur even if her hair wasn't black like Linda's, it did look nice all braided an pinned up in thet new chignon style. An thet coral dress Aunt Jane had stitched with all them fancy ruffles made her feel all growed up like. Now, fur thet new shawl—

But the shawl wasn't draped on the hook where Katie had left it. Puzzled, she searched her row of hooks, lifting one garment after another in an effort to locate the missing wrap. To no avail. Slapping a last dress back into place, Katie glowered. Drat it all, she had to look good fur this evenin. It wasn't often thet Bonnie invited her to supper. An this wasn't to be jist any old meal, cause Bonnie had told her to dress up like.

"What fur?" Katie had asked.

"It's a surprise." And Bonnie's blue eyes had twinkled.

Well, whatever Bonnie's surprise was, Thane was bound to be there. Course Linda wouldn't be. Bonnie hadn't invited her. Biting her lip, Katie recalled how awful she'd felt when she first introduced Bonnie to her cousin. She'd been so sure her friend would take to Linda. But Bonnie hadn't. She'd said a polite, "Hello there," then turned and walked away. Katie had stood staring after her friend, her fists dug into her sides. What was the matter with Bonnie, anyways? Couldn't she see thet Linda was somethin special like?

But Bonnie hadn't seen. She'd continued to ignore Linda whenever possible. And now she'd invited only Katie to supper. Linda wasn't—

Linda. As Katie stared at the clothes heaped on the bed, suddenly she knew. Linda had "borrowed" her new shawl.

Hands at her waist, Katie strode toward the bed. For the next several minutes she rummaged through the assortment of peasant style clothes. But the shawl wasn't there. She'd simply have to do without it. An she'd wanted so bad to look somethin special like fur Bonnie.

But to Bonnie she *was* special. "Oh, Katie, you're beautiful. Why, I'll bet every feller in town noticed you on your way over here."

Katie flushed, then spun about, her arms outstretched. Bonnie grabbed her hands then and they whirled about the parlor, until finally they landed on the sofa, exhausted and laughing. And then Thane appeared, his blue eyes taking in the giddy girls.

Instantly, Katie sat up, disgusted with herself for behaving so childishly. Drat it all, what must Thane think of her, anyways?

But Thane apparently didn't mind her silliness. For he gave that shy, lopsided grin that made Katie lightheaded with pleasure.

"Gosh, Katie, you're lookin awful purty this evenin." He blushed then and glanced down at his boots. But that didn't bother Katie. Thane thought she was purty, an he'd said so right off like. Nothin else mattered.

The fried chicken supper was delicious, and Katie might really have enjoyed herself if it hadn't been for Will glowering at everyone as he sat at the head of the table. What was the matter with him, anyways?

"Tell me, Will, has this new dry goods store affected your business much?" It was Randall Dalton speaking from his place beside Bonnie.

"Matter of fact, it has. I don't see what business some outsider has comin in here an buildin new stores. What's thet uncle of yours aimin to do, drive the rest of us out of business?" Will glared at Katie.

"Now, Will, really—" Minnie Chapman reproved her son.

"Uncle James is helpin us out at home," Katie snapped. "He opened thet dry goods to help pay fur his an Linda's keep. An as fur Aunt Jane's shop— Why my goodness, she was mopin around an actin purt nigh done in fur several weeks there. Course it didn't make no sense to me. Still, someone needed to do somethin. An Uncle James did. Settin Aunt Jane up to sell hats an dresses has made her a new person like."

Several moments of silence followed Katie's outburst. But she didn't care. Uncle James was wonderful. Really an truly he was.

"Well, there's going to be lots of new businesses coming to town soon," Randall spoke again. "Brownsville's going to have its very own newspaper. *The Banner*, it's to be called. The office will be on Miller Street."

"When's the first issue comin out?" Thane asked.

"Couple of weeks." Randall paused, took a drink of water, then turned to Bonnie's mother. "I've been hired as the feature writer," he said proudly.

"Oh, Randall, thet's wonderful!" Bonnie beamed as she placed a piece of grape pie before him.

"Speaking of wonderful, I sure do love grape pie."

"I know." Bonnie grinned as she reseated herself beside him.

Randall dug into his pie then and everyone else followed suit. After he'd finished his second piece, he leaned back in his chair and smiled at Bonnie. Then, directing his attention toward Minnie again, he said, "Mrs. Chapman, I would like to request something of you."

"Why yes, Randall, what is it?"

"Your daughter's hand in marriage." And he stilled Bonnie's fluttering hand with his own.

"Why my gracious. Why yes, I suppose—"

"No!" Will banged his fist on the table. "She can't marry you."

"An jist why not?" Bonnie's blue eyes shot sparks at her older brother.

"Cause Mr. Dalton was a secessionist, thet's why. An you *know* what they did to our Pa. Why—"

"Oh fur cryin out loud," Bonnie exploded. "Thet's all over an done with."

"Not fur some of us, it ain't. It sure as the world ain't over fur *them*. Don't loads of them come here purt near ever day to parade around on *our* Spring Grounds?"

"Now, Will, really—"

At this, Randall stood up and clapped his hands smartly. "May I have your attention please."

Silence.

"Now then, Mr. Will, with all due respect, I believe you are out of order. I did not seek *your* permission in this matter. I asked your mother. Now, Mrs. Chapman, may I be given permission to wed your daughter next summer, or whenever you think fit?"

"Why, yes. Of course you can. Thet is, if Bonnie wants to."

"Why gracious sakes, course I do. Oh, Mama, thank you, thank you, thank you." And Bonnie hugged her mother. Then, skipping to the other side of the table, she hugged Katie.

"Oh, Katie, I'm so glad you're here. I could die, I'm so happy."

"Oh please, don't do that." Randall's voice cut in. "And while you're passing out the hugs, don't I get one?"

"Oh, Randall, don't be silly. Course you do." And, lifting her skirts,

Bonnie raced back around the table. Stopping before him, she grinned. Instantly, Randall took her in his arms and kissed her soundly.

Katie, thrilled for her friend, stared at the two with envy. Minnie set down her coffee cup with a clatter as she murmured, "Oh, my." Thane blushed to the roots of his chestnut hair. And Will shoved back his chair, rose and stalked from the room.

"Katie?"

"Yes?" Katie answered softly, hoping Thane would speak of love. He did. Sort of.

"Are you happy fur Bonnie an Randall?"

"Why my goodness, course I am. Why, it's only right seein as how they love each other an all."

"Yes. Well, I wonder— Thet is— Oh, gosh Katie, what I mean to say is, have you ever been in love?"

Ever been in love? Oh my goodness, Thane was askin if she loved him. Course she did. She—

CRASH. Drip. Drip. Drip.

Katie started as noise from the kitchen invaded the privacy of the back porch.

"It is a mess, *si*?"

Drat it all, why did Linda have to pick this moment to upset the dishpan, anyways? Couldn't she be more careful like?

"Thet's okay, Katie. I—I shouldn't have asked."

And then, before Katie realized what was happening, Thane had risen.

"I'd best go along now."

Katie stood then too, wishing the swish of thet rag mop wasn't so loud. Drat it all, she'd hoped Thane would kiss—

"You—you really are purty, Katie." An then he was pullin her close like, an kissin her hard.

"Oh my goodness—"

But Thane was gone. Runnin he was, down West Street. Leaving Katie to sigh and gingerly finger the place where his mustache had brushed her lips.

Chapter 22

Jane Douglas strolled along Main Street delighting in the bright October sunlight and the envious glances of the town's leading ladies. Fur once thet blamed birthmark didn't matter. Nothin mattered this mornin but her clothes. Fur today *she* was asettin the style fur Brownsville.

Land sakes, it felt good to be awearin poplin stead of calico. Gold her dress was, with slim sleeves on the basque an a bustled skirt with lots of pleats an ruffles. The buttons an fringes was cinnamon colored. The ribbon astreamin from the back of her tiny hat was cinnamon too, while them little feathers was gold an white.

Course she owed it all to her brother, James. Fact was, he purt near insisted she open a millinery an dress shop next to his new dry goods place. Downright pushy, he was. Leastwise it seemed thet away to her. Land sakes, she'd wanted to run off an hide when he first brought it up. Why, she didn't even have the gumption to comb her hair or dress nice. How could she possibly think on sellin fancy things to folks? Still an all, she needed somethin to git her agoin again. An if James supposed he'd given her thet somethin , she reckoned she'd let him think it.

But it wasn't James who'd rescued her from despair. It was Claudia. For upon hearing of Robert's death, Jane had hurt so deeply that finally, in desperation, she'd sought her old friend out. And this time, Claudia had been true. Quiet as always, she had merely listened as Jane poured out her longing to be married. An Robert was gone. There'd never be no one else to love. It was downright unfair, thet's what it was.

But Claudia wasn't convinced. Course she didn't *say* so. She simply ran a roughened hand across Jane's disheveled hair an patted her arm. She gave her a piece of fresh peach pie an a cup of tea too. An as Jane prepared

111

to leave, Claudia gave her the nicest gift of all. A smile. Course it looked kinda poor like, with all them teeth amissin. An thet once smooth skin was creased as a dried –up apple. But it healed Jane's heart jist the same. Fur behind them toothless gums an thet wrinkled skin was the Claudia of her childhood. Thet skinny little girl who'd clung to her, agivin her the strength to tell Kentucky good-by.

Nearing her shop, Jane sighed. Fashion was somethin special all right, but what she wanted more than anything was fur Claudia to live next door. Like she used to. Course it couldn't never happen. Still an all, she thanked the good Lord fur lettin them visit now an again.

Pausing before her square store front, Jane frowned. Land sakes, she'd been so caught up these past days astitchin up her finery she'd furgot to speak to Mamie bout helpin out. An she simply had to have help. Why, even with thet new Singer sewin machine, she couldn't keep up. Already she had six dress orders awaitin to be done. She'd jist have to git Mamie to wait on trade. Fur whether she wanted to or not, thet girl was agoin to work.

Thomas felt as gloomy as the morning itself. Puffing his corncob pipe, he gazed through the rain–spattered kitchen window to the nearly bare branches of the cherry tree flapping in the wind. Buffeted he was, jist like them branches. For ever since he'd read that Robert E. Lee had died, Thomas had been disturbed.

Course he'd never served under the famed General. Still, it made a feller feel uneasy like knowin the man was gone. Fur thet Virginian had personified the feelins of every true Missourian. A state had the right to decide its own destiny. Yet, they'd lost. Virginia in the East; Missouri in the West. An deaths like Wade's hadn't made a lick of difference.

Still, the gossips at Crawford's store claimed this next election would fix things up a bit. "With them fool Republicans split, things is bound to git better," Tevis had said. An maybe they would. Fact was, Thomas was hopin this Brown feller would be elected governor. *He* wasn't goin to vote though. Thet would be plumb stupid after the ass he'd made of himself in '68. Course he wasn't sorry. He'd never be sorry. Them dang Feds deserved any tormentin they got. Still, if Julia ever caught wind of somethin like thet again, she'd never forgive him. An he needed stayin close like to Wade.

Suddenly, as he stood before the window, Thomas felt restless. Thet Katie an Linda were chatterin like magpies as they washed up them dishes.

Actin silly they was, an he was sick an tired of hearin them. He'd a mind to mosey on up to Uncle James' store, despite thet rain.

Ten minutes later Thomas pushed open the door to his uncle's store only to encounter the steely eyes of Uriah Martin.

"Mornin," Thomas spoke through taut lips as he attempted to sidestep his old friend.

But Uriah blocked his way. "Quitters ain't welcome here, see?"

"Now, jist a minute. My uncle runs this place—"

"Somethin the matter, boys?" James Douglas' eyes narrowed as he slipped from behind the counter and strode toward them.

"Yep. This here nephew of yours came bustin in here like he owns the place."

"Now, jist a minute, you rascal. I—"

"Mercy sakes, I had you two figured fur friends. Fact is, if you're right smart, you'll made amends real quick like. See you later, pal." And he slapped Uriah on the back before returning to wait on trade.

"Sure." Uriah grinned then, a smirk playing across his beefy lips. "So long, *friend*." And he brushed past Thomas, nearly knocking him over.

Thomas stared after him, his legs straight as sticks. Dang, but he itched to tell thet bastard a thing or two. Jist what gave him the right to buddy up to Uncle James, anyways? Made a feller feel uneasy like, it did. And right now Thomas didn't need anything else to make him feel uneasy.

Chapter 23

It was snowing and bitterly cold that Christmas morning of 1870 when Harvey Fudd climbed the steps to the Lewis' living quarters. Rapping on the door, he waited until Daniel drew him inside.

"A mite cold out there," he ventured, handing a tattered coat and hat to his host. He placed a green peppermint stick in his mouth, then crossed the room to the woodbox.

"Uh, Harvey, personally, I think it's warm enough in here already. Don't you?"

"I guess so. Thet is, if you say so, Mr. Daniel, sir." And Harvey turned to find a chair. And sniffed. "Hey, it smells like ham in here."

"Sure does. My father's fixing ham and roasted sweet potatoes, apples, biscuits and gingerbread. It's a feast, pure and simple."

Harvey nodded, then rose to follow Daniel into the kitchen, his head shaking as always. "Mornin, Mr. Lewis, sir. Merry Christmas."

Livingston nodded, puffing his Havana as he bent to remove a pan of biscuits from the oven. Though a far cry from the light ones his mother used to make, these at least were brown on top. And they smelled delicious.

Sliding the bread onto a warmed plate, Livingston placed them and a dish of apple butter on the table. The latter was a gift from Minnie Chapman. Biting down on his Havana, Livingston sighed. In recent months he'd gotten the distinct feeling that Mrs. Chapman was looking for a new husband. Well, she would just have to look elsewhere. For Livingston had no intention of loving again. He was glad, more glad than he could say, to be free from such involvement. He did wonder though, why Daniel hadn't married. Come to think of it, his son was thirty years old now. Course he had to admit he'd rather see Daniel remain a bachelor than take up with that oldest Fitzsimmons girl. Lord, but she was a sly one. A mighty sly one. And Daniel was tempted. More than once he'd noted how Daniel's fingers had gripped the planer more firmly when she slinked past the shop window. Afterward, he'd even hum a bit, something he seldom did anymore. Come to think of it, he hadn't hummed a tune since little Joy was alive. It was as though Daniel was falling in love. Livingston shuddered. Ah well, the boy must decide these things for himself.

Tossing his Havana into the stove, Livingston removed his apron and sat down at the head of the table. Once Daniel and Mr. Fudd were seated, Livingston paused. Surely since it was Christmas, a prayer would be in order. He didn't know why he should even think of God just now, unless it was because of that unopened letter lying on his bureau.

Surprising himself, he said, "Let's bow now for prayer." Then quickly, he recited. "Father God, we thank thee for this our daily bread and for thy Holy Scriptures which nourish our souls. Amen."

Harvey immediately stabbed a piece of ham and grabbed a biscuit. But Daniel didn't move. He simply sat, his bearded chin resting on his laced fingers, and stared at his father. Though he never said a word, Livingston could sense his unspoken question.

Livingston sighed. "Well, Son, I know it's unusual for me to pray. Even so, this *is* Christmas. And since all three churches are holding services today, it seemed only right that I acknowledge our Maker."

"Four churches," Daniel corrected. "Baptists have started holding services at the Presbyterian–Methodist Meeting House."

"All right, four then." Livingston speared a sweet potato, sliced it open and smothered it with butter. Lord, he wished now he hadn't prayed. Wished he hadn't repeated his father's words as though they were his own. They weren't, of course. How could they be when he had no time for God? Ah well, he wasn't going to let a little prayer spoil his good dinner.

After they'd eaten, the three men worked together straightening the kitchen, though Livingston could have done without the old man's help. For despite his good intentions, Mr. Fudd was clumsy. Once, when he nearly dropped the sugar bowl, Livingston gasped. He was glad, more glad than he could say, when that dish was dried and safely in the cupboard. For it was a fine piece. A mighty fine piece. He'd bought it as part of a set for Verna Marie in the early years of their marriage. He shuddered to think it might have been broken.

The dishes done, the men moved into the sitting room. There, Daniel presented Harvey with a blue wool muffler.

"Merry Christmas," he said.

"Fur me?"

Daniel nodded.

"Oh my, why thank you, Mr. Daniel, sir," he said, wrapping the band of wool about his neck. And then, before Livingston realized his intent, Harvey hurried to the potbellied stove, yanked open the door, and threw several sticks inside. "There, keep us warm." And he fingered the fine blue wool.

Oh, Lord, Livingston groaned, must I roast in my own home too?

Evidently Daniel sensed his mood, for he took out a checker game, suggesting they play on the kitchen table.

"Oh my, I—I'm not very good." Harvey flushed.

"Neither am I," Daniel smiled. "So that makes us even." And he led the way to the slightly cooler kitchen.

But Livingston didn't follow. Despite the fact he was beginning to sweat, he didn't want to play checkers. At least not now. He didn't want to do anything but sit and cool off. Come to think of it, his bedroom was the coolest room of all. And once there, he could read the letter. If he wanted to. But did he?

Biting down on his Havana, Livingston closed his eyes. And groaned. For he could picture all too clearly a summer evening in 1832. After running errands all afternoon with his friend, he'd rushed into the house, starved. A growing boy of fourteen, he seemed always to be hungry. And this evening the smell of sizzling ham was especially mouthwatering. Mother would make red–eye gravy and some of her high, light baking powder biscuits and they'd have a fine meal. Only there was no ham or gravy or biscuits. There was only water and half a loaf of stale bread.

"Your father took supper to the Andersons," Mother explained.

Ah yes, the Andersons, the Freelings, the Browns, the *poor*. Father had taken the Lewis' supper and given it to "those less fortunate". Lord, how many times had he, Livingston, gone to bed hungry while Father fed the poor? Ah well, what did it matter now?

Slowly, Livingston rose and trudged into the bedroom. But despite the cooler temperature, he wasn't comfortable as he slit the envelope with his letter opener. Settling on the side of the bed near the window, he drew out a single sheet and read.

Dear Son,

> *I take my seat this morning to write you of a change
> in my life. I have remarried.*

What? His father getting married? Let's see now, he must be seventy— seventy three at least. Puffing on his Havana, Livingston read on.

> *Her name is Althea. She's a bit younger than myself, but a wonderful companion given me by God.*

> *The wedding was small. Just us and her brother, Ira. And the minister, of course. I confess that when I repeated those solemn vows, I could not but remember the many couples I united in holy matrimony.*

Ah yes, his father hadn't preached since well before the War. But then it was his own fault he was banned. If he hadn't been so outspoken against slavery— Lord, but he was glad, more glad than he could say, that he was away from there. For Livingston would never be able to tolerate darkies the way his father did.

> *Son, I hope you're not angry with me for what I've done. I loved your mother as I loved my own life. But that was long ago.*

Ah yes, 1835 was a long time ago. And Harrisonburg was a long ways away. But not so far away that he, Livingston, had forgotten. He could never forget the pain inflicted by his mother's death. Pain so deep it numbed his insides. Yet somehow, he'd managed to stumble to his father's study in search of comfort. What he found only further anesthetized his spirit. For there was his father sprawled unconscious across his desk, an empty bottle on the floor. Silently, he'd turned away. From his father and God and love. He hadn't loved again until a year later when he met Verna Marie.

> *I'm old now, Son. Old and feeble, and perhaps a bit wiser.*

> *Let me hear from you sometime. Tell Daniel I think of him often.*

> *Your father,*
> *Jeremiah Lewis*

Biting hard on his Havana, Livingston slowly refolded the letter and slipped it back into the envelope. Crossing the room, he opened a bureau drawer and placed the letter alongside some frilly handkerchiefs which had once been special to Verna Marie.

He left the cool bedroom then for the heat of the sitting room and kitchen. And to find out who'd won that game of checkers.

Chapter 24

Beneath the April sun Katie twirled upon the grass, a newly washed sheet billowing from her extended arms as she spun around and around, reciting from Browning.

> *The year's at the spring*
> *And day's at the morn;*
> *Morning's at seven'*
> *The hill–side's dew–pearled;*
> *The lark's on the wing;*
> *The snail's on the thorn:*
> *God's in his heaven—*
> *All's right with the world!* [1]

Goodness, but she was happy. Why, she reckoned she'd never been this happy in her whole life. For Katie was in love. Really an truly she was. An even more wonderful, Thane loved her. Jist thinkin on it made Katie all giddy like. Why, she'd purt nigh swooned when Thane had whispered them words last night.

"Katie, I—I love you." He'd trembled then as he pulled her to him. "I wonder, thet is—oh, gosh Katie, do you love me too? Even a little?"

"Oh my goodness, yes." And Katie had raised her lips for his kiss.

He'd claimed them as though he had a right to, kissing her with such passion that at first Katie was startled. Then gradually, she gave herself up to him until she lost all sense of everything but the two of them. And then, as he had so often before, he abruptly lifted his head and stepped backward, his arms falling to his sides.

"I'd—I'd best git along now. Good night." And he had disappeared into the darkness, leaving Katie to wonder at the inconsistency of it all.

Drat it all, why did he always have to run off fur,anyways?

But the mist of last night's doubts had evaporated beneath the warmth of this morning's sun. Thane loved her. Really an truly he did. Nothin else mattered.

"You're happy, *si*?"

It was Linda, smiling as she advanced toward the clothes line, a snowy pillowcase in hand.

"Happy? Course I'm happy. I'm in love."

"Oh, *prima* Katie, thet's wonderful." And Linda hugged her.

Katie reached to hug her cousin in return but already Linda was pinning the pillowcase to the line. And before she knew it, Katie felt Linda snatch her sheet and hang it too.

As Katie watched her cousin skip back to the rinse tub on the porch, she wondered at her resilience. Why, only yesterday she'd stood beside the bed, holdin up one slashed garment after another, while tears poured down her face.

"They're ruined, *si*"

Course they was ruined. There was no fixin them dozen skirts an blouses which had been sliced to ribbons. Whoever did it intended to destroy. How had it happened, anyways? They'd all come down to breakfast as usual, Linda gettin there first to help My Ma set things on.

Course Mamie was a tad late. But then she had to look extra purty these days, workin fur Aunt Jane an all. She'd set right to helpin the minute she stepped into the kitchen, bein nice to everyone, specially Linda. It didn't seem possible thet she'd taken shears to Linda's special clothes. But she had.

Drat it all, what was *wrong* with Mamie, anyways? Jist cause Linda found them marbles—It didn't make no sense to Katie. After all, Linda had found them while cleanin Aunt Jane's room. Course her own chin had trembled at the sight of thet small leather bag sittin on her chest of drawers. Still—

"Pretty, *si*?" And Linda had picked out green, pink, and blue spheres.

Katie nodded. Them was Patrick's marbles. Clasping her arms about herself she recalled the many days she'd seen her brother play with them beside the log bench underneath the oak tree. She vaguely recalled him an Thomas scratchin a circle in the dirt an puttin the marbles inside it. Mostly though it was him an Mamie thet played. Hour after hour they'd hunker, seein who could win the most of them little clay balls. Patrick usually won. But thet never stopped Mamie from tryin. She loved thet game, jist like she loved Patrick.

Hanging another sheet, Katie glanced at her cousin. Already, Linda wore a new skirt. For once her tears were dried, she'd marched up to her pa's store an bought a whole basketful of yard goods. Why my goodness, if she stitched up even half thet stuff, she'd have more clothes than she'd had before.

"I like your new skirt," Katie said.

"It's pretty, *si*?" And Linda swished the ruby ruffles as though nothing had ever happened.

❖ ❖ ❖

It was nearly noon when Daniel emerged from Chapman's Dry Goods, mail in hand. Fingering the single letter addressed to his father, he frowned. It was from his grandfather. Personally, he longed to meet the old man. But his father wouldn't hear of it. The truth was, his father seemed angry with his grandfather for some reason. Ah well, there was nothing he could do to change things. Even so—

His hand was on the door of his own shop when a feminine voice cut into his thoughts.

"Good mornin, Mr. Lewis."

Daniel turned to greet Mamie Fitzsimmons. The green dress she wore, with its bustled skirt and black braid trim, darkened her eyes to the color of emeralds. And rays of topaz sunlight brushed her wavy, upswept hair to the sheen of copper. For a second Daniel let his gaze wander over her tall, slim figure. God, but she was lovely! Then realizing he'd yet to speak, Daniel swept off his stovepipe hat.

"Good morning to you, Miss Fitzsimmons. You're on the way home to dinner no doubt."

"Oh yes. An I do so enjoy workin in Aunt Jane's shop."

"Business good?"

"Wonderful. Seems like every lady in town wants a new dress or hat."

"Well, if all the dresses are as pretty as yours, I can see why."

"Why thank you, Mr. Lewis." And she fluttered eye lashes the color of mahogany.

Tightening his fingers about the brim of his hat, Daniel swallowed hard. "Well, I suppose I'd best go see if my own dinner is ready." And he pushed open the shop door. "Perhaps we'll meet again soon."

"Of course." And Mamie turned toward home.

Watching her slink along, Daniel gripped his hat even harder. God, but he wanted to follow her. To lay his arm across her small shoulders, to look deeper into those green eyes, to kiss those sensuous lips— Daniel stopped, chagrined at his own thoughts. Then entering the shop, he admitted to himself what he'd known for some time now. Harvey Fudd was a wonderful old man. But he was a friend, pure and simple . And the truth was Daniel needed more than that. He needed a wife. For he was lonely. Lonely for that special comfort that only a woman can give.

Chapter 25

Sunday dinner over, Jordana stood before her bureau, studying herself in the square mirror. The tiny hat, the tassel–trimmed basque, the bustled skirt looked fine, she reckoned. Though she was plumb tuckered out after gettin it all on. Still, she'd best look like a lady if she wanted James to take her to them Spring Grounds. He'd refused to consider it two weeks before when she'd appeared in an old calico.

"Mercy sakes," he'd exclaimed, "you can't go out lookin like thet. Folks will think you're from hick town."

And so she'd had Jane stitch this gitup, makin James pay fur it. She was right glad she'd done it too, despite feelin a mite uncomfortable. After all, what was a little discomfort compared with the contentment of visitin them lovely Spring Grounds?

Outside, James handed her into his handsome new surrey and they set off. For a moment Jordana wavered. Was it right, leavin Michael standin there by the rail fence? Course there wasn't room fur three in this fancy contraption of James'. An he had invited *her*. She reckoned she was bein jist plumb silly to worry about Michael.

At the Spring Grounds, James slowed the horses to a walk, driving pretentiously among the newly finished cottages. Finally, he drew to a stop beneath the grove of oak trees.

Though she longed to rush across the bridge, into the Pagoda and down the steps, Jordana walked sedately, her hand on James' arm. In the pagoda, James seated her. Then taking two tin cups, he disappeared down the broad stone steps. He returned seconds later, handing her a drink of cold, spring water.

Forgetting for a moment to behave like a lady, Jordana gulped the water, letting its cool sweetness filter into her being. My but thet was good! She held out her cup for more. Frowning, James handed her his own.

This time Jordana sipped slowly. Glancing at her brother, she said, "My but things has changed round here since you an Linda came."

"Is thet so?"

Jordana nodded. "Everything's better. Take Thomas, fur instance. Why, he hadn't been to church fur years till you came."

"I'm a good influence, eh?" James smiled sardonically, pushing back his sombrero.

"Reckon so. He sets great store by you. Course he might be goin jist to see thet Crawford girl. He's spoilin to marry her, thet's fur certain. It's natural I reckon, her brother bein his best friend an all."

James nodded. "Killed at Wilson's Creek."

"He told you?"

"Sure. We're friends. Jist like you an Carrie used to be."

"Carrie? You remember Carrie?" Jordana nearly dropped her cup in surprise.

"Mercy sakes, Sis, don't look so startled." He playfully shook a finger at her. "Course I remember thet towhead. She was my cousin too." He paused, then added, "I was sorry to hear she passed on."

Swallowing hard, Jordana wiped her eyes with her handkerchief, wishin them cool fingers round her heart would find somethin else to bother. Deliberately, she focused her attention on the milling crowd. There was gittin to be lots of folks comin here now. Lots of horses, surreys, buggies. Lots of buildins too. Them cottages, the sanatorium— Why, she'd even heard they might put up a hotel. She hoped not.

"Somethin wrong?"

Jordana shrugged. "This—this here is gittin a mite overdone. It ain't much like the Big Spring no more."

James laughed. "Course it's not like Big Spring. Never could be. This here's a newer state, newer land, newer opportunities."

Jordana stared at her brother, the fingers turning icy. Confound him! What was wrong with James, anyways? Didn't he ever miss Kentucky?

As though reading her mind, James laughed softly. "Mercy sakes, Sis, I had you figured fur better than thet. What was so good about Kentucky, anyhow?"

The fingers warmed briefly. "It was home," she said simply.

"Sure. But I wasn't sorry to leave it."

"Was—was you sorry when Pa died?"

"Only cause I figured thet nigger, Adrian, killed him."

"I was glad. Jist plumb glad." There, she'd finally said it. Finally told someone thet she hated Pa. An it felt good.

James nodded. "I figure you had a right to be." His deep set eyes held hers for a moment as though telling her he understood.

James knew. Had known all along. Then confound it, why didn't he do somethin?

"Sorry, Sis, but I couldn't do nothin about it. Mercy sakes, I was no match fur Pa. He was strong, remember? Besides, there was Ma to think of—"

Silence.

"Like another drink?" James stood and reached for her cup.

She nodded, thankful thet the fingers were brushin lighter now. Maybe after more of thet Sweet Spring water they'd disappear fur good.

After they'd finished their second cups, James picked up a stone jug. "Reckon I'd best fill this here before we go."

Jordana stood then and stepped to the edge of the Pagoda. Seeing that spurt of clear water, she longed to follow James. But thet wouldn't be ladylike. Besides, there was some highfalutin men down there. An they was fillin cups an laughin, like they owned the place.

James waited politely for the men to move so he could fill his jug. But they continued joking, oblivious to his presence. Finally, he cleared his throat and spoke distinctly. "Pardon me, Gentlemen, I'd like to fill this here jug."

The men continued laughing.

Angry, James elbowed a pudgy man aside. "Pardon me," he bellowed, "I'm here to fill this jug."

At this, the laughter ceased and a tall, insolent man stepped in front of James. "And just who do you think you are, taking from our spring?"

"Your spring? I'll have you know I live here."

"You don't say. Well, you could have fooled me. I thought this was Missouri." And he laughed, the others joining in .

At this, James removed his sombrero. Eyes narrowing, he shook his finger at the older man who stood just below him. "Let me tell you somethin, Mister. I was thirteen years old when I came to Saline County. How old were *you*? Or were you born here alongside the Osage an Fox?"

For a moment the air was so tense Jordana wondered if the man would strike James. Confound them city folks. Why did they have to spoil things fur, anyways?

But the man evidently decided James wasn't worth a fight. With a sneer, he turned aside.

James filled the jug then, but he was angry. He didn't take kindly to bein put down.

He smiled though, as he handed her again into the surrey. Jordana smiled back. After all, James was her brother. An he was right. Them Sweet Springs did belong to the locals as well as to city folks.

Later, as the horses clopped along the dusty street, Jordana sighed. Confound it, things jist hadn't gone right today. If only she'd had the freedom to hike her skirts an run down them steps to thet spring. If only she could've set there an felt thet cool, sparklin water splash about her feet. If only Carrie had been there, bucket in hand, to fetch her a drink.

As she watched her brother and sister set off for the Spring Grounds, Jane frowned. It wasn't right them two goin off thet away. James was actin too high–n–mighty fur this family. No tellin what kind of deals he was amakin with the local big wigs. An Jordana. Land sakes, she was gittin purt near upity herself. Course she did look mighty fine in thet new dress. An she would made a good advertisement fur Jane's shop. Still an all, Jane didn't cotton to the idea of givin your family the cold shoulder.

An thet's jist what her sister was adoin. Leavin them all behind like they was nothin. Fur herself, she didn't care one bit. But them girls needed her. Why land sakes, Jordana hadn't hardly noticed when Mamie cut up all them clothes of Linda's. An Katie. Why, Katie had been atryin fur days to tell her ma she was in love with Thane Chapman. But Jordana jist treated her like she wasn't even there. It seemed to Jane her sister didn't think of anyone anymore. Except fur James. Even Michael was left to fend fur himself. But if Michael felt slighted he didn't say so. Course he did take extra sips from thet there jug now an then.

An that's what he was doing when Jane joined him on the back porch.

"Aye, Lass, it's a warm day to be sure." Michael took one last swallow, then corked the jug and set it beside his rocker.

"Sure is," Jane agreed settling into a cane–bottom chair. "Why land sakes, I purt near roasted along with them taters myself."

"Aye, Lass, I'm thinkin I should've gone to git more spring water this mornin. Course Colleen will bring back plenty, to be sure."

Jane nodded.

For a long time they sat in silence, Michael with his eyes half closed, his burly shoulders moving slightly.

"Aye, Lass, I'm troubled to be sure. I know thet thet spring back in Kentucky was real special like, mind. An there was somethin about a cousin—"

"Carrie was more than jist a cousin to Jordana," Jane snapped. "Why land sakes, they was best friends. Course we didn't see her much, except in the summer time, cause she lived in Glasgow. But always when we went there Carrie an Jordana would traipse off to thet Big Spring. An they'd come back alaughin like a couple of hyenas." Jane paused, her voice softening. "Jordana sure did cry when we left there. Course Carrie passed on back in the 1850s."

"Aye, Lass, I'm rememberin now about a letter comin round thet time. Me Colleen cried right bad after readin it. Course I tried to be extra kind like. Still—"

There was silence then, broken only by the chirping of birds and the clatter of pans in the kitchen.

"Land sakes, thet Linda sure is somethin else," Jane said. "She can do more work than anyone I ever seen. An now she's got Katie likin to do dishes too."

"Aye, Lass, Linda's fine to be sure. But Katie now, she's special like."

Jane nodded. "Course she's awful happy jist now."

Michael chuckled. "Aye, Lass, thet Chapman lad has got her attention, to be sure."

Jane frowned, brushing the birthmark on her cheek. "I— I reckon it must be nice like, bein loved an all. Leastwise Katie's thrivin."

"Aye, Lass, she'll be fine."

"When she's married, you mean?"

"Not necessarily, mind. I'm thinkin Katie has yet to learn thet lovin folks, dispite a heap of hurts, is always worth the cost. Meself, I understand. It takes time, thet bein sure. But Katie— Aye, she'll learn I reckon. An then she'll be right happy, to be sure."

Chapter 26

The wedding was beautiful. At least Katie thought so. Fur Bonnie was lovely. Really an truly she was. Cause thet pale blue dress jist made her eyes look darker than ever. An them tiny pink mums, woven among her chestnut curls, made her cheeks seem all rosy like.

A hush descended on the parlor as Bonnie and Randall came to stand before the fireplace. Though the afternoon was too warm for a fire, the starkness of the hearth was relieved by bowls of pink and white chrysanthemums on the mantle. A bowl of white flowers stood on the pump organ too. But the organ was silent. For it had been Bonnie's Pa who played, and of course he was gone.

> *May God be gracious to us and bless us, and make his*
> *face to shine upon us, through Jesus Christ our Lord.*
> *Amen.*[1]

The minister was beginning now and Katie relaxed, leaning back against the cushioned velvet of the sofa. Fingering the white lace shawl in her lap, she smiled. How much nicer this gift was than them lumpy mittens she'd knitted fur Bonnie on thet Christmas years ago. So much had changed since then. An yet, so much had stayed the same. Like her friendship with Bonnie. *Thet* would never change. Cause she an Bonnie cared fur each other. Really an truly they did.

> *Husbands, love your wives, even as Christ also loved the*
> *church, and gave himself up for it...Nevertheless do ye*
> *also severally love each one his own wife even as himself;*
> *and let the wife see that she regard her husband.*[2]

Katie stole a glance at Thane who sat between her and his mother. As though feeling her gaze, he turned and gave her that shy, lopsided smile

127

she'd come to know so well. Then quickly, he reverted his attention to the couple before them.

Katie turned her attention too, wondering as she did so how it would feel to be married. If she married Thane would she still be the same old Katie, or would she be different like? Course he hadn't asked her. Not yet anyways. But he would. An when he did—

> *Forasmuch as you, Randall, and you, Bonnie, have covenanted together in the presence of God, and of this company, to live together in holy marriage and have pledged the same...I declare you to be husband and wife...*[3]

"Oh, my." Minnie spoke tearfully as Randall kissed his bride. Then lifting her bulk from the sofa, she hurried to embrace her daughter. Turning to Randall, she said, "Welcome to the family, Son."

Smiling, Randall shook her hand, then went to the writing table where he signed his name in the family Bible. After Bonnie signed hers and thanked the minister, she crossed the room to Katie.

Throwing her arms about her friend, she exclaimed. "Oh, Katie, I'm so happy I could jist die. An I'm so glad you're here. Why my gracious, you're my best friend in the whole world."

Katie smiled as she returned the hug. "You're my best friend too. Really an truly you are. An I made you somethin special like." With that, she held out the shawl.

"Why, Katie, thet's beautiful! " And despite the warmth of the day, Bonnie slipped the shawl about her shoulders. Then linking her arm with Katie's, she said, "You'll come to visit me, of course. In fact, I thought to have you an Thane over fur supper sometime next week."

"Oh my goodness, thet's wonderful. I'd love to come. Wouldn't you?" And she turned to Thane.

"Why, gosh Katie, I reckon so." Then coming closer to Bonnie, he kissed her lightly on the cheek. "Congratulations, little sister. I—I love you a lot, you know."

"Why thanks, Thane. An you know what? I love you a lot too."

"And so do I." It was Randall, speaking from behind them. "And I also love eating. So let's have some supper." They all laughed then as they trooped into the kitchen.

The table, laid with Minnie's best dishes, groaned beneath platters of fried ham and chicken, bowls of mashed potatoes, cream gravy, string beans and squash, and baskets of cornbread and biscuits. But before anyone ate, they bowed for prayer. It was Thane who led.

"Dear God, we thank thee for the occasion of this day. Bless Bonnie— and Randall. And bless the food we partake of. Amen."

Katie looked up just as Thane lifted his head. Seein them chestnut waves an them blue, blue eyes, she felt purt nigh overcome with pleasure. Without thinking, she reached out to touch his sleeve. Again, he gave her that shy, lopsided smile before accepting a platter of ham from Randall.

They were halfway through the meal when the back door opened and Will stomped in. Crossing to the washstand, he ladled water into a basin and washed his hands. Then abruptly, he seated himself at the head of the table. Without a word, he began filling his plate.

"Have a good day, Son?" Minnie asked.

"Hardly. Too much trade an too little help." He scooped half a dish of grape preserves onto his already heaped plate.

Seeing the dismay in Bonnie's eyes, Katie understood. Them preserves was mostly fur Randall. After all, Bonnie had labored all day over a hot stove jist to give her love somethin special like. An drat it all, Will was shovelin it into his mouth like there was no end.

As if sensing the girls' eyes on him, Will ceased chewing and demanded sharply, " What's the matter? Am I eatin too much of your weddin feast? I didn't git no dinner, you know. *Someone* had to mind the store."

"Oh, Will, fur cryin out loud. We—"

"It's fine, Will. Eat all you like," Randall cut in. "And thanks for working. Though we did miss you this afternoon."

"I'll bet you did," Will sneered, then resumed eating.

Katie bit her lip, wishing Will had stayed away. Still, it was Bonnie she loved. An Thane. An as long as she had them beside her nothin else mattered.

The bedroom is dark, except for a shaft of moonlight. And quiet, except for the rhythmic breathing of Linda. But to Katie, kneeling before the open window, it's as though the sun shines upon scarlet leaves and birds sing in sweetened air. Fur Thane has asked her to marry him.

> *The voice of my beloved! behold, he*
> *cometh leaping upon the mountains,*
> *skipping upon the hills.*
> *My beloved is like a roe or a young hart:*
> *behold, he standeth behind our wall, he*

> *looketh forth at the windows, shewing*
> *himself through the lattice.*
> *My beloved spake, and said unto me, Rise*
> *up, my love, my fair one, and come away.*
> *For, lo, the winter is past, the rain is over and gone;*
> *The flowers appear on the earth; the time*
> *of singing of birds is come, and the voice*
> *of the turtle is heard in our land;*
> *The fig tree putteth forth her green figs,*
> *and the vines with tender grape*
> *give a good smell. Arise, my love, my fair*
> *one, and come away.*[4]

Thane has asked her to marry him! Stretching her arms into the cool darkness, Katie can scarcely contain her joy. The milky glow of moonlight and the silvery gleam of stars, pale when compared to the brilliance which suffused her when Thane proposed.

An them kisses. Why my goodness, they made her feel a need inside she'd never knowed she had, so that even now she sways sensuously in time with the maple limbs across the way. An his voice. Whisperin her name over an over, urgin her to come away an be his love. An afterward, he'd strode away less quickly than before.

> *Arise, my love, my fair*
> *one, and come away.*[5]

Oh, Thane. My wonderful, wonderful Thane. Yes. Yes. Yes!

Chapter 27

For once Katie failed to appreciate the Sabbath morning hymn. With tomorrow bein Christmas an Thane comin fur dinner today, she could hardly contain her excitement. She an Thane were engaged. Promised they was, since My Pa had given consent.

"Aye, Lass," he'd said, "you'll be right happy, to be sure." He'd tousled her hair then, as he'd done so often in them long ago days when she was a child. And Katie had felt blessed.

And it came to pass in those days, that there went out a decree from Caesar Augustus, that all the world should be taxed...And Joseph also went up from Galilee, out of the city of Nazareth, into Judea, unto the city of David, which is called Bethlehem...[1]

Glancing across the aisle to where Thane sat, Katie smiled. He was *so* handsome. Really an truly he was. Them broad shoulders filled out his frock coat real nice like. An them chestnut waves curled real purty jist above his collar. Course she couldn't rightly see them eyes jist now, but oh my goodness, they was beautiful. Like the early night sky they was—clear an dark.

Katie stretched her arms, reveling in the delicious feel of love. She could hardly wait fur dinner time today an fur Christmas dinner tomorrow. Both times she'd be in company with Thane. An maybe tomorrow evenin she could manage a talk with Bonnie. After all, Bonnie knew all about married life now. She knew about Thane too. Katie reckoned Bonnie could answer all her questions.

The minister had barely ended his sermon when a shrill whistle split the air.

131

"Somethin wrong, *si*?" Linda whispered, her dark eyes wide with apprehension.

"Land sakes, thet must be the train acomin."

Even as Jane forgot herself and spoke out loud, several men got up from their seats, hurried toward the back door and went out.

Whoo–ooo. Whoo–ooo–ooo.

Course thet was the train comin in. It was bound to be seein as how the Fitzsimmons men—an Mamie too—had headed fur thet new depot this mornin. Even Uncle James had passed up church to be on hand when thet engine came in.

Throughout the congregation curious glances changed to whispers, which in turn evolved to outright conversation. What is this here train, anyways? This'll put Brownsville on the map, sure enough. They say thet engine eats loads of wood. Drinks lots of water too. They say—

"Ah–hum." The minister cleared his throat. "Let us bow before our Lord in prayer."

But neither Katie nor anyone else heard that benediction. The railroad was completed; a train was pulling in. Even the Lord seemed commonplace by comparison.

❖   ❖   ❖

A large crowd had gathered by the time the Lewis men and Harvey Fudd reached Lexington Avenue. Most of the folks were milling in front of a platform, set up just to the east of the depot. It was a day for politics, pure and simple.

Glancing about, Daniel noted a number of darkies had gathered on the other side of the tracks. His father was certain to be uneasy about that. But if the elder Lewis noted them, he didn't let on. Instead, he faced east, puffing his Havana leisurely as he waited for his first glimpse of the steam locomotive. Harvey Fudd faced east too. In his excitement he sucked his peppermint stick with unusual vigor, his head shaking slightly.

Watching the two of them, Daniel felt a sense of pride. He was proud of his father for being an expert craftsman and an honest businessman. He was proud of Harvey for trying so hard to please. He loved them both. Even so—

Despite the fact the train was coming, Daniel went in search of Mamie Fitzsimmons. Before long he saw her, standing beside her father near the platform.

She evidently saw him too, for as he neared, she strolled to meet him. They met just as a long whistle rent the air. Despite the clamor which followed, they had eyes only for each other.

"Good morning, Miss Fitzsimmons," Daniel removed his stovepipe hat.

"Good mornin, Mr. Lewis. It's nice to see you again."

"It's a pleasure to see *you*. Pure pleasure." Daniel gripped the brim of his hat as he studied the figure before him. Did Mamie truly care for him, or did that lovely face cloak a mercenary soul?

As though sensing his uncertainty, Mamie inclined her head and smiled.

Relieved, Daniel smiled in return. "No doubt your family has plans for tomorrow?"

"Nothin special. Katie'll be at the Chapmans. The rest of us'll jist set about the fireplace an chat like families do."

Crushing his hat brim with aching fingers, Daniel spoke smoothly. "Then perhaps it would be convenient for me to drop by?"

Placing a gloved hand on his arm, Mamie purred. "I'd like thet, Mr. Lewis."

"Daniel," he said, loosening the hold on his hat. "Just call me, Daniel."

❖   ❖   ❖

To Thomas the morning was wonderful. Standing beside Tevis, he puffed contentedly on his new Charatan Supreme pipe, a gift from Uncle James. Made a feller feel plumb good standin in the crisp air, waitin fur the sight of thet there train. Brownsville had finally gone an done it.

An Uncle James too, from the looks of things. Important like he was today, minglin with local dignitaries on thet platform. Course Uncle James deserved recognition. Why, he'd talked more than one businessman into buyin county bonds fur thet railroad. Though fact was, he hadn't bought none himself. Still, he'd invested plenty in this town. More than most.

"Well, would you look who's over there," And Tevis nudged Thomas with his elbow.

"Who?"

"Our old friend, Uriah."

"He ain't my friend."

"So it seems. An if the gossip I hear is true, he's out to bring you down. Fur quittin the gang an all."

At this, Thomas, his legs straight as sticks, snarled, "Damn thet bastard, anyways. I hate him."

"Jist fillin you in pal, thet's all." And Tevis strode off.

Watching his friend go, Thomas felt abandoned. Alone. Friendless.

He stood for some time, his legs stiff, and pondered life. What was the use of it all, anyways? With Wade gone—

Whoo–ooo. Whoo–ooo–ooo.

A piercing blast from the train sliced into Thomas' cogitation. Thet engine would be pullin in any minute now. He'd best git a closer look. Maybe over there, behind Crawford's store.

He was perhaps twenty feet from Julia and her papa when Julia turned and beckoned him with a slim hand. Thomas froze. Fur somethin about thet wave caused his heart to stand still. He'd seen it before, the summer he was ten. He'd sneaked out of the smithy thet mornin an high–tailed it up to the creek, hopin to find someone to play with. An he did. He was still several feet from the bank when he saw Wade Crawford. Lookin up, Wade saw him too, an beckoned. "Hurry, Thomas. Look! It's a snake. Copperhead, I think."

Thomas had froze. For one brief second his heart had ceased beating. Cause he was scared. Not of thet snake, of course. He wasn't afraid of a rascal like thet. It was Wade thet scared him. Fur thet wave called him to friendship.

"Come on, Thomas, hurry!"

Thomas' heart had begun to race then as his legs sped toward the bank. He would be a friend to Wade. He *would*.

Lifting his left sleeve to his eyes, Thomas shifted uneasily. Fur the person beckonin now wasn't Wade. It was Julia. Urgin him to her. Or so it seemed. Yet, Thomas stalled, his lips taut, his heart scarcely beating. Why was love seekin him out again? Darn it all, anyways. If he'd ever lose Julia the way he lost Wade—

Whoo–ooo! Whoo–ooo–ooo!

Julia was beckoning again, a question in her violet eyes.

Damn, but he wanted to run away. To turn an skedaddle back to home an safety. Yet, Julia was there before him. Right purty she was too, with them blonde curls peepin out from neath thet tiny hat. An them fine lips parted in excitement over thet comin train.

Whoo–ooo!! Whoo–ooo–ooo!!

Thomas' own lips curved upward then. His body relaxed, he moved forward. By the time he reached Julia, his heart was pounding. Beatin in his ears, it was.

"Nice day, Son," Mr. Crawford offered.

Thomas nodded. "Thet's fur certain." And he smiled at Julia.

Another blast from the whistle and the crowd surged forward.

"Can you see all right?"

"Almost. If thet man over there would move—" Julia waved a gloved hand.

"Furgit him. Jist stick to me." And Thomas pulled her to his left side, edging through the crowd for a better view.

Stopping just shy of the platform, he spoke around his pipe. "How's thet?"

"Fine."

At that moment it happened. A black steam engine chugged into view, smoke pouring, whistle blaring. The crowd roared its approval as the iron wheels rolled closer, until at last, hissing steam and belching smoke, it screeched to a halt beside the depot. Folks went wild then, clapping, waving, stomping. But Thomas refrained. Whether he waved his arm or danced about wouldn't make a lick of difference anyways . An, fact was, with his arm about Julia even thet train seemed less outstandin like. Fur he was in love. Nothin else seemed important.

PART III
1872-1875

LOSSES

"...it was the winter of despair..."
— Charles Dickens
A Tale Of Two Cities

Chapter 28

She couldn't believe it. Jane just couldn't believe that Claudia was dead. But she was. Claudia, Andrew, Rachel, the boy, Adrian, little Leah, even Rachel's surly husband—they was all dead. Land sakes, it didn't seem possible.

Running her fingers through her disheveled hair, Jane smiled wanly. It was downright uncanny thet she should be asittin in the same rocker she'd set in thet day Claudia had moved off. Still an all, the heat of thet July day in '66 couldn't compare with the frost of this January evenin in 1872. Fur the sun wasn't shinin now. An she couldn't peer through the window to watch her friend go away. All because of thet blamed Ku Klux Klan. They'd swooped down on northern Brownsville, mutiliated their victims, then flew off again, disappearin as quick as they'd come. It'd been purt near a week now an still no one knowed how it happened.

Rubbing the birthmark on her left cheek, Jane sighed. She wished she'd gone to see Claudia more often. Half a dozen times in two years didn't amount to much. Still an all, thet last visit at Christmas had been a happy one. Fur Claudia had talked more in thet afternoon than Jane could ever remember. Land sakes, she spoke of her ma, her pa, Kentucky, an even her sister, Dinah. An her face seemed to lose twenty years when she looked at Andrew. Later, she'd served tea an dried apple cake. An when Jane left, she'd given her an extra piece to take home. Land sakes, even now Jane could taste thet treat. Full of sliced apples an broken pecans it was, an spicy with cinnamon an jist a pinch of nutmeg. How she'd savored thet second piece, eatin it leisurely after a long day at the shop. An now—

"Aye, Lass, them Klan folks is a sorry lot, to be sure."

At the sound of Michael's voice, Jane started. Land sakes, she'd been athinkin so much about Claudia she hadn't heard no one else come in. Yet there was Michael, asittin in his rocker beside the fireplace, his head bowed as he studied his hands folded across his ample waist.

"They're an impudent bunch all right," Jane snapped. "They've no cause to kill folks thet away. It's downright sinful, thet's what it is."

"Aye, Lass, I reckon you're right. Meself, I miss Andrew right bad. He was always so special like."

"Course you miss him. I miss Claudia too. Why land sakes, we grew up together. It was Claudia I clung to when we left Kentucky. It was Claudia I turned to when Pa was killed, an when Ma died. Why, we was *friends!*"

"Aye, Lass, thet you was. Meself, I took to Andrew right off when Uncle Patrick brought him home. Mind you, I was but a lad of twelve at the time. Me Dad—Me Dad had jist passed on. I was feelin right bad I reckon, till I saw thet new slave. 'He's yours,' Uncle Patrick said. Aye, Lass, but thet tall, shy black boy was never my slave. I've a mind thet from the beginnin we was friends. Fur years we worked side by side in the smithy. I loved thet man, to be sure. Thet's why it hurt right bad when he up an moved off sudden like. I've a mind he thought I'd done him wrong someway. But I never did. I couldn't."

"Course you didn't do Andrew no wrong," Jane snapped. "It was Thomas thet did."

"Aye, Lass, you bein sure?"

"Course I'm sure. Land sakes, it was Thomas thet raped Rachel an got her in the family way."

For a moment Michael appeared stunned. He sat unmoving, staring at Jane as though he hadn't heard right.

"Land sakes, don't look at me thet away. It's true. Anyways, thet's all over with now. Rachel had a fine boy. He looked—he looked jist like Thomas, only darker."

Still, Michael sat motionless. Yet, them lines about his chin seemed to deepen. An them hazel eyes darkened with moisture. For the first time ever Jane thought he looked downright old. More than his fifty two years.

"They named him Adrian." She spoke more gently now. "At first Claudia was angry. Andrew too, I reckon. But they seemed to git over it in time. Both—both of them loved thet youngin."

"Aye, Lass, I've a mind they did. Meself, I would've too, had I aknown."

At the quaver in Michael's voice, Jane frowned. Land sakes, she'd only now realized thet Adrian was Michael's grandson too. An he never got to see him.

"I'm sorry, Michael. It was downright unkind of me to tell you thet away. Fact is, I should've kept quiet like."

"Aye, Lass, you meant no harm, to be sure." But his voice still quavered, and his thick shoulders heaved as he sat staring at his hands folded across his middle.

Thomas sat on the edge of the bed smoking his Charatan pipe and studying the flag draped above his headboard. The Stars and Bars. Dusty now, that cloth still symbolized what he believed in. Dang it all, them Feds had no *right* to tell Missourians how to live. Thet rascal Fremont had no *right* to free them slaves. Course Andrew never left, anyways. After all, he was My Pa's friend. Leastwise thet's what they'd always thought.

The corners of Thomas' mouth turned up slightly as he thought of the former Fitzsimmons' slaves. He reckoned he ought to be sorry they was dead. But he wasn't. He was sick an tired of niggers settin up trade an actin like they was good as white folks. Served them right, bein murdered. Even if his one–time friend Uriah had been a party to it, he was glad.

Standing, Thomas walked to the row of hooks and reached for his nightshirt. Then changed his mind. He was hungry. Maybe My Ma had some of them fried apple pies left.

Downstairs, My Pa sat alone at the kitchen table. The light from the coal oil lamp revealed his flushed, puffy face and the jug in his hand.

"Aye, there's me lad, Thomas. The one who chased me friend away."

"You're drunk, My Pa. You'll be a sight better in the mornin." And Thomas reached for the jug.

But Michael jerked it away. He belched, took another swig and belched again. "Aye, Lad, I know all about it to be sure."

"About what?"

"About what?! Aye, Lad, I don't take to lyin."

"Now, wait jist a minute. I ain't no liar an I don't know what you're talkin about."

"Aye, Lad, but you do. You hurt us right bad when you took thet young Rachel an used her fur a breedin cow."

At this Thomas shifted uneasily. How had My Pa got wind of thet? Anyways, thet was so long ago he'd plumb furgot it happened.

"Aye, Lad, an I know about the wee one. A wee brown lad, in a wee tiny shack, in a wee dark settlement up north." He chuckled then as he swigged more whiskey.

"What wee one?" Thomas demanded, his lips taut.

"Aye, Lad, the one you sired to be sure."

The one he'd— Thomas shifted again, his mouth growing dry with fear. Why, he'd never fathered a child. Anyways, he'd only taken Rachel thet once. In all his born days he'd never heard anything so silly.

"Aye, Lad, he's dead now. Thet wee one thet was lookin like you. Dead, to be sure. Andrew an the wee one is dead. Dead. Dead. Dead." And he took another swig from the jug.

Thomas, his mouth still feeling like cotton, sidled toward the stairway door. He was nearly there when the thick voice halted him.

"Aye, Lad, I love you , mind."

Thomas didn't answer. Instead he shifted uneasily, then hurried on upstairs. In all his born days he'd never seen My Pa so bad hurt. Course he never heard him say, "I love you," before neither. It made a feller feel all choked up like. But then the older man was bound to say somethin foolish like. After all, he was drunk. Jist plumb drunk.

Chapter 29

As she placed the last dish in the cupboard and hung the tea towel to dry, Katie sighed. Drat it all, what was the matter with her family, anyways? Jist cause them slaves got killed was no reason to take on so. Why, look at Aunt Jane. Mopin around she was, refusin to git dressed an go out. Course thet meant Mamie had to mind the shop an do the sewin. An Mamie wasn't one to stand fur too much workin. Why, jist awhile ago she'd spouted right off like.

"Oh fur heaven sakes, Aunt Jane, stop actin like your best friend died. Them niggers was gittin too uppity fur their own good. Anyways, if you don't git back to work soon, you can jist kiss thet shop good–by. Cause I ain't no seamstress, an I *ain't* goin to sew much longer."

Katie winced at the hurt she'd seen in Aunt Jane's eyes as Mamie stalked from the room. Sad she looked, as she sat there rubbin thet birthmark. Real sad. Still, *someone* had to take her in hand. An it jist as well be Mamie, she reckoned.

Drat it all, why couldn't Aunt Jane git over things easy like the way My Pa did? Course he'd mourned fur Andrew aplenty. He'd got drunk several evenins at first. But then he'd put thet liquor jug aside an went on like nothin ever happened. But Aunt Jane seemed all done in like. Nigh onto a month it'd been an she still acted like it was yesterday.

Climbing the stairs, Katie shook her head. There was no accountin fur some folks, she reckoned. Fur herself, she was goin to bed early an dream of Thane. Jist thinkin on thet man made other things seem easier like.

In the bedroom, Katie lit the lamp and began to undress. She was in her nightie when she realized she'd have to clear the bed before sleeping. Drat thet girl. Why couldn't Linda pick up her clothes fur, anyways?

Crossing the room, Katie began flinging clothes aside. Skirts, blouses, sashes galore hit the floor as Katie made ready for bed. She did like Linda. Really an truly she did. Fur Linda, with her course dark hair an easy smile, was somethin special like. Still, Katie wished she'd be a tad more neat. She wished—

Katie stopped, staring at the doll on the bed. Her chin quivering, she lifted the limp figure, clad now in a swirling skirt and peasant blouse. Molly. The one friend who had always been there. Fur it was Molly thet Katie had clung to when Thomas went off to war. It was Molly she'd slept with after they took My Pa away. Molly had been there too, to ease the pain of losin Patrick. An now, Linda had taken her away.

For a long time Katie hugged her old friend close. Then laying her back on the bed, Katie went to the window overlooking Main Street. Kneeling, she stared through cold glass to the moonlit world beyond. She'd jist as well let Molly go, she reckoned. But drat it all, why did it have to hurt so bad fur, anyways?

Her chin quivering, Katie hugged herself as she stared at the naked branches of the maple tree across the way. Outlined by moonlight, they looked as bereft as she felt. Lonely they was, fur the comfort of leaves. Leaves thet had withered an died. Yet, even now them limbs is stretchin, reachin as though beckonin fur new leaves to come.

Katie's chin ceases quivering as she rises to her feet. It's all right about Molly. Really an truly it is. There'll be other friends. After all, she has Bonnie. An Thane. Slowly, Katie stretches her arms and smiles.

Chapter 30

Large snowflakes fell thickly, causing Daniel to shiver as he strode west on Main Street. My but it was cold this evening. Even so, he was glad to be out. Clutching his volume of Browning, he smiled. It would be pleasure, pure pleasure, to read poetry to Mamie. Of course others would be there too, but it was Mamie he courted. It was Mamie he'd bought the card for.

But it was Katie who answered the door. A lovely Katie clad in a ruffled pink poplin.

"Good evening, Miss Katie." Daniel removed his stovepipe hat.

"Oh." Katie reacted with a start. "Oh my goodness, yes. Do come in, Mr. Lewis. Furgive me fur actin startled like. I was expectin Thane."

"Think nothing of it," Daniel smiled as he removed the card from his greatcoat and handed the latter to Katie. "I brought along some Browning," he fingered the volume tenderly.

"Oh, thet's wonderful. Thet'll give us somethin special like."

In the parlor, Daniel seated himself on the sofa.

"Mamie'll be down in a minute," Katie said, then slipped from the room leaving Daniel alone with Linda. Watching the Mexican cousin shell corn into a wire popper, Daniel noted again her robust beauty. And again, he compared her with Mamie. Though Linda was vibrant, Mamie embodied the delicate beauty that stirred his soul.

As though she'd heard his thoughts, Mamie slinked into the room, her topaz skirts swaying.

Tightening his grip on the card in his hand, Daniel rose to meet her.

"Good evening, Mamie. I've brought you something."

Taking the proffered card, Mamie read it slowly.

"Why, Daniel, a Valentine. My but it's lovely." And she stroked the lace–trimmed card before placing it on the writing table.

Sittingon the sofa, she turned to Daniel, a smile on her sensual lips. "Thank you. Thank you very much."

"You're welcome," Daniel swallowed hard, a band tightening about his chest. God, but he cared for this woman.

"I hope you like popcorn." Mamie stroked his coat sleeve as she spoke.

"I sure do." Daniel relaxed a bit then, watching those hard kernels explode into white fluff as Linda shook the popper above the flames in the fireplace.

Soon Thane arrived and took a chair opposite Daniel.

"How's things at the shop?" he asked.

"Fine. We've more orders than we can possibly fill."

"Why, thet's wonderful," Mamie interjected, patting the back of Daniel's hand.

"We think so." Daniel surreptitiously covered her fingers with his other hand.

Katie passed a bowl of apples then, and reluctantly Daniel disengaged his hand to take one.

"This is good, *si*?" Linda spoke around a mouthful of apple.

"*Si,*" Katie answered and everyone laughed.

"Corn is good too," Thane teased, nodding toward the roasting pan.

"You want some?" And she scooped out a bowlful and handed it to Thane.

"Why gosh, thank—thank you, Linda." Thane blushed to the roots of his chestnut hair as he accepted the heaped bowl. After munching several handfuls, he turned to Katie, who sat at his knee, and smiled. "This is real good, you know. Jist awful good."

Katie smiled in return, stretching her hand to touch his. Minutes later she rose, and taking up a book, stood before the fireplace.

"This evenin we're goin to read poetry." She smiled again. And something about this smile reminded Daniel of the girl who had once stood in the post office and accepted a gift from Bonnie. For Katie was radiant as she opened the book and began.

Tell me not, in mournful numbers,
   Life is but an empty dream!
For the soul is dead that slumbers,
   And things are not what they seem.

Life is real! Life is earnest!
  And the grave is not its goal;
Dust thou art, to dust returnest,
  Was not spoken of the soul....

In the world's broad field of battle,
  In the bivouac of Life,
Be not like dumb, driven cattle!
  Be a hero in the strife! ....

Let us, then, be up and doing,
  With a heart for any fate;
Still achieving, still pursuing,
  Learn to labor and to wait.[1]

"Thet's beautiful, *si*?" Linda burst into the stillness which followed. "Let me, *prima* Katie." And rising, Linda took the book from her cousin. Leafing through it, she stopped and smiled. "I read this one?" Then swaying slightly, she began.

Half a league, half a league,
Half a league onward,
All in the valley of Death
  Rode the six hundred.
"Forward the Light Brigade!
Charge for the guns!" he said.
Into the valley of Death
  Rode the six hundred....
Cannon to right of them,
Cannon to left of them,
Cannon in front of them
  Volley'd and thunder'd....[2]

Daniel grimaced. Though he loved the poem, Linda was butchering it. She didn't have the rhythm right and she mispronounced half the words. He was glad when she finished and gave the book to Mamie.

Turning a few pages, Mamie stood, slinked toward the fireplace, and spoke. "I ain't much fur poetry really. Not like Katie, anyways. But seein as how Linda started with Tennyson, I guess I'll read from him." She smiled then at Daniel and began.

Sweet and low, sweet and low,
Wind of the western sea,
Low, low, breathe and blow,
Wind of the western sea,
Over the rolling waters go,
Come from the dying moon, and blow,
Blow him again to me;
While my little one, while my pretty one, sleeps...[3]

A hush fell over the room as Mamie closed the book. Daniel, swallowing hard, clutched his book of Browning. As he stood, it seemed everyone looked at him expectantly. Mamie had as good as said she loved him. It had been pleasure, pure pleasure, to hear her sweet voice directing those words toward him. Now, he supposed, he must respond in kind. It didn't take long to find the poem he wanted.

She should never have looked at me
If she meant I should not love her!
There are plenty...men, you call such,
I suppose...she may discover
All her soul to, if she pleases,
And yet leave much as she found them:
But I'm not so, and she knew it
When she fixed me, glancing round them....[4]

Daniel paused, the tightness in his chest shortening his breath. His fingers gripping the book, he looked directly at Mamie. She smiled. The band in his chest loosened then and his fingers relaxed. His bearded face took on its own smile as he continued.

Such am I: the secret's mine now!
She has lost me, I have gained her;
Her soul's mine: and thus, grown perfect,
I shall pass my life's remainder.
Life will just hold out the proving
Both our powers, alone and blended:
And then, come the next life quickly!
This world's use will have been ended.[5]

No one spoke as Daniel returned to sit beside Mamie. But he knew that they knew that he was in love with Mamie. And she with him.

Gradually, the focus shifted from Daniel to Thane. The latter blushed as he stood and strode to the writing table. Taking up the family Bible, he opened it to Song of Solomon and read.

*The voice of my beloved: behold, he
cometh leaping upon the mountains...
...Rise up, my love, my fair one, and come
away....* [6]

Daniel knew the words were meant for Katie. No doubt everyone knew. Yet for some reason, Thane read on without once looking up. And when he'd finished, he laid the Book aside and sat down where he was instead of returning to Katie. If Katie minded, she didn't let on and soon the buzz of conversation reduced the strain in the atmosphere.

Himself, Daniel wanted a closer look at that writing table. It was a simple piece, yet expertly crafted. The diamond designs on the drawers especially intrigued him. Satiny to the touch, its mahogany surface gleamed. And then beneath the lace–edged cloth, his sensitive fingers detected an indentation. And another. Mystified, he lifted the cloth, then dropped it. UNION. The letters had been carved crudely, marring the perfect finish. God, who had done such a thing?

Soldiers, no doubt. *Union* soldiers. Hadn't his father told him that troops ransacked this house? They'd gone so far as to take Mr. Fitzsimmons from his family. And killed the younger son.

Daniel's fingers curled about the edge of the table then, as for a moment he envisioned a bloody saw and his own hands severing a gangrenous limb. For a second he stared hollowly at the cloth–covered table. Then, placing his hand over his eyes, he covered the tears he couldn't hold back. God, but war was awful!

It was some minutes before he regained his composure. When he did, he strode quietly to the sofa and sat down.

"Like our table?" Mamie asked, her green eyes suspiciously moist.

"It's lovely. Beautiful wood, excellent craftsmanship–"

"It used to be perfect."

"It most definitely was. Personally, I think it could be again. Perhaps I could sand it down, refinish the top?"

"Oh, would you?" And the smile on Mamie's face caused Daniel to relax and smile in return.

Jane was nearly asleep when Mamie opened the door and tiptoed in. Without bothering to light a lamp, she began undressing in the dark. Leastwise thet's what Jane guessed she was adoin. Still an all, thet rustlin sounded more like paper than petticoats. Fact was, she seemed to be tearin somethin like. What was thet girl up to, anyways? Course Jane couldn't fault the girl too much. Why land sakes, if Mamie hadn't given her a tongue lashin last week she'd still be mopin stead of sewin. Still an all, Mamie had never acted right since thet War. An now, she was actin strange again. Jane sighed. Fact was, fur all her outward charm, she guessed thet inside Mamie still bled. Fur Patrick.

Chapter 31

Whoo–ooo. Whoo–ooo–ooo. The 7:10 freight train pulled out of Brownsville, its whistle floating through the cool evening air and into Thomas' bedroom where he stood before the mirror combing his dark hair. He was plumb proud of himself jist now. May was still a week away an already he had the garden in. So tonight, he was goin to see Julia.

Laying aside his comb, he took up his pipe and slipped it into his left coat pocket. Tonight he would see Julia, but more than thet he would ask her pa fur permission to marry her.

His mouth dry, he blew out the lamp and descended the stairs. Jist plumb scared, he was. But determined. Why, it'd been over six years since he first called on Julia. It was high time they got hitched.

In the Crawford's parlor Thomas sat quietly while Julia played the piano. His left ankle crossed over his right knee, he puffed his pipe and watched the girl he loved. She was beautiful, thet was fur certain. Why, it made a feller go purt near crazy watchin them tiny hands roam the keyboard an them gold hairs curl about her neck.

Finished, Julia smiled at her papa, then came to sit beside Thomas on the sofa.

Thomas, his feet shifting on the carpet, looked across the room to the plump, balding man who was Julia's pa. It wouldn't be easy convincin Mr. Crawford thet his daughter was essential to Thomas' own happiness. Still, he had to.

Removing his pipe, Thomas leaned forward and cleared his throat.

"Mr. Crawford, sir, I—I wish to ask a favor of you."

"Yes?" The older man simply returned his gaze as he pressed the ball of his foot to the floor and rocked.

151

"I wish to claim your daughter's hand in marriage. You see, I need her somethin awful. An I love her. She's— she's plumb beautiful."

"Yes. Can't say but what I agree with you there. But tell me, Son, how're you fixed fur money?"

"Well, Sir, fact is, I'll inherit the home someday."

"Any money?"

Thomas shook his head, his mouth dry with fear. "Course Uncle James is purt near rich. He lives with us an contributes regular like. He's right smart about money, Uncle James is. Too smart to invest in them worthless railroad bonds."

"An smart enough to con others into investing, is thet it?" Mr. Crawford frowned.

"I reckon so. But fur all thet, he's a good man. He keeps our family goin like."

"So at least your family's well off." It was a statement.

Thomas nodded.

"You plan on blacksmithin when your pa's gone?"

The question took Thomas by surprise. Without thinking, he blurted.

"No. I don't take to the smithy. Makes a feller feel all cooped up like. Fact is, I've a mind to tear thet down an plant an apple orchard."

"Not in the near future." Again, it was a statement.

"No, sir."

"Well then, so much fur money. You been doin any more of this here bushwhackin nonsense?"

"No, sir, I ain't."

"I see. An what of thet Klan?"

"The Klan?"

Mr. Crawford nodded, his rocker moving slowly.

"Why, no Sir, I reckon them rascals ain't up to no good." Thomas paused then, his lips taut. Fact was, he was a mite worried about Uncle James. More than once he'd seen him an Uriah talkin. Last time he'd been so bothered like, thet he'd up an asked his uncle what it was all about.

But Uncle James had merely laughed, wavin his ringed hands expansively. "Mercy sakes, boy, it was nothin. Talkin about them Crawfords, thet's all. An I'll have you know they're fine folks. Absolutely fine."

Course Thomas had agreed. Still, he had an uneasy feelin about his uncle an Uriah.

"Son?"

Mr. Crawford's frown jerked him back to the present.

"Why, no sir, I ain't never takin up with the likes of them."

"I see. Well then, seein as how you love my daughter—" Mr. Crawford ceased rocking, leaned forward and looked straight at Julia. "Julia, dear, do you wish to make this man your husband?"

Julia looked up from her embroidery then, her violet eyes wide with apprehension. "Why I suppose so, Papa. Thet is, if you think it's all right."

"I see. Well, young man, I guess you have your answer."

For a second Thomas' mouth went dry. Then leaning over, he kissed Julia on the lips. He would have kissed her a second time, but Mr. Crawford cleared his throat.

"Thet's enough now, Son."

Chagrined, Thomas drew back. But his eagerness could not be entirely checked. "When can we be married?" He smiled expectantly at Julia.

"Oh, a year from June, I suppose."

"A *year*?!" Thomas burst out. "Why, thet's impossible. A man could go plumb crazy waitin thet long."

"Can't say but what I agree with you there. Still, it's the lady's choice. Women ain't like us, Son. They need time to git ready fur such things. Ain't thet right, Julia, dear?"

"Yes, Papa. I have ever so much to do. Embroiderin all them linens, makin my trousseau—"

Thomas had no choice but to agree. Still, when he kissed her good night, he took his time. And for once, Julia didn't resist.

❖   ❖   ❖

Seated on the log bench beneath the oak tree, Thomas crossed his left ankle over his right knee and smiled. He was gettin married. Puffing his Charatan pipe, he looked up at the star–studded sky, and marveled at it all. He, a man of purt near thirty years, with only one arm an no money, was gettin married. To the woman he loved. Jist thinkin on it made him feel plumb happy like.

An Julia. How did she feel, anyways? She didn't seem to mind thet he was eight years older than her or thet he wasn't a businessman. Course she did like purty things, thet was fur certain. Still, he reckoned she was set to do without, fur a time, anyways. An his missin arm. Did thet bother her? Shifting his feet in the dirt, Thomas had to admit he didn't know. She'd never *said* anything, of course. Still, she did always manage to sit on his left side. An she always laid her head on his left shoulder too. But fur all thet, she had agreed to marry him.

Recrossing his legs, Thomas decided that maybe next summer wasn't so far off after all. By then Julia was bound to feel more love fur him. By then she'd be eager to be his wife an the mother of his children.

His lips taut, Thomas shifted uneasily. He already had a son. Dead now. But his, nonetheless. All because of thet nigger, Rachel. Darn it all, why had she been so purty fur, anyways? An so fertile? He hadn't wanted a son. Leastwise not a dark one. A man could be plumb embarrassed by a son like thet.

But a white son now, thet would be dandy. One with big violet eyes an gold curls. One thet would toddle about the garden, pattin the dirt with a chubby hand. One thet would laugh an reach fur his pipe. Now, thet would be a son worth havin. Cause thet would be Julia's. An his.

Chapter 32

Livingston Lewis sighed as he entered his cabinet shop on the last Friday in May. He was afraid of what he'd find. And sure enough, several finished pieces had scratches on them. Nothing major, just enough grazing to mar the finish. Just enough tracks to require resanding and restaining.

Picking up a rocker whose spindles would need to be redone, Livingston spotted a washstand with a letter engraved on the side. Oh, Lord! Biting hard on his Havana, he knelt to examine the damage. An F. The letter F had been carved with precision. Indignant, the older Lewis ran his hand over the damaged wood. He was angry, more angry than he could say. With Harvey Fudd. And with Daniel. It was all right to befriend a man in need, but Daniel had gone too far. He'd given that eccentric old man access to their shop, their supplies, even their living quarters. And look what happened. He'd turned on them.

With a groan Livingston prepared to repair the damage. Lord, but he wished Daniel was here. Not only did he need his help, he wanted to settle this thing about Mr. Fudd. But Daniel was out helping the street crew this morning. Ah well, after tomorrow Daniel's four days of service would be up. *Then* they'd decide the fate of that nuisant old man.

Puffing on his Havana, Livingston began sanding a spindle. Come to think of it, this damage reminded him of the bushwhacking escapades of a few years back. Even so, it couldn't be Secesh doing. They'd forsaken the shenanigans of vandalism for the baseness of murder. He chuckled. Well, so long as their victims were darkies, he wouldn't condemn them. The Klan may be brutal but at least they rid the earth of unwanted scum. He'd been glad, more glad than he could say when they'd killed those darkies up north. Even so—

The door opened and Harvey Fudd walked in.

"Mornin, Mr. Lewis, sir. It's a mite warm out there."

Livingston ignored the man. But if Mr. Fudd was bothered by his employer's foul mood, he never let on. Extracting a pink peppermint stick from the cigar box, he went in search of the broom. Seconds later he was sweeping, scattering sawdust everywhere.

Biting hard on his Havana, Livingston refrained from castigating the man. Time enough for that when Daniel returned. In the meantime—

In the meantime he missed his son. He missed the privilege of watching him at work. For Daniel was a craftsman. A fine craftsman. Those gentle hands of his touched wood reverently, as though it was a living, breathing being. Those long fingers traced the grain, feeling for the slightest flaw. And his bearded face would inevitably light with a smile when a job was done to his satisfaction.

Drawing on his Havana, Livingston sighed. Daniel had been especially happy in recent weeks. Even so, Livingston couldn't bring himself to be glad. Somehow, he'd felt sad, more sad than he could say, when Daniel came home last evening, singing an old ballad.

> *There is a charm I can't explain*
> *About a girl I've seen,*
> *And my heart beats fast*
> *when she goes past*
> *In a dark dress trimmed in green.*
> *Her eyes are bright as evening stars*
> *so lovely and so shy,*
> *And the folks all stop*
> *and look around*
> *Whenever she goes by...*[1]

Lord, he couldn't believe it. Daniel was singing. Such a far cry from the Daniel who rarely spoke and whose eyes seemed void of life. Even so, Livingston wasn't happy. For Daniel's singing could mean only one thing—he was in love with Mamie Fitzsimmons. She was pretty enough, for that matter, with her green eyes and auburn hair. But Livingston didn't like her. He simply couldn't imagine her cooking for Daniel, stroking his hair, or rocking his child. Come to think of it, he couldn't imagine Mamie loving Daniel at all. Ah well, if Daniel wanted her, it must be right. After all, he was happy. And more than anything else, Livingston wanted his son's happiness.

❖   ❖   ❖

The fragrant scent of apple blossoms wafted into the kitchen, a breeze stirring the muslin curtains beside the table. Before long the moon would be up, its soft glow casting a silent benediction on a lovely spring day. But for Livingston, a prayer for patience was more in order. Lord, but the day had tried his. Or rather, Mr. Fudd had. Every time he moved, that man was in the way. Whether he was whipping sawdust with a broom, fanning sweat with his straw hat, or cleaning rags with turpentine, he was invariably under Livingston's feet. Finally, in late afternoon, he'd sent the man home.

Pushing his half empty plate aside, Livingston took out a new Havana and snipped off the tip. Lighting it, he sighed. There was no use putting this off any longer.

"Son," he said, "we've got to talk."

"Talk?" Daniel looked up, a buttered biscuit balanced in his hand. "What about?"

"Mr. Fudd."

"Harvey? Why? He's not in the way or anything, is he?"

Livingston groaned. "Of course he's in the way. He's *always* in the way, you know that."

Dolloping jelly on his biscuit, Daniel blanched. "Personally, I know nothing of the kind. I like Harvey, pure and simple. And let me tell you right now—"

"Ah yes, you like him," Livingston cut in. "Even so, you've got to face the facts. Your friend's been scratching our furniture."

"No!" Daniel crushed the biscuit in his hand, oblivious to the jelly which oozed over his sensitive fingers. "Harvey would never do a thing like that. He's my *friend!*" With that Daniel threw his mashed biscuit onto his plate and shoved his chair back from the table. Rising, he glared at his father. "I won't listen to this accusation another minute. The truth is, Harvey is simply a nice old man and you know it."

Removing his Havana from between his stained teeth, Livingston sighed. "Look, Son, I know how much you like Mr. Fudd. That's why I've not told you before this."

"You mean this has been going on for some time?" Daniel drummed his fingers on the back of the chair.

Livingston nodded. "Off and on for a couple of months."

"Why didn't you tell me?"

"Lord, Son, I already explained that. I know you love Mr. Fudd. And your happiness means a lot to me. More than I can say."

"What about the furniture? You didn't sell it scratched up." It was a statement.

"Of course not. I simply redid it. I'll admit though that I've been angry. More angry than I care to say."

"I suppose so." Daniel gripped the chair back. "Thanks though, for refinishing things."

"It's all right, Son. Only now we've got to do something. The scratches have turned into carving. You understand?"

Daniel nodded. "All right. No doubt I'll think differently in the morning. Just now we need to wash up these dishes. I'm going to Mamie's this evening."

Puffing his Havana, Livingston sighed. He had to admit spending another evening alone wasn't his idea of pleasure. Why didn't Daniel consider his feelings as well as his own? Ah well, let him have all the enjoyment he could. Things would be difficult enough when Harvey Fudd was forced from the shop.

❖   ❖   ❖

Daniel stood alone in the shop, his hands clenched at his sides. God, but his father was right. Someone was destroying their work. Crossing to a newly finished table, he turned as pale as the first rays of sunlight peeping through the windows. For there, carved into the smooth oak surface were initials. An A and an R. Pressing his fingers into the grooves, Daniel swallowed hard. It had to be Harvey. But why? God, but he'd been good to that man. He'd rescued him from the ridicule of the Secesh. He'd given him work to do. He'd even given him a family life of sorts.

And Harvey? He'd taken pride in doing well the few things that he could. He'd been a good helper, pure and simple. The truth was the old man seemed incapable of such destruction. Even so, the evidence was there.

Gazing at the ruination of his handiwork, Daniel feels as though a band has been slipped about his chest. Tighter and tighter it's drawn until he can scarcely breathe. God, but he hurts.

Running his fingers once more over the satiny oak table, Daniel goes to open the front door. As he does so, he deliberately ignores the old cigar box sitting on the counter. The one filled with an assortment of peppermint sticks.

Chapter 33

It was raining and Thomas was glad. A feller couldn't possibly pick cherries in this gullywasher. Course he could mosey on up to Crawford's store if he'd a mind to. Catch up on the gossip like, an see Julia.

But it was Uncle James, not Julia, Thomas spotted the moment he entered the store. Surprised, Thomas strode to the counter where his uncle, chewing on a licorice whip, was talking with Julia's pa.

"Why hello there, Thomas." James tipped back his sombrero. "I had you figured to stay inside on a day like this."

"I aim to," Thomas grinned as he took out his pipe. "Thet's what I'm here fur."

James laughed at that, then forestalled his nephew as he felt for tobacco.

"Mr. Crawford, give this young feller here some of your best English tobacco."

Minutes later, puffing his Charatan pipe, Thomas gazed longingly at Julia. My but she looked dandy this mornin. Jist plumb purty she was in thet blue dress an all. Fact was, he had a mind jist to go right up an kiss her on the lips. Course he didn't. But he smiled at her all the same.

And Julia, looking up from the cornmeal she measured, smiled shyly in return.

"Say, Miss Crawford," Uncle James cut in, "how about half a pound of thet horehound candy? My sister's right fond of it."

"Sure, Mr. Douglas." And Julia hurried to fetch the candy.

As she did so, Thomas turned to his uncle. "Thanks, Uncle James, fur the tobacco an candy? Things sure are a sight better around here since you came along."

159

"Mercy sakes, I ain't done nothin much." James waved his hand as he spoke. "Anyhow, you're a mighty fine bunch. An I reckon my time is comin. Cause someday, you'll be givin somethin special like to me." And he took the bag of candy from Julia.

Chapter 34

Daniel shivered as he lighted the lamp on his chest of drawers. Replacing the chimney, he stared at his reflection in the mirror. God, but he had aged. His normally slender face had a gaunt look that made him seem ancient. His cheek bones were mountainous protrusions while his eyes were sunken valleys. His charcoal hair and beard were streaked with gray. And his frame had been pared until his clothes hung in folds about him.

Clenching his bony fingers, he told himself not to brood. After all, this was 1873. A new year, a fresh beginning, another chance.

Another chance? For what? Having his heart crushed all over again?

Lifting his hands to his face, Daniel wept. Copious tears streamed from his eyes, flowing between his fingers and dripping off the backs of his hands. Over six months it had been and still his heart was like an open wound. He'd tried withdrawing, pulling himself inward until only his shell touched the world outside. But that which had enabled him to survive before eluded him now. Try as he might, he simply couldn't escape the pain. He couldn't stop *feeling*. All because one he loved had betrayed him.

It had been warm that last evening in May and he'd decided to call on Mamie. Humming, he closed the door to the sitting room and descended the steps. He was in love, pure and simple. Perhaps this evening he could persuade Mamie to set a date for their wedding. Personally, he wanted to be married soon. But Mamie—

Daniel stopped. A lamp was burning in the shop. And scratching sounds filtered through the air. Clenching his fist, Daniel hesitated. God, but he hated to confront his friend. Even so—

Reluctantly, Daniel entered the shop, then gasped in horror. For there, carving figures on top of a washstand, was a slender figure with auburn hair.

"Mamie?"

For a second the paring knife halted, then with renewed vigor it chiseled—PAT

"Mamie! My God, what are you *doing?*"

The figure never answered. Never turned. Instead, small fingers moved faster, as though frantic to finish the job. RI

"No!" Daniel crossed the room in three strides. Grabbing the cotton clad shoulders, he pulled her away.

Instantly, Mamie was over the stand again, clawing at the walnut stained wood. C

"Mamie!" Again Daniel grasped her shoulders, but not before she'd scratched a K.

"God, woman, what *are* you doing?"

"Doin?" The figure whirled to face him, taking him by surprise.

"Doin?" The voice rose higher, the green eyes glittered. "I'm payin you damned Feds back, thet's what I'm doin." And she lunged at Daniel.

He grabbed her arm just before the knife plunged into his chest. For a moment Mamie froze. Then grinning wickedly, she inched the knife closer. For many minutes they grappled, Mamie trying to stab him, Daniel trying to restrain her without inflicting pain. Finally, when the knife grazed his cheek, Daniel threw caution aside and shoved her to the floor. Before she could recover, he was on top of her, pressing her face into sawdust.

"Drop that knife or I'll suffocate you."

With a whimper, the fingers uncurled, letting the knife fall free.

Instantly, Daniel snatched it up. Then standing, he hurled it toward a pile of new lumber stacked in the corner. The blade sank to the handle in a pine plank.

Turning to where Mamie still sprawled in the sawdust, Daniel nudged her with the toe of his boot.

"Get up," he commanded.

Slowly, Mamie complied, brushing sawdust from her face.

"Why?" Anguish filled his voice as he asked the simple question.

"Oh fur heaven sakes," she sneered. "You can't be *thet* stupid. I *hate* you."

Stunned, Daniel stared at her.

"But why? We love each other. We planned—"

"You love me. I never cared one whit fur you."

"But you acted like you did."

Mamie smiled then and arched her body toward him. "Course I did. And you fell fur it, hook, line, an sinker."

Daniel blanched, clenching his fists.

"I can see you're hurt. Serves you right fur bein such a meany."

"A meany?" God, what *was* she talking about?

"You're a Fed," she snarled. "An I hate Feds. A damned Fed shot my brother. Killed him."

"But I didn't—"

"Listen, Mr. Nice Guy, you killed other State boys jist like him. An a Fed's a Fed far as I'm concerned."

"But Mamie, that was a decade ago. That War's over."

"Not fur me, it ain't. When my brother was killed, I vowed I'd git the one who done it. An you're as stinkin as any Fed I know. You got this comin to you." And she gestured toward the washstand.

A band tightened about Daniel's chest. Mamie didn't love him. She never had. She'd used him, pure and simple. She'd taken pleasure, pure pleasure, in taunting him. All because a decade ago some impetuous Union soldier shot her favorite brother. Gazing at the beautiful form before him, Daniel felt the band drawn tighter. He'd been played for a fool. He'd given his heart away only to have it clawed, then flung bleeding into his face.

"Get out!"

Mamie had left then, still grinning over his hurt.

And now, half a year later, he still hurts. Clenching his fist, Daniel blows out the lamp and strides from the room. He simply can't bear any more pain. At least not this evening. Taking up his greatcoat, he leaves his living quarters in search of solace.

Biting hard on his Havana, Livingston looked at the clock on the candlestand and groaned. Eleven thirty. Daniel would be returning any time now. A very drunk Daniel, singing and laughing like the world was his oyster. Lord, but it hurt to see his son so torn up. It made him sad, more sad than he could say. Even so, he had to admit he'd expected as much from that Fitzsimmons girl. He'd never liked or trusted her. He'd never thought she was right for Daniel. For that matter, he'd—Stomp. Stomp. Clatter. Stomp.

The Union forever,
Hurrah! boys, hurrah!
Down with the traitor—[1] oops.

Clatter. Bang. Thump. Thump. THUMP.

Biting his Havana nearly in two, Livingston rose from the chair and went to the door. Opening it, he held up his lantern. Sure enough, there was Daniel at the bottom, collapsed in a disgraceful heap. With a groan, Livingston started down the stairs.

Daniel looked up then and a stupid grin split his beard. "Why, hello, Father. When did you come to Missouri? We won that War, you know. We beat the tar out of those Secesh." And he beat at the air with clenched fists. "I even cut one up with a knife. It was pleasure," hick, "pure pleasure, to watch them go down."

"Come on, Son, get up." Setting the lantern down, Livingston slipped his arms beneath Daniel's shoulders.

"Leave me alone!" Daniel snapped. "Can't you see I'm getting married. To that one over there with the red hair and—" Daniel slumped to the floor, unconscious.

Watching his snoring son, Livingston chomped on his Havana. Lord, he wanted to cry. To sit right down on these steps and bawl like a baby. But he couldn't. He had to get Daniel upstairs and into bed. Lifting the thin frame gently, Livingston began slowly to ascend the stairs. He would be glad, more glad than he could say, to see tomorrow come. For tomorrow was another workday and Mr. Fudd would arrive early. (To get the fire going, of course.) And if there was anyone who could possibly make his Daniel feel better it was that eccentric old man.

A howling March wind coupled with shadows cast by a coal oil lamp created an ominous atmosphere in the upstairs room. Yet to the figure seated on the bed, the world had never looked more promising.

Puffing contentedly on his Charatan pipe, Thomas stroked the curved handle of the revolver on his lap. A Smith & Wesson Schofield .45. It made a feller feel plumb proud to own a gun like this. Put him in the same class as them James Boys. Course if Julia's pa was to git wind—

"He won't!"

Just saying the words made Thomas feel better. More in charge of things like. Anyways, after they was married what Mr. Crawford thought wouldn't make a lick of difference. Till then Thomas would jist sit quiet like, leavin folks alone.

Rising, Thomas strolled to his chest of drawers and laid the revolver on top. Then opening the first drawer, he took up the gun, studied it once more and placed it carefully inside.

Chapter 35

It was Saturday, May 17, 1873. A beautiful day with sunny skies, green grass and blossoming trees. A perfect day for a wedding.

> *Rise up, my love...*
> *For, lo, the winter is past,*
>   *the rain is over and gone;*
> *The flowers appear on the earth;*
>   *the time of singing of birds is come...*
> *Arise, my love, my fair one, and come away.*[1]

"Drat it all, stop thet!" Katie spoke aloud as she hugged herself, rocking back and forth, back and forth. Fur there wasn't goin to be no weddin after all. She an Thane wasn't gittin married. Not today. Not ever.

Scooting her rocker away from her bedroom wall, Katie bit her lip to keep her chin from trembling. Her weddin day. Her *weddin* day an here she set, rockin like an old maid.

She should have knowed of course, thet Thane would call it off. But she had hoped. After all, Thane *did* think her somethin special like. An he loved her. Really an truly he did. Then why?

"Why, gosh Katie, I—I don't know. I jist don't know." He'd bent his chestnut head then to study the toes of his boots.

They'd been in the parlor on a cool April evening. Katie had held her hands to the flames in the fireplace, feelin all warm an cozy like. An then Thane had plunged her into ice water with the announcement thet he wouldn't marry her.

"It's—it's Will, ain't it?" Katie had stammered, wrapping her arms about herself and collapsing into a chair.

"Will?" Thane's blue eyes had blinked rapidly.

165

"Yes, Will. He's bound to think I'm not good enough, my family bein State folks an all."

"Aw, Katie, thet's stupid. Jist cause Will an me don't see eye to eye on things don't mean he tells me what to do."

"Well, why then?" Katie's chin trembled so, she could scarcely speak.

"Like I said, I—I jist don't know."

"Thet's no reason. Leastwise it don't make no sense to me. After all, you did kiss me lots, an—an you *said* you loved me. You made me feel somethin special like. An— oh drat it all, anyways." And Katie began to sob.

She quieted when she felt a handkerchief placed on her lap. Looking up, she met Thane's blue eyes. Filled with tears they was, an lookin straight into hers.

"I do love you, Katie," he said. "Thet's the trouble." He turned away then and walked to the fireplace. Placing his hand on the mantle, he bent his head toward the flames. "I guess maybe I jist love you too much."

"Too *much*? Why, thet's jist plain silly. Either you love someone or you don't."

"Thet's true fur you maybe. But not fur everyone. I— I— oh gosh, what I mean to say is thet it was okay at first, lovin you jist a little. But now—" He turned to face her again, the corners of his mustache drooping. "I jist can't, Katie. Thet's all. I jist can't."

Katie had stared at him then, her heart too full for words, until at length he'd slipped quietly from the room.

Katie had given way to tears again as she realized it was over. Thane wasn't goin to marry her. She'd sobbed for hours then until the logs in the fireplace had burned to ashes and the sun poked flaxen fingers through the windows.

>   *Rise up, my love, my fair one,*
>   *and come away...* [2]

"Oh drat it all, stop. Please!" Katie bent double in her effort to put the words from her mind. She remained hunched over for what seemed like hours. It was nearly dusk when she rose from the chair. She'd best gather them eggs, she reckoned. She couldn't sit here furever, drownin in her tears. Besides, My Ma had asked her specially to gather them before supper.

Passing through the kitchen, Katie averted her face. She wasn't givin her family the satisfaction of knowin how bad she hurt. Even if this was her weddin day, she—

Drat it all, anyways. Thet egg basket wasn't in its usual place on the back porch. Well, she wasn't goin off to search fur it seein as how time was gittin on. She'd jist gather up her skirt like, an use it. What difference did it make, anyways?

Opening the door to the chicken coop, Katie slipped inside. Phew! She hated this place. All smelly an hot like. Hastily, she checked the nearest nest. Empty. Then another. Empty. And another. Empty. By the time she'd made the rounds she was sweating and angry. Drat it all, someone had already been here. An they never told her. Backing out the door, she felt her shoe squash something soft. She knew by the smell it was chicken manure. Thoroughly disgusted by now, she stalked toward the house. On the back porch, she sank into the old rocker and laboriously unbuttoned her shoes. Kicking them aside, she stomped into the kitchen.

And stopped. And stared. Fur there was Linda, singin as she scrambled up eggs fur supper. Eggs? Eggs. The very ones *she* was supposed to have gathered.

"Drat it all, Linda, why didn't you tell me?"

"Tell you?" Linda looked up, her dark eyes full of innocence. "Tell you?" she repeated. Then, picking up the wooden grinder, she ground pepper into the eggs. "I make nice supper, *si?*"

It was too much for Katie. Biting her lip until it bled, she turned aside to the washstand. Ladling water into a basin, she soaped her hands with lye soap, her tears forming pools in the suds. It wasn't fair. Her weddin day an everything was goin wrong. Course she knowed she shouldn't feel sorry fur herself, but drat it all, she loved Thane. An he had left her. Gone away. Jist like Thomas did fur thet War. An My Pa. An Patrick. Did the ones you love *always* go away? Course not. After all, she still had Bonnie.

With the thought of her friend, Katie's features softened. Bonnie was the best friend in the whole world. Course Bonnie was a mother now. But havin little David didn't keep Bonnie from carin fur Katie. Why, jist last week she'd invited Katie over fur dinner. An after Randall had gone back to work, Bonnie let Katie rock the baby.

Holding the warm bundle, Katie studied the sleeping face. My but he was a sweet one. Somethin special like with all them tawny curls. An the way he held his tiny mouth reminded her of Thane. In no time he'd be smilin thet beautiful, lopsided smile.

"Katie, what's wrong?"

At the sound of Bonnie's voice, Katie realized her chin was tremblin. "It's Thane, ain't it?"

Katie nodded.

"Well, I think it was right mean of him to do you this way. Even if he is my brother, I'm mad at him."

"It—it's all right. Really an truly it is."

Baby David grew restless then and Bonnie lifted him from Katie's arms to place him in the cradle. Reseating herself, she took her friend's hand.

"Katie, I'm so sorry fur what's happened. But jist cause Thane left you don't mean I will. I'll *always* be right here to take care of you."

"I know." Katie spoke the words aloud as she rinsed the soap from her hands. And the mere remembrance of Bonnie's faithfulness, lightened her spirits. Things was bound to git better. Why, even Linda wasn't so bad. Unless of course, she'd a mind to put half thet pepper in them eggs.

Forcing herself to smile, Katie joined the family for supper.

Chapter 36

It seemed a perfect evening. Gentle breezes rustled cherry leaves, amber sunlight spilled through open windows, cooling temperatures soothed tired bodies. Refilling water glasses at the supper table, Jane breathed a sigh of contentment. Today had been downright wonderful. Busy, but wonderful. Fur more an more women was buyin from her shop. Why land sakes, if trade kept increasin this away she'd have to hire another seamstress. Things was lookin thet good.

Forking the first bite of cherry pie into her mouth, Jane chewed slowly, savoring the tart flavor. Mm. Mm. Nothin was better than fresh fruit pie. An cherry was her favorite. Katie's too. Course this evenin thet child wasn't gobblin it up any. Starin at her plate like she was, with arms folded across her chest.

Poor child, no wonder she wasn't eatin. She'd been hurt aplenty these last months. An thet Thane Chapman was to blame. Land sakes, he'd been downright mean to break things off like thet. Why, Katie already had half her trousseau made before thet man broke her heart. It was unfair an she'd a mind to tell Thane so. Still an all, it wasn't none of her business. She reckoned she'd best jist try to help Katie feel better like.

Laying down her fork, Jane placed a hand on her niece's arm.

"Land sakes, Child, you're missin the best cherry pie in the world. Eat up now, fore Thomas takes it all."

"I'll try." And Katie slowly reached for her fork.

Jane returned to her own piece then, wondering if this was all she'd get. Land sakes, she wasn't akiddin bout Thomas. Even if it wasn't his favorite apple, he was eatin like a house afire. On his third piece he was, an still shovelin it in. Course Thomas was happy jist now. Happy an in love.

169

The corners of his mouth never drooped nowadays. Cause he was gittin married.

It was dusk by the time dessert was finished. Jordana lit the lamp while Linda cleared the table. Jane busied herself filling coffee and tea cups. For several moments the family sat in silence, content at the end of the day. The lull came to an end when James pushed back his chair and stood to his feet.

Watching him in the glow of the lamp, Jane felt a rush of gratitude. Course she never had cottoned to him the way Jordana did. Somehow, she never could furgive him fur rapin Claudia all them years ago. Still an all, he was her brother, an he had been good to her. Settin her up in business had been downright generous. He was handsome too. Leastwise she thought so. Why land sakes, it didn't seem possible he was old. But he was. Purt near fifty, she reckoned. He—

"Mercy sakes, you're a quiet bunch this evenin. But you're wonderful jist the same. Thet's why I know you'll be happy to hear thet I'm fixin to marry."

"Marry? When?"

"Saturday, Sis. Day after tomorrow."

"Why, thet's wonderful!" Jordana threw aside her tea towel and hurried to her brother's side. Reaching up, she hugged him. "You know I set great store by you, James. An, I'll love your lady too. You'll be livin here, I reckon."

"No. Fact is, I'm movin in with her. She keeps house fur her pa." He laughed, waving a finger in Jordana's face. "Mercy sakes, it ain't the end of the world. Why, in no time we'll be visitin back an forth like we never parted."

"Aye, Brother, congratulations is in order, to be sure." Michael pushed aside his empty tea cup. "What's the name of this lass you're hitchin up to?"

"Julia Crawford."

For a second the name hung suspended in the air. Then it dropped, severing the feeling of unity. Jumping to his feet, Thomas jerked his pipe from his mouth. "NO!"

The word carried such force that Jane started. Land sakes, thet boy was angry. Purt near beside himself, he was.

"No," Thomas repeated, his taut lips barely checking his rage. "Julia's mine. We're gittin hitched next week."

James laughed, waving a ringed hand. "Mercy sakes, Thomas, I had you figured fur a smart feller. So if I was you, I'd change plans right quick like."

"No." Advancing toward his uncle, Thomas doubled his fist and swung.

"Confound you,Thomas, stop thet." And Jordana reached for her son. But her arm was clasped in midair by a burly hand.

"Aye, Colleen, me lad's a man, to be sure. Leave him be."

"But—"

Wham! This time it was James who struck, splitting Thomas' chin, causing him to reel backward. But Thomas righted himself, stiffened both legs and came at his uncle again.

Laughing, James caught the doubled fist in both his own powerful hands. "Mercy sakes, Thomas. Don't carry on so. Miss Crawford an I are gittin married. Thet's all there is to it."

"Like hell you are. You're plumb crazy if you think you can steal my girl. I don't care if you are somebody important like around here, you ain't gittin Julia. She's mine. See?"

At this, James' eyes narrowed. Clearing his throat, he spoke distinctly. "Fact is, I don't see. I'll have you know thet *I'm* goin to marry up with Miss Crawford. Now, if you still don't understand, I suggest you talk to the lady in question."

For a long moment, Thomas stood straight as a rod, his thin lips taut. Then looking his uncle straight in the eye, he spoke savagely. "All right, I will. An you'd best be ready to back down. Cause I mean to tell you here an now thet *you* ain't never goin to marry Julia."

With that, Thomas turned and strode from the room, leaving the family aghast and his Charatan pipe on the table.

Thomas was trembling. In all his born days he'd never been as mad as he was right now. Rage coursed through him until he could scarcely light the lamp on his chest of drawers. Damn Uncle James, anyways. Damn him to hell.

Crossing to his bed, Thomas dropped to the quilt–covered mattress, his heart racing. He loved Julia. An she'd promised to marry *him*. Course her pa had never been too fond of him. Still, it made a feller choke up like, when he'd preferred Uncle James to himself. "A mature man with good money an a stable future," was the way he'd put it. Shifting his feet on the floor, Thomas allowed himself a sardonic smile. Mature, my foot; Uncle James was jist plumb old. But thet didn't make a lick of difference to Mr. Crawford. Or to Julia.

"Damn!" Thomas lifted his left sleeve to his eyes. He needed Julia somethin awful, an she had throwed him over fur Uncle James. Changed her mind, she'd said, blinkin them violet eyes an lookin scared. Changed her mind?! Well, he'd show her a thing or two. He'd meant it when he said Uncle James wouldn't marry her.

Rising, Thomas strode to the chest of drawers. Angrily, he grasped the knob on the top drawer and jerked it open. The short barrel of the Smith & Wesson Schofield .45 gleamed in the lamp light.

Carefully, Thomas lifted the gun. It was loaded. He'd kept it thet way on purpose. A feller never knowed when he'd need purtection like. An this evenin he aimed to purtect the woman he loved.

Michael had barely settled his head on the pillow when Jordana, already in bed, grabbed his arm.

"James?"

"Aye, Colleen, it's me, Michael."

"Michael? Where's James?"

"Lyin in the cemetery, with Patrick."

"Cemetery?"

"Aye, Colleen, he's been dead fur weeks now. He was hurt right bad, to be sure."

"No!" Jordana sat up.

"Aye, Colleen, lie down now." And Michael pulled her down beside him.

But Jordana turned away, shaking her finger in the air. "James? Confound you, come back here." And she began to sob.

Long into the night she carried on, crying and pleading for her brother to come back. And all the while the man who loved her lay silent, his own thick shoulders heaving.

Chapter 37

His legs crossed Indian–style, Thomas sat on the dining room floor near the fireplace, puffing his corncob pipe. Glancing up to where Julia sat in Aunt Jane's sewing rocker, he sighed with satisfaction. It made a feller feel right proud to be married to a lady like thet. An to be expectin a youngin too—why, he'd never been so happy in all his born days. Unless it was last summer.

He'd been pickin string beans thet day in July when a soft voice called his name.

"Thomas?"

Startled, he'd turned to see Julia standin at the end of the row.

"What you doin here fur, anyways?" He tried to sound gruff, though fact was, his throat was purt near dried up with fear.

"I—I—can we talk?" Her violet eyes were wide with apprehension.

"Here?" He nodded toward the smithy where the metallic blow of hammers, the rumble of human voices and the neighing of horses combined in a cacophony which nearly forbade serious conversation.

"I—I—Whatever you say."

Thomas had dropped a handful of beans into a bucket then and led her around the house to the log bench beneath the oak tree. Seating himself beside her, he shuffled his feet in the dirt. He couldn't bring himself to look at her. Not after—

"Thomas? I—I'm sorry thet I hurt you. Thet is, since James—since James—" she paused, sniffled several times, then went on. "What I mean is, I—I'm lonely. Do you—do you still want to marry me?"

For a second Thomas thought he hadn't heard right. Anyways, why did he want her now? She'd betrayed—

173

"Please?"

He looked at her then, an saw them delicate hands thet lay in her lap, palms up an fingers curlin, as though beckoning him to her. His heart racing, he leaned over and kissed the honey–colored hairs curling about her neck.

"I reckon so. But what of your pa? Don't he still fancy you marrin up with a 'mature man with money an a good future'?"

"Well—yes, I suppose so. But—but jist you leave Papa to me. All right?"

And so they'd got hitched thet very week in a quiet ceremony at her home. His home now. An he liked it. Enabled a feller to keep in touch like, workin in thet store all day. Leastwise—

"James?"

Thomas groaned. It was My Ma, callin fur Uncle James again. How many times had she done thet, anyways?

"Aye, Colleen, he's not here. He's in the cemetery with Patrick."

"Dead?"

"Aye, Colleen, to be sure."

"It was them men thet done it," Jordana's voice rose as she leaned forward in her chair.

"Aye, Colleen, what men?"

"Them at the Spring Grounds. Why, they jist plumb hated James. Threatened him like. Confound them all, anyways." And she began to cry.

"Aw, My Ma, Uncle James had a passel of enemies." Thomas shuffled his feet as he spoke. "Lots of folks in Marshall got mighty upset like, when he tried to git them representatives to give us Brown County."

"Aye, Lad, he lost friends there, to be sure. Meself, I took to the idea of a new county with Brownsville fur its seat. But, I reckon folks in them other seats didn't see it thet away."

Oh, fur heaven sakes." It was Mamie, speaking from where she sat on a hassock opposite Thomas. "It was them God–awful Feds thet killed Uncle James. An I think you're a bunch of meanies not to say so."

"But James wasn't a States man." Julia spoke softly, her knitting needles clicking.

"James was fur Kentucky. An determined like, he was. Confound it, James, come back here." And Jordana started crying all over again.

"Aye, Colleen, James was born in Kentucky, to be sure. But he was from California too. Meself now, I'm thinkin he was mostly fur Mr. James."

"Thet's—thet's not true, Mr. Fitzsimmons."

The plaintive note in Julia's voice caught Thomas' attention. His lips taut, he studied her face by lamplight. But her unfurrowed countenance gave no clues to her innermost feelings. Darn it all, anyways. Why was he bein uneasy fur? It was jist plumb silly fur him to be jealous of a dead man. Anyways, Julia was his now. He smiled up at her, touching her knee with his hand.

To Thomas' relief, she smiled back, her violet eyes focused on the booties she was knitting.

"Aye, Lass, I meant no offense, to be sure."

"Well, James *was* from Kentucky," Jordana interrupted, forestalling further comment from Julia. "Douglas folks always lived there. You hear me?" And she waved a finger at the room in general. "My ma, my pa, James, an me—an Carrie too. We was all from Kentucky." She paused, frowning. "Confound it, I furgot to write Carrie. She'll be right sad to hear about poor James."

Thomas sighed then and struggled to his feet. If My Ma was goin to keep livin in some never-never land, he was goin to mosey on home. Served her right though, to go crazy like. Why, it was plumb stupid to love someone like she did Uncle James an her cousin, Carrie. Why, a feller could git hurt lovin like thet. Hadn't he purt near gone crazy himself when Wade got killed?

Touching his wife's shawl–clad shoulder, Thomas' lips grew taut. Julia was the only person in the world worth lovin. An love her he would. Cause *nobody* was ever goin to take her away from him. Nobody.

Chapter 38

Sandwiched between two feather ticks, Katie shivered. Nineteen years old she was, an feelin like thirty. If only she could be happy again she might feel young like. But she reckoned thet would never happen seein as how she still loved Thane.

Rise up, my love, my fair one, and come away...
For, lo, the winter is past...[1]

Katie shivered. Drat it all, winter wasn't neither past. Anyways, it wasn't the cold in the room thet chilled her heart. It was what Thane was doin. Courtin Linda he was, an treatin Katie like she was nothin special at all.

In her whole life Katie doubted she'd hurt like she did early thet evenin when Thane called fur Linda.

Arise, my love, my fair one, and come away...[2]

She'd been unable to blot the words from her mind as she watched Thane settle a wool shawl about Linda's shoulders. An Thane? What was he thinkin when he placed his soft–brimmed hat over them chestnut curls an opened the door fur his date? It was purt nigh impossible to know, seein as how he kept them blue eyes lowered.

Wrapping her arms about her cotton–clad shoulders, Katie sighed. Drat it all, why did Linda have to like Thane fur, anyways? Couldn't she jist pretend he wasn't there, send him away like? Anyways, she'd trusted Linda. Counted her as a friend. An now she was stealin Katie's love. An Katie was mad. Really an truly she was.

Course Katie did sort of feel sorry fur her cousin. First, she'd lost her ma out in California. Then Uncle James had got killed. Thet must have hurt somethin awful. She reckoned she'd never seen anybody so tore up like as

176

Linda was when they told her Uncle James was dead. She'd screamed an stomped somethin terrible. Vowed to see the murder hanged, she had. Only she hadn't, cause no one knowed who done it.

Still, it must of been hard to take over runnin her pa's store. But Linda had. An soon she was talkin an laughin like nothin ever happened. An now she was seein Thane.

Envisioning the two of them together, Thane's chest–nut head bent near her raven one, Katie bit her lip to keep her chin from trembling. Drat it all, she'd been a fool to care fur Thane. She'd been jist plain stupid to open her heart to him. Fur he had tore it all apart like, then muttered, "I'm sorry," an walked away. He'd left her all done in an hadn't even cared. An it hurt. It hurt somethin awful.

Tightening her arms about herself, Katie allowed a tear to trickle down her cheek. If only she hadn't loved in the first place. Well, she'd learned her lesson good. From now on she wasn't lovin no one but Bonnie. Specially not some man. Drat it all, she'd jist be an old maid. A spinster, like Aunt Jane. After all, thet was better than feelin all tore up like inside. Lots better.

"*Prima* Katie? *Prima* Katie, guess what?"

Slippered feet danced about the moonlit room as Linda Douglas prattled on.

"Oh, *prima* Katie, it was wonderful. *Don* Thane, he kiss me, *si?*"

But the form on the bed never answered. Never opened her eyes. Never moved.

At a corner table in the Sweet Springs Saloon, a lone figure sat staring at the whiskey glass held between his fingers. It moved. Angrily, he tightened his grip. And still the glass moved, its amber contents sloshing. For with three drinks already inside him, it was his hands which shook. Slender hands he had, with long, sensitive fingers. Hands which delighted in the satiny feel of wood. Hands which had once carved the flesh of soldiers. Hands which, until recently, had stroked auburn hair and caressed smooth cheeks. Hands whose trembling betrayed the refuge he sought in drink.

God, but he hurt. The rips in his heart were as raw and bleeding as—

"What's the matter there, fella? Little woman throw you over?"

At the contempt in the voice behind him, Daniel whirled from his chair. Whiskey glass in hand, he briefly studied the man before him. Short, beefy and unkempt, the man's sneer was like sandpaper, scraping across his lesioned heart.

"Let me tell you right now, Mr., that my affairs are none of your business." With that Daniel drew his right hand back and let the contents of his glass fly into the face of his tormentor.

Then, before the surprised agitator could react, Daniel plunked down the empty glass and strode from the bar.

Chapter 39

It was raining when Livingston Lewis emerged from the post office on Lexington Avenue, a letter in hand. Frowning, he shoved the envelope into his pocket and strode toward Spring Street. Now, why would his step–mother be writing to him? She'd never written before. Unless—

Livingston stopped, oblivious to the rain pelting his hat and shoulders. His father. His father was ill. Ah yes, his father was ill and wanted Livingston to come. Biting his soggy Havana, Livingston commenced walking. He couldn't make a trip right now, not even if he wanted to. Someone had to mind the shop and Daniel.

Lord, but his son was mixed up these days. Drink was turning him into a stranger. A stranger who grew angry at the slightest provocation. Even the well–intentioned Mr. Fudd could make Daniel lose his temper. Like last week. It had been unseasonably warm that day, the temperature reaching to sixty five degrees. But despite the warmth outside, Mr. Fudd had fired up the stove as usual. When he'd moved to add still more wood, Daniel had thrown down his stain rag and shouted, "For God's sake, Harvey, stop that! It's like an oven in here already."

For once, Livingston had felt sorry for the old man. The poor thing had dropped the fagot back into the woodbox, his head shaking so bad he almost lost his peppermint stick. But if Daniel noticed, he never let on. With trembling fingers he'd retrieved his cloth and continued applying walnut stain to a table leg.

Approaching the shop, Livingston groaned. He was sad, more sad than he could say, at the inferior quality of Daniel's work these days. Stain too thickly applied, sanding less than smooth, planing misshapen and uneven. Lord, he'd worked far into the night more than once lately trying

179

to rectify his son's mistakes. And still Daniel drank.

He was drinking again that evening, a bottle of bourbon accompanying his supper. Biting his Havana, Livingston ignored the whiskey the best he could, clearing the dishes and washing them. Placing the plates into a second pan, he poured scalding water over them and returned the teakettle to the stove. Daniel, attempting to be helpful, took up a tea towel and with trembling fingers, grabbed up a steaming plate. Instantly, he dropped it, the porcelain crashing to the floor.

"God damn!" Daniel swore as he stared at the shards of glass at his feet.

At that, something inside Livingston snapped. Jerking his Havana from between his teeth, he turned on his son.

"All right, Son, that's enough. The problem is *you,* not the plate. You know that. I'll admit I feel sorry for you. And I'm sad, more sad than I can say, that you got hurt. But I won't condone you damning the Almighty."

At this, Daniel glared at his father, his fingers toying with the tea towel. "And I suppose you condemn me for drinking too. No doubt you're so righteous *you* never tipped a bottle."

"Come to think of it, I never did. Your grandfather did, though."

"He did? But he was—"

"A minister. I know. Even so, after—after Mother died, he got blind drunk. Passed right out in his study."

"And what did you do—pray for him?"

Biting hard on his Havana, Livingston met his son's eyes straight on. "No, sir, I ran away. I left Harrisonburg and went to Romney and Uncle Hayward. And I never went back."

At this, Daniel laughed. "So brave, so brave," he muttered and reached again for the bottle.

His hands once again in the dishwater, Livingston refrained from answering. Ah well, perhaps he had been a coward back in '36. Even so, he could never forgive his father for being drunk at a time when he'd needed him the most. Not even if he was ill. And he must be or his wife wouldn't have written. Well, time enough to deal with that after he'd read the letter.

Twenty minutes later, Livingston sat in the overstuffed chair beside the double–drawer candlestand, the letter in hand. Puffing his cigar, he pried open the seal on the cream–colored envelope and drew out a matching sheet.

Dear Livingston,

> *I take my seat this morning to write you some distress-*
> *ing news. Your father passed away a week ago.*

So, his father was gone. Was he supposed to be sad? Maybe even cry? He couldn't. Come to think of it, he'd felt no emotion for the man in years.

> *He died in his sleep. A peaceful death, so fitting for the*
> *life he'd lived.*

Peaceful? Livingston shuddered. The man who'd whipped him for allowing Nettie to be trampled by cattle hadn't been peaceful. He hadn't been in control at all for that matter.

> *Neighbors and friends have been most kind. My table is*
> *simply loaded with baked goods and home cured ham.*
> *Nigh a hundred people passed through the house before*
> *the funeral. Most all had kind things to say. He'd given so*
> *many of them food, clothes, and his prayers across the*
> *years.*

Ah yes, food from his mouth, clothes from his back had gone to benefit "the poor".

> *I should like to continue living here, if you don't mind.*
> *My brother lives nearby.*

Mind? Why should he? His mother was gone.

> *Your father spoke of you often. He wanted me to meet*
> *you sometime. I think I would like that. For if you are*
> *anything at all like Jeremiah, you are a fine man.*

Biting his Havana, Livingston groaned. Lord, he hoped he wasn't like his father.

> *The day before he left us, your father spoke tenderly of*
> *your mother and your little sister, Nettie. I think now that*
> *he must have known he would be seeing them soon.*

> > *Write to me when you have time. I remain*
> > *Sincerely,*
> > *Althea Lewis*

Livingston didn't realize he felt so deeply until his thigh began to burn. Lord, he'd bit his cigar in two and the ashes had burned a hole in his trousers. Hastily, he scooped up the remains of the Havana and tossed them into the stove, his mind still on the letter. Nettie and his mother. Lord, he wished he could see them again. For they were the first people he'd dared to love. And they had gone away.

With a groan that shook his entire being, Livingston slipped the letter back into the envelope and blew out the lamp.

❖   ❖   ❖

The dress shop was quiet as Jane sat in the back room stitching lace onto an evening dress for Mrs. Simpson. Pulling the single thread carefully, she frowned. Land sakes, but trade was slow. Had been fur several weeks now. Course trade had fallen off everywheres, not jist her shop. Still an all, it'd been quite a setback after months of brisk sales. Yet despite the recession, she couldn't complain none. Why land sakes, her family was purt near rich these days compared to how they'd been right after thet War. They had food galore, stylish clothes an a house thet had been refurbished jist last year. Course thet was before James got killed.

The thought of James caused Jane to sigh. Jordana still hadn't got over losin their brother. She'd taken to her bed fur weeks after it happened, leavin Katie to run the house. Then when she did git up, she blamed Michael fur not purtectin her brother. As if Michael or anyone else could've told James how to do. Why land sakes, it'd been James who always done the tellin. Still an all, Jordana carried on. Asked fur James often, she did. An talked of cousin Carrie like she was still alivin.

Holding her needle up to rethread it, Jane squinted. Land sakes, she couldn't hardly see thet little hole. Purty soon she'd have to wear specs like some old lady. Still an all, at least she wasn't losin her mind like Jordana. Course her sister might not carry on so if the marshal could find the feller thet killed James. But thet didn't seem about to happen. Cause no one around here had thet new kind of gun he'd used. Most had only shot guns or a Navy Colt .36 like Thomas.

Ting–a–ling. Ting–a–ling. The bell over the door sounded like music to Jane's ears. And so did the sound of Mamie's voice offering to help a customer. With a smile, she bent over her work. Maybe she'd make a sale today after all.

Chapter 40

It was a mild, sunny day with a gentle breeze which bore the fragrance of blossoming fruit trees. Yet the corners of Thomas' mouth turned downward as he sat on the log bench smoking his corncob pipe. From the kitchen came the clink of utensils against ironstone as the family sat at Sunday dinner. Yet, even the warm sounds of conversation failed to move him. For Thomas wasn't hungry. Not for food; not for family.

A baby's cry caused his frown to deepen. Fur thet youngin was his son. *His* son? Like hell he was. Let Katie care fur him. After all, she'd named him, hadn't she?

Gazing across the dirt road, Thomas sighed. It didn't seem possible thet jist three months ago he'd been happy. Proud too. Why, it made a feller purt near feel like struttin to be married to Julia an to be the father of thet youngin growin inside her belly.

Thomas jerked his pipe from his mouth and spat on the ground as though to rid himself of a bad taste. Three months ago, it was. Three months last night since he awoke to hear Julia moanin. Instantly he'd sat up, his mouth dry with fear.

"You all right?" he asked.

She answered with another groan. "Doctor. Get the doctor. I—I—The baby's comin. Hurry!"

Somehow, he'd managed to dress in record time, then stumbled into his father–in–law's room. After waking the older man, he'd grabbed a cloak an ran fur the doctor.

The next fourteen hours was one gigantic nightmare. Why, a feller could go plumb crazy jist thinkin on it. Fur Julia had groaned an screamed till he itched to tell thet doctor to stop it or he'd kill him. He'd sat with both

183

feet on the floor, too distraught even to smoke his pipe. An thet stout tea
Mr. Crawford kept forcin him to drink made a feller want to vomit. Julia
was hurtin. Nothin else seemed important.

It was nearly sunset when, after an especially piercing scream, the cry
of a newborn was heard. Mr. Crawford broke into a smile, but Thomas
lifted his left sleeve to mop his eyes. Damn, it made a feller choke up like.

"Mr. Fitzsimmons, you have a son."

Thomas had looked up then into the haggard face of the doctor.

"Why, thet's wonderful. How's—how's Julia?"

"Weak. Very weak. She wants to see you. But only a few minutes,
mind."

His heart racing, Thomas made his way to the bedroom. Inside he
stopped, his mouth dry with fear. Fur Julia looked as white as them sheets
she was layin on.

"Thomas?" She held out a dainty hand.

Kneeling beside the bed, Thomas grasped the proffered hand with his
left one.

"It's a boy."

He nodded. "Are—are you all right?"

"Awful weak is all."

"Well, thet ain't somethin easy like you done."

She tried to smile.

Thomas' heart beat so rapidly he could scarcely breathe. Jist lookin at
thet heart–shaped face an all thet gold hair made him feel plumb crazy like.
An then he saw the baby. A tiny mite with dark hair, he tugged at Julia's
breast.

"Thomas, I—"

"Hush. I reckon you need your rest now."

"But I have to tell you—" Her violet eyes pleaded.

"What dear?"

"The—the baby's name. It's James. After—after his father."

For a second Thomas merely stared at her. Then jerking his hand free,
he stumbled to his feet. Stiffening his legs, he glared down at her.

"Why you dirty, double–crosser. You're nothin but scum. Jist rotten,
stinkin scum." With thet, he'd strode from the room. He'd grabbed up his
cloak an stomped out the door. Fur hours he'd walked, tryin to shake off
the notion thet Julia had tricked him. But she had. An like an idiot, he'd
played right into her hands. He'd made an honest woman of her. Thet was
all. She didn't love him. An he needed her somethin awful.

On an on he walked. Down by the mill, up by the depot, down Locust Street, across Ray— It was near midnight when he returned. Fur all his anger, he still loved Julia. An it was high time she was lovin him too. Fact was, she jist might come around, now thet she'd confessed.

Mr. Crawford sat alone in the kitchen, his round body slumped over the table. At the sound of Thomas' footsteps, he roused.

"You heard, Son?" he asked, his voice quavering.

"I heard."

For several seconds neither spoke. Then Thomas moved toward the bedroom door. "Is Julia sleepin, or can I see her now?"

The older man rose. "But I thought—that is, Julia's—"

As Mr. Crawford broke into sobs, Thomas' heart began to race. Julia! Somethin was wrong. Jerking open the bedroom door, he stopped cold. Fur there was a woman he'd never seen before bendin over his wife. Washin her she was, like—

"Git away from her," Thomas roared as he grabbed the woman's shirt–waist and spun her around. "What do you think you're doin? Who are you, anyways?"

"Why—why, I'm Mrs. Taylor from over yonder. The Mr. asked if I'd lay out—"

Lay out? Lay out! Lay out. She was here to lay out the dead.

"NO!" Shoving aside Mrs. Taylor, Thomas reached for Julia's hand. It was cold. He touched her face. It was cold. Throwing back the covers, he touched her now flat belly. It was cold.

"No! No! No!" In all his born days, Thomas had never hurt as he did in thet moment. He felt like a knife had been plunged into his heart, an twisted. With his left hand he tried to wrench it free, tried to stop the anguish he knew only too well. Anguish he'd endured when he buried Julia's brother on Bloody Hill. But this time it was his own blood thet was leakin out. Spillin from his heart an flowin over thet lovely form on the bed. Julia. The only person in all the world thet he loved. An now she was gone, takin with her his own life.

So it was thet his heart scarcely beat when he viewed her again, all purtied up like. His heart made no movement at all when folks came to call. Not even Katie could make him respond. Nor the preacher. When he said thet "Our dear Sister is now at peace with God", Thomas ignored him. Julia wasn't with God. She was with him, Thomas. In his heart.

Only now, his heart hurt again. The sound of a baby's cry issuing from the kitchen twisted the knife once more. An this time it was worse. Fur the blade of memory gouged his senses until he felt plumb crazy. Memories of violet eyes, gold hair, a sombrero–clad head an ring–covered hands. Memories of Julia. Of Uncle James. Of love. Of betrayal. Memories thet slit the membrane of his soul.

Jerking his pipe from his mouth, Thomas lunged from the bench, his fist clenched. Then glaring at the turquoise sky above, he screamed, "Why does it have to hurt so bad fur, anyways? Why?"

The whisper of oak leaves and the twitter of birds provided the only reply.

Chapter 41

Seated in the rocker beside the bed, Katie studied the baby in her arms. Purty he was, with all thet dark hair an them deep blue eyes. Good too. Why my goodness, he hardly never cried or took on like most youngins. Not even the heat seemed to bother him much. He jist stared about him solemn like, as though takin in the whole world.

Stroking Benjamin's soft, dimpled arm, Katie's chin quivered. Drat it all, this youngin was wonderful—but he wasn't hers. He belonged to Thomas. An Katie wanted a baby of her own. Really an truly she did. A youngin with chestnut curls an a lopsided grin. A youngin thet would be bashful, yet carin. A youngin jist like his pa. Only she'd never have thet. Not ever. Fur Thane was marryin Linda. Right this very minute he was, down there in the parlor.

Course Linda was purty an all. Pirouetting about the room earlier that afternoon, she'd asked. "I look fine, *si?*"

"Yes, you look fine," Katie had snapped. An Thane was bound to think so too. For dressed in her full–sleeved white blouse and billowing white skirt, Linda had never been more lovely.

"You wear fine dress, no?" Linda pointed to Katie's own calico.

"No. I'm not goin."

"Not goin? But *prima* Katie, you must. *Don* Thane would want—"

"Drat it all, leave Thane out of this!" Katie had taken up Benjamin then and plunked herself in the rocker.

Linda left then and a few moments later a pair of heavier footsteps halted in the doorway. Looking up, Katie saw My Pa. Despite her hurt, she smiled. Fur My Pa did look a tad uncomfortable in them fine trousers an thet frock coat. She reckoned he wouldn't never take to nothin but workin

187

clothes. Still, thet moon–shaped face an them thick shoulders was a comfort.

"Come in." She motioned him toward her.

Crossing the room, he stopped beside the rocker and stared down at Benjamin who sucked contentedly on a sugar tit. And then, he reached a burly hand to tousle Katie's hair. "Aye, Lass, I know you're hurtin, mind."

Katie didn't answer. Instead, she hugged Benjamin tighter and bit her lip to keep her chin from trembling.

"Love's like thet, to be sure. Meself, I'm thinkin it's worth the trouble. Not the bad, mind. But the good. Bein sure about love makes life somethin special like."

But Katie wasn't so sure. Course she loved My Pa an Bonnie. But she loved Thane too. Really an truly she did. Only right now he was vowin to love Linda.

The voices downstairs were animated as they drifted up from the parlor window. Katie heard Linda's laughing comments and Thane's deep replies.

> *The voice of my beloved! behold, he*
> *cometh leaping upon the mountains,*
> *skipping upon the hills...*[1]

Drat it all, if only she could furgit Thane, shut him out like. But she couldn't. When the sounds moved to the kitchen, she envisioned them all, chattering, smiling, happy to see Linda married. Glad to welcome Thane to the family.

Her chin trembling, Katie rises from the rocker and places the now sleeping Benjamin on the bed. Then quietly, she moves to the window overlooking the back porch. Taking a ruffled curtain in hand, she looks on as Linda emerges from the porch, laughing. And she watches as Randall and My Pa lift Linda's trunk to the slot behind the seat of Thane's buggy.

Thane's buggy. Katie digs a fist into both her sides. Why my goodness, Thane hadn't owned a buggy, when he'd courted *her*. Course he'd only worked fur Will then. Now he's the boss, runnin Linda's store. Still, it's infuriatin to see thet fine buggy sittin in the afternoon sun. An open buggy, it is, pulled by a bay Morgan.

An Thane, how does he feel about things, anyways? Does he still—

"Aye, Lad, take care."

Katie winces at the warmth in My Pa's voice as he lays a hand on Thane's broad shoulder. Drat it all, he needn't be so happy like.

Thane blushes then, a crimson glow stealing from the top of his snowy collar to the roots of his chestnut hair. Silently, he hands Linda into the buggy. Then coming around to his own side, he pauses, glancing about. What's he lookin fur, anyways?

Her. She knows the instant their eyes meet. Hers a sad gray, his a somber blue. For several moments their souls seem to lock. Then slowly, Thane disengages himself. And Katie watches as from a distance when he turns again to his bride.

> *Rise up, my love, my fair one, and come away.*
> *For, lo, the winter is past, the rain is over and gone;*
> *The flowers appear on the earth; the time of singing of birds*
> *is come...*[2]

But drat it all, it isn't the birds she wants to hear, it's *his* voice. His voice callin her away. His voice—

But the lips beneath thet chestnut mustache is still. An them eyes is lowered now as he climbs into the buggy an flicks the reins.

Katie drops the curtain then and turns away. Hugging herself, she walks around the bed to sit once more in the rocker.

❖   ❖   ❖

"Katie."

It was Thane. An he was callin her. Callin from someplace far off like.

"Here. I'm here." Katie tried to reply, but her voice sounded all fuzzy like. "I—I'm here." Katie tried again, holding out her arms to welcome him.

And he came. "Katie." The voice was closer now an she could see them beautiful chestnut curls an them deep blue eyes.

"Katie."

Somethin was wrong. The voice didn't sound right. An why was he shakin her fur, anyways? She did love him. Really an truly she did.

"Katie!"

With a start Katie awoke to stare into worried blue eyes.

"Well, it's about time you came around. Are you all right?" And Bonnie shook her arm again.

"Course I'm all right," Katie snapped. "Really an truly I am."

"Well, you really was sleepin hard, thet's fur sure." Again Bonnie eyed her friend with concern.

"I was jist dreamin like. An purt nigh thought you was—" Katie turned her face away, not wanting to show her pain. An there was Thane again, tormentin her with thet lopsided grin thet made her go all giddy like. Only it wasn't Thane. Fur this smile wasn't shy like. It was playful, bubbly, eager. It was the smile of a toddler.

"Baby." Little David Dalton was standing beside the bed tickling Benjamin's bare feet. And Benjamin was fussing.

"Oh fur cryin out loud, David, stop thet." Bonnie pulled her son away from the bed and handed him a tiny carved horse. "Here. Play with this."

Still smiling that lopsided grin, David plopped onto the floor to study his toy.

Bonnie turned back to Katie then, her freckled face a mask of concern. "Oh, Katie, I'm so sorry."

Katie nodded, knowing Bonnie wanted to help. But nothin helped. Nothin could stop the tearin she felt inside. Comin apart like she was, jist like she'd done years ago when them Feds took My Pa away. But My Pa had come back. Thane wouldn't. He was married now to Linda. Fur life.

"Katie, you know you're my best friend in the whole world. If there's anything I can do—" Bonnie left the sentence dangling, then as she picked up her son and tiptoed from the room.

And Katie, watching her friend go away, longed to run after her. To tell her she loved her and would always be her friend. But she couldn't. Her legs refused to budge. She could only sit alone and hug herself. And weep.

Chapter 42

Livingston Lewis let the *Brownsville Herald* slip from his fingers and onto the floor. Biting his Havana, he sighed. Lord, he was tired. More tired than he could say. He'd spent fourteen hours in the shop that day and still he wasn't caught up.

Glancing through the window, he noted the myriad of stars and frowned. Another clear night. And they needed rain so badly. The summer had been so hot and dry that gardens had produced little. Of course he hadn't much time for working outdoors. Even so, he usually managed to have some sweet potatoes. But not this year. He'd bought his yams from that new grocery business on Lexington until last week. Then even that supply was gone. Sold out. Now the only potatoes left were Irish ones. And while boiled or fried these potatoes were good, they were a far cry from sweet potatoes. Golden yams baked until the outside was crusty, then slit open and daubed with butter and a sprinkling of brown sugar. Nothing was better than that.

Ah well, he'd survive of course. Even so, it didn't help that business had dropped off too. Several customers were turning to the ready–made furniture now being sold in town. But, even the new competition wasn't Livingston's greatest concern. It was Daniel. So far Livingston had managed to keep the quality of work at a premium, but he couldn't alter his son's basic moods. Surly he was, and unfriendly. A far cry from the kind, sensitive man who had once smiled at customers. A far cry from the young man who cared about his work.

Glancing at the clock, Livingston saw that it was after eleven. Rising from his chair, he trudged to the kitchen. Adding another stick of wood to the stove, he ladled cold water and coffee into a pot and set it on to boil.

He might as well have it ready when Daniel returned. He was certain to need it.

Biting on his Havana, Livingston had to admit he'd rather not face the next hour. Any moment now his son would come clomping up the stairs, singing. Or rather warbling, about how the Union won the War. And then he'd laugh and point and say, "I'm going to marry that red head right over there."

Only this night was different. For Daniel wasn't singing. He was weeping. Jerking open the door to the sitting room, he walked in, cold sober. But Lord, he looked awful. His shirt was ripped, his hair tangled and his left eye swollen.

"Daniel? Why, Son, whatever is the matter?"

"Harvey." The name came out in a sob. "They put Harvey in jail."

"Oh, Lord. Well, come on into the kitchen and tell me about it."

Seconds later Daniel sat at the table, the coffee before him untouched.

"It was because of me," he said, meeting his father's gaze. "I was down at the saloon, drinking. I'd already had one whiskey, maybe two, when Harvey came in and sat down beside me. His head was shaking so he could hardly speak. But, he did. 'Thet's not fur you, Mr. Daniel, sir,' he said. And he snatched the glass from my fingers."

Daniel paused, tapping those same fingers on the table. "The truth is, I'm ashamed of what I did then. I snatched it back and told him to—to go back to his peppermint sticks and leave me alone." Daniel allowed himself a brief smile. "But that Harvey is a persistent old codger. He just reached for the glass again. 'No, Mr. Daniel, sir, it ain't fittin.'"

"Well, I thought this would all blow over. But Harvey wouldn't let it. He tried to grab the glass again. And this time he got himself seized from behind."

Daniel paused, running his fingers across the table. "Some giant of a man—I've no idea who—just jerked Harvey right off his chair. 'The gentleman spoke, pal. Leave him alone,' he said."

"Harvey was scared then, I could tell. His face turned white like it does and his eyes grew large. But that didn't stop him. Most definitely not. 'Hey, Mr., quit thet,' he said. 'Mr. Daniel's my friend.' Of course the man didn't quit. And then I realized that he really intended to hurt Harvey."

Daniel paused and placed a hand before his face. When he drew it away, tears glistened above his beard. "I—I jumped up then and shouted for the man to leave Harvey alone. But that only made things worse. Another man joined the first one, punching Harvey like it was pleasure, pure pleasure. And that's when I got angry. I threw that whiskey glass on the floor and grabbed the second man. I hit him once, twice—I don't know how many times. I just know that I was angry with him for hurting Harvey. I—I guess that's when some others got involved. Pretty soon everyone was hitting everyone else. And then the marshal strode in. He waved his nightstick and shouted for order. When it all stopped, Harvey— Harvey was lying on the floor."

Again Daniel stopped and covered his face. Sniffling, he went on. "I—I thought he was dead at first, he looked so still. But he came around, when the bartender poured water on his face." Daniel paused, clenching his fist. "He looked so bewildered, blinking and shaking his head. I—I started to help him up. But the marshal shoved me away. 'We'll handle this, Sir,' he said. And then he hauled Harvey to his feet and out the door. When I started to follow, that giant that started it all blocked my way. 'Let the old coot go. A night in jail will teach him a thing or two!'"

Daniel stopped then and stared at Livingston. "They had no right to do that. Harvey hadn't hurt anyone. Besides that, he's my *friend*."

"Yes, Son, I know that. And he does too. He'll be back in the shop soon, ready to help out."

"You really think so?"

Livingston nodded.

"Thanks, Father, for understanding." Daniel reached out and briefly patted the older man's shoulder. Then rising from the chair, he crossed the kitchen and disappeared into the back bedroom.

Biting hard on his Havana, Livingston trembled with suppressed delight. Lord, but it had been years since Daniel had reached out to him like that. And it felt good, more good than he could say, to be close to his son.

Chapter 43

Katie poured scalding water over the supper dishes and sighed. Drat it all, why did everything have to be so gloomy fur, anyways? Even the sky looked purt nigh done in, with all them dark clouds rollin around. An March only a week away. Why my goodness, it ought to be springtime like.

Course Katie didn't feel much like springtime. Not lately, anyways. What she mostly felt was anger. After all, why should *she* have to do all the work around here? But then someone had to cook an clean an wash. Linda wasn't here to do it. An My Ma spent purt nigh every wakin minute sittin by the window waitin fur Uncle James to come. Course Aunt Jane was willin enough. But seein as how she did sewin most evenins, the best she could do was keep an eye on Benjamin. So thet left Mamie.

An it was jist plain silly to count on Mamie fur helpin. Why my goodness, she hadn't lifted a finger to help cook supper. Course she worked all day modelin hats at the shop. Still, if she'd a mind to she could of helped. After all, sellin hats wasn't exactly back–breakin work. Why, brushin thet mop of hair every evenin seemed to take more energy than anything else. An thet's what she was doin now. Strokin them auburn tresses like they was fine fur, she was. While she, Katie, struggled to git the dishes done. Drat it all, couldn't thet girl think of anyone but herself? After all, she was twenty six. A tad old to be so lazy like.

Placing her hands on her hips, Katie turned toward her sister. "Drat it all, Mamie, stop thet brushin an come dry dishes."

But Mamie, bending forward from the waist, continued brushing her hair which almost touched the floor.

"Mamie, did you hear me?"

"Oh, Katie, fur heaven sakes be quiet. A body gits tired of bein fussed at all the time."

Turning back to the dish pan, Katie shook her head. Drat it all, what was the matter with her sister, anyways? Jist cause she an Daniel—

"Ouch!" Katie yanked her hand from sudsy water to see a tiny red stream flowing from her index finger. Drat it all, she'd cut herself. What a mess. An it hurt too. Really an truly it did.

"Mamie, git over here an do these dishes while I fix my finger."

When Mamie failed to answer, Katie fumed. Here she was all done in like, an Mamie was still brushin her hair. There was simply no accountin fur her sister's selfishness. Well drat it all, she had to fix her finger whether them dishes got washed or not. She couldn't jist stand here an bleed to death.

Crossing the room, Katie shoved Mamie aside and jerked open the door below the washstand.

"Katie! Fur heaven sakes be careful."

But Katie paid no attention. Let Mamie take on all she wanted to. *She* was goin to fix her finger. Rummaging with her left hand, Katie finally found a clean rag and a bottle of turpentine. Dropping into a nearby chair, she pulled the stopper from the bottle and doused her rag. Then grimacing, she slapped it on her finger and tied the rag about her hand. This done, she sat quietly, her chin trembling. Goodness, but thet hurt. Still, now she wouldn't have to do them dishes.

"Mamie?"

"What?"

"You've got to do them dishes."

No answer.

"Mamie!"

Throwing her mass of hair back over her shoulders, Mamie glared at her sister, her green eyes glittering. "Oh fur heaven sakes, be quiet. All you've done fur months now is gripe. No man can be worth all thet."

Stunned, Katie bit her lip to keep her chin from trembling. Drat it all, Mamie had no right to talk to her thet way. Jist caused she loved Thane—

"Well my goodness, it sounds like the pot callin the kittle black to me. Anyways—"

Mamie's shrill laugh cut her off. "Oh, Katie, you really are a simpleton. Why, I never loved Daniel."

"You didn't? Then why—"

"Because I'm too smart to love, thet's why. A body can jist take so much hurt. An losin Patrick was enough to last me furever."

"But Daniel— Why?"

"Fur Patrick, stupid."

"Patrick?"

"Oh, Katie, fur heaven sakes stop bein so dumb. Daniel was a Fed, wasn't he?"

Katie nodded. But it didn't make no sense to her. It was jist plain silly to hurt a nice man like Daniel on account of thet stupid War. Why, no wonder he'd taken to spendin his evenins at the saloon. To lose someone you loved could hurt somethin awful. After all—

Whoo–ooo. Whoo–ooo–ooo.

"What's thet?" Katie nearly jumped from her chair at the sound.

"The train whistle, silly."

"I know *thet*. An I ain't silly. The Lexington run ain't due fur an hour yet."

Whoo–ooo. Whoo–ooo–ooo.

"Well, maybe its early."

"Now who's bein silly? Thet train ain't never been this early before. Why—"

Thomas burst into the kitchen, panting from his rush down the stairs. "What's goin on, anyways?"

"Oh fur heaven sakes, Thomas. You an Katie is such simpletons—"

But Thomas ignored Mamie as he strode into the dining room.

Whoo–ooo. Whoo–ooo–ooo.

"Aye, Lad, thet might be best."

It was My Pa's voice. And then he and Thomas were in the kitchen, grabbing cloaks from over the woodbox.

An hour later they returned, shivering. "Aye, Lasses, it's bad news to be sure."

"What happened?"

"A cyclone hit Houstonia this afternoon," Thomas spoke from around his corncob pipe.

"Land sakes, was anyone hurt?" It was Aunt Jane, standing in the doorway, a sleeping Benjamin on her shoulder.

"Aye, Lass, we don't know."

"Reckon it was a dandy, though." Thomas warmed his hand over the stove as he spoke. "Accordin to the engineer the town's purt near wiped out. Business houses all tore up like. Even the depot got blowed away."

"My goodness, how awful." Katie looked down at the pink bandage on her finger. Though the cut still stung, it would heal. Anyways, she'd be purt nigh over it by tomorrow. But to be knocked down by thet roarin wind. Why, thet would be terrible. Lots of cuts, broken bones, death. Katie shuddered. She did hope no one was hurt. Really an truly she did.

❖ ❖ ❖

The house was dark, the hour was late and Jane was tired. Why land sakes, she'd done purt near a day's work after eight o'clock this evenin. All thet parin an choppin an mixin. All thet stirrin over the kitchen stove. Still, it was worth it to send soup to them poor folks in Houstonia. Even Mamie had consented to help. Though Jane had watched her like a hawk. Land sakes, they couldn't have her aspittin in the kittles or afloatin a hair in the soup. Still an all, she'd been downright helpful even if she did give Katie the cold shoulder.

Frowning, Jane fluffed the feather pillow beneath her head. She did wish them girls would git along. Land sakes, they both bristled like porcupines at the least inconvenience. Course Katie was still asmartin over losin Thane—

"Patrick? Patrick, are you there?"

With a sigh, Jane turned toward the figure lying next to her. Mamie was at it again. Adreamin bout Patrick an the War.

"Patrick? Fur heaven sakes, Brother, git back in here."

Mamie was sitting up now, reaching out her hands.

"Patrick? Those God–awful Feds are out there. Can't you see them?"

Frantic now, Mamie clawed the air.

"Mamie." Jane gently touched a flailing arm. "Mamie, it's all right now. Land sakes, Patrick's asleepin quiet like. It's downright silly fur us to be astirrin ourselves this away."

"Oh." Mamie's arms went limp then and she laid back down. But her voice continued to punctuate the darkness. "Patrick? You know I think you're jist an old meanie. Now, look what you've done. You've gone an got yourself killed an I—I—"

As Mamie's sobs filled the air, Jane stared into the darkness. Land sakes, thet girl was ahurtin. Still an all, love was like thet. Hadn't she purt near died when Claudia did? Course all the hurtin in the world wasn't nothin compared to them good times they'd shared. Specially thet last visit. Sittin in thet shanty asharin apple cake an memories with her friend had lifted life's cares from her shoulders. Real peaceful like, she'd felt.

An now, even with Claudia gone an Mamie acryin, Jane knew that peace again. Why land sakes, lovin could be downright wonderful.

Chapter 44

Thomas dropped the last of the peas into the ground and tamped the earth lightly over them with his foot. There. Thet was all he was goin to do this afternoon. Why, a feller could git plumb wore out workin too hard. He was ready fur somethin easy like. Like sittin neath thet old oak tree. But as he approached his favorite spot, he stopped. Katie was already there. An thet youngin with her. Pattin thet split log bench he was, like it belonged to him. Removing his pipe, Thomas spat on the ground.

Katie jumped. "My goodness, Thomas, you scared me. Didn't think you'd be done plantin so soon. Anyways, come on an sit down."

But Thomas stood some feet away, his legs stiff, his lips taut. Darn, but thet youngin looked like James with them large dark eyes an thet dark brown hair. Course thet oval face an rounded chin could jist as well belong to My Ma. Still, fact was—

"Thomas, is somethin wrong?"

"What's thet youngin doin out here fur, anyways? Ain't he supposed to take a nap or somethin?"

"He already had a nap. Now, come on sit down."

Reluctantly, Thomas sat, puffing his corncob pipe. It made a feller uneasy like the way thet youngin looked at him. Studyin him like with them large, solemn eyes. Then shyly, reachin a chubby hand to pat his knee.

Instantly, Thomas shoved him away. A feller could go crazy like buddyin up to everyone thet reached out a hand.

"Thomas! Why, thet was jist plain mean. What'd you do it fur, anyways?"

"Cause I wanted to," he snapped. "Anyways, he's not hurt."

True enough, Benjamin hadn't cried. He simply sat in the dirt where

198

---

he'd landed, his small face registering confusion. Then slowly, he turned his attention to a jagged stick which he promptly put into his mouth. Katie jerked it from him.

"No, no," she scolded. "Thet's nasty. Here." And she took from her apron pocket a string of wooden beads. Benjamin studied it soberly a moment before he reached to take it.

"James? Confound you, James, come back here. You hear me?"

Katie groaned. "I'd best go settle My Ma. But drat it all, why can't she jist accept things like? After all, it's been purt nigh two years since Uncle James got killed. Anyways, it don't make no sense to take on so." Rising, she started for the back porch.

Hey!" Thomas called after her. "Ain't you takin this youngin with you?"

Turning, Katie placed her hands on her hips and glared at her brother. "Drat it all, Thomas, I can't do everything around here. *You* watch him. Anyways, he's your youngin, not mine."

"Damn!" Thomas planted both feet on the ground and glared at Benjamin. Thet youngin had robbed him of the woman he loved, an he was supposed to *like* him?

"Why, hello there, Thomas."

Thomas started at the sound of a familiar voice. Without bothering to rise, he acknowledged his one–time friend. "Hello, Uriah. Why'd you sneak up fur, anyways? You could scare a feller plumb out of his skin doin thet."

"My, my, touchy ain't we? Anyways, I jist left my horse at the smithy. Thought I'd mosey on over an see an old friend." His voice held contempt.

His lips taut, Thomas let that pass. No use stirrin up trouble like.

"How's the flour business these days?"

"Purty fair. Things has been better since we moved down there on the Blackwater. Pa puts out about 1000 bushels of flour a day now. Course we may be in fur a sight of competition. Seems they're fixin to build a new steam mill right across the tracks from the depot."

Thomas nodded. "Tevis said as much."

For a moment neither spoke. Then Uriah nodded toward Benjamin. "I see you got what you wanted."

"Pardon?"

"Hey, old boy, you got what you wanted."

Still mystified, Thomas studied his one–time friend. Dang it all, what was he talkin about, anyways?

"Aw come on. You married thet purty Crawford gal, didn't you?"

Thomas nodded, shuffling his feet in the dirt.

"Well, you could have knocked me down an called me sassafras when I heard it. I jist figured them Crawfords would go fur a more established man," Uriah smirked. "Like your uncle."

"Now, wait jist a minute—"

"No, you wait. See, old boy, I figured Miss Crawford, bein more refined an all, would take to a more polished man. Fact of the matter, I may have said somethin of the kind to your uncle myself."

"No!" Thomas jumped to his feet then, his legs straight as sticks, his anger boiling. "I'm sick an tired of you tormentin me this way. So let me tell you a thing or two–"

Uriah shrugged. "No use jawin at me. I don't pay much mind to quitters. Figured Miss Crawford wouldn't neither."

At that, the lid flew off Thomas' patience and his anger spewed over. His left hand shot out and grabbed Uriah's collar. Giving it a yank, he exploded. "Why, you dirty rascal. You're nothin but a low down, stinkin bastard!"

Uriah merely laughed. "Hey, calm down, old boy. Things ain't so bad."

"Not bad! Not bad? Course things is bad. Julia's dead an—an— An I've a notion to kill you."

At that, Uriah's eyes turned to steel. "Like you killed your uncle." It was a statement.

Stunned, Thomas let go the collar and stepped back. He knew. Uriah *knew* about Uncle James.

Uriah laughed. "You're not only a quitter but naive, old boy. If you was fixin to do thet right you should have asked me to help. But never mind thet now. Jist so long as you stay out of my way, things'll be fine, see?" Uriah gave Thomas a not–too–playful shove then and left.

Thomas, shifting his weight from his right leg to his left and back to his right again, stared after him. Dang it all, anyways. Thet feller used to be his friend. An he'd betrayed him. Buddied up to Uncle James an pulled the wool over his own eyes. It was enough to make a feller choke up like. Enough to make a feller quit on life.

Jane Douglas was embarrassed. Acutely self–conscious she was, as she strode along Main Street toward home. And not even her new mint dress with its slim front panel and its modified bustle could keep her from feeling like a dowdy old maid. It was them spectacles thet done it. Why land sakes, them wire–rimmed things made her feel all of fifty, a full decade older than she was. Still an all, she could see a mite better. And what she saw as she crossed West Street to her own back yard was baby Benjamin sittin alone in the dirt beside the split–log bench. Achewin on a string of beads he was, astarin at the world like it was some kinda mystery.

"Land sakes, youngin, what you adoin out here fur, anyways? Ain't your Aunt Katie awatchin you at all?" Unmindful of her new dress, Jane stooped and picked up the young Benjamin. She smiled then and patted his cheek. But Benjamin remained solemn.

"Aunt Katie." It was spoken matter–of–fact like.

But Katie was standing in the dining room, her fists dug into her waist as she glared at Jordana, who sat in her rocker, her face turned toward the window.

"Drat it all, My Ma, Uncle James is dead. An it's jist plain silly fur you to keep on watchin fur him."

"Dead? James dead? No. He can't be. Carrie? Carrie, git your bucket." And Jordana got up and trudged to the kitchen.

"Let her be," Jane put a restraining hand on Katie who would have followed. "Land sakes, we can't make her see if she ain't a mind to. Here. Take this youngin an wash him up. I got to change clothes an fix supper."

An hour later Jane took a skillet of cornbread from the oven and sighed. "Land sakes, where's your pa?" She addressed Katie who was filling the water glasses.

"Why my goodness, how should I know? Anyways, he's bound to be along shortly. Thomas too."

But five minutes gave way to ten, and still no Michael. Land sakes, what ailed thet man, anyways? Why, sounds from thet smithy had ceased purt near as soon as she'd taken the cornbread from the oven. Somethin was wrong.

"I'm agoin to look fur your pa," Jane removed her apron and strode past Katie. "You all go on an eat."

Outside, Jane took a few steps off the back porch and stopped. Through her new specs she could make out a figure in the dusk. It was Michael. By the root cellar he was, an kneelin over another man.

"Aye, Lad, I know you're hurtin, to be sure. But I'm thinkin you'd best come around now." With that Michael patted his son's ashen face. But Thomas slept on, snoring lightly.

"Aye, Lad, I reckon you can't." Michael grabbed his son beneath the armpits then and heaved. Standing, he flung the limp figure over his burly shoulders and turned toward the house.

Whether he noticed her or not, Jane couldn't tell. But as he staggered by, she noted his drawn countenance an heaving shoulders. Suddenly, she was angry. Land sakes, it was downright disgustin the way Thomas was acarryin on. Makin an old man out of his pa an an orphan out of his son. All because of thet gal. Why, she'd a mind to tell him a thing or two. After all, lots of folks lost someone they loved. An most of them didn't git drunk as a skunk because of it. Scowling, Jane turned and marched toward the house.

Chapter 45

Katie stood before her bedroom mirror, adjusting a small hat over her brunette hair. Satisfied, she pinned it into place and smiled. She did look somethin special like with them dark pink ribbons trailin down over her chignon–style braids. An her pale pink dress with its puff sleeves an wide lace trim made her feel purt nigh beautiful. Course it did seem a tad unusual to be dressin fur church on a weekday. But then Governor Hardin had set aside this third day of June, 1875 as a day of prayer. Fur grasshoppers of all things. Why my goodness, there wasn't no more of them this year than usual. But thet hadn't stopped Aunt Jane from closin up her shop.

"Land sakes, jist cause we ain't overrun with them critters don't mean everybody's got it good. Why, thet paper says eastern Missouri is purt near covered with them things. Jist eatin the crops right up, they are."

So Katie hadn't argued. Anyways, she liked gittin all dolled up. After all, Bonnie would be there. An maybe Thane— Drat it all, why *couldn't* she furgit thet man. It was jist plain silly to take on so.

Sighing, Katie took the toddling Benjamin by the hand and made her way downstairs. Aunt Jane was all ready, lookin jist plain lovely in her peach–colored satin dress. Even Mamie looked purty, the green in her gown makin her eyes seem somethin special like.

"Drat it all, I wish My Pa would stop workin fur a bit an join us. Or Thomas even," Katie said, as she stopped by the oak table in the dining room.

"Land sakes, Child, you know your pa's no church goer. Livin by the Good Book has always been his way. As fur Thomas—" Jane shook her head.

"Oh fur heaven sakes you two, stop your jawin so we can git on with this thing. Where's My Ma, anyways?" Mamie glanced toward the empty rocker.

"She's gittin ready," Aunt Jane snapped. "Land sakes, Girl, jist be glad she's agoin."

Shaking her head, Katie wasn't sure she agreed with her aunt. After all, My Ma had only been to church a few times in the last two years. An the last time she'd purt nigh done them all in by askin folks if they'd seen Uncle James. It had been awful embarrassin. Really an truly it had. An now, My Ma was fixin to go again. Only time was flyin an she wasn't ready.

"Land sakes, I'd best hurry her up a bit." And Aunt Jane strode through the kitchen and into the bedroom beyond. Seconds later, she reappeared, frowning.

"Land sakes, girls, your ma's gone. Disappeared like, she has."

"Aw, don't carry on so, Aunt Jane. She's probably jist outside." Mamie waved toward the back porch.

But Jordana wasn't outside. Not in the back, not in the front, not on the log bench by the oak tree.

Worried, Katie ran to the smithy. Easing herself through the crowd near the doorway, she found My Pa.

Michael ceased pounding on the poker he was straightening at the sight of his daughter. "Aye, Lass, you're a sight fur sore eyes." He rubbed the small of his back as he stood, his hazel eyes shining.

"Oh, My Pa, we can't find her. We've searched an searched an—"

"Aye, Lass, slow down now." Michael placed a burly hand on Katie's forearm. "I reckon you're lookin fur your ma?"

Katie nodded.

"Meself, I'm thinkin she took your Uncle James' surrey."

"The surrey? What fur?"

"Aye, Lass, it's them Spring Grounds, to be sure."

The Spring Grounds? Why, thet was jist plain silly. Unless— Unless—

Leaving My Pa to his customers, Katie sped to the barn. Sure enough, Uncle James' surrey was missin. There was nothin to do but hitch old Dobbin to the wagon an go after her.

Benjamin treated the trip as an adventure, peering between the slats of the wagon bed, his usually serious face alight with joy. But the women were disturbed.

Drat it all, she'd got all dressed up fur nothin, Katie fumed as they jolted along. Now she'd miss seein Thane an even worse, Bonnie. What was the matter with My Ma, anyways?

It wasn't hard to spot Uncle James' surrey. Even among the better carriages it stood out, its six–inch gold fringe dancing in the breeze. But it was empty.

Drat it all, how were they supposed to find My Ma in all this crowd? Why, in her whole life Katie reckoned she'd never seen so many folks gethered in one place. They spilled from the doors of the newly opened Sweet Springs Hotel. They lounged on the seats of the octagonal Pagoda. They strolled about on dusty streets. Why my goodness, everywhere she looked there was gentlemen wearin high–top hats an pin–stripped trousers, an ladies sportin bustled gowns an frilly parasols.

A tug on Katie's skirt caused her to glance down at Benjamin. Meeting her gaze, he said solemnly. "Maw—maw," and pointed. Following the direction of the chubby finger, Katie sighed. It was My Ma all right, dressed in an old calico an carryin a wooden bucket.

Drat it all, she was pretendin like Kentucky again, Katie thought as she quickly moved toward her mother.

But Jordana seemed unaware of her daughter and her grandson as she stopped a smartly dressed couple. "Have you seen my cousin, Carrie?" she asked eagerly.

Assuring her they hadn't, they started to walk on. But Jordana grasped the woman's arm. "Confound you, don't run off like. I need to find Carrie. She's a little girl with long flaxen hair an—an she loves thet Big Spring."

"I'm sorry, Ma'am, but we haven't seen her," and the man hastily steered his wife away.

"You come back here, you hear me?" Jordana shook a finger at the backs of the departing couple.

"My Ma?"

"Carrie?"

"No. It's me, Katie. We've come to take you home."

"Confound it, I ain't goin nowhere till I find Carrie."

"But My Ma—"

Jordana didn't hear. Already she was moving through the crowd, swinging her bucket, calling for her cousin. This time it was Jane who intercepted her.

"Carrie?"

"Carrie's awaitin at home," Jane snapped, as she guided her sister through the trees toward the wagon. But Jordana insisted on riding in the surrey.

"James?" she called as she settled on the upholstered seat. "Confound it, James, where are you?"

"Land sakes, Jordana, stop shoutin. James is awaitin fur you at home. Right beside Carrie, he is." And Jane flicked the horse with the reins.

❖　　❖　　❖

The afternoon was hot. So sultry that even the breeze failed to cool Katie as she stood at the graveside holding Benjamin's hand and listening to the minister.

> *"The Lord is my shepherd; I shall not want.*
> *He maketh me to lie down in green pastures: he leadeth me*
> *beside the still waters.*
> *He restoreth my soul..."*[1]

Katie shook her head. She wanted to believe them purty words about God bein kind like a shepherd. Really an truly she did. But God had purt nigh disappeared. Gone away like he had, takin My Ma with him. If only Katie didn't hurt so bad things mighten seem so awful like. But My Ma was gone. An nothin could bring her back. Course Katie never had loved her the way she did My Pa. Still, she'd always reckoned thet someday My Ma would accept her like she did Mamie. Now, she never would. An thet hurt. Really an truly it did.

Katie bit her lip to keep her chin from trembling. It didn't make no sense what had happened to My Ma. Why, she'd been purt nigh crazy them last few days. Even My Pa couldn't do nothin to fix things. Course he tried. He'd sat all night holdin My Ma's hand, callin her "Colleen", tellin her he loved her. Yet in the end, it was Uncle James she'd called fur.

Katie sighed, wishin My Pa would jist go ahead an cry. But he didn't. He jist stared at thet wooden box, his heavy shoulders heavin.

> *"Surely goodness and mercy shall follow me all the days of*
> *my life: And I will dwell in the house of the Lord forever."* [2]

Katie turned away. As she did so she caught sight of her brother's face. Strained it was, the corners of his mouth curvin down. An his eyes was empty. Jist like they'd been fur weeks now. Course he tipped thet stone jug a good bit. Still, corn liquor wasn't what made him withdraw like. It was losin Julia. An now My Ma.

But she reckoned it was Mamie who missed My Ma the most. Tears flowed from them green eyes landin on the toe of her shoe as she kicked at the mound of dirt beside the opened grave. An them tears turned to sobs as Aunt Jane began to sing

> *"On Jordan's stormy banks I stand,*
> *And cast a wishful eye*
> *To Canaan's fair and happy land,*
> *Where my possessions lie."* [3]

The service ended, Katie joined the others in tossing clods onto the wooden casket. She would miss My Ma. Really an truly she would. Still, she was glad My Ma rested peaceful like beside Patrick an Uncle James. All thet talk about movin the cemetery up north hadn't amounted to much. Unless you counted thet new split–rail fence over there alongside Locust Street. She reckoned the talk had brought thet about.

The grave filled in, Katie felt a hand on her shoulder. She knew without lookin it was Bonnie. Unable to control herself any longer, Katie turned to the welcoming embrace an bawled like a baby.

Her tears spent, she looked up into the sympathetic face of her dearest friend. My goodness, how could she *ever* survive without Bonnie? Them blue eyes an chestnut curls, thet bubblin personality, an thet carrin, lovin heart was like a balm to Katie's wounded soul. Fur Bonnie was to her like thet friend in the sonnet she read jist the other day.

> *When to the sessions of sweet silent thought*
> *I summon up remembrance of things past,*
> *I sigh the lack of many a thing I sought,*
> *And with old woes new wail my dear time's waste; Then*
> *can I drown an eye, unused to flow,*
> *For precious friends hid in death's dateless night,*
> *And weep afresh love's long-since cancell'd woe,*
> *And moan the expense of many a vanish'd sight. Then can*
> *I grieve at grievances foregone,*
> *And heavily from woe to woe tell o'er*
> *The sad account of fore–bemoaned moan, Which I new*
> *pay as if not paid before:*
> > *But if the while I think on thee, dear friend,*
> > *All losses are restored, and sorrows end.* [4]

"Oh, Katie, I'm so sorry. It jist ain't fair fur life to do you this way. You know I'd fix it if I could. But I can't. I can only give you my love. Please, come see me soon. We'll have a right fine visit. All right?"

Katie nodded, too overcome for words. She would go see Bonnie. An they would talk about My Ma. An Thane. Then maybe things wouldn't seem so awful like. Then maybe she could go on.

Chapter 46

The morning was warm and close. Laying aside his staining rag, Livingston Lewis reached into his trouser pocket for a handkerchief. Removing his Havana, he mopped his forehead and sighed. Lord, the joints in his fingers hurt. Even so, work had to be done. For customers like Mr. Miller wouldn't wait.

Ten minutes later, the door opened and Mr. Fudd hurried in. Puffing his Havana, Livingston nodded in greeting. Daniel, on the other hand, ceased sanding a chair seat and smiled at the elderly man.

"Good morning, Harvey." Daniel, his dark head bent above his work, seemed happier just having the man here.

"Mornin to you, Mr. Daniel, sir, an Mr. Lewis, sir." Harvey stopped at the small counter, opened the old cigar box and selected a blue peppermint stick. Placing it between toothless gums, he moved behind the work bench to get the broom.

Biting his Havana, Livingston sighed. Lord, he wished that just this once Mr. Fudd would forget the sweeping. At least until that new varnish was dry. But of course, he wouldn't suggest such a thing. For despite the mess he made in trying to be helpful, Mr. Fudd was invaluable.

Watching his son now as he ran those sensitive fingers over the smooth chair seat, Livingston breathed a sigh of relief. He was thankful, more thankful than he could say, to have the old Daniel back. Come to think of it, he hadn't touched a drop of whiskey since the night Mr. Fudd rescued him from the saloon. He'd remained sober, worked diligently and enjoyed life once again.

Daniel did worry about the old man though, of that Livingston was certain. And with good reason, he supposed. For Mr. Fudd had been jailed a second time. Ostensibly for "disturbing the peace". In reality, Livingston suspected several merchants hadn't forgotten the fracas last fall. And since Mr. Fudd was the cause of that, he must be the reason why trade had dropped off for Main Street business houses in recent months. Personally, Livingston saw the railroad as the culprit. For merchants on Lexington Avenue did a thriving business. Come to think of it, several houses had recently moved from Main to Lexington.

Lord, he wished folks would leave Mr. Fudd alone. Course he had to admit, the old man wasn't much to look at. But being spindly and constantly shaking one's head was no crime. For that matter, behaving like an eccentric old fool didn't make him guilty of breaking a city ordinance either. A far cry from the likes of those James' Boys, Mr. Fudd seemed like a child—eager to please, satisfied with simple things.

As the dust began to swirl beneath Mr. Fudd's broom, Livingston puffed gently on his Havana and smiled. Let the old man help. Time enough to worry about messes later. For now it was enough to have the old Daniel back. Because that made him happy, more happy than he could say.

❖   ❖   ❖

They were working late that evening, trying to get a wardrobe finished for Charles Hamilton before his wedding at the end of the week. Standing alongside his father, Daniel rubbed mahogany stain into smoothly sanded wood, his mind on the man beside him. He worried about him, pure and simple. For his father wasn't as spry as he used to be. Rheumatism was affecting his knees and his fingers as well. True, he hadn't complained. But then he never was one to voice his feelings. Not about himself or others. Take Harvey Fudd, for example. Personally, Daniel knew his father merely tolerated the man. That's why he'd sent his old friend home earlier in the day.

Now, as he watched his father puff gently on his Havana, Daniel wished he would remarry. Because the truth was, that someday the older man would simply be unable to work. He'd need someone then to look after him, fuss over him, love him.

Of course Daniel had no doubt that his father wished he would be the one to marry. But Daniel wasn't looking for a wife. After having his heart clawed to shreds by Mamie, he wasn't about to offer it to someone else.

Both doors of the wardrobe finished, Daniel looked up to see a woman peering into the windows. It looked like Jane Douglas, outlined in the early evening light. She disappeared then, and seconds later opened the door and strode in.

"Land sakes, Mr. Daniel, I purt near couldn't believe my eyes. You aworkin like thet while your friend is abein picked on. Thet's downright shameful. Why, thet Mr. Fudd is a nice—"

"Harvey? Somebody's bothering Harvey?" Daniel clenched the staining rag in his hand. "When? Where?"

"Why, right now. Folks all over is arunnin down to Lexington. Couple of fellers say they're agoin to teach Mr. Fudd a lesson. They say—"

Daniel heard no more. Throwing down his rag, he hurried outside and across to Spring Street. "What happened?" he snapped to Mr. Owens, the barber, who hurried along in the same direction.

"Don't know fur sure. Seems like the marshal sent two men to arrest thet there Mr. Fudd. Said he was disturbin the peace again."

"He was *not!*" Clenching his fists, Daniel began to run. If anyone tried to take Harvey again, they'd have *him* to deal with.

Arriving at Lexington, Daniel stopped. He had to. Such a crowd had gathered he couldn't get through. And he needed closer. For there, right beside the depot, a platform had been assembled. And a noosed rope swung slowly from the overhead beam.

Daniel swallowed hard as a band tightened about his chest. They planned to hang Harvey, pure and simple. For already, two men were propelling the old man onto the platform. Well, they wouldn't. *He* wouldn't let them.

Angrily, Daniel elbowed the people on either side and shoved the ones in front. He had to get through. But try as he might, he couldn't get closer. And now, he was hemmed in from behind as well.

Forcing himself to look up at his friend, Daniel felt the band pull even tighter about his chest. Harvey. His wiry frame trembled and his face turned white with fear. Laughing, one of the men slipped the noose over Harvey's shaking head. Daniel saw his friend's eyes grow huge as the rope was tightened.

"NO!" Again, Daniel flailed at the people around him. To no avail. The truth was, he simply couldn't get through.

Burying his face in his hands, Daniel began to weep. He loved that old man, pure and simple. And those men up there had no right to take his life. Harvey hadn't hurt anyone. Daniel doubted he was capable of such action. Harvey was kind, he was loving, he was—

"Say, what's going on here, anyway?"

At the sound of a business-like voice, Daniel jerked his head upright. He saw then a well-dressed man, his hand raised to shield his eyes from the lowering sun, striding from the direction of the City Hotel.

"Why, we're jist fixin to rid this town of a no–good trouble maker."

"Well, you can just stop." The man strode onto the platform, glaring at the men.

"Hey, old man, you'd best back off. This critter's been arrested by the marshal, see?"

"I don't care who's charged him with what. *I'm* the prosecuting attorney of this county and I say no one in Brownsville has committed a crime deserving of death. Now, you loosen that noose right now and come along with me. We'll see who gets arrested."

The crowd turned then and yelled for the arrest of Uriah Martin and Melvin Duncan. Sensing they were beaten, the two men quickly loosened the rope about Harvey's neck.

Once the rope cleared the old man's head, the crowd began to dissipate. Daniel, the band snapping from his chest, raced to the platform. Without a word, he embraced his friend. God, but Harvey was quaking. And his eyes had a vacant, haunted look. He was terrified, pure and simple.

"Are you all right?"

Harvey tried to nod but his head was shaking nearly out of control.

Daniel forced himself to smile. "Think no more of this now. It'll soon blow over and be forgotten. For now, you can come home with me. Father will have a good supper cooked, fried chicken and biscuits. Oh, and I just happen to have one of these along." And reaching into his trouser pocket, Daniel pulled out a peppermint stick.

Chapter 47

It was a hot afternoon in early August when Katie decided to visit Bonnie. Fur weeks now she'd been too busy to leave home. Until today. She decided this mornin thet it was jist plain silly to be washin, cookin an cleanin when she needed Bonnie somethin awful. And so after she'd rinsed the dinner dishes, she washed Benjamin's hands and face, changed her own dress and set out.

Impatient to get to her friend, Katie resented Benjamin's slow pace. Drat it all, couldn't thet youngin walk any faster? Then looking down at the dark brown head bobbing beside her, Katie felt ashamed. Course he was doin the best he could. After all, he was only sixteen months old. If she wanted to go faster she'd jist have to carry him. But drat it all, it was too hot fur thet. Anyways, if he'd jist hold to her hand—

But Benjamin let go.

Exasperated, Katie turned to see him squatting on the plank walk studying something shiny. Drat it all, what was thet youngin after, anyways? With a sigh she hunched beside him, her poplin skirt arching behind her. Taking the dusty coin from Benjamin's equally dusty hand, Katie frowned. A silver dollar. What was it doin on the boardwalk, anyways?

Rising, Katie decided she'd best check with the nearest merchant. Most likely it belonged to one of them. Entering the cabinet shop, she immediately sneezed. Goodness, there was dust galore in here.

"That's all the sweeping we need done for now, Harvey," a kind voice said.

Katie looked up from her handkerchief to see Daniel Lewis coming toward her. "Good afternoon, Miss Katie, may I help you?" He smiled as he carefully wiped the sawdust from his fingers.

"I guess so," Katie paused. Drat it all, it was jist plain silly fur her to come traipsin in here like this. Still, the dollar must belong to him—

"My nephew found this on your boardwalk." And she handed him the silver coin.

Taking the proffered money, Daniel wiped it with his cloth, then studied it carefully. "It's a Liberty Seated, pure and simple. We don't see as many as we did. Most people use trade dollars or greenbacks now," he smiled. "The truth is, this could belong to anyone. You say the chap found it?"

Katie nodded.

Daniel reached out a hand then to tousle Benjamin's dark hair. In return Benjamin, his finger in his mouth, solemnly studied the tall stranger. Then slowly, he smiled.

Grinning, Daniel returned the coin to Katie. "Save it," he said, "for the chap."

"Why thank you, Mr. Lewis."

Daniel held up a hand. "Think nothing of it. It's a pleasure, pure pleasure, to see a nice boy like this one… And, Miss Katie, next time just call me Daniel. After all, I was almost your brother once."

❖   ❖   ❖

In Bonnie's warm kitchen Katie rocked slowly, a sleepy Benjamin in her arms. Watching her friend slip skins and seeds from large, purple grapes, Katie sighed. Goodness, but it must be somethin special like to have a husband to bake fur. Course Katie didn't mind Bonnie bein married. After all, a friend as sweet as her deserved a family. But drat it all, Katie wanted a family too. She wanted—

"You're awful quiet, Katie. Is things all right at home?"

"No. Between Thomas an My Pa tippin thet liquor jug I'm purt nigh done in. Course Thomas don't take on nigh as bad as My Pa. Still, he jist lives to smoke thet stinkin pipe an mind them trees an garden. Why my goodness, Bonnie, he don't pay no attention to Benjamin. Ignores him he does, like he ain't even there."

"Oh dear, thet sounds bad. Course the youngin's got you. An I bet you're a right nice ma too." Bonnie smiled, a look of pride in her bright blue eyes.

"Thanks, Bonnie," Katie bit her lip to keep her chin from trembling. Then glancing down at Benjamin, she managed a smile. "Looks like he's asleep."

"Thet's good. You can lay him on the bed, then we can talk."

Katie rose from the rocker and carried Benjamin to the bedroom. Gently, she placed him on Bonnie's patchwork quilt, careful not to disturb little David who slept in the trundle bed.

Tenderly, Katie removed Benjamin's shoes and stockings. On impulse, she kissed a chubby foot. Goodness, but he was precious. Really an truly he was. She should be happy like, the way Bonnie was. But drat it all, she wasn't. Fur Bonnie had more than thet tawny–headed youngin sleepin so peaceful like. She had his pa fur a husband.

Her chin quivering, Katie placed the tiny shoes on the floor and returned to the kitchen. Settling into a chair beside her friend, she reached into the crock filled with slippery grapes and removed a handful. For several moments both women sat, preparing grapes for the pie that was to be Randall's desert that evening. It was Bonnie who broke the silence.

"You mentioned your brother awhile ago," she began. "He's not the only one who lost his ma. How are *you* doin?"

Katie bit her lip. "I sort of miss her, I reckon. Not like I'd miss My Pa if he died. Course My Ma seemed all done in like ever since Uncle James got killed. She talked a lot about her cousin, Carrie, too. An Kentucky. There must have been somethin special like about thet place. Still, I thought she shouldn't take on so. An now My Pa's doin it."

"He's missin your ma right good." It was a statement.

Katie nodded. "He's purt nigh to drink himself to death over it. Course My Pa always did have his jug. Laces his tea with liquor purt nigh ever day. Still, I ain't never seen him take on like this before. He's always been so— so happy like. Now, he starts chuggin soon as supper's over with. An he don't quit till he's asleep in his chair. Why my goodness, most nights Aunt Jane has to put him to bed."

"Sounds awful." Bonnie began sifting flour as she spoke.

"It is. An if thet ain't bad enough, there's Mamie. She took on so bad fur awhile thet Aunt Jane finally lit into her. Told her, 'If you don't stop mopin in thet shop, you can jist stay home an cook. Land sakes, lots of folks lose loved ones.'"

"I'll bet Mamie was right mad about thet," Bonnie said, cutting lard into her flour with two case knives.

"Course she was. She scampered from the room like she was bein chased. Still, she must have had a mind to change. She's still sellin hats."

They were silent then as Bonnie rolled out a crust and fitted it into a pan. Then Katie spoke.

"How's your ma been lately?"

"Not very good. I thought to make her quit thet store. But, she won't. Mostly cause Will's right cheap an won't hire no more help. An without Thane helpin, it's jist too much—" Bonnie stopped and raised grape–stained fingers to her lips. "Oh, Katie, I'm sorry. I didn't mean to do you this way. I jist wasn't thinkin. I—"

"It's all right. Really an truly it is. Why, it's jist plain silly fur me to take on so." Katie's chin trembled as she spoke. Drat it all, when would she *ever* git over thet man? Why, he an Linda had been married more than a year now. Course they didn't seem anxious to have no youngins. But still—

"Katie?"

"Yes."

"Katie, fur all your life you've loved folks. An I'm glad. It's right nice to care fur others. Only sometimes you git hurt. Like—like when Thane quit you. Katie, I thought— Oh fur cryin out loud, let me finish this pie, then we'll talk."

Minutes later, the pie in the oven, Bonnie wiped her hands on her apron and disappeared into the dining room. She returned with a scrap of newspaper. "I thought of you, Katie, when I first saw this. It's called 'First Love'. Now, you jist shut your eyes an listen. All right?"

Katie closed her eyes then and let the words seep into her pain–racked soul.

> *Whom first we love, you know we seldom wed.*
> *Time rules us all. And life indeed is not*
> *The thing we planned it out ere hope was dead;*
> *And then, us women cannot choose our lot.*
> *Much must be borne which is hard to bear.*
> *Much given away which it were sweet to keep,*
> *God help us all who need indeed His care;*
> *And yet I know the Shepherd loves His sheep.*[1]

The words stopped and Bonnie's own impatient voice cut in. "Oh, Katie, don't you see? It's right natural to hurt some. But you can git over it. You can go on. You can even take to someone else. Love again."

"No!" Katie's eyes flew open as she wrapped her arms about herself. "I ain't never lovin no one again. It hurts too much when they go away. Really an truly it does."

"Oh, Katie, fur cryin out loud. *Course* it hurts right bad. Thet's why you need God to help. Like this poem says." She shook the paper toward her friend. "Oh, Katie, can't you see? Knowin God cares can make things all right. He can fix your heart up so good you'll jist go right on lovin like before."

But Katie wasn't convinced. Drat it all, what did Bonnie know of love gone awry, anyways? An if God could fix her heart up proper like, why hadn't he already done it? No. Much as she loved this friend with her kind blue eyes an carin ways, she wasn't a mind to believe her right now. Hugging herself tightly, Katie shook her head. She wasn't goin to love again. Not *ever*. An not Bonnie or God or anyone else tellin her to would make a tad of difference.

Chapter 48

Thomas Fitzsimmons sat on the edge of his bed, puffing his corncob pipe and staring at the wooden plank floor. He couldn't believe it. Tevis was dead. Shot by a nigger, he was. Damn, but it made a feller choke up like, jist thinkin on it. Course his friend had attacked the nigger first. An thet was dumb, jist plumb dumb. Even if the bastard did deserve it, a feller could git into a heap of trouble fur pullin a stunt like thet. An now he was dead. Gone. Jist like Wade.

The thought of Wade caused Thomas to raise his left hand to his eyes. Damn! He'd never git to be with thet dandy feller again. *Never*. His lips taut, Thomas closed his eyes and saw again the blood–soaked clumps of dun–colored hair wrapped in his own red bandanna.

His eyes open again, Thomas stood slowly and studied the flag which hung above his bed. An thet plaque. CSA. It was over. Done fur. Finished. The dream of savin Missouri from the Feds was gone. Climbing onto the bed, Thomas removed the plaque and dropped it onto the quilt.

But thet flag. Hanging limply in the humid August air, the Stars and Bars represented all that Thomas had fought for and lived for. Though the white had turned to gray and the red to russet, Thomas had still clung to it as a symbol of hope. Until now. But with the death of his bushwhacking friend, Tevis, had gone the last shred of promise.

Blowing the dust from a red corner, Thomas lifted the fabric to his face. Even now it was soft and fragrant. Lovely it was, like thet special woman who stitched it. Julia. A feller could purt near go to pieces jist thinkin on her. Why, them gold curls had bound up his heart real easy like. Them shapely breasts had aroused his manhood somethin fierce like. Thet sweet face had captured his soul, makin him almost crazy like. An she was

217

gone. Her pa too had died, leavin no one with the Crawford name to remind him of what had been.

Slowly, Thomas lifts the flag from its hooks. Slowly, he steps to the floor. Awkwardly, he folds the seven stars and three bars. In all his born days he's never felt so alone. Fact is, ever love in his life is gone. An without Wade, Julia, an Tevis, it don't make a lick of difference thet them Feds won the War.

Gently, Thomas places the plaque on top of the flag and lays them inside the chest of drawers, beside his Smith & Wesson Schofield .45. Then, slowly, he closes the drawer.

❖   ❖   ❖

Supper over, Daniel settled into the overstuffed chair beside the window and reached for *The Brownsville Herald*. *The Herald* had been out for about a year now, and he enjoyed reading it. Rumor had it that *The Banner* was about to fold. The truth was, he didn't care much one way or the other so long as he had a paper to read.

Glancing over the front page, his eyes came to rest on a poem at the top of column two, "A Poetical Slander on Missouri". Holding the paper loosely, Daniel began to read.

> *Stretching from the Mississippi out*
>   *toward the Golden Gate,*
> *You may know it as Missouri, you may*
>   *know it as the State*
> *Where the hardy, jean–clad peasant, when*
>   *not lynching some dear friend*
> *Is—with chances in its favor—himself*
>   *curing on the end....* [1]

His eyes returning to that sixth line, Daniel's fingers clenched the paper. Within seconds he was on his feet. Wrapping the paper tightly, he hauled back with his right arm and hurled the offending pages across the room. If that was someone's idea of humor, he must be mad. For it was torture, pure torture, to see a friend prepared for lynching. God, it wasn't funny. It wasn't funny at all.

Chapter 49

Thud. Thud. Thud. Thomas dropped ears of sweet corn into the wooden bucket beside him. At the end of this row he'd be done. All done. Fur this was the tail end of the corn crop. Made a feller feel almost sad like to think of summer endin. Still—

Clip. Clop. Clip. Clop. Thomas paused as two men on horseback stopped before the smithy. Made a feller feel kinda anxious like, when strangers rode in. Armed they was, with revolvers an shot guns. An his own revolver was stuck away in thet drawer upstairs. Darn it all, he hoped they hadn't a mind to make trouble. The older one dismounted then, and led his horse into the smithy.

Thomas returned to picking corn, surreptitiously eyeing the lone stranger. His square jaw, stubby beard an cowboy hat looked familiar like. Could it be? Naw. What would he be in Brownsville fur, anyways?

Thud. Thud. Thud. The last of the ears landed in the bucket. Yet, Thomas remained in sight of the smithy. He was rewarded minutes later when the second man emerged minus his horse. The younger man dismounted then, and tied his own animal to the hitching post. Then loosely carrying their shotguns both men strode toward Thomas.

"Howdy, stranger," the younger man spoke, blinking his bright blue eyes.

"Hello there. Name's Thomas. Thomas Fitzsimmons," and he reached out his left hand to shake.

Both men ignored the gesture.

"Reckon you lost thet other arm fightin fur Missouri." It was a challenge.

"Sure did. Right there beside thet Anderson house in Lexington," he

219

paused, shifted from his right foot to his left, then back to his right again. "Thet was after I lost my best friend at Wilson's Creek. Still, we whupped thet bastard, Lyon. Made a feller feel plumb good, seein him fall like thet."

Thomas sensed then a subtle shift in the men's attitudes, confirming his suspicions. So these were the notorious James Boys. Again, he extended his hand. This time Frank shook it.

"So you won't mind feedin a couple of Missouri boys then." It was Jesse, issuing an order.

Darn, but Thomas despised thet tone. Still, a feller had best oblige the man.

"Feed good Missourians? Course we can. My sister will russle up some dinner in no time." As he spoke, Thomas glanced toward the sky. Not quite noon. If they hurried they could eat before My Pa decided to break fur dinner.

"Come along." Thomas picked up the bucket of roastin ears and led the way to the porch. "Hope you fellers don't mind comin this way. The family uses the back door." He set the bucket down then and entered the kitchen.

"Katie, I brought a couple of fellers fur some dinner."

At the sight of two men totin shotguns, Katie gasped. "Oh my goodness!"

"Pleased to make your acquaintance, Ma'am," Jesse swept off his hat, revealing thick, dark hair.

"Me—me too," Katie stammered as she turned back to the stove where chicken sizzled in a skillet. "Dinner's purt nigh ready."

"No hurry, Ma'am."

Thomas gestured to the washstand. "Wash up if you've a mind to," he said, glancing toward the door. Made a feller feel uneasy like, knowin Aunt Jane or Mamie could show up any minute.

"Not now, Benjamin," Katie pleaded, disentangling the toddler's fingers from her skirts. But Benjamin, apparently frightened by the strangers, persisted in trailing after her. Finally Katie sighed, stopped stirring gravy and handed the boy a wedge of cornbread. "Go sit by the woodbox now, an eat it."

Benjamin, his dark eyes wide, studied first his aunt, then the strangers. At last, reluctantly, he accepted the morsel and settled on the floor.

"Nice youngin you got there," Jesse said as he laid down his shotgun to wash.

"Sure is." The corners of Thomas' mouth turned up. "Havin a son makes a feller feel plumb proud like."

Neither man responded to the comment as they took seats at the table.

"Hope this chicken is plenty done," Katie said as she placed a platter on the table. String beans, Irish potatoes, gravy, corn bread, light bread, butter, jam, and pickles rounded out the meal.

Both men ate heartily, though they kept their shotguns within easy reach. And Thomas noted that Jesse kept one eye on the door.

"Nice town you got here," Frank offered.

"Sure is."

"Must have a nice school somewheres. Leastwise someone likes to read." He nodded toward the volume of poems that lay on the edge of the washstand.

Katie blushed. "Mostly I'm the one thet takes to poems. Course, I didn't git much schoolin. Had to quit after Andrew's family moved up north. Andrew an Claudia was our slaves," she added.

Frank nodded. "Readin is fun though. Ever read any Shakespeare?"

"Some."

"Or Francis Bacon?"

Katie nodded. Her normally gray eyes took on a sapphire hue then as she began to chant.

"The world's a bubble and the life of Man
Less than a span;
In his conception wretched, from the womb
So to the tomb;
Curst from his cradle"
Here Frank joined in—
"and brought up to years—"[1]

"SHUT UP!"

Both Katie and Thomas jumped and Benjamin's large eyes registered fear. But Frank resumed eating as though nothing was amiss.

It was only when Katie served peach pie that Thomas felt the tension lift. So thet rascal Jesse James really could git tough. He jist hoped them Boys skedaddled out of here before anyone else caught wind of them. Evidently his face showed something of his fear, for Jesse eyed his suspiciously .

"Somethin botherin you, Thomas?"

Darn, but thet feller was sharp.

"Naw. Jist thinkin on somethin sad like. The youngin's ma—" he nodded toward Benjamin. "She—she died when he was born."

Evidently satisfied with the explanation, Jesse quickly finished his pie and stood up. "We'd best git along now. Thanks, Ma'am, fur the meal." He put his hat on, picked up his shot gun and headed for the door. Frank followed suit, still chewing a last bite of pie.

They'd just stepped out when Thomas heard Aunt Jane's voice .

"Land sakes, where'd you fellers come from? Who are you, anyways?"

"Good day, Ma'am." Both men tipped their hats to Aunt Jane and Mamie, then disappeared around the back of the house.

"Thomas?" Aunt Jane called, marching into the kitchen. "Thomas, was them there fellers those outlawin James Boys?"

Thomas nodded, then went to the window facing the smithy. Puffing his pipe, he watched as Jesse stood guard while his brother went for his horse. Outlaws, fur certain. Yet fur all thet, Thomas itched to tell them a thing or two. Didn't them fellers know the War was over? Didn't they know there was nothin nor no one worth fightin fur? Didn't they know thet lovin always gits you hurt? Evidently not, for they seemed bent on revenge as they rode from view down Main Street. And for that, Thomas thought they were stupid. Fur it was jist plumb dumb to care. Plumb dumb to love.

Chapter 50

Icy raindrops spattered the sitting room window as Livingston settled into the overstuffed chair to read the paper. He shivered.

"Son, put another stick of wood on the fire, will you?"

Even as Daniel moved to comply, Livingston shuddered. Imagine being cold after a sweltering day in the shop. And this November chill was a far cry from the icy temperatures that usually predominated the winter months. Even so, he had to admit he was beginning to need the warmth of Mr. Fudd's roaring fires. Rheumatic fingers and knees ached less when shielded from the cold.

Puffing his cigar, Livingston scanned the paper, looking for some good news. He found it.

Brown, the negro who murdered Philip Pfaar and ravished his wife in St. Louis not long ago, hangs today. Desperate efforts were made by his counsel to save him, but fortunately without avail.[1]

Biting his cigar, Livingston smiled. It was mighty good to hear of a darkie being hanged. Mighty good. Lord, he hated them. Every since that old barber had nicked his father's face—

Ah well, that was years ago. And in Harrisonburg too. Even so, he still felt an inward thrill whenever a darkie hung. Personally, he'd love to see every last one of them dead. He'd been glad, more glad than he could say, when that black buck, Harry, had been strung up for raping Verna Marie. Of course he had to admit, that hadn't helped his wife any. Even so—

Turning a page, Livingston winced. His fingers were stiff again.

"Son, put another stick of wood on the fire. I'm cold."

❖ ❖ ❖

Jane closed her shop early on a sunny afternoon in November and strode briskly toward home. Land sakes, she had more important business to attend to there than at the shop. An she'd finally got up the gumption to do it. She'd jist sneak upstairs quiet like, change into an old calico an hurry to thet root cellar. Though she didn't cotton to what she was agoin to do, she did need to hurry. Michael closed the smithy early these days.

Twenty minutes later, Jane began lugging stone jugs from the cellar. Puffing, she set two on the ground, then entered the cellar for more. Land sakes, who'da thought Michael would have all this liquor stashed away. There was purt near a dozen jugs here already an more to come. Still an all, she wasn't afixin to quit now.

Unstopping the first jug, Jane hastily poured its contents on the ground, then set it aside and took up a second one. She emptied this one too. Then another. And another. And another.

"Aye, Lass, thet's a sorry sight, to be sure."

Startled, Jane looked up, spilling whiskey on her dress. "Land sakes, you scared the livin daylights out of me. An ruined my dress too."

Michael snorted. Then as Jane emptied yet another jug, he said, "I'm thinkin you've gone an joined up with them temperance ladies out there in Ohio."

"I have not. Why land sakes, what would I want with the likes of them, anyways? You know I ain't against you havin a swig now an then. I jist ain't a mind to put you to bed ever night fur the rest of my life. I got work aplenty without thet."

His eyes moist, Michael turned aside. "Aye, Lass, I've been a fool, to be sure. But me Colleen, she—she was somethin special like. I loved her."

"Course you loved her. We all did. But land sakes, the rest of us ain't passin out every night from corn liquor cause she's gone."

"Aye, Lass, you're right, to be sure." Michael started to leave, then turned back.

"Jane."

Jane started. Why land sakes, he'd never called her by name before. He must be real serious like.

"Aye, Lass, you mean well, to be sure. But I'm thinkin you don't understand. I reckon you might if you was married."

"Ain't my fault I'm not."

Michael's eyes widened. "You bein sure?"

"Course I'm sure. Land sakes, jist cause I wear specks an have a red cheek don't mean I ain't got no feelins."

"Aye, Lass, you have it right bad, I reckon."

"I reckon."

"Who?"

"None of your business. Anyways, thet's over with by now. Only— only I'm still acarin about folks. Leastwise I try to."

"Aye, Lass, you do, to be sure."

He turned away then and plodded toward the house. Still, it seemed to Jane that his heavy shoulders shook less than they had of late.

Chapter 51

The evening air was cold. So cold that Katie's breath created a cloud of steam as she stood on the platform at the train depot. Biting her lip to keep her chin from trembling, she hugged herself fiercely. Bonnie was leavin. Goin away she was, an takin the last rays of sunlight with her.

"All aboooard!"

At the porter's call Randall Dalton boarded the eastbound train, carrying a sleeping David on his shoulder. Bonnie followed, her pale blue skirts looking almost green beneath the glow of swaying lanterns. Seconds later she waved from a lighted window.

Waving in return, Katie forced a smile she didn't feel. Drat it all, why did this have to happen fur, anyways? Why couldn't Bonnie stay in Brownsville where she belonged? Why my goodness, it was plain as day thet she was needed here.

But Randall needed her too. Leastwise thet's how Bonnie had put it a week ago when she broke the news to Katie.

"We're movin," she said, "cause Randall's got a new job."

"Movin? Where to?"

"Sedalia."

"Sedalia? Why, thet's—thet's way off like." Katie waved in the general direction of southeast.

"Nonsense. It ain't thet far. An it's a right nice town from all I hear."

"But why? Why can't you stay—"

"Oh fur cryin out loud, Katie, I already told you. Randall's got work there. *The Banner* folded, you know."

Katie nodded. "What about thet *Herald?* Couldn't he work there, close to home like?"

226

Bonnie shook her head. "They don't need reporters. The *Sedalia Democrat* does. So—

"So you're movin. When?"

"Soon. I thought to be settled by Christmas."

Again Katie nodded, biting her lip to keep from crying.

"Jist cause I'm leavin don't mean we can't be friends no more," Bonnie said. "Why, we can write lots of letters. You can tell me all about your Aunt Jane's shop an how thet youngin's growin. I can tell you what a nice place Sedalia is. An I'll be back to visit, thet's fur sure. Cause— cause my ma's been right poorly of late."

Katie began to cry. Drat it all, Bonnie's ideas jist wasn't good enough. She was movin an nothin would ever be the same again.

"Oh fur cryin out loud, Katie, what're you blubberin fur? In a minute you'll have me bawlin too." And Bonnie began to sob. Loud, heart–wrenching sobs they was, makin Katie feel all done in like.

At last Bonnie ceased weeping, blew her nose on a handkerchief and smiled at Katie. "There. I'm fixed up fine now." She reached for her friend's hand. "Katie, you know I hate doin you this way."

Katie nodded. Still—

Whoo–ooo. Whoo–ooo–ooo.

"All abooooooard!" The porter picked up the step from the platform and climbed onto the slowly moving train.

Whoo–ooo. Whoo–ooo–ooo. Steam poured from the engine as the train gathered speed, taking the Daltons farther and farther from the trembling figure on the platform.

> *When to the sessions of sweet silent thought*
> *I summon up remembrance of things past,*
> *I sigh the lack of many a thing I sought,*
> *And with old woes new wail my dear time's waste...*
> *But if the while I think on thee, dear friend,*
> *All losses are restored, and sorrows end.* [1]

Oh, Bonnie, why did you have to go fur, anyways? Why?

"Katie?"

Katie bites her lip as a hand touches her arm. It's Thane of course, ready to escort her to the carriage where his ma already waits.

Thane. The one man in the world she truly loves. The brother of thet friend she jist waved good–by to. Yet, as she slips her gloved hand through the crook of his arm, her heart seems to come apart like. Fur Thane holds himself aloof, makin him seem a stranger like.

As she stumbles toward the carriage, Katie allows a tear to creep down her cheek. Fur every one has left her: Thomas, My Ma, Thane, an now, Bonnie. Drat it all, it don't make no sense to her why folks have to go away like. But they do. They always do.

Leaning her forehead against the cold glass of her bedroom window, Katie stares into the dark world beyond. Out there somewheres Bonnie is movin toward Sedalia. Bonnie has gone away an left her behind.

Wrapping her arms about herself, Katie rocks on her knees, her whole being aching from the loss. It hurts somethin awful like. Her insides seem to be comin apart, splittin an tearin an bleedin. She clamps her teeth over her bottom lip an still the tears come. Buckets full pour down her face and onto the floor. Bonnie, oh Bonnie, please come back to me. Please!

"Aunt Katie?"

Katie mops her face with a handkerchief and turns toward the owner of the voice. It's Benjamin, standin at the end of the bed, his finger in his mouth. Swept away by the tide of her grief, Katie hadn't heard him come in. And now, as she looks into that solemn face, she knows the youngin needs her. Wants her to rock him an pat his dimpled limbs. Well, she *won't!* She's had enough of carin fur folks. Let his pa mind him fur once.

Turning back to the window, Katie stares again into the darkness. Drat it all, why does it have to be nighttime fur, anyways? Why can't it be sunny like, so she can see thet tree? She needs it somethin awful like. She—

Grunting, Katie shoves on the window frame until it's raised above her head. Br–r-r. It's cold out there. Still, Katie leans on the sill and listens. She hears them then, them naked limbs snappin an swayin. An she can almost see them too. Really an truly she can. They're stretchin mighty far like, an reachin fur the sky.

"Aunt—Aunt K—Katie?" It's Benjamin. Calling.

With a start, Katie slams down the window. What's the matter with her anyways, lettin all thet cold air in? She turns then and looks toward her nephew. Why my goodness, thet youngin's tremblin.

"Benjamin?" She smiles now and stretches a hand toward him.

But the boy, his dark eyes like two question marks, simply studies her.

"Benjamin? Please come to Aunt Katie." She opens her arms then and waits.

Slowly, the boy takes his finger from his mouth and smiles. His legs break into motion then as he scampers across the wood floor.

Folding him close, Katie kisses the top of his dark head.

"You're a good boy, Benjamin. Really an truly you are. An I—I love you."

Chapter 52

Daniel was worried. He was worried about Harvey Fudd, pure and simple. He'd been uneasy about the old man for some time now. Actually, his concern stretched back to that night the marshal had first arrested him for "disturbing the peace". Lately though, Daniel had been more than concerned. He was worried. Really worried. For every since the evening of that near lynching, Harvey had been subdued. Though he'd done his work as conscientiously as ever, he'd never quite regained his amicable disposition. That haunted look which filled his eyes on the evening he slumped to the wooden platform had never really disappeared. Until yesterday.

Why the day before, Harvey had been the picture of his old self: friendly, kind and caring. And Daniel had taken pleasure, pure pleasure, in watching his old friend clean rags and feed the fire, the peppermint stick in his mouth bobbing as he worked. But that was yesterday. Today he hadn't showed up. It was nearly noon now and still there was no sign of him.

Throwing another scrap of wood into the pot–bellied stove, Daniel sighed. He needed Harvey, pure and simple. For feeding the fire himself meant time stolen from his craft. Personally, he'd just as soon have the room cooler. But his father most definitely needed the warmth. Even so, the older man worked at a snail's pace. And judging by the way he frequently bit down on his Havana, Daniel had no doubt he was in pain. Not for the first time, Daniel wondered how much longer his father would be able to work. True, for a man of fifty–seven years, his mind was active enough. His hazel eyes were clear too. And only a few strands of gray were apparent in his dark, wavy hair. But rheumatism most definitely was getting the best of him. Why, some days his knees were so stiff he could scarcely get out of his chair. And his fingers. They were so swollen that even sanding had become difficult. It was depressing, pure and simple. Ah well, he'd deal with his father's deteriorating health when he was forced to. Just now he was more worried about Harvey.

By early afternoon when the wiry old man still hadn't come in, Daniel decided to check on him. No doubt he'd taken ill. A cold maybe. Or influenza. Laying aside his sandpaper, Daniel took a clean rag from his pocket and wiped his fingers thoroughly.

"Quitting early, Son?" Livingston asked as he laboriously rubbed walnut stain on a chair leg.

"I'm going to find Harvey. The truth is, I'm afraid he's taken ill. You know he never misses work."

Puffing gently on his Havana, Livingston managed a smile. "Come to think of it, he hasn't. I'll have to admit he does take his job seriously."

Daniel nodded, tossed a chunk of wood into the fire, and went out. Outside, he clasped his cloak more firmly about him and shivered. Br–r–r. It was cold, pure and simple. And if the overcast sky was any indication, there'd be snow before the week was out. He just hoped the freezing temperatures wouldn't make Harvey's cold worse.

Turning down Blackwater Street, Daniel frowned. God, a person could lose his footing along here. With no boardwalks, the icy ground was slick as glass. Once, he stepped onto a sheet of ice suspended over a dried up mud hole. The crack echoed hollowly in the frigid afternoon air. It was quiet, pure and simple. Even the Blackwater was muffled by a thick blanket of ice. Daniel shivered, then stopped before a one room log cabin. It too, was silent. Desolate. Tapping his gloved fingers on his cloak, he strode toward the door and knocked. No answer. He tried again, rapping soundly on the wooden panel. Again, no answer. Frowning, he turned the knob and pushed his way inside.

"Harvey? Harvey, are you all right?"

No answer.

Glancing about, Daniel saw that the bed, its cornshuck mattress a myriad of lumps, was empty. The fireplace too, was barren, except for a lone pot which hung suspended in the center, much like a rotting tooth filling the gap of an ominous grin. "Harvey?" Again, no answer. God, where could the old man be? Drumming his fingers impatiently on a warped table, Daniel turned and hurried outside and around back. Maybe his friend had gone for water and fallen. Maybe he was lying frozen somewhere. Maybe— Daniel stopped, stunned by the sight just ahead. For there, swinging from the limb of a pin oak, was the body of his friend. "God, but I'll kill whoever's done this!" Then clenching his fist, he ran to the frozen corpse. Before the body, he stopped. A paper protruded from the pocket of the worn jacket. Removing his gloves, Daniel reached for it, his long fingers trembling. Slowly, he unfolded the note.

> *My time is cum to die an them guys in town is the cause. They laugh at me an think I ain't fittin. Maybe I ain't. Onliest Mr. Daniel loves me. He's my bestest friend, cept fur my poor old ma. My pa, he didn't never want me, so I guess God don't neither. Anyways, I ain't fittin fur the likes of this town. So I'll jist go away quiet like an not bother folks no more.*

Daniel stared at the paper clenched in his chapped hand. God, he hurt. That band was tightening about his chest again, squeezing his heart, pure and simple. Flinging the paper aside, he buried his face in his hands and wept. Harvey was dead. That dear old man, who'd given him the courage to love again, was gone. All because he was a little different from others. And it was agony, pure agony, to think it had come to this.

At length, the band still constricting his chest, Daniel forced himself to breath deeply and look into the face of his old friend. It was awful, just awful. That round head which had once been in perpetual motion was still now, hanging permanently to one side. And those eyes, which had registered so many emotions, were like glass balls, staring from ashen skin. But the mouth. It was the mouth that wrung Daniel's heart. For those gaping lips and the stubble which surrounded them, were covered with fine crystals. Red and white crystals, that were sticky to the touch.

PART IV
1876-1880

GAINS

"My heart is open wide tonight
For stranger, kith or kin.
I would not bar a single door
Where Love might enter in."

— *Kate Douglas Wiggin*
The Romance of a Christmas Card

Chapter 53

Jane was tired. Land sakes, she'd worked all day, an still there was sewin to be done. Fur the family this time. Course they was buyin a mite more ready-made things nowadays. Especially the men. Still an all, there was some garments Jane felt was best stitched at home. Like a new shirt fur Benjamin.

Settling in the sewing rocker in the dining room, Jane frowned. Thet heat from the fireplace did seem a mite much this evenin. Why land sakes, even if it was January, the air outside felt like springtime. Course it wouldn't last long. Still an all, she enjoyed the break in the cold spell.

Picking up the white cotton fabric, Jane wished, not for the first time, that she had a sewing machine at home. Land sakes, she could whip up this shirt in no time on a machine. The way it was, she'd jist have to make do. Threading her needle, Jane thought about the youngin this was for. Purt near two years old he was, an growin fast. Still an all, he was a shy one. He much preferred playin by the woodbox in the kitchen to runnin through the house. An them dark eyes was so solemn they sometimes made Jane feel downright uneasy. Fact was, them eyes an thet oval face reminded her of Jordana.

Jane sighed. She did wish her sister had alived. Why land sakes, her life could of been downright wonderful if she'd had the gumption to care. But Jordana never cared a bit fur anyone, except James an Carrie. An of course, all her youngins. Except Katie. Thet child had jist been born at the wrong time. Why land sakes, Jordana hadn't hardly stopped cryin fur the mite she'd lost when Katie popped into the world. No wonder she didn't cotton to her right off. Still an all, Katie was downright special. An if Jordana hadn't been such a stick–in–the–mud she'd aseen it. But then her

235

sister never had seemed to see nothin good in life.

Stitching a fine seam, Jane frowned. Land sakes, Jordana had been blessed aplenty. Why, she'd married the best man in the whole world. Leastwise Jane thought so. Why, Michael was downright wonderful. Looking up from her work, Jane glanced across the room to where he sat on the other side of the fireplace. Dozin he was, his fingers laced across his protrudin belly.

Watching him, Jane felt her heart beat faster. Why land sakes, thet forehead ashinin in the lamplight an them burly shoulders astrainin at the seams of a flannel shirt looked downright attractive. Course she couldn't know what he was athinkin on nowadays. Jordana might still be on his mind. Still an all, he hadn't done more than nip thet jug since the evenin she'd poured whiskey on the ground. But thet didn't mean he cottoned to her. Why land sakes, he might think her downright ugly since she'd took to wearin specs. Or he might not be athinkin on her at all.

Course he *had* noticed her thet once. Near Christmas time it was, an Jane had a mind to attend the big dinner them Presbyterian ladies was aputtin on at the Central Hotel. Only she couldn't go alone. Why land sakes, a lady couldn't jist walk out of an evenin by herself. Oh my, no. Why, the marshal would arrest her quicker than you could say "scat". Course now, if Katie an Mamie were both agoin—but they wasn't. Jist flat out said no. Both of them. Purt near rude they was too.

"I ain't goin to no church dinner," Mamie hissed as the family sat at supper a few evenings earlier. "Anyways, there's no use carryin on about God an Christmas when it was God thet took My Ma away."

No one had replied to that, but later, as they sat together in the dining room, Michael offered to escort Jane to the dinner.

"Why land sakes," she'd exclaimed, "them ladies will purt near pass out if you come awalkin in. You sure you've a mind to do this?"

"Aye, Lass, I reckon I am. Providin they don't go to preachin, mind."

And so the two had gone. Jane, wanting to make a good impression, had dressed with special care. She'd worn one of her own creations, a green velvet gown that was slim in the front and only slightly flared in the back. She took special pains with her hair too, braiding it, then pinning it up, Chignon style. And she'd topped it all with a hat that sported wide, frilly lace, green velvet bows, and a fawn–colored feather. Eyeing herself in the mirror, she smiled. Why land sakes, she looked downright purty. Except fur them blamed specs an thet unsightly red splotch she might even be beautiful. But would Michael think so?

Evidently he did, for his hazel eyes lighted at the sight of her. "Aye, Lass, you're a sight fur sore eyes, to be sure."

Jane's heart had hammered in her chest then as she grasped the sleeve of his dark frock coat. What they ate fur dinner Jane couldn't rightly remember. Still an all, the evenin had been downright wonderful. An by the time she an Michael had bade each other good–night, Jane's heart purt near sang fur joy. She was in love. Fur the second time in her life she had a mind to git married.

But with the passing of days, Jane's heartbeat returned to normal and she chided herself for counting her chickens before they'd hatched. Cause Michael hadn't paid her no special attention since thet night. And now, as she sat watching him doze, she wondered if this love too would remain one–sided. Would she jist have to mosey along through the days an months an years only to have Michael die off like Robert Saylor had done? Land sakes, jist the thought of thet ahappinin was depressin. Still an all—

As though he knew she'd been watching him, Michael stirred and opened his eyes. His moon–shaped face looked flushed in the firelight. Yawning, he spoke contritely. "Aye, Lass, I'm a bit sleepy this evenin. Not proper company, to be sure."

"Well, I don't blame you none. Why land sakes, there ain't nothin wrong with restin," Jane snipped a thread as she spoke. "Leastwise not when you work downright hard all day."

"Aye, Lass, thet I do. You makin somethin fur the wee lad?" He gestured toward the cloth in Jane's lap.

Jane nodded. "A shirt fur church goin. Why land sakes, thet youngin takes to church like a duck takes to water. Jist loves them songs an things. Course he won't always cotton to sittin with us women folks. Too bad his pa don't go no more. Course a grandpa would be purt near as good."

Michael sighed. "Aye, Lass, you know how I feel about church goin. I'll teach the lad about the Good Book an about lovin folks, but I ain't goin to church. Jist cause I went to thet fancy dinner don't mean I take to religion. Meself, I'm thinkin God likes me well enough."

"Land sakes, course he does. He ain't uppity like us humans is. Still an all, I cotton to church goin. I guess I always will. Course I was bein downright impudent to talk to you thet away. Please—"

"Aye, Lass, no harm done. I know you're jist carin like. Meself, I take to folks like thet." He paused, then continued softly. "Aye, Jane, you're a bonny one, to be sure."

Unnerved by the compliment, Jane stitched faster. And stuck her finger. "Ouch!" She sucked it quickly lest the blood stain the fabric.

Michael chuckled. "Aye, Lass, you needn't hurry. Meself, I'm thinkin you're a right fine woman." His voice took on a tender note then. "Aye, Jane, would you be thinkin on maybe marryin up with me?"

For once Jane was speechless. And her heart was hammering so hard she could scarcely get her breath.

"Aye, Lass, you needn't answer now. There's time, to be sure."

Jane laid down her sewing. "I— Oh my, yes. Course I'll marry you. Providin its soon."

Michael studied her a moment, a frown creasing his brow. "Aye, Lass, you bein sure?"

"Sure? Course I'm sure. Why land sakes, Man, I love you."

Michael smiled then, his eyes moist. Rising from his rocker, he crossed to where Jane sat. "Aye, Jane, it's settled then."

Jane, her heart pounding, took his proffered hand and rose to her feet. Letting the half finished shirt fall to the floor, she gazed into Michael's kind face.

"Aye, Lass, like I said, you're a bonny one." And he lightly brushed the birthmark on her left cheek with his full, sensitive lips.

Chapter 54

The day was chilly and damp. Not the frigid cold that accompanied most winters, yet cool enough for Livingston's joints to ache. Especially those in his fingers.

Laying aside his staining rag, the elder Lewis hobbled across the shop to the woodbox. Bending, he seized several sticks of wood. Then flexing the fingers of his right hand, he managed to grasp the handle on the door to the stove and pull. Dumping the wood inside, he shoved the door closed and trudged back to the finishing table. Again, he flexed his fingers. Lord, they hurt.

Biting hard on his Havana, he retrieved his rag and continued staining a spindle. Mr. Smith would be calling for his chair tomorrow and it must be ready. Even so, he couldn't hurry. For those swollen stubs attached to his equally swollen hands were a far cry from the nimble fingers which had once served him so well.

Glancing down the table to where Daniel stained the seat, Livingston groaned. Lord, but he wished that boy wasn't so withdrawn. It made him sad, more sad than he could say, to see his son oblivious to all but the wood before him. And for that matter, angry too. Of course Daniel was hurting. He'd lost a good friend. Even so, it would seem that he could at least pay attention to those about him. But except for an occasional grip on the piece he was finishing, his son gave no sign he had any feelings at all. Ah well, at least he'd stayed away from the saloon this time. Come to think of it, he hadn't brought home any bourbon either. All things considered, Livingston supposed the present situation was the best he could hope for.

Puffing heavily on his Havana, he sighed. He had to admit that Harvey Fudd had been good for Daniel. Even so, the boy should not have cared so much. Loving like that wasn't worth the grief it inevitably caused. Personally, he'd known that for over forty years. He'd known since the day his little sister, Nettie, was stampeded by cattle that the cost of love was too high. And it made him sad, more sad than he could say, that Daniel hadn't learned that lesson.

Ah well, he couldn't live his son's life for him. The man of thirty five was a far cry from the boy of fourteen. If Daniel hadn't learned to guard his heart by now, he probably never would. Even so, it pained Livingston to watch the younger man suffer. Never a heavy person, Daniel had become rail thin during the past few weeks. His face too, seemed slimmer. And haggard. It made him sad, more sad than he could say, to see those cheek bones jutting like Virginia hills while the flesh beneath his beard seemed daily to melt away. Only his hands remained unaffected. Those slender, sensitive fingers touched wood with the same gentleness they always had. Wood had become Daniel's world. Except of course, for those scraps in the box by the stove.

Biting hard on his Havana, Livingston waited. He waited for Daniel to glance up, to indicate he felt the shop growing cool. But Daniel, rubbing pecan stain into the smoothly sanded chair seat, worked as though he was alone.

With a groan, Livingston finally disengaged his fingers from his own staining rag and shuffled once more to the woodbox.

❖   ❖   ❖

It was Sunday. And so mild that Daniel had opened his bedroom window. He stood before it now, watching as worshipers gathered at the church next door. Not for the first time, he wondered if religion held any hope for those who took it seriously. No doubt his grandfather had found comfort in his beliefs. Yet, his father despised church, pure and simple. Harvey believed in God. Yet, he'd died thinking he had no right to love.

Remembering his kind old friend, Daniel felt the familiar band tighten about his chest. He'd loved that man, pure and simple. He'd loved him more than he'd loved anyone since his little sister, Joy, had strangled on sawdust. Even Mamie, with her green eyes and feline ways, had not claimed his heart the way Harvey had. For Harvey had given love as freely as a child. And it had given him pleasure, pure pleasure, just to be around the man. Only now, he was gone.

Running his fingers over the window sill, Daniel stifled the urge to cry. He simply *couldn't* give way to his feelings. He must keep the armor about his heart intact. For if he allowed his battered ego room to breathe, he'd go straight to drink. And he couldn't afford such luxury. Not this time. For his father was no longer capable of running the shop alone. He had to stay sober, pure and simple. Yet, at times he felt he'd die for lack of space. He needed room. Room to move, to think, to *feel*. Room to agonize, to weep, to bleed. Room to love.

And those people down below. As they moved from a noisy world into the quiet of God's sanctuary, did they struggle on the inside as he did? Will Chapman, for instance. Beneath that proud exterior, did he still mourn the loss of his father at the hands of Secessionists? And Minnie Chapman. Did she cry in the night for the companionship of her only daughter who'd moved away? And Thane, with his Spanish wife, Linda. Did they give themselves wholly to each other? Or did one or both of them build a cage about the heart? Did loving have the power to lacerate the soul, even in marriage?

And Miss Douglas. Was she really prepared to open her life to her former brother–in–law? Or would loving a man, even one as kind as Michael Fitzsimmons, prove too costly? There was Katie too, smiling at the youngster who held her hand. She loved that chap, pure and simple. Did that mean she was prepared to watch him go away later on?

Suddenly, as the last worshiper slipped inside the door, Daniel decided to join them. He needed strength, pure and simple. Strength enough to endure the pain of a heart lacerated by the lash of love. Strength to break through the barriers which encased his emotions. Strength to care again for another human being.

❖   ❖   ❖

Inside the small frame church, Daniel slipped into the back pew on the west side of the aisle. Apart from the others, he sat with head bowed, eyes closed. The truth was he couldn't bear to watch the faces of those who sang with such assurance.

> *What a friend we have in Jesus, All our sins and griefs to*
> *bear!*[1]

Suddenly, Daniel is weeping. Silent sobs shake his thin frame as tears trickle through his fingers, splashing onto the wooden floor. God, can it really be true? Is there really someone who can understand his grief of losing a best friend? Or will this feeling all blow over once the service is ended?

> *...but this one thing I do, forgetting those things which are*
> *behind, and reaching forth unto those things which are*
> *before...*[2]

It is agony, pure agony, to think on these words. Yet, he must. For in that instant Daniel knows he must forget Harvey, pure and simple. Not the Harvey who traded walnuts for peppermint sticks or the one who fed fagots to an already glowing fire. No, that Harvey will remain in some corner of his heart forever. It's the Harvey who betrayed him that he must forget. The one who took himself away. But how? How can he wipe from memory that frozen figure dangling from the branch of a pin oak tree? How can he ease the tightness in his chest so that he can feel again?

"Sir."

Daniel looks up to see a deacon standing at the end of his pew. Noting the proffered plate of bread fragments, Daniel hesitates. God. Does he really believe?

Take, eat: this is my body, which is broken for you...[3]

With trembling fingers, Daniel grasps a few crumbs and places them on his tongue.

The deacon offers the cup then. Taking it, Daniel notes it is nearly empty; the others have partaken.

This cup is the new testament in my blood... [4]

Touching the glass to his lips, Daniel throws back his head and drains the contents. Returning it to the deacon, he smiles. For in that moment the band about his chest begins to loosen. Slowly, he inhales, filling his heart with the essence of God. And with that Being comes a surge of strength. Strength to endure the pain of separation. Strength to reach out and love again.

Chapter 55

Inside Smith & Ferguson's Hall, Katie stroked the volume of poems in her hand and wished that Bonnie was here. Why my goodness, she didn't know none of them folks sittin behind thet long table over there. Course she saw Mrs. Brewster at church every week. An Mr. Gordon. Still, they wasn't friends like. Purt nigh strangers, they was. Yet, seein as how she'd a mind to attend this meetin, she reckoned she'd best find a seat.

Slipping between the rows of wooden chairs, Katie took a seat near the middle. Within minutes the room was half filled, making her feel better. She wasn't alone in thinkin a library association would be somethin special like, after all. She—

"Oh, *prima* Katie, it is good to come, *si?*"

It was Linda, flouncing into the seat beside her, her dark eyes snapping with excitement.

Clutching her book to her bosom, Katie forced a smile. "Course it's good to be here. Books an learnin are somethin special like. I—"

Katie paused, biting her lip. For there, seating himself on the other side of Linda was her husband, his chestnut curls looking almost amber beneath the glow of lantern light.

"Hello, Katie." Thane smiled briefly, then turned to greet Daniel Lewis who was joining them.

Thane. Katie stretched her hand for a moment as though to capture that lopsided grin. As though she could somehow coax from those full lips the words she longed to hear.

Rise up, my love, my fair one, and come away.
For, lo, the winter is past, the rain is over and gone;
The flowers— [1]

243

"Oh, stop it!"

Katie didn't realize she'd spoken aloud until Linda turned to her.

"*Prima* Katie, you all right?"

"Course, I'm all right," Katie snapped. She clutched her book close once more, pressing it to her heart. Fur this book was somethin special like. It was the one her best friend had slipped beneath the grille in the old post office the Christmas when she was twelve years old.

Oh Bonnie, why did you have to go away fur, anyways? Why couldn't you jist stay here? Drat it all, I need you somethin awful like. Really an truly I do.

"*Prima* Katie?"

It was Linda again, reminding her it was time for the meeting to start.

Katie, forcing her mind to the present, paid attention then as a temporary chairman stood to his feet.

"U–hum. Welcome to each of you who've come this evening. Tonight we will be electing officers and adopting a constitution for the Brownsville Library Association. U–hum. Our regular meeting time has been set for the third Friday of the month at 7:00 p.m. Our purpose is to cultivate an appreciation for the arts and for education in general. We will be featuring such things as debates, lectures, essays, concerts, and readings. U–hum. We will now consider ourselves in business session."

Ninety minutes later, upon adjournment, Katie followed Linda to the cloakroom.

"My goodness, thet was wonderful. Don't you think so?"

"*Si*" Linda located her red shawl among the other wraps. "You come alone, *prima* Katie?"

"Course not," Katie snapped. "Thomas saw me here. He'll be back to take me home."

But Thomas didn't return. Finally, after twenty minutes of waiting, Katie knew she'd have to go alone. Drat it all, she should have gone with Thane an Linda like they asked her to. Now she'd jist—

"Miss Katie?" It was Daniel Lewis smiling down at her, his hat in his hands. "Do you need an escort home?"

Chagrined, Katie nodded. "I reckon thet Thomas ain't comin after all. There's jist no accountin fur thet man these days. Sorry to put you out this way."

"Think nothing of it," Daniel put his hat on then, and picked up his lantern.

Outside, a mild breeze cooled Katie's burning cheeks. Drat it all, she'd a mind to light into Thomas good when she got home. She didn't take to bein left to fend fur herself this way. In her whole life she reckoned she'd never been so ashamed. What must Daniel think of her, anyways?

But Daniel apparently wasn't thinking of her at all. He spoke quietly of the meeting they'd just left. "Personally, I enjoyed it," he said.

"Me too," Katie agreed. "An thet next one is bound to be somethin special like."

"No doubt it will be. What do you think of the idea?"

"Thet education should be mandatory?"

Daniel nodded.

"Why my goodness, yes. Everyone needs learnin. Course I only had a tad myself, seein as how My Ma needed me at home. I was purt nigh done in like, havin to quit thet way. I jist love them words an how they can make you see an feel, even hear things like. I reckon I could spend hours thinkin on them."

"No doubt you could. The truth is, I could too."

"Why my goodness, thet's wonderful!" Without thinking, Katie reached out and touched Daniel's coat sleeve. Then hastily withdrew. "I— I don't mean to take on so. Still, I love them poems. An—an I'm hopin Benjamin will too."

"He's the young chap, isn't he?"

Katie nodded. "He's Thomas' youngin. But I reckon I'll be carin fur him. Thomas don't take to him none."

"I'm sad to hear that. I liked him, pure and simple."

"He is somethin special like," Katie agreed.

They walked in silence then, passing Daniel's shop on Main Street.

"I reckon your work is somethin special like too," Katie said. "Leastwise My Pa thinks it is."

"I'm glad to hear that," Daniel said. "The truth is, I get pleasure, pure pleasure, in taking a plain piece of wood and making something useful out of it. But I'm afraid there's hard times ahead."

"Hard times?"

Daniel nodded, tapping his fingers on the side of his coat. "My father's failing," he said simply.

"Oh my goodness, thet sounds awful like."

"It is. In the first place, he suffers so—" Daniel swallowed hard, clenching his fist. "No doubt he'll have to quit work. I—I wish he had a wife. Someone to care for him."

"I reckon thet would be nice. You know My Pa an Aunt Jane is fixin to marry?"

Daniel nodded. "I—I guess most people need someone to love, pure and simple."

At this, Katie pulled her cloak more firmly about her. Drat it all, would she *never* furgit Thane? Why, even now she could see them deep blue eyes as they looked at her this evenin. Full of love they was, before he'd turned away. An it made her come all apart like, knowin he married Linda instead of her.

"Miss Katie? You're awfully quiet. Did I say something wrong?"

Katie shook her head. "No. It's jist thet—thet lovin hurts somethin awful like."

"I *know*."

The words came out with such force that Katie started. Drat it all, what was the matter with her, anyways? Course Daniel hadn't never got over what thet Mamie done to him. An then losin his best friend an all. Why—

"Oh my goodness, I'm sorry. Really an truly I am. I reckon I furgot about—about Mr. Fudd. You must be hurtin somethin awful like."

"I was. Actually, I'm better now."

"Thet's good."

They were nearing the Fitzsimmons' house now and both fell silent. At the front door, Daniel lifted his hat. "It's been a pleasure, Miss Katie. Would you like for me to call before the next meeting?"

"Oh my goodness. Why, yes. Yes, thet would be somethin special like. An thanks fur this evenin too. Good night, now."

"Good night." Daniel replaced his hat then and strode back along Main Street, the glow of his lantern bobbing in the darkness.

Chapter 56

It was snowing. Flakes fell thickly through the darkness, creating a curtain between Katie's bedroom window and the maple tree across the way. Wrapping her arms about her robe–clad body, Katie sighed. Drat it all, why did it have to snow fur, anyways? It was jist plain silly fur it to be snowin like this in March. Anyways, thet cold white stuff comin on top the weddin made her feel all done in like.

My Pa an Aunt Jane. It didn't make no sense to her. Course she loved them both, but marriage at their age seemed jist plain silly. Why my goodness, they was *old*. Still, they seemed happy enough. Really an truly they did. Why, My Pa had actually beamed when he said them vows. An Aunt Jane had looked all sparkly like when they'd joined hands.

> *Forasmuch as you, Michael, and you, Jane, have covenanted together in the presence of God, and of this company, to live together in holy marriage and have pledged the same... I declare you to be husband and wife...*[1]

Katie bit her lip as the snow continued to fall beyond the window. Drat it all, why was she always attendin someone *else's* weddin? Why did she have to be an old maid fur, anyways?

> *Rise up, my love, my fair one, and come away.*
> *For, lo, the winter is past—*[2]

Katie put her fingers in her ears, and closed her eyes. Maybe this way she could shut out the sound of Thane's voice an the sight of thet snow. Maybe she could pretend thet Thane still loved her, an thet the grass was greenin. Maybe—

Drat it all, she wished Bonnie was here. Fur Bonnie always could

247

make things seem a tad better like. But Bonnie, like Thane, had left her.
She'd simply got on thet train an rode off in the darkness, leavin Katie
alone. Course she did write letters. An they helped. Really an truly they did.
Cept fur when she mentioned Thane. Why my goodness, thet one last week
had been real newsy like, until thet part at the end.

> *Like I told you, Katie, Sedalia is a right nice town.*
> *Course it is a good bit bigger than Brownsville. Why, I*
> *have to ride in a carriage purt near everywhere I go. But*
> *it's worth it. Specially fur church goin. Why, in all my life*
> *I ain't never been so glad fur anything as I am thet*
> *church. Them folks take to us right nice like. Fact is,*
> *they're mostly what keeps me goin.*
>
> *Oh, Katie, sometimes I miss home so much I could*
> *die. I'm not near as happy as Randall. Course his family's*
> *all gone. I'll bet never knowin his ma made him more*
> *independent like. Losin his pa in thet war was right bad*
> *too. Anyways, he seems right happy here even if he is*
> *busier than a bee. Why, I thought to have him home more*
> *often. Stead he's workin, workin, workin. In all my life I*
> *never knowed a daily paper could be so much work. Oh*
> *fur cryin out loud, I sound like a regular sob sister.*
> *Course it's right nice here.*
>
> *David loves it. He specially likes thet big clock*
> *standin on Ohio Street. Purt near every day he begs his*
> *pa to see "thet clock thet's this big". (He always makes a*
> *right big circle with his arms.) An at least once a week*
> *Randall puts him in the carriage an takes him off fur the*
> *mornin. In all your life did you ever hear of such a thing?*
> *Why fur cryin out loud, he'll spoil thet youngin right bad.*
>
> *Course I thought to have another youngin by now.*
> *Another baby to hold. It'd be right nice to have a little*
> *girl. But, oh my, I don't guess I'll ever have a youngin*
> *thet favors the Chapmans more than David does. Cept fur*
> *them lighter curls, he's the spittin image of Thane. Them*
> *big blue eyes an wide shoulders. An thet special lopsided*
> *grin. In all your life you never saw such a handsome*
> *youngin. Course he don't act like Thane...*

Katie hugged herself tighter. Course thet three–year–old didn't act
like Thane. Why my goodness, thet boy was always movin an talkin. Thane

was more quiet like. A tad bashful, even. But kind. Them deep blue eyes was never boastful or scornful or rude. An thet mellow voice was never churlish or surly or crude. Why, Thane was jist plain good to everyone. Cept her.

Two giant tears trickled down Katie's cheeks as she rose from the window and blew out the lamp. Padding across the room, she removed her robe and slipped between the feather ticks. Outside, it was still snowing.

❖   ❖   ❖

By the light of a coal oil lamp, Jane and Michael sat at the kitchen table drinking tea. That is, Michael was drinking. Jane just kept stirring hers. Round and round she moved the spoon, the metal making an occasional clink as it touched the sides of the cup. It was her wedding night and Jane was nervous. Why land sakes, she'd never been with a man before. An she was downright scared. How was she supposed to act, anyways? What if Michael changed his mind, decided she didn't amount to much after all? What if—

"Aye, Lass, you ain't bein sorry are you?" Michael spoke as he laced his second cup of tea with whiskey.

"Land sakes, no. Course I ain't sorry. I jist—"

Michael smiled. "I'm thinkin you're a wee bit scared. Tis normal, to be sure. Only you needn't be. I won't hurt you, mind."

"Why land sakes, I should hope not."

At this Michael chuckled, his moon shaped face looking friendly in the glow of lamp light.

"Aye, Lass, you're a plucky one, to be sure. Run along now, an dress fur bed. I've a mind to have some more of thet apple pie before I turn in."

"Thanks." Breathing a sigh of relief, Jane slipped from her chair and scurried to the bedroom.

It seemed strange to be in Michael's room. Course she'd been in here before. Still an all, this was different. This time the room was partly hers. An the man who shared it was her husband.

Laying her specs on the bureau, she carefully removed her hat. Holding it, she glanced about the room. Why land sakes, she'd furgot to bring down a hat box. Well, she'd jist have to make do. Rummaging through the drawers of the bureau, she found some clean linen. Unfolding a pillowcase, she laid it over her hat. There—thet would keep the dust off till mornin.

With trembling fingers she unfastened the pearl buttons on her basque and slipped it off. Cream colored satin it was, an trimmed with lace. The skirt was satin too, with a short train an fringe trim. Laying both pieces across the rocking chair, she removed her petticoat and unlaced her corset. Slipping the latter off, she breathed a sigh of relief. Land sakes, it felt good to git thet tight thing off. Purt near squeezed the life out of her, it did. Slipping her new nightdress over her head, Jane buttoned it carefully. Only then did she remove her lace–trimmed drawers and stockings.

Thrusting her feet into slippers, Jane turned toward the mirror above the bureau. Removing the pins from her hair, she unbraided it and let it fall loosely about her shoulders. Brushing the brunette tresses, she smiled. Land sakes, except fur a few strands of gray, her hair looked like thet of a young woman. Downright purty it was, long an thick. Would Michael—

As though he'd heard her thoughts, Michael appeared in the doorway. Their eyes met in the mirror; his bright with desire, hers clouded with apprehension.

"Aye, Lass, you're a bonny one, to be sure." He turned then and began to unbutton his shirt.

As Jane continued brushing her hair, she watched her new husband remove his outer clothes and carefully hang them up. Then clad only in his small clothes, he climbed into bed. Pulling the covers to his waist, he watched her for some moments. At length, he spoke.

"Aye, Lass, you've brushed long enough, mind. Put the light out now, an come to bed."

At his words, Jane laid aside her hairbrush and reached for her lace–trimmed nightcap.

"Aye, Lass, I'm thinkin you won't need the cap."

Blushing, Jane let the article fall from her fingers onto the bureau, then carefully blew out the lamp. Groping her way to the bed, she stood for a moment watching the snow fall beyond the window.

"Land sakes, is it agoin to snow all night?"

"Aye, Lass, I reckon it might."

Jane removed her slippers then and shyly crept into bed. She had scarcely stretched out when Michael's arms were around her. Strong arms they was, yet his hands was gentle. Gentle as they stroked her hair, her face, her throat. Gentle as they lifted her nightdress to caress her breasts.

With a sigh of longing, Jane surrendered to his amorous advances. She returned his kisses, first diffidently, then eagerly. Land sakes, he was astirrin up feelins she'd never knowed she had. Good feelins they was, too.

Thus Jane received her husband with a heart full of love and a body suffused with longing. She received him as though she'd waited all her life for just this moment. Even so, she was nearly overwhelmed by the intensity of his passion. Why land sakes, he took her like he'd never knowed a woman before. Bellered like a bull, he did. And afterward, he buried his face in her hair, his thick shoulders heaving. He kissed her then, again and again and again.

"Mavoureen, oh my bonny mavoureen! Aye, Jane, I thank you. Indeed, I do."

Chapter 57

By the end of March the snow had finally stopped falling, leaving a good six inches on the ground. Yet, despite this accumulation, Katie was going out. Why my goodness, she couldn't let a tad of thet white stuff interfere with a library meetin. It was bad enough havin the last one canceled. Besides, she felt purt nigh done in from bein cooped up inside this house fur days. An with them newlyweds at thet.

Course Katie was happy for My Pa and Aunt Jane. Really an truly she was. Why my goodness, they loved each other somethin awful like. Fact was, in her whole life Katie reckoned she'd never saw My Pa so happy. Up early in the mornin's he was, whistlin while he shaved. An in the evenins his round face purt nigh glowed when he came in from the smithy an kissed Aunt Jane. An instead of nappin in his chair like usual after supper, he'd taken to holdin two–year–old Benjamin on his lap an tellin him stories about "a wee little lad who lived in a wee little house in a wee little town in Tennessee".

Aunt Jane too, seemed awful content like. Why my goodness, she looked purt nigh beautiful when My Pa touched her shoulder an called her "Mavoureen". An she stitched them dresses like it was playtime. In the dinin room she sewed on thet new machine My Pa had got her. Course Katie couldn't complain none. Why my goodness, she never had to cook at noon anymore. Fur Aunt Jane always stopped sewin in time to "cook dinner fur Michael".

Yet, despite the happiness emanating from My Pa and her aunt, Katie was disgruntled. Drat it all, why did other folks have all the luck, anyways? Course Mamie wasn't married either. But then Mamie didn't want to be. Katie reckoned Mamie wouldn't never love another man like she'd loved their brother, Patrick. An thet was silly. Jist plain silly. Cause thet War was over an done with. Still, there was no accountin fur Mamie's behavior these days. Why, jist the other day, she took on somethin awful when Aunt Jane insisted she wade through thet snow to the shop. Threw a regular fit she did, till Aunt Jane took her in hand.

"Why land sakes, girl with all them new shops openin up, we need ever bit of trade we can git. Now, scat!" And so Mamie had gone, whimpering all the way.

An now, as Katie opened the front door to admit Daniel, she wished thet Mamie had *stayed* at the shop. She didn't like the way Daniel deliberately avoided lookin toward the kitchen where Mamie performed her usual ritual of brushin her hair. She'd a mind to light into both of them fur makin things so awkward like. Still, Daniel had come fur *her*, so she'd jist make the best of it.

Outside, Katie lifted her skirt in an attempt to avoid the snow. But despite her best efforts, the hem was soon wet. Drat it all, an this was a nice dress too. Indigo it was, makin her eyes look all blue like. An now it was ruined.

"Do you suppose we'll have that discussion about education this evening?" Daniel asked, apparently oblivious to Katie's soggy skirts.

"Why my goodness, I hope so," Katie said. "Thet's what I'm goin fur."

But the discussion did not materialize. For fewer than ten people showed up at the hall. The president waited fifteen minutes past starting time, then rapped the gavel on the table. "Meeting dismissed for lack of a quorum."

"Well drat it all, I was lookin forward to this meetin." Digging her hands into her waist, Katie glared at the receding back of the president.

"Me too," Daniel agreed. "But I'm afraid this whole idea is going to blow over. Ah well, we needn't waste the entire evening. Personally, I'd like to read some poetry. How about you?"

"Why my goodness, yes. Thet sounds real special like."

"We'll go to my place then." And Daniel set off back south on Spring Street.

Inside the Lewis sitting room Katie immediately shed her wraps. Goodness, it was hot in here! An Daniel was addin *more* wood to the fire? Why, it was purt nigh as hot as the smithy in here already.

"I'll make some coffee and find some sweets to go with it," Daniel said as he disappeared into the kitchen.

Coffee? Katie felt purt nigh done in jist thinkin of somethin hot. Still, it was nice of Daniel to offer. Really an truly it was. Glancing across to where the elder Mr. Lewis sat in an overstuffed chair reading the newspaper, Katie sighed. Drat it all, what should she say to him, anyways? It was jist plain silly sittin here all quiet like. Still—

"Here we are." Daniel returned bearing a tray of coffee and a box of chocolates.

Chocolates? Katie stared at the confection Daniel held out to her. Why my goodness, she reckoned she'd never had any bought before. An thet purty lady on the box—

"The dishes were my mother's." Daniel spoke quietly as he stirred two spoonfuls of sugar into his own coffee before joining her on the sofa.

"Oh, they're lovely. Really an truly they are." And Katie sipped politely from a dainty cup edged with sunken scroll–work.

They sat in silence for a time then, until Daniel rose and went to the glass–enclosed bookcase. Pulling open a door, he selected a couple of volumes and returned to the sofa.

"Personally, I like Robert Browning. But I thought you might like this." And he handed her a volume simply labeled, *English Poetry*. Eagerly, Katie took the proffered book, her short fingers brushing his longer, slender ones. Opening it, she squealed in delight. "Oh my goodness, here's "Paul Revere's Ride". And without waiting any further she began chanting:

> *"Listen, my children, and you shall hear*
> *Of the midnight ride of Paul Revere,*
> *On the eighteenth of April, in Seventy five;*
> *Hardly a man is now alive*
> *Who remembers that famous day and year.*
> *He said to his friend, 'If the British march*
> *By land or sea from the town tonight,*
> *Hang a lantern aloft in the belfry arch*
> *Of the North Church tower as a signal light,— One, if by*
> *land, and two, if by sea;*
> *And I on the opposite side will be*
> *Ready to ride and spread the alarm*
> *Through every Middlesex village and farm... (Thus) booted*
> *and spurred, with a heavy stride On the opposite shore*
> *walked Paul Revere.*
> *Now he patted his horse's side,*

Now gazed at the landscape far and near,
Then, impetuous, stamped the earth,
And turned and tightened his saddle–girth;
But mostly he watched with eager search
The belfry–tower of the Old North Church....
And lo! as he looks, on the belfry's height
A glimmer, then a gleam of light!
He springs to the saddle, the bridle he turns,
But lingers and gazes, till full on his sight
A second lamp in the belfry burns!
And so through the night went his cry of alarm,
To every Middlesex village and farm,—
A cry of defiance and not of fear,...
The midnight message of Paul Revere."[1]

"Thet's beautiful. Don't you think so? Now, you read one."
Smiling, Daniel opened his book to a "Song from Pippa Passes."

"All service ranks the same with God:
If now, as formerly he trod
Paradise, his presence fills
Our earth, each only as God wills
Can work—God's puppets, best and worst,
Are we; there is no last nor first.
Say not 'a small event:' Why 'small'?
Costs it more pain than this, ye call
A 'great event', should come to pass,
Than that? Untwine me from the mass
Of deeds which make up life, one deed
Power shall fall short in or exceed!"[2]

Swallowing hard, Daniel closed the book.
Katie waited several moments before she quietly began—
"It was many and many a year ago,
In a kingdom by the sea
That a maiden there lived whom you may know
By the name of Annabel Lee..."[3]

For over an hour they read: Tennyson, Shakespeare, Shelley, Scott, Wordsworth, Byron and of course Browning. At last Katie stretched her arms, sighing happily.

"This has been such fun. Really an truly it has."
Daniel smiled. "I've enjoyed it too, pure and simple. We'll most

definitely have to do it again sometime."

Katie nodded. "Oh, thet would be wonderful, seein as how the library meetin is purt nigh done in like." She paused, then asked shyly, "Fur now, can I read jist *one* more poem? One sort of fittin like?"

At Daniel's nod, Katie read softly—

"The day is done, and the darkness
Falls from the wings of Night,
As a feather is wafted downward,
From an eagle in his flight.
I see the lights of the village
Gleam through the rain and the mist,
And a feeling of sadness comes o'er me
That my soul cannot resist...
Come, read to me some poem,
Some simple and heartfelt lay,
That shall soothe this restless feeling,
And banish the thoughts of day...
Read from the treasured volume
The poem of thy choice,
And lend to the rhyme of the poet
The beauty of thy voice.
And the night shall be filled with music,
And the cares, that infest the day
Shall fold their tents, like the Arabs,
And as silently steal away." [4]

❖   ❖   ❖

Livingston lay in his large bed trying desperately to sleep. But he couldn't. For despite the extra comforter an the hot bricks at his feet, he ached. Lord, but he ached. His swollen fingers and swollen knees fairly throbbed with pain. And his heart ached too. Imagine Daniel taking up with that younger Fitzsimmons girl. It made him sad, more sad than he could say.

Katie was a nice enough girl, he supposed. Even so, she was a far cry from the woman he'd envisioned for his son. Personally, he thought her too young. Why, she couldn't be much more than twenty. Surely Daniel knew that.

Ah well, what business of his was it if Daniel cared for someone who was inexperienced in life? None, he supposed. Even so, he shuddered at the possibility of Daniel getting hurt again. For kind, sensitive–natured Daniel seemed destined for hurt. That gut–wrenching kind that comes from caring for another. That soul–scathing kind that Livingston himself had endured when his sister, Nettie, was killed. And again when his mother died. And yet again when Verna Marie withdrew from his affections. It was this kind of suffering he vowed to avoid in the future. And it was this kind of suffering he longed to spare his son.

Chapter 58

Jeweled drops of water glistened on pale green leaves as Thomas stood surveying the damage from the previous day's storm. Lightning, hail and high winds had broken several branches from his apple trees. The one nearest the barn had lost a fair–sized limb. It lay pointing toward the hump of the root cellar, the blond wood of its split end a sharp contrast to the pea–green leaves and smoky–gray bark of its upper end.

The corners of Thomas' mouth turned downward as he puffed his corncob pipe. Darn it all, anyways. Why did the things he liked always seem to end up broken? Course he wasn't the only one hit by the storm, thet was fur certain. Word had it thet them winds had knocked down the smokestack out at Eagle Mills. Thomas shrugged. He didn't give a lick about thet mill. Not anymore.

It was the old mill thet housed his memories. Memories of whilin away time with Tevis an Melvin while Uriah waited on trade. Closing his eyes, he could still see Uriah, his swarthy face beaded with sweat as he lugged a twenty–pound sack of flour to the wagon of a customer. An he could still see the four of them meetin on evenins to chug corn liquor an stomp to ballads like "Joe Steiner".

The corners of Thomas' mouth turned down even further. Fur all thet, they'd split apart. Made a feller feel plumb empty inside seein thet abandoned mill at the end of the street. Made him choke up like, thinkin on Tevis lyin over there on Locust Street while Uriah an Melvin rode off with them James an Younger Boys. An him? He was nothin but a one–armed widower with a bastard son.

Pressing his left sleeve to his eyes, Thomas sighed. It was useless, jist plumb useless to care. Fur carin brought pain. An he didn't aim to hurt again. Ever. He'd jist as soon back off an be alone.

Sighing, Thomas picked up his saw and set to work on the branch.

Chapter 59

Daniel was lonely. In the weeks since he'd reopened his heart to love, he'd felt a growing need to have someone to care for. Not a woman, of course. He wasn't *that* needy. Not his father either. True, he felt closer to the older man than he ever had. But his father was ingrown, reticent, incapable of giving love. And he wanted someone to love; someone who would love him in return. Someone like Harvey Fudd. Curling his long slender fingers about a roughly sculptured chair leg, Daniel sighed. He missed Harvey, pure and simple. For Harvey accepted love as simply as a child, and gave it as eagerly in return.

A child. Why hadn't he thought of that in the first place? A child was most definitely what he needed. A child he could love as he'd loved his little sister, Joy, so many years ago. For that relationship had been pleasure, pure pleasure. Only he didn't know any curly–headed little girls. The only child he'd really noticed was that nephew of Katie's. A shy chap, no doubt. Even so, he seemed like a loving youngster. One capable of giving and receiving affection. But what would Katie think? For instance, would she assume him too forward in wanting to befriend Benjamin? Would she feel he had no right to the affections of a child not his own?

Ah well, there was only one way to find out, he supposed. Ask her. And he would, on Sunday after church.

❖   ❖   ❖

Daniel left the shop early, a spring in his step as he strode down Main Street toward the Fitzsimmons' house. A trainload of circus animals was due to arrive within the hour and he wanted Benjamin to see them.

He had no trouble getting the boy to accompany him, for every since late spring he and Benjamin had been friends. And now, as they stood on the depot platform, Daniel felt a warmth inside he hadn't felt in months. True, he enjoyed the sight of those golden cars lining the track for blocks. And he enjoyed the sights and sounds of several hundred animals being unloaded. Mostly though, he enjoyed Benjamin.

God, he loved that chap. Loved him, pure and simple. He loved the way he stood, a finger in his mouth, as he studied the parade of horses. Or the way his lips curved upward at the sight of baby monkeys. He seemed frightened though, as the cage door was opened to release an Indian elephant. Though he made no sound, Benjamin's blue eyes widened until they seemed to claim half his face, and he squeezed Daniel's index finger until the latter winced. Kneeling, Daniel placed his hands on the two–year–old's shoulders.

"It's all right, Son. That's an elephant, pure and simple. He's got floppy ears and a long trunk, but he can't hurt you. See, that man over there is herding him into that pretty wagon. There, he's locked in now."

Benjamin's eyes grew smaller then, but there was still a trace of fear in them as he looked back at Daniel. Without hesitation, Daniel scooped the boy into his arms. Standing, he smiled.

"Would you like a ride on my shoulders?" he asked.

Benjamin nodded. And his face broke into a grin as Daniel hoisted him above the crowd. They stood for some time then, Daniel grasping the ankles of the chap, while Benjamin tousled his hair in return. The sun had begun to set before they finally turned to leave. But when Daniel stooped to let Benjamin slide from his shoulders, the boy protested.

"No." And he shook his solemn, oval face, his straight brunette hair swishing.

But Daniel insisted. "Listen, Son, there's nothing to fear. You can hold my hand if you'd like."

Benjamin did like, for he clung to Daniel's fingers all the way home. And Daniel could still remember the grip of that small hand as he prepared for bed that evening. He loved that boy, pure and simple. Just as he would love his own son or daughter.

His son? God, what was he thinking of? For children of his own meant marriage. And he most definitely was not planning to marry. Swallowing hard, Daniel blew out the lamp. Try as he might, he could not think of marriage apart from Mamie. And thoughts of Mamie invariably led to heartbreak. It was torture, pure torture, to think of loving a woman again. Even so, he'd have to consider marriage if he wanted children of his own.

Ah well, he'd consider it further tomorrow. Just now what he needed most was sleep.

❖   ❖   ❖

Katie was excited. Pinning a straw hat over her crimped hair, she positively glowed. She was goin to the circus! Why my goodness, in her whole life she'd never been to one before. An now, she was goin. With Daniel Lewis, of all people. Course she reckoned she'd been an afterthought. It was Benjamin he really took to.

Her toilet completed, Katie skipped down the stairs just in time to open the front door for Daniel.

"Good evening, Miss Katie," Daniel removed his stove–pipe hat, then turned to Benjamin. "Hello, Son, I brought you something." And he reached into his pocket to remove a peppermint stick. Hunkering, he extended the red and white confection, his long fingers trembling.

Eagerly, Benjamin took the proffered candy, placed it between his baby teeth and chomped.

"Fur goodness sakes, youngin, not like thet. Suck it."

But Daniel stopped Katie from taking the sweet. "Leave the chap alone," he said. "He has a right to what he wants."

Thus Benjamin continued chomping even as Daniel placed him in the front seat of the surrey. He was still chomping when Daniel turned down the driveway to the Spring Grounds.

"Oh my goodness, did you ever see such a thing?" Katie pointed excitedly toward the Big Top.

Daniel smiled. "It is most definitely impressive."

Impressive for sure. And not just the size of the tent, but the crowd as well. Why my goodness, Katie reckoned half the town had turned out an all them highfalutin politicians as well. It was jist plain silly to think they'd git a seat. But they did. Close to the ring, even.

Sinking into a cushioned opera seat, Katie clapped her hands. This was wonderful! Really an truly it was. Specially them horses prancin about with ladies doin tricks on their backs. An camels. Why my goodness, Katie didn't reckon she'd ever seen one of them before. But there they was with Arabs ridin on their humps, wavin spears somethin crazy like. Next came the elephants, their huge gray bodies dwarfing the men who rode them.

"It's all right, Son. They won't hurt you."

Katie jerked her attention from the animals to see her nephew bury his face in Daniel's knees. Why my goodness, what was the matter with thet youngin, anyways? He was bound to git sticky on Daniel's houndstooth trousers since he'd had yet another peppermint stick.

Katie reached out to pull Benjamin away, when Daniel stopped her. Not by words this time, but by the look on his face. Tender. That was the only way to describe Daniel's countenance as he looked at the boy. And his sensitive fingers were gentle as he caressed Benjamin's head. Then bending his own dark head, Daniel spoke quietly. "Look, Son, the seals are playing ball."

Benjamin looked up then, a smile creasing his usually solemn face. "Ball." And he pointed to the rubber sphere the seal was balancing on his nose.

Daniel smiled, his heart in his face. And Katie, looking on, wondered how this normally quiet, self–contained man could care so much fur a youngin. But he did. He pulled Benjamin onto his lap and showed him how to crush a peanut shell. Benjamin's dark eyes sparkled then as he took the nut from Daniel's fingers.

Leaving the males to themselves, Katie turned her attention back to the ring where a lady prepared to walk the tightrope. Katie held her breath as the lady left the side and slowly made her way toward the center. Oh my goodness, she would fall! Yet, even as the performer continued taking steps, Katie admired her. If only she could traipse across a rope like thet. If only she had the gumption to try somethin darin like. It all looked so excitin. So rewardin. So fulfillin.

Benjamin was asleep by the time they returned home.

Tenderly, Daniel gave the boy to Katie who took him upstairs to bed. When she returned, Daniel was sitting in My Pa's rocker.

"Would you like some coffee in the parlor?" she asked.

Daniel shook his head. "I'm fine, thank you."

Katie sat in Aunt Jane's rocker then, realizing as she did so that both chairs had been made by Daniel. Nice they was, too. Why my goodness, she guessed there wasn't nothin more special then a golden oak rocker. Why—

"Miss Katie?"

Katie started at Daniel's voice. All serious like, it was.

"Yes?"

"I hope you enjoyed the evening. Personally, I had a good time."

"Oh my goodness, yes. Course I enjoyed it. Really an truly I did."

"Actually, I'm wondering how well you enjoy my company."

"Why my goodness, I think you're purt nigh special, seein as how you take to Benjamin an all."

"Am I special enough to act as a father to him?"

"Be his pa, you mean?"

Daniel nodded.

"If he takes to you, I reckon so."

"And you? Do you take to me enough to become my wife?"

"What?" Katie clasped her elbows with her hands as she stared at him.

Daniel flushed. "I'm sorry, Miss Katie, I had no right to ask that. But the truth is, I want to marry. I want children, pure and simple."

Katie bit her lip as she stared at the man in the other rocker. Old, he was. Leastwise he was lots older than her. An Thane. Katie's chin trembled. Drat it all, course she wanted children too. She wanted her own youngins somethin awful. But she wanted them to be Thane's. She wanted—

"Forgive me, Miss Katie. No doubt I was being selfish to ask you. But I just supposed that since you have no attachment—" His voice trailed off.

"Oh fur goodness sakes, stop bein sorry like. Course, I ain't got no attachment. But thet don't mean I'm up fur grabs."

The moment she'd said the words, Katie regretted them. Course Daniel was assumin too much. Still, he was kind. Really an truly he was. An he was bound to make some woman a good husband. So what if he didn't love her? She didn't love him neither. Still, they both wanted youngins. An they both loved readin them poems—

"I'm sorry I took on so, Daniel. After all, I wasn't fixin to marry soon. But I'll think on it. Really an truly I will."

"Thank you." Daniel relaxed then and stood to leave. At the door he quickly leaned down and brushed his lips across Katie's cheek. Then donning his hat, he went out.

Watching the tall figure climb into his surrey, Katie bit her lip. Drat it all, what kind of a kiss was thet supposed to be, anyways? Why my goodness, Thane always kissed her like he meant it. Made her feel somethin special like. Course Daniel didn't claim to love her. But then, Thane didn't neither. Not anymore.

Chapter 60

It was clear and cold this first evening of 1877. So cold, in fact, that despite the flames dancing in the fireplace, Jane shivered. Scooting her rocker closer to the blaze, she commenced hemming a skirt. Land sakes, she was busy. Sewin all day an half the night, she was. An thet new seamstress worked hard at the shop too. Still an all, they seemed downright slow. Why land sakes, she hadn't even started on Katie's trousseau.

Snipping a thread, Jane frowned. She had a mind thet somethin wasn't right about this comin weddin of Katie's. Even though purt near everything seemed in order, she reckoned it was a marriage of convenience. Fur Daniel's eyes didn't shine like they had when he'd come acourtin Mamie. An Katie? Why land sakes, thet girl was bein downright practical. No moonin around an whisperin poetry like she'd done when she cared fur Thane. An thet seemed shameful. Jist downright shameful. Fur a marriage without love was kinda like asmellin fresh–baked apple pie without atastin it. Fact was, Jane couldn't imagine not lovin Michael. Why land sakes, he was wonderful.

Looking up from her sewing, Jane smiled. Fur Michael was tellin thet youngin another one of them "wee" stories. This time it was about a "wee little man who toted bricks on his wee little back, to make a wee little courthouse fur a wee little town in Tennessee". Course thet was all about Rogersville, where Michael had growed up. Where Michael lost his pa, an found Andrew.

A knock on the door brought the story to a halt. Thet would be Daniel of course, comin to fetch Katie fur the dance. Comin to give Benjamin some candy too. Shyly, the boy slipped from his grandpa's knee and inched toward the doorway as Katie ushered Daniel inside. An then Daniel was asmilin an areachin inside his pocket fur a peppermint stick. Benjamin smiled in return as he chomped the sticky sweet.

Daniel turned his attention to Katie then, assisting her with her wrap. Settling the cape on her shoulders, he paused, gripping the fabric beneath his fingers. For several seconds he stood, his eyes riveted on something in the kitchen. Land sakes, what was he athinkin on, anyways? After all, thet kitchen was purt near dark—except fur thet lamp on the shelf near the washstand. The one Mamie burned while she brushed thet mop of hair.

Pushing her specs more firmly on her nose, Jane studied the tall man across the room. Land sakes, he was astandin mighty still. There, he was abreathin deep now an alookin back at Katie. And a tiny smile slit the beard on his face, making him seem almost handsome.

❖　　❖　　❖

Outside, Daniel stepped jauntily, swinging his lantern and chanting—

"The year's at the spring
And day's at the morn;
Morning's at seven;
The hill–side's dew–pearled;
The lark's on the wing;
The snail's on the thorn:
God's in his heaven—
All's right with the world![1]

He was free! He was free from the ghost of Mamie, pure and simple. God, it felt good. For the truth was, that until this evening he'd never really gotten her out of his system. That auburn hair and those emerald eyes had actually dug into his heart and stayed there. Now, it was different. For this evening as he stood in the Fitzsimmons' dining room, he had come face to face with the *real* Mamie. The Mamie whose eyes had locked with his. And in the slits of those green eyes he'd seen the soul of a suffering woman. He felt sorry for her, pure and simple. The kind of sorrow one feels for a neighbor or distant relative whose been badly hurt. But sympathy is not love. And that realization broke forever the cord with which she had bound him. He was free.

"The year's at the spring
And day's at the morn—"[2]

Abruptly, Daniel stopped. Chagrined, he turned to Katie. "Miss Katie, forgive me, please. I was behaving like a child, pure and simple. Actually, it's night instead of morning, and winter instead of spring. Though personally, I suppose God's still in his heaven."

"I reckon so," Katie conceded. "But I do think a new year is kinda like the mornin—all dewy an special like. Don't you?"

"Sure."

They resumed walking then, a pleasant silence falling between them.

"I sort of wonder what this new year will be like," Katie spoke as they crossed Main Street to Spring. "It's bound to be a tad excitin, us fixin to marry an all."

Daniel didn't answer. Personally, he was having second thoughts about the impending marriage. Though he most definitely wanted children, he felt he really had no right to claim Katie when love was missing. True, she had agreed to his proposal. Even so, he felt like a user, pure and simple.

At the hall, Daniel hung their wraps, then guided Katie onto the dance floor. Gliding to the music of Strauss' "Roses From the South", Katie looked up at him and smiled. Daniel returned the smile, noticing as he did so her even teeth and flawless complexion. Her skin was lovely, pure and simple. Actually, he'd never seen this much of it before. And what he saw, he liked. For Katie's silk dress featured a V neckline which barely covered her shoulders. Her arms were bare too, below lace–trimmed puffed sleeves. Personally, he liked pink and Katie most definitely looked good in it. And those cherry ribbons around her neck and in her hair merely accentuated the flush in her cheeks. A flush that suffused her face as she radiated warmth. Yet, when Daniel asked if she cared to rest awhile, Katie shook her head.

"Oh no, I'm not done in at all. I'm havin fun. Really an truly I am."

And Daniel was too. It was pleasure, pure pleasure, holding a woman in his arms. And Katie was a woman, pure and simple. For unlike the slender Mamie, she was full–figured. The swell of her ample breasts was clearly outlined by her form–fitting dress. And her cleavage was barely concealed by a layer of ruffled lace. He could feel the curve of her hips too, beneath his hand at her waistline, despite the whalebones in her corset. And the knowledge that she was to be his caused him to swallow hard. For in less than a year they would be married. Married? God, but—

"Ouch!"

Daniel stumbled then, only now realizing that his fingers had been gripping hers unmercifully tight.

"Oh, Miss Katie, I'm so sorry. I—"

"Oh fur goodness sakes, stop bein sorry. An please, stop callin me *Miss* Katie. Thet's jist plain silly, seein as how we're fixin to marry an all."

The exasperation in Katie's voice stung Daniel like a slap. And the sparks in her gray eyes told him she thought he was a dolt, pure and simple. No doubt he was. At least where women were concerned. For try as he might, Daniel couldn't seem to understand them. They were most definitely fickle. For instance, only an hour ago he could have sworn Katie liked him. Her eyes had actually looked blue as she smiled into his face. And now she scorned him, stiffening herself in his arms, pulling back from him as far as she could. Why was she like this when all he wanted was to be kind? To show her he appreciated her sensitive spirit, her caring heart? To show her he valued her person? To show her he loved—

No! Swallowing hard, Daniel wrenched his thoughts from Katie. Glancing about, he tried to concentrate on other things: the crowd gathering to sample eggnog, the young girl turning the pages of music for the pianist, the kaleidoscopic blend of brightly colored gowns and the subdued tones of pin–stripped trousers and cutaway coats.

"Ouch!"

This time Katie jerked her hand away and stalked from the dance floor.

For a moment Daniel simply stared after her, the band about his chest beginning to tighten. God, but he—

"Pardon me."

Chagrined to realize he stood in another couple's way, Daniel strode toward the cloak room. He had to get away. To think. To gain control of himself. He had to cage his feelings before he did something he'd regret. (Like smothering Katie's face with kisses.) But it was torture, pure torture, trying to assemble his armor again. For he'd come to value unrestricted emotion, the kind that allowed him to reach out, to touch, to care. The kind that allowed him to *feel*.

"Daniel?" It was Katie, concern written on her lovely face. "Are you all right?"

All right? Of course he wasn't all right. All right meant touching, kissing, loving. All right meant holding his arms out to Katie, gathering her close, whispering how much he cared. All right meant junking the armor and breathing free. All right meant—

"Daniel?"

As Katie stepped closer, Daniel snapped the breastplate into place. His fingers uncurled then as he reached for their wraps.

"Ah–yes, Katie, I'm fine. But I think we'd better go now."

Outside, Katie shivered. Without thinking, Daniel placed his arm about her shoulders. Instantly, he realized his mistake. Letting his arm fall back to his side, he winced. God, but he couldn't take this. Eventually, he'd have to declare himself to Katie. But not now. Not tonight. The feeling was too new. And the truth was, he was afraid of being hurt again. Of having his heart clawed to shreds, then flung bleeding into his face.

"Daniel?"

Chagrined, Daniel realized they'd arrived at Katie's doorstep. And Katie was waiting.

"Won't you come in fur coffee?"

"No. That is, thanks for asking, but not tonight." He tipped his hat then and left abruptly without bothering to kiss her or even say goodnight.

Chapter 61

It was another gloomy day in March, and Jane sighed as she hand stitched a bit of fringe on a waist for Katie. Land sakes, it rained enough nowadays to float Noah's ark. Well, at least it hadn't started yet this mornin. And Katie, hoping it would hold off a couple hours more, had taken Benjamin and gone to the shop to buy herself a summer hat.

Turning up the lamp, Jane thanked the good Lord for the reprieve from the rain and for the blessing of silence. Why even Thomas outside now, aharrowin the garden. Course he was disgruntled, fussin cause plantin was so late this year. But fact was, Thomas was purt near always a mite out of sorts about somethin. Had been ever since Julia passed on.

Snipping a thread, Jane sighed. She did worry about thet boy. Michael did too. Why land sakes, Michael was always aputtin himself out fur him. Tried downright hard he did, to show Thomas he cared. But Thomas didn't pay no mind. Jist went along quiet like, agiven his pa the cold shoulder. Still an all, Michael kept atryin. Why jist a few weeks ago, he had returned to the smithy to work after supper. An worked so late thet by the time he came in, Jane was already in bed.

"Michael?"

"Aye, Mavoureen, it's me."

Listening to her husband undress in the dark, Jane's heart beat faster.

"Awful late to be aworkin, ain't it?"

"Aye, it is, mind."

Jane felt the feather tick move as he climbed into bed beside her. Automatically, she lifted her head so he could slide his arm about her shoulders.

"Ain't you agittin a mite old to be aworkin so long?"

"Aye, Mavoureen, I am, to be sure." He sounded tired and the kiss he gave her was more perfunctory than passionate.

"Then what you adoin it fur, anyways? Why land sakes, what's so important it can't wait till mornin?"

"Thomas' plow. He'll be needin it soon, mind. An them blades was dull as ditch water."

Jane had stroked his bristly cheek then, her heart beating hard. It was fur things like this thet she loved him. Course Thomas never noticed. Why land sakes, he never even had the gumption to tell his pa thanks. An thet made Jane angry. Downright mad, she was. Purt near mad enough to grab him by the collar an shake him till he stopped bein so blamed selfish. Course she didn't. After all, Thomas was thirty–four years old now, an not to be treated like some youngin.

Sighing, Jane snipped a final thread. Holding the basque in front of her, she smiled. It was lovely. Jist the right shade of rose to bring out Katie's silky complexion.

Upstairs, she laid the garment on Katie's bed beside the matching under–skirt. There. Soon now thet child's trousseau would be done. She jist hoped thet Daniel had a wardrobe big enough fur all them clothes. An a heart big enough fur lovin Katie.

Turning from the clothes, Jane started back downstairs. Crossing Thomas' room, she glimpsed a bit of something white sticking out from a chest drawer. A streak of crimson ran along one edge. Land sakes, had thet boy hurt himself an not told no one?

Swiftly, Jane crossed the room and jerked open the drawer. She almost laughed in relief. Why, it was nothin but thet old Stars an Bars. Gazing at the thick bars and seven stars, Jane shook her head. Land sakes, she reckoned she'd never furgit the time Thomas brought thet flag home an smuggled it up here. Downright impudent he'd been, agoin behind his pa's back thet aways. Fur Michael had wanted to make amends, to furgit fightin an start lovin. But Thomas had a mind to keep thet War agoin. Leastwise it had seemed thet away at the time. But now—

Folding the rumpled flag, Jane started. For her fingers encountered something hard. Something cold and hard and ugly. Even before she saw it, she knew what it was. A gun. A Smith & Wesson Schofield .45 revolver. One of them kind thet outlawin Jesse James used. One of them kind thet had killed her brother, James.

Trembling, Jane hastily shoved the contents back inside the drawer and slammed it shut. But she couldn't seem to slam the door to her mind.

Thomas had murdered James. Why? What had given thet boy the gumption to do such a thing?

Julia. They both loved her. Leastwise Thomas did. Jane doubted her brother had really cared. James seemed a mind to love no one but himself. Why land sakes, he'd been ahurtin women fur a long time before he cottoned to Julia. Touching her birthmarked cheek, Jane felt again the terror she'd known that night so many years ago. 1843 it was, when James had stomped to the loft of their Missouri farm house and shouted at Claudia.

"You dirty nigger. You think you're right smart, don't you? Well, I'll have you know *someone's* goin to pay fur your pa killin mine. Someone's goin to pay an pay an pay."

He'd beat Claudia then and raped her. And the screams in her friend's soul had reached Jane as surely as if she'd shrieked them aloud.

Course Jane never believed old Adrian had murdered their pa. But James had sold him jist the same. An kept thet young Harry. Kept thet uppity young buck thet Jane never trusted. An years later, after James had sold out an gone West, Harry had raped Mrs. Lewis.

An James? James had stayed in California until a few years ago. But prosperity hadn't changed him a mite. He was still downright selfish. Enough to steal his nephew's woman an defile her. Turning from the drawer, Jane sighed. It purt near made sense now, why Thomas hated little Benjamin.

Descending the stairs at a snail's pace, Jane made up her mind. She'd tend her own business fur now, an never tell a soul what she'd found. Specially not Michael. Why land sakes, she loved thet man. Loved him so much she couldn't bear to break his heart by tellin him his son was a murderer.

Chapter 62

Katie trembled as she stood before the mirror in her bedroom on an afternoon in June. Biting her lip, she closed her eyes as Bonnie fastened a strand of pearls about her neck. Her weddin day. The day she was to marry Daniel Lewis. The day she had both looked forward to an dreaded.

"There, Katie, you look right nice now. Beautiful, in fact. Why, I'll bet Daniel will purt near bust with pride when he sees you." Bonnie gave a final pat to Katie's shoulder as she spoke.

Opening her eyes, Katie stared at her reflection. Why my goodness, she did look purty. Thet new princess–style gown Aunt Jane had stitched up was beautiful. Silver white it was, with layers of lace–trimmed ruffles extendin to a short train in back. Lace trimmed her off–the–shoulder neckline too, an edged the long sleeves which came to a point over her hands. An them rosettes. Made from the same satin as her gown, they'd been fashioned into a wreath an pinned atop her floor–length veil. A larger one rested at the V in her neckline. An them pearls. They was beautiful. Almost as beautiful as thet diamond ring which weighted her left hand. Daniel must be purt nigh broke after payin fur all thet. He really was somethin special like. If only—

"Fur cryin out loud, Katie, *smile*. After all, it's your weddin day. An I'll bet by this time next year you'll be expectin a youngin of your own."

Katie did smile then as she turned to face her friend. "Furgive me fur takin on so. Course I'm goin to have youngins of my own. Lots of them. Jist like you." And Katie reached a hand toward Bonnie.

Grasping the proffered hand between her own, Bonnie smiled. Yet tears glistened in her bright blue eyes as she said, "Oh, Katie, you're the best friend in the whole world. An I'm jist so happy I could die. Expectin another youngin has purt near made me go silly. Fact is, I'm hopin hard fur a little girl this time. Course another boy would be right nice too. Even if he is as lively as David."

And David *was* lively. For it was four–year old David Dalton who spoke first when Katie entered the parlor carrying her bouquet of pink roses.

"Wow, your Aunt Katie sure does look purty!" And he nudged Benjamin who sat on the sofa beside him.

Everyone laughed then. Except Katie. For Katie was biting hard on her lip to keep her chin from trembling. She dared not look at David. Why my goodness, thet curly–headed youngin was somethin wonderful. An thet lopsided grin of his could make her fall apart like inside. In her whole life Katie reckoned she'd never felt so done in as she did jist now. If only—

Shaking her head, Katie tried to rid her thoughts of Thane. Fur Daniel was standin by the preacher, waitin. An a different Daniel he was too. One she'd never seen before. Why my goodness, he looked purt nigh handsome in thet charcoal cutaway coat an them matchin trousers. An his cream–colored vest an snowy shirt sure did make thet dark tie stand out. But it was his face that brought Katie up short. For his long jawline and jutting chin were in plain view. Daniel had shaved! Cut thet beard right off he had, leavin only a thick, black mustache above his upper lip.

Daniel smiled then and Katie stopped trembling. Why my goodness, he did think she was purty. Fur them gray eyes said she was somethin extra special like. His voice said so too, when later he answered the preacher.

> "Daniel, will you seal your sacred troth by the giving of a
> ring in pledge that you will faithfully perform your
> vows?"
> "I will."
> "Katie, as a token and a pledge that you will faithfully
> perform your holy vows, will you so receive and wear this
> ring?"
> "I will." [1]

Katie's voice sounded hollow, even to herself. Why my goodness, what must Daniel think? But Daniel seemed aware of nothing more than their hands as he slipped the ring into place above the diamond. He gripped her fingers so hard then, she almost cried out.

> "And now may he who walked in intimate companionship
> with the first human pair...make your house a habitation
> of love and peace...Amen." [2]

With shaking fingers Daniel lifted her veil then and kissed her softly, much the way he usually kissed her good night. And just as gently, he took her hand and tucked it into the crook of his arm as they moved into the dining room. Here, Bonnie served up slices of frosted white cake while Aunt Jane poured tea and coffee.

Over the rim of her porcelain cup, Katie watched My Pa as he stirred whiskey into his tea. Seein as how his thick shoulders heaved, Katie left Daniel and went to him. Stretching a hand, she patted his coat sleeve. Instantly he smiled, his round face lighting with pleasure.

"Aye, Lass, you're a bonny bride, to be sure. An I reckon you could use somethin new." Setting aside his cup, he disappeared into the kitchen, returning with a foot–long wooden box. Placing it in Katie's hands, he spoke, his voice husky with emotion, " Aye, Lass, I'm thinkin you could use them in your new home."

Katie lifted the hinged lid then and gasped. "Oh, My Pa, they're lovely! Really an truly they are." For there in the box were kitchen utensils: a ladle, a pancake turner, a sieve, and a long–handled fork and spoon. Hers they was, an My Pa had made them. Fur the second time in her life My Pa had given her a gift from his smithy. A gift from his very own hands.

Laying the box on a corner of the table, Katie stretched her hands toward My Pa. He kissed her then and patted her head.

"Aye, Lass, take right good care of thet new husband, mind."

"I will," Katie promised. Then turned quickly to see if Daniel had overheard her answer. Why my goodness, she couldn't have him thinkin—

"Congratulations, Katie. You're lookin awful purty like, thet's fur certain." And Thomas kissed her briefly, his breath reeking of burley tobacco. "Makes a feller feel plumb old seein his little sister git hitched." He moved off quickly then, raising the cuff of his left sleeve to dab at his eyes.

Staring after him, Katie's heart seemed to come apart like. Fur Thomas was somethin wonderful. Really an truly he was. Leastwise he had been before thet stupid war. These days he seemed purt nigh an old man. Why, my goodness it was jist plain awful watchin him shrink up like. Seein them thin lips always turnin down. Seein him back off from folks he used to love. If only she could—

"Miss Katie?" Katie turned her attention then to Daniel's pa. He was standin there quiet like, smokin thet big cigar an studyin her like he couldn't rightly figure her out.

"The weddin was awful purty, don't you think so?"

Mr. Lewis nodded. "Ah yes, and you make a pretty bride. A mighty pretty bride. Just treat my Daniel right is all I ask. And I'll be glad. More glad than I can say."

"Why my goodness, course I'll treat Daniel right. Why, already I think he's somethin special like. Really an truly—" Katie's voice trailed off as Livingston turned and limped away. Hands on her hips, Katie glared after him. Drat it all, why did he have to spoil things fur, anyways? Jist cause she didn't love Daniel was no reason to think she'd be mean to him. After all—

"In–law troubles already?" Mamie's purr brought Katie around with a start.

"Drat it all, Mamie, what you fixin to do—ruin my weddin day?"

"My but you do carry on, don't you? What a shame, you lookin so purty an all." And Mamie stroked the crown of rosettes in Katie's hair.

But Katie wasn't in the mood for Mamie's underhanded ways. Before she could reply, however, Aunt Jane slipped an arm about her waist.

"Land sakes, child, you look a mite upset. An on your weddin day too. Smile now, fore your new husband flat out leaves you. There. Thet's better. Why land sakes, you look downright purty when you've a mind to. Fact is, you're purt near as special as if you was my own youngin."

Katie bit her lip then as she grasped the older woman's hand. "Furgive me, Aunt Jane. I reckon you're somethin special like yourself. An I thank you fur makin this dress. In my whole life I've never had one so nice. I love you. Really an truly I do."

"Thanks, Child." And Jane took Katie's face in her hands and kissed her.

"Aunt Katie?" It was Benjamin, tugging at her gown.

Looking down, she saw a chubby hand clutching a yellow peppermint stick. And dark eyes, asking what his lips couldn't manage to say. Kneeling, Katie placed her hands on his shoulders.

"My goodness, in all the excitement I purt nigh furgot you. But I don't aim to. You know thet, don't you?"

Benjamin nodded.

"Still, I—I have to leave now. Daniel—Daniel too. But I'll miss you somethin awful like. Course if you've a mind to you can come to my new house tomorrow."

"Uncle Daniel said I could." It was a statement, accompanied by a lick on the peppermint stick.

"An Uncle Daniel's right. Why my goodness, I reckon you're purt nigh my own youngin now." And Katie hugged her nephew to her breast.

She hugged Bonnie too, clinging to her friend.

"Oh, Bonnie, I wish you didn't have to go. I'm feelin purt nigh done in like already. Why, in my whole life I don't reckon I've needed you this bad. You're so helpful, an kind, an happy."

"Hush, Katie, or Daniel will hear. Jist cause you're not madly in love don't mean you can't have a right nice home. You know I'd have fixed things with— I mean, fixed your heart if I could. But I can't. Course I can pray fur you an love you. An maybe—maybe you'll have some youngins thet'll make you feel right good."

They clung to each other then until Katie finally pulled herself away and climbed into the front seat of Daniel's waiting surrey. Biting her lip and hugging herself, Katie closed her eyes. She must take herself in hand an furgit the past. She must furgit the home she was leavin with Aunt Jane an My Pa. She must furgit Thomas an Bonnie. An—she must furgit Thane.

"Katie, are you all right?" It was Daniel, concern rougheninng his voice.

"Course I'm all right. An jist where are you takin me to, anyways?"

"The Sweet Springs Hotel. I– Actually, I thought you'd enjoy a wedding supper there. Even so, if you'd rather not–"

"Course I want to go there. Why, my goodness, I ain't never been inside thet place. But I hear it's really somethin special like."

An special it was. Claret colored carpeting muffled their footsteps as they walked through the gas–lit parlor to the dining room. Here there were twenty round dining tables, each covered with a snowy linen cloth. Leading them to one in the corner, a white–coated waiter seated Katie in a plush, morocco chair. Seconds later, another waiter poured sparkling spring water into crystal goblets. Handing them each a menu, he spoke crisply. "May I suggest the fresh Blackwater trout?"

"Oh my goodness, that sounds wonderful."

They agreed then on the trout and an assortment of vegetables. "We'll have pastries later." And Daniel dismissed the waiter with a flick of his hand.

Once the waiter had disappeared, Katie glanced about nervously. Goodness, she'd never seen so many diners in one place before. Or so many gas lamps. Or dining chairs. Or candles. An she'd never seen a red napkin folded like the one before her. Looked like a pointed hat it did. Picking it up, she carefully unfolded it and spread it over her white satin skirt.

She looked up then, only to meet the eyes of her new husband. For Daniel, his hands folded beneath his chin, was studying her as though to memorize her features.

My goodness, I wish he wouldn't stare at me thet way. Why, it makes me feel all embarrassed like. Like I wasn't dressed right or somethin. Surreptitiously then, Katie's right hand stole to her neckline. Feeling the round smoothness of pearls, she smiled. *Good. Thet necklace was all right. Her veil too—*

Her veil! Katie panicked when her fingers failed to grasp the white tulle. *An thet crown of rosettes? Where was they? Mamie. Course thet selfish minx had taken them. Slipped them right off, she had, without Katie even knowin it. An now, she was sittin in this highfalutin place with nothin coverin her head. What must Daniel think of her, anyways?*

"You're beautiful." The words seemed to slip unintentionally from her husband's lips.

"What? Why, thet's jist plain silly. Look at me— Why, I ain''t even dressed right. An if Mamie was here I'd light right into her."

"Mamie?"

"Course, Mamie. *She* took my veil an rosettes. An now, I look somethin awful."

Daniel shook his head. "Personally, I like your hair that way. Those curls falling on your shoulders are lovely, pure and simple. And—" Daniel stopped, as though aware he'd said too much. He fussed with his napkin then, unfolding it on his lap.

Katie hugged herself and looked away, trying to focus on the piano sonata drifting in from the parlor. But music did little to calm her emotions. *Somethin awful was happenin; Daniel was actin different than he used to. More like—*

"Here we are." And a waiter set a platter of baked trout before Katie. Glad for the distraction, Katie took up a silver–plated fork and dug in. *Um. It was good.*

An hour later, Katie pushed aside her plate and groaned. *Goodness, she'd eaten like a pig. Carrots, string beans, hot breads, cherry pie—an all of it yummy.*

But Daniel had saved the best for last. Pouring champagne into long–stemmed glasses, he handed her one. "To us," he said and drank his down.

Katie sipped hers, grimacing as she did so. *Why my goodness, this stuff tasted sour like.* Still, she finished it before the waiter brought out finger bowls.

Outside, the sun was sinking behind the oak trees, casting gems of amber and vermilion on the clear Blackwater River. Taking Katie's arm, Daniel guided her to the Pagoda. Seated on a marble bench, Katie noted recent changes in the structure. Purty it was, with them stained–glass windows at the top an them marble fountains from which bubbled thet spring water.

"Care to dance?" Daniel touched her arm as a nearby orchestra drifted into the "Blue Danube".

"No. No thanks. Not this evenin." And she turned to study the sunset. But eventually the sunset gave way to dusk and Katie knew she must go.

> *Rise up, my love, my fair one,*
> *and come away...*[3]

"Drat it all, stop thet!"

"Katie, are you all right?"

"Course I'm all right." And Katie strode from the Pagoda, leaving a bewildered Daniel to follow.

❖   ❖   ❖

In Daniel's living quarters, Katie glanced nervously about the sitting room. Was thet bedroom jist beyond the stove hers?

As though he'd heard her unspoken question, Daniel took Katie's hand and led her to the bedroom.

"This used to be my parent's room," Daniel spoke matter–of–factly as he lit a lamp on the candlestand.

"My goodness, it's purty. Really an truly it is. An I love this bureau." Katie reached to touch the elaborately carved walnut wood which surrounded the rectangular mirror. "It's all like fruit an leaves an things."

"My father made the set for my mother, shortly after we came to Missouri. And—and I made this for you." He gestured toward a walnut chest which stood at the foot of the bed.

"Oh my goodness, a blanket chest!" Kneeling, Katie ran her hand over the satiny smooth surface. Then slowly, she raised the lid and smiled. For the spicy fragrance of fresh cedar rose to meet her. "It's beautiful. Really an truly it is. I—I don't know how to thank you." She looked up at him then and was immediately embarrassed. For Daniel was blushing. Purt nigh red his face was, like he didn't know what to say.

Chagrined, Katie rose and closed the lid. "Tomorrow I'll unpack my trunks an fill up this purty chest."

"No doubt you will. The truth is, it was pleasure, pure pleasure making it. Oh, and uh—I have something else for you too." Daniel pulled out a bureau drawer then and removed a white box. "I—I hope you like this." His fingers trembled as he extended it to her.

"Why my goodness, course I will. Only—" But Daniel was gone. Disappeared into the sittin room he had, closin the door behind him.

Mystified, Katie pulled the lid from the box. And there, gleaming up at her was a silk nightdress. Pale pink it was, with lots of lace trim an ribbons to tie beneath her breasts. It was beautiful. Really an truly it was. Why my goodness, she'd never had no clothes cept what Aunt Jane made before.

Twenty minutes later, Katie stood before the dressing glass gazing at her reflection. Almost purty she was, in her new nightdress. And her thick, brunette hair still held the suggestion of curl despite the vigorous brushing she'd given it.

Laying aside the brush, Katie studied the rings on her left hand. Should she take them off? After all, thet birthstone one was heavy like. Course Daniel—Drat it all, I ain't Daniel's slave. And Katie jerked off both rings and plunked them on the marble top of the bureau. She'd put them away tomorrow in her little K box. Jist now—

Katie paused, staring at the rings which glittered beneath the lamp light. Why my goodness, there was somethin written inside thet weddin one. A message like. Picking up the gold band, Katie leaned closer to the lamp.

Silence and passion, joy and peace...[4]

It was Browning, of course. But why had Daniel put it there fur, anyways? Unless—No! Love wasn't no part of this here marriage. They'd agreed to thet right off like. Still, them words sounded like lovin to her. Course *she* didn't have to love. An she didn't have to think about them words neither.

Hastily, Katie shoved the wedding ring back on her finger. There. She'd wear it after all. Leastwise thet was better than readin them words ever day. Why, it was jist plain silly–

A knock on the door caused Katie to start.

"C—come in."

Daniel entered then, minus his coat, vest, and tie. Closing the door behind him, he crossed the room to Katie.

"Daniel, I—I— Thank you fur the nightdress."

For a long moment Daniel said nothing. Then huskily, he spoke. "Katie, you're beautiful, pure and simple." He lapsed into silence again as his slender fingers began to caress her face. Gently, he stroked her forehead and cheeks. Tenderly, he touched her nose and traced the line from her jaw to her rounded chin. And then those fingers were pressing her lips.

Katie trembled. Drat it all, he *said* we weren't lovin each other. But thet's what he was doin. Lovin her. With them gentle hands an dark eyes. An it wasn't fair. It jist wasn't fair. Not when she cared fur—

Daniel dropped his hand then and spoke brusquely. "It's time to put out the light."

Without a word, Katie scrambled into the huge bed, the cotton sheets feeling cool to her skin. Daniel extinguished the light then and moments later slipped into bed beside her. Without a word he reached out and pulled her to him.

Katie stiffened. Why my goodness, he was naked. Hot too.

"Katie?"

"Yes."

"The truth is, I care for you, pure and simple. I'll most definitely be gentle. Even so, it may hurt. Please, tell me if it's too much and I'll stop."

But Katie said nothing. She couldn't. Why my goodness, she reckoned she'd never been this scared in her whole life before. And then Daniel was kissing her. Gentle like, then harder. An then he was whisperin her name an touchin her breasts. He, *Daniel*, was lovin her. Not Thane.

Afterward, she cried. Giant tears rolled down her cheeks as she struggled to suppress her sobs. Drat it all, she didn't love this man. Why had she married him fur, anyways? Why—

"Katie? God, if I've hurt you—" And he stroked her tear–streaked cheeks as gently as if she was a child.

"It's—it's all right. Really an truly it is."

Only, it wasn't. Katie knew it wasn't. And as Daniel sighed and turned away from her, Katie sensed that he knew too. And was disappointed.

Chapter 63

The afternoon was more than a little warm. Yet, Daniel was thankful for the heat. For his father most definitely functioned better in warm weather. Even so, Daniel could tell by the way the older man bit down on his Havana that he was in pain. Yet, the glow in his hazel eyes and the reverence with which those gnarled hands stroked the sanded wood caused Daniel to swallow hard. His father was a craftsman, pure and simple.

Daniel was too. At least he tried to be. And he'd never tried harder to create a perfect piece than he was trying now. The truth was, he wanted to win that six–dollar prize at the Sweet Springs Fair. The one to be given for the most outstanding piece of creative work. Personally, the money didn't mean much to him; it was for Katie he wanted it. He wanted to give her some money, pure and simple. And a new piece of furniture for the sitting room. He did hope she would like the secretary. She could surely use it for writing letters to her friend, Bonnie. As for the money—Ah well, he'd just have to work hard and hope for the best.

Gripping the piece of wood with his left hand, Daniel reached for the sandpaper and began the laborious task of smoothing the drop leaf. God, but he loved Katie. Loved her, pure and simple. Yet, he felt that band tighten about his chest whenever they were together. For Katie didn't love him. Of course, they'd agreed that love was unnecessary to their relationship. Yet, Daniel felt cheated. He longed for Katie to want him, to crave him the way he craved her. True, Katie never spurned his advances. Yet, she didn't enjoy lovemaking either. She wanted a child, pure and simple.

Sighing, Daniel looked up to see a small face pressed against a square of window pane. It was Benjamin, chomping on the inevitable peppermint stick. Daniel paused and waved at the boy, feeling guilty as he did so. For

Benjamin wanted to observe him close up; he wanted to be in the shop with him. But Daniel had been adamant in his refusal. Three years old was too young to be allowed in the wood shop. Hadn't his own sister, Joy, choked to death on sawdust?

Even so, Daniel swallowed hard at the sight of those large dark eyes studying him so closely. For he loved that chap, pure and simple. Maybe in another year or two he would let Benjamin into the shop. In the meantime, he would love him the best way he knew how. And he would love his aunt too, like he'd never loved anyone before.

❖   ❖   ❖

Stepping inside the large tent, Katie gaped at the enormous display before her. Why my goodness, she'd never seen so many pieces of needlework in one place before. Embroidered pillow cases, crocheted doilies and tablecloths, knitted sweaters and hand–made quilts dominated the scene. Even the tiny sacque she'd made was there. Course she hadn't won no prize. She hadn't aimed to. After all, her knittin, though much nicer than them ugly mittens she'd made years ago, still wasn't good enough fur most folks. But Katie hadn't made the sacque fur most folks. She'd made it fur Bonnie's comin youngin. Running her hand over an especially pretty pillow case, Katie bit her lip to keep her chin from trembling. She mustn't cry here, seein as how no one would understand. Still, Bonnie was her best friend an Bonnie was hurtin somethin awful.

> *Oh, Katie, it's unfair fur God to do me this way. I'm so*
> *sad, I could die. Losin this youngin has purt near made*
> *me go crazy. In all my life I've never been so cross as I*
> *am these days. Fact is, I snap at Randall like it was all his*
> *fault. An it ain't. Why fur cryin out loud, he's hurtin too.*
> *You know, I'd fix things if I could. But, Katie, I can't.*
> *Cause more than anything I want a right nice little girl.*
> *an I ain't goin to git one. Leastwise not right now…*

Katie turned away from the displays and emerged from the tent. Poor Bonnie. If only she could've had thet youngin. If only she wasn't feelin so done in like. If only she—

"Hello, *prima* Katie. You have a nice time, *si?*"

Jerked from her reverie, Katie blinked at her cousin. Drat it all, why was Linda so happy fur, anyways? An why did she have to show up jist now when Katie needed to be alone?

"*Prima* Katie, you all right?"

"Course I'm all right," Katie snapped.

"You git a nice prize, no?"

"No, I didn't git no prize. Did you?"

"*Si*. Fur my good canned chilies."

"Congratulations."

"*Gracias*."

Katie, wanting nothing more than to be alone, would have turned away then, but Linda went on talking.

"You bring thet little one, *si*?"

"Benjamin? Course I did. Only he's with Daniel now, watchin the horse show."

"Horses nice, *si*?"

Katie nodded, then bit her lip. For there coming toward them was Thane. Wearing a frock coat and houndstooth trousers, he was as handsome as ever.

"Afternoon, Ladies," Thane blushed as he removed his light brown derby.

Katie stammered a reply, nearly undone by the sight of them chestnut curls. Beautiful they was, with thet sun makin them look all reddish like. Course she'd like to see them blue eyes too. But Thane kept his eyes downward, studying the toes of his highly polished boots. Drat it all, she reckoned she'd have to say somethin to him. Somethin nice like.

"How's your ma doin these days?"

At this Thane looked up, his blue eyes registering concern. "Not—not too good. But then it's no wonder she's havin a rough time of it. Oh, gosh Katie, what I mean to say is she sure does miss Bonnie. Course we're all purty down–in–the–mouth over her leavin."

"Me too. Course she writes letters ever now an again. She's—she's feelin a tad poorly jist now."

"Nothin serious, I hope?" Thane's eyes blinked an his mustache drooped.

Katie shook her head. "She's fine. Really an truly she is. She'll be writin your ma sometime soon."

But Katie's words failed to reassure Thane. He remained sober, his fine face drawn, until Linda shook his arm.

"*Marido*, you worry too much, *si*? Buy me some lemonade an be happy."

Blushing, Thane pulled free from his wife. "Lemonade sound good to you, Katie?"

At Katie's nod, Thane left to find the refreshment. He returned in a matter of minutes carefully balancing three cups. Once they were all sipping the cool liquid, Thane seemed more at ease.

"How's Daniel these days?"

"Fine. He an Benjamin are over visitin the horse show jist now."

"Sounds like fun. An thet secretary he made is real nice. Jist real nice. You must be real proud of him fur winnin the big prize."

"Course I am," Katie asserted, trying to look pleased. Nevertheless, she was indignant. Drat it all, why hadn't Daniel mentioned he was enterin a piece? An a secretary too. Why my goodness, she'd wanted one of them things fur as long as she could remember.

An jist like Thane said, it was beautiful. Really an truly it was. Yellow pine, she reckoned it was, an stained to match the sittin room furniture. Running her hand over the smoothly finished top, Katie felt a glow of pride. Her Daniel had made this. Her Daniel had won the big prize. Cause her Daniel really was somethin special like.

❖   ❖   ❖

A warm breeze blows through the window, ruffling Katie's unbound hair and the lace on her silk nightdress. Seated on the massive bed, she fingers the two gold coins in her hand. Six dollars. An all hers. Why my goodness, how will she ever spend thet much, anyways? Fact is, she feels purt near guilty jist havin it. Fur Daniel had given it with love. An it makes her feel all sad like inside seein as how she don't love him in return. Still, she has the money—

> *Oh, Katie, in all my life I've never felt so lonesome. Fact*
> *is, I'd give most anything fur a right nice visit with you...*

A smile creases the corners of Katie's mouth as she clutches the coins. Rising, she crosses the room to the bureau. Why my goodness, course thet's what she'll do. Instead of goin to church next Sunday, she'll jist buy herself an Benjamin train tickets to Sedalia. An with what's left over she'll buy Bonnie somethin real special like.

Feeling considerably happier, Katie lifts the lid to her K box and places the coins inside. Right beside her pearl necklace and her diamond ring.

Chapter 64

Katie didn't travel to Sedalia that fall after all. Instead, she spent her days in the large master bed, so ill at times she could scarcely raise her head from the pillow.

Drat it all, why was she so sick fur, anyways? Why my goodness, she spent more than half her time throwin up in thet chamber pot. An she went fur days without combin her hair or puttin on a dress. Tied to this bed she was, fur she hadn't no strength to git up. Why, in her whole life she reckoned she'd never felt so awful. Done in she was, an worried besides.

Daniel worried too. When Katie failed to rally after a few days, he decided to send for the doctor. But Livingston forestalled him.

"Lord, Son, you don't need a doctor. There'll be time enough for that later on. For that matter, I've seen your mother like this several times. It was worse with you than the others."

"With me?" Daniel tapped impatiently on the table as he spoke.

Livingston nodded, his thick lips forming a smile around the ever present Havana. "Katie's in the family way, Son. All things considered, she'll be fine."

But Daniel got the doctor anyway. And he remained worried even though the kindly man assured him his wife would be fine. He hovered over Katie, trying to coax her into drinking chicken broth or tea. He smoothed the covers and patted her pillow. And he emptied the chamber pot frequently, without complaint. Still, Katie remained ill. Until November. Then as swiftly as it came, her illness began to pass. And the first day she sat up, she wrote to Bonnie on the new secretary in the sitting room.

Drat it all, I'd a mind to see you this fall; to have a
special visit like. You're bound to be hurtin an I aimed to

help. Only now I can't cause I'm a tad done in myself.
Why my goodness, Bonnie, I'm expectin a youngin of my
own. An it's jist plain silly fur me to be havin one now
seein as how you lost yours like. Still, I'm purt nigh happy
now thet I'm feelin better.

Sighing, Katie put down her pen. Drat it all, she did hope Bonnie would take to the idea of her expectin a youngin. But Katie needn't have worried. For Bonnie's reply only made her friend seem more dear.

Fur cryin out loud, Katie, I won't quit you jist cause
you're havin a youngin an I'm not. I think it's right nice
fur you to have one. Fact is, I'm hopin you'll have a little
girl. Mostly I'm hopin it'll be all healthy like, like my
David.

Oh, Katie, David is such a comfort to me jist now. An
you're purt near as special. I mean it when I say you're
the best friend in the whole world. An I'm right glad
you're feelin better too.

Katie smiled. She loved Bonnie jist about better than anybody. Really an truly she did.

❖   ❖   ❖

It was a snowy day in January when family and friends gathered in the parlor of the Chapman home. For a time the snapping of flames in the fireplace provided the only sound. Even Linda was subdued as she handed around pie and filled tea cups. No one felt like talking. For these mourners had just returned from burying Minnie Chapman.

Seated on the sofa beside Bonnie, Katie bit her lip to keep her chin from trembling. She had to be strong fur Bonnie's sake. But drat it all, why did this have to happen fur, anyways? Course Bonnie's ma had been failin fur sometime now. Still, no one expected her to *die*. Why my goodness, at Christmas time she seemed jist fine. An Bonnie had pulled herself together like after seein her ma. She'd even smiled as she boarded the train fur her return home.

"Oh, Katie, I don't know what I'd ever do without you an my ma. It's a good bit easier facin thet empty cradle after bein here. Have a right nice winter now."

Bonnie had left then, not dreaming she'd be back so soon. And now she sat again in the family parlor, twisting her handkerchief an trying not to cry. Katie ached for her friend. Really an truly she did.

She ached for Thane too. Why my goodness, his face had been white as a sheet ever since his ma passed on. An them full lips hadn't smiled once.

"Thanks—thanks fur comin, Katie. Daniel too." It was Thane, stopping beside the sofa, his gaze traveling from Katie to Daniel, who stood behind her, and back to Katie again.

"Course I came, Thane. Why my goodness, you're my friends." And Katie stretched out her hand.

Thane grasped it, his blue eyes looking suspiciously moist before he lowered his gaze.

How long they remained that way, Katie didn't know. She only knew that Thane needed her. Really an truly he did. An she needed him too, somethin awful like. Why my goodness, hadn't she loved him purt nigh furever? Half her life it seemed like she'd been waitin fur Thane to claim her love.

But Thane pulled away then to shake hands with those who were leaving. Even Will was going. Had to mind the store, he said.

"Oh fur cryin out loud," Bonnie exclaimed. "Can't you furgit thet business fur even one day?"

Will turned to face her then, his jaw set, his thin nostrils flaring. "No, as a matter of fact, I can't. Someone has to work, you know. We can't all sit around, bawlin all day."

Once he'd gone, Bonnie turned to her friend, tears shimmering in her bright blue eyes. "I don't bawl all the time, do I Katie?"

"Course not," Katie snapped. Then slipping her arms about her friend, she spoke soothingly. "Don't pay no mind to thet Will. He's jist plain silly to be takin on like thet. Why my goodness, it's all right to cry now an again. After all—"

But Katie's words were lost as Bonnie began to weep. Deep, heart-rending sobs shook her friend until Katie was frightened. Why my goodness, she'd never seen Bonnie take on so. She reckoned her friend had loved her ma somethin awful like.

"Oh, Katie, why does it have to hurt so bad fur? Why?"

Katie didn't answer. She couldn't. After all, hadn't she hurt times galore herself? Why my goodness, every time she heard someone callin her to love, she answered. An then later when she was all carin like, them folks went away. Drat it all, it jist wasn't fair. Fur her or fur Bonnie.

Why? She didn't know why. She jist knew thet lovin hurt somethin awful. An knowin made her wonder if carin was worth the effort.

Chapter 65

Daniel couldn't sleep. Try as he might, he couldn't shake the feeling that he was being smothered. It was torture, pure torture, trying to sleep in a nightshirt. God, he hated the thing. His chest, his legs, his arms seemed trapped—caught between layers of flannel that seemed to squeeze the breath from his body. Yet, night after night he encased himself in its folds. All because of Katie.

Listening to his wife's easy breathing, Daniel felt the band about his chest tighten even further. God, but he loved her. And hated himself for doing so. Clenching his fist, Daniel smiled wryly. It most definitely was a good thing that Katie was already with child. Otherwise there wouldn't be any. For he could never make love to a woman whose heart belonged to someone else. And Katie's belonged to Thane Chapman.

It was the day of Minnie Chapman's funeral that he made the discovery. Actually, he hadn't given the Chapmans much thought at the time. It was Katie he felt for. God, but he longed to ease her pain as she held her friend that day. He wanted to love her, pure and simple. But then as they prepared to leave the Chapman home, Katie had turned to Thane. She held out her hand, telling him how sorry she was about his mother. And as Thane grasped it, Daniel saw Katie's eyes change from a somber gray to a brilliant blue. And the smile that creased her lovely lips was one of pure joy.

Daniel was stunned. It was agony, pure agony, to watch his wife offer her affection to someone else. Not since the day he'd found Harvey Fudd swinging from a pin oak had the band about his chest been so tight. Of course he knew that Thane had at one time courted Katie. But that was a long time ago, and he had just supposed the relationship had all blown over. Evidently, it hadn't. For Katie loved Thane, pure and simple.

God, but he hurt. His emotions, his heart, his very being was so constricted he was certain that if the band about his chest was pulled any tighter, he'd cease breathing altogether. Sitting up, Daniel swung his legs over the side of the bed. He was strangling, pure and simple. He had to find relief. Thrusting his feet into slippers, he grabbed up his wrapper and stumbled to the sitting room. Lighting a lamp, he crossed to the bookcase where he yanked open a glass door and began pulling out books. Grasping a bottle of bourbon and a small glass, he turned to the overstuffed chair. God, but he needed a drink. Anything to ease that terrible tightness in his chest.

His hands shaking, Daniel poured a shot, then drank it straight down. He poured and drank again. And again. And, he was pouring yet again when a bright light demanded his attention. At first he supposed it to be merely a reflection of his own lamp. But, as the light grew larger, he knew it was flames, pure and simple.

Fire!

"Oh, my God—" Daniel plopped his glass and bottle onto the candlestand, then ran to the bedroom. Throwing off his wrapper and nightshirt, he jerked on his clothes. He was nearly dressed when Katie roused.

"Daniel?"

"Go back to sleep."

"But you're gittin dressed. What time is it, anyways?"

"Three o'clock."

"Oh my goodness. Where're you goin? An what's all thet light fur?"

"It's a fire, pure and simple."

"A fire? Where?"

"Chapman's Dry Goods. Now, go on back to sleep."

"Chapman's? Oh my goodness, no. Daniel—" But Daniel was gone before she could say any more.

❖　　❖　　❖

Katie huddled in the chair, a quilt covering herself and the solemn–faced Benjamin. Purt nigh two hours it'd been an still thet bucket brigade was workin somethin fierce like. Why, my goodness, thet fire was goin to burn down the whole place. Then where would Thane be? With Linda, of course. Drat it all, why couldn't she remember thet the Chapman store was all Will's now? An why couldn't she seem to remember thet Thane was married? Thet he—

"Aunt Katie, is Uncle Daniel all right?"

"Course he's all right." Katie forced a smile as she gazed through the window into the early morning darkness. Darkness illuminated by myriad flames, ever stretching orange fingers beyond the reach of water. Katie sighed knowing that Daniel would stay out there until the fire was under control. Daniel would do his duty.

Pressing Benjamin's dark head against her breast, Katie shook her head. Goodness, but Daniel was withdrawn these days. Like livin in a shell, he was. Why, he hadn't even the gumption to speak to her unless she spoke first. He never touched her no more neither, or kissed her. An it was jist plain silly the way he looked in thet nightshirt. Why my goodness, he looked more like a spirit than a person with thet thing flappin about his legs when he walked. But he wasn't, of course. Fur Daniel's spirit had gone away like. Jist disappeared, leavin him unapproachable. Why, he'd even stopped goin to church. Stopped smilin too. An carin. Cept fur Benjamin. He loved thet youngin somethin awful like. Why, he'd even takin to lettin him help in the wood shop. An him jist four years old. It didn't make no sense to her.

His pa didn't make no sense neither. Drinkin, he was, on the sly like. Why my goodness, she'd purt nigh passed out when she found thet bottle behind them books. Whiskey, it was. Real whiskey, not thet home–brew stuff My Pa always had. Course My Pa an Thomas drank. But thet was different. They sipped thet jug right there in plain view. She reckoned thet was what bothered her so about Daniel's pa—his sneakin around like. Why my goodness, he whisked thet bottle off the candlestand this mornin like he'd been caught stealin. Course she'd pretended not to see. She—

"Miss Katie?"

It was Daniel's pa standin in the kitchen doorway an lookin like he'd never been to sleep all night.

"Would you like some breakfast?"

Katie started to shake her head. She didn't want eggs or biscuits or coffee. Still, with the baby an all—

"Course I would. But I reckon I'd best git dressed like first."

Livingston nodded. "Here, let me take the boy." And he scooped up the sleeping Benjamin and limped acrossed the room to the sofa.

Half an hour later Katie sat at the kitchen table sipping coffee, and wishing Daniel was here. Drat it all, *he* knew she preferred tea. At least he used to.

"Looks like that fire's about out," Livingston puffed his Havana as he spoke. "It sure did a lot of damage though. An awful lot of damage."

Katie nodded. "I reckon thet crabby Will Chapman will have to quit workin now. Leastwise fur awhile."

Livingston said nothing as he opened the oven door and placed a batch of biscuits inside, his swollen fingers nearly dropping the pan.

Katie sighed. She knew she should be cookin more, but drat it all, Daniel's pa seemed so in charge like—

A draft of cool air touched Katie's back causing her to turn around. She gasped at the sight of her husband. For he looked awful. Really an truly he did. Why, his hair was all rumpled like an smellin like singed feathers. An them gray eyes was swimmin in pools of blood. His face was blistered an his clothes was muddy. He looked purt nigh done in as he stood there starin straight ahead.

"Oh my goodness, you're hurt!" Katie jumped from the table and ran to him.

But Daniel waved her off with a hand that oozed blood. "I'm fine. But I'm hungry, pure and simple."

"Well, eat then," Katie snapped as she returned to the kitchen. What was the matter with Daniel, anyways? Why my goodness, them hands was burned somethin awful. They needed fixin right off like. An she aimed to do it. Thus after the meal, she rose and collected a fistful of rags.

"Daniel, I've a mind to treat them hands. They're hurt somethin awful like."

"Actually, they're fine. Now, if you'll excuse me—"

"They ain't neither fine. Why my goodness, they're bleedin on your clothes even. Now, you jist—"

"Katie, for God's sake, can't you see I'm in no mood to be fussed over? Now, leave me alone. All right?"

"No, it ain't all right, an I ain't leavin you alone. Drat it all, man, what's got into you, anyways? Now, I aim to fix them hands, so I reckon you'd best sit down quick like before I light into you real good."

Daniel sat. But he kept his face averted while Katie bathed his hands, smeared them with grease and wrapped them in rags, being careful to wrap each finger separately. Why my goodness, she couldn't let his fingers grow all together like. Duck's feet was good fur swimmin, but not much else.

"There. Now, I'll jist git thet nightshirt an some hot bricks—"

"God, Katie, I can't just leave the shop—"

"Course you can. Drat it all, Daniel, you're a grown man an you can rest if you've a mind to. Now, stop takin on so while we git them stinkin clothes off." And Katie began unfastening his shirt.

Chapter 66

"Oh my goodness— Oh–h–h–h!" Katie groaned as yet another contraction seized her body. Blindly, she reached for Aunt Jane's hand.

"There, there. Why land sakes, Child, you're adoin fine. Fact is, this youngin can be born purt near any time now. Ain't thet right, Doc?"

"Looks like it." A kindly face smiled down at Katie.

But Katie wasn't in the mood for a doctor's smile or Aunt Jane's chatter. Why my goodness, what did they know about havin youngins, anyways? They'd never had one. But Bonnie had. And it was Bonnie Katie longed for. Why, she reckoned she wouldn't feel so done in like if Bonnie was here. Fur Bonnie would understand. She'd know it was all right to take on now an again seein as how—

"Oh my goodness—Oh–h–h–h—Ah–h–h–h!" Even as she groaned again, Katie scolded herself for wanting Bonnie. For Bonnie couldn't come to Brownsville. Why my goodness, she had her own husband an youngin to care fur. Besides, she'd been home again the last week in February. To attend another family funeral. This time it was Will. Unable to accept the loss of the family store, he'd loaded a revolver and shot himself in the head. The note he left said simply—"I failed Pa."

Poor Bonnie. They'd stood on the depot platform the day after the funeral and wept. Cried somethin awful like they had, before Bonnie boarded thet train an left again. Katie had stood for a long time then, waving at the disappearing cars, before hurrying home alone. Drat it all, why did Bonnie have to leave fur, anyways? An why did the weather have to be so awful? All thet rain, an mud an cold. Why my goodness, in her whole life, she reckoned she'd never seen so many wagons an carriages gittin stuck on Main Street.

But winter eventually passed, an now it was May. Jist right the weather was, if only—

"Oh my goodness—Oh–h–h–h—Ah–h–h–h–h–h!" Again Katie gripped Aunt Jane's hand as sweat poured down her face.

"Daniel?" Drat it all, where was thet man, anyways?

"Daniel ain't here," Aunt Jane snapped. "Why land sakes, we got enough to tend to without him bein underfoot. Still an all, I guess he ain't far off. In the sittin room, most likely."

An drinkin too, no doubt. Why my goodness, Katie felt jist plain awful to think she'd suspected his pa of boozin. But drat it all, how was she to know it was her husband who took to whiskey? Course she'd heard them rumors about the saloon after he'd broke off with Mamie. But thet was a long time ago. Fact was, she'd never *seen* Daniel drink. Till one night last March. It was the wind thet woke her up thet night. Whinin an rattlin the window it was, loud enough to raise the dead.

"Daniel?" Frightened, Katie had groped for her husband. Only to find his side of the bed empty.

"Daniel?" Katie called again, her chin starting to quiver. "Daniel! Drat it all, man, answer me."

But there was no answer.

More indignant now than frightened, Katie slipped from the bed and strode to the closed door. Opening it, she stared into the sitting room. Oh my goodness, it *couldn't* be! But it was. For there sat Daniel, a whiskey bottle in one hand, a shot glass in the other. Purt nigh done in he was, his right hand shaking so that Katie feared he'd pour the amber liquid on himself or the floor. He didn't though. And when he set the empty bottle on the table, Katie noticed his hands again. And winced. Ridges of scar tissue stood out on their backs, especially on the right one. Jist plain ugly, they was. Yet, Katie was grateful too. For she had saved the palms and fingers. Thus Daniel still carried on a love affair with wood. Cept when he'd been drinkin. Why my goodness, his pa had scolded him somethin fierce like fur messin up a table. Had quite a row they did, one night. An still Daniel drank.

"Oh my goodness—Oh–h–h–h–h I *can't!* Oh my goodness. Ah–h–h–h–h!" Katie lost control then, screaming until she was hoarse. She was dyin. Really an truly she was. Somethin awful was happenin, causin her to come all apart like. Huge fangs were tearin at her insides, pullin an rippin till she purt nigh blacked out. Done in she was, an bleedin like a stuck hog. "Oh, my goodness. Oh oh–h–h–h–h—I can't. Please, oh, please—STOP!"

Katie went limp then as the world faded away. She awoke to find an anxious Aunt Jane bending over her.

"Katie? Well it's about time you come around. Why land sakes, Child, you gave us an awful scare. But you're fine now. An you've got a girl youngin. Downright purty she is too."

"A girl?" And she faded away again.

The next time she awoke it was to find a tiny form resting on her arm. A girl. Katie smiled then at the heart–shaped face and rosebud mouth before slipping into a natural sleep.

When next she awakened it was to see Daniel kneeling beside the bed, gazing at the tiny form beside her.

Daniel?"

Daniel looked at Katie then, his gray eyes empty.

"Oh my goodness, don't you like her?"

"Sure I like her."

"Let's name her fur your folks seein as how she's got your dark hair an all. What was your ma's name, anyways?"

"Verna Marie."

"Oh my goodness. Verna is an ugly name, don't you think?"

Daniel didn't answer.

"If you've a mind to, let's jist call her Marie."

"All right." Daniel rose then and strode quickly from the room.

Staring after him, Katie grew indignant. Why my goodness, he never even asked if she was mendin nice or nothin. An he never said thank you or—

Little Marie began to whimper, her tiny mouth opening like a baby bird in search of food.

"Oh my goodness, you're hungry." Smiling, Katie opened her night-dress and offered her daughter a breast. "There. I reckon thet'll keep you now."

And it did. For minutes later, Marie ceased sucking and returned to sleep. Kissing the soft head, Katie smiled. This youngin was wonderful. Really an truly she was.

"Aye, Lass, it's a lovely mornin, mind."

"My Pa!" Katie turns to see the balding, middle–aged man standing in the doorway. "Come on in an see this here youngin."

Michael crosses to the bed then and looks down at the sleeping child. "Aye, Lass, she's a bonny one, to be sure. Though, I reckon, her mom is bonnier still."

"Why my goodness, My Pa, don't say thet. You know I ain't purty. Leastwise not now. Why, I'm messed up somethin awful like."

"Aye, Lass, I reckon you have looked better. Still, you're bonny." And to Katie's surprise, he reaches down and strokes her disheveled hair. He straightens then and gazes down at her, his eyes suspiciously moist. And it occurs to Katie that he must have looked down on another mother and child twenty three years ago with that same mixture of love and pride.

Chapter 67

Katie's steps quickened as she neared the end of the block and home. It all looked so invitin, so peaceful like with My Pa an Aunt Jane rockin on the back porch an Thomas sittin on thet log bench beneath the oak tree. It reminded her of the old days when she had been one of them. Fact was, she reckoned she still belonged there. Leastwise she wanted to. Why, my goodness, she felt purt nigh a stranger among them Lewis men. Fur neither one paid her a tad of attention. An it hurt. Really an truly it did. It hurt somethin awful like. Still—

"Land sakes, Child, hurry up an let me see thet youngin." It was Aunt Jane, holding out her arms as she spoke.

Smiling, Katie followed Benjamin up the path and handed Marie to her aunt. Then sinking into a split–bottom chair, she stretched a hand to My Pa.

"Goodness, but it's nice to see you. I reckon you're feelin fine seein as how you look good."

"Aye, Lass, I reckon I am. A bit tired, mind, but right good jist the same." He withdrew his hand then and lifted Benjamin onto his ample lap. Seconds later he was telling of "a wee little lad who saw a wee little President in a wee little town in Tennessee."

Katie watched her pa with glowing eyes. For that story was a familiar one. Why, my goodness, she reckoned he'd told it to her half a dozen times. All about Andrew Jackson it was, an how he'd stopped in Rogersville on his way to be inaugurated President. An despite the added lines on his face and the added inches to his belly, My Pa still reveled in the tellin . Fur he thought it somethin special like to see a President, even if he was jist a "wee lad" at the time.

The story finished, Benjamin climbed down and seated himself on the edge of the porch, his short legs dangling over the side.

For several moments no one spoke. Katie relaxed to the chirp of sparrows and the squeak of Aunt Jane's rocker, her hands laying limp in her lap.

"Aye, Lass, how's things goin with Daniel?"

At My Pa's question, Katie stiffened, placing her hands on her elbows. "Fine," she lied. "Anyways, it would be if them ready–made furniture places hadn't started up. Still, some folks is willin to pay extra fur hand–made things."

Michael nodded. "Meself now, I reckon I'll always take to hand–crafted pieces. They jist seem better made, mind."

Katie agreed. Though right now, Daniel's work suffered. Still, he an his pa put out some fine lookin furniture. Why—

"Why fur land sakes," Aunt Jane burst out, "this youngin is soppin wet. She needs attendin to right now."

At this, Katie started. Oh my goodness, she'd furgot them extra didies. Come right off without them, she had. But drat it all, she'd been so anxious to git away from Daniel—

"I'm sorry, Aunt Jane. Really an truly I am. But I jist plain furgot them extra didies."

"Oh, my. Well, we'll jist have to make do. Why land sakes, I've a mind to use them old tea towels in there. They'd make downright good pants fur a youngin." And with that she disappeared into the kitchen.

Staring after her, My Pa chuckled. "Aye, Lass, I reckon me Mavoureen would make a right good mom."

"She's been awful good to me," Katie said.

"Aye, Lass, I reckon she has."

At the tenderness in My Pa's tone, Katie winced. If only Daniel would speak of her like thet. If only he thought she was somethin special like, the way he had when they was first married. If she couldn't have Thane— Biting her lip, Katie reprimanded herself. Drat it all, what was she thinkin of *him* fur, anyways? She reckoned she'd best change the subject right quick like, before she started bawlin.

"How's things goin at the smithy these days?"

If My Pa noticed the catch in her voice he didn't let on. He sighed though, making Katie wonder if he was more than "a bit tired".

"Aye, Lass, I enjoy it, to be sure. Course I'm a bit slower, mind. Can't work like I used to. Still, I'm thinkin thet the smithy's goin to end with me."

"But My Pa—"

"Aye, Lass, I reckon it's fur the best. Some folks is sayin we'll all drive a horseless carriage someday, anyways."

"Oh, thet's silly. Jist plain silly. We'll always need horses. Leastwise we'll always need you."

"Aye, Lass, I do thank you. Still, I reckon you could do right fine without me."

"Oh, My Pa, I couldn't. Why my goodness, I love you somethin awful like."

"Aye, Lass, I reckon you do. Still, I'm thinkin I'd like to go quiet like. Not like some of them folks in Richmond."

"Richmond, Missouri? Why thet's way off like." And Katie waved toward the northwest. "What happened there, anyways?"

"Cyclone."

"Like thet one in Houstonia awhile back?"

Michael nodded. "A right bad one from all I hear. Fourteen folks killed an purt nigh half the town tore up."

"Oh my goodness. Why, it must be somethin awful like to git hit by one of them things." Katie hugged herself, wishing that My Pa hadn't brought the subject up. It made her come all apart like inside jist thinkin on it. Course thet wasn't likely to happen *here*. Leastwise not—

"Aye, Lass, we're borin the lad, to be sure." And Michael nodded toward Benjamin.

Katie relaxed then as she watched her nephew take hesitant steps toward the log bench and his pa. Drat it all, she wished Thomas had the gumption to speak to thet youngin. Smile at him, anyways. But Thomas seemed oblivious to the boy who had stopped beside the bench. He continued smoking his corncob pipe and staring silently into space. He never moved. Not even when Benjamin crawled up on the bench beside him. He never so much as acknowledged the four-year old who looked up at him with eager eyes.

"Drat it all, I've a mind to light into Thomas good. What's the matter with him, anyways?"

"Aye, Lass, I wish I knew."

The sadness in My Pa's voice curbed Katie's anger. "He never really got over thet War, did he?" she asked softly.

"Aye, Lass, I reckon not. But he's a right good lad, mind."

Katie's chin trembled as she reached out to pat My Pa's hand. And the roughness of his skin caused a tear to slid down her cheek. Why my goodness, he worked somethin awful like. Toiled hard he did, day after day in thet smithy.

> *Under a spreading chestnut–tree*
> *The village smithy stands;*
> *The smith, a mighty man is he,*
> *With large and sinewy hands...*
> *Week in, week out, from morn till night,*
> *You can hear his bellows blow;*
> *You can hear him swing his heavy sledge,*
> *With measured beat and slow...*[1]

Katie longed to put her arms around My Pa, to tell him how much she loved him. Fact was, he seemed the only thing thet kept her goin these days what with Daniel actin so withdrawn an all. Still, she couldn't find the words to say how she felt.

"Aye, Lass, I reckon you're purt nigh the best daughter a man could have. Right good, you are. An I'm thinkin you're gittin better all the time."

Katie squeezes My Pa's hand then as a second tear slips from her eyes. He knows! My Pa knows thet I love him an he's grateful. Why my goodness, I reckon I never felt this close to no one else before. Love sure is somethin beautiful like. Really an truly it is.

Chapter 68

It is cold, bitterly cold, on this twenty-fourth day of December, 1878. Christmas Eve and Daniel is alone. Staring at the half–emptied glass in his hand, he wishes he had gone next door with the others. He'd been invited of course, by Katie and Benjamin. And it was pain, pure pain, to turn down the chap's request to hear him sing, "Away in a Manger". But he had. For the truth was, he feared meeting Thane Chapman and seeing Katie's face light up in his presence. So he'd taken the coward's way out.

Sipping his drink, Daniel wonders about his father. For he too has gone to see the Christmas program. And that is astonishing, pure and simple. Why, he can't even remember a time when his father attended church. Of course he'd prayed off and on through the years. But never on a regular basis. Until recently. Now it seems his father has definitely turned religious. For instance, he's begun saying a prayer at bed time. Not in front of anyone, of course. He just mumbles to himself as he heats bricks on the kitchen stove. Even so, Daniel is surprised that he consented to attend the program. In the first place, he'd been raised a Methodist, not a Christian. Besides that, he'd hated his preacher father and the God he stood for. Ah well, his father is noticeably older these days. Older and in considerable pain. No doubt that accounts for the change.

For himself, Daniel is tired. Tired of reaching out and loving. Tired of being hurt, pure and simple. For, try as he might, he never can hold onto the ones he loves. His mother; his sister, Joy; his Union buddy, Russell; the lovely, slender, Mamie; his eccentric old friend, Harvey—And now, he's losing Katie. And he hasn't the strength to try and win her back. Even God can't help him now.

Or can he? Wasn't it God who met him on a Sunday morning after

Harvey Fudd died? Wasn't it God who gave strength through bits of bread and a sip of wine? Wasn't it God who enabled him to reach out and touch the solemn–faced Benjamin?

Daniel's hand trembles as he sets his glass on the candle–stand. Rising, he leaves the sitting room, his feet faltering on the stairs. In the back room of the shop he takes his time putting on his greatcoat and stovepipe hat. He pulls on his gloves slowly, pressing the leather between each finger. Then taking up the lantern, he proceeds toward the door and outside.

Inside the small, frame church, Daniel stands at the back. Seeing Katie with Marie on her shoulder causes the band to tighten about his chest. With effort he shifts his gaze to the men's side of the aisle. Thane's there as he knew he would be. His own father too, minus his usual Havana. Clenching his fist, Daniel turns his attention to the group of children filing toward the platform. Benjamin is there. And the smile on his face when he spies Daniel is as glowing as the lighted candles on the evergreen tree.

"Away in a manger, no crib for a bed,
The little Lord Jesus laid down his sweet head…" [1]

Daniel watches as an older girl places her doll in a homemade manger beside the tree. A doll that reminds him of his own tiny Marie.

"Be near me, Lord Jesus, I ask Thee to stay
Close by me forever, and love me, I pray…" [2]

Love. Tears sting Daniel's eyes. For it is love he craves, pure and simple. A love to heal his pain–racked heart. A love to permeate his entire being. A love that will conquer his fear of losing dear ones.

"And the Word was made flesh, and dwelt among us…" [3]

Ah, yes, this is it. The Christ Child is God, pure and simple. God becoming human just to say I love you.

Placing a scarred hand over his face, Daniel weeps. "Oh God, it's been torture, pure torture, living like this. And the truth is, I can't bear it any longer. Please, give me yourself so that I can love for always."

"Joy to the world! the Lord is come;
Let earth receive her King;
Let every heart prepare him room…" [4]

Daniel wipes his face with a handkerchief, but he doesn't sing. He can't. For tonight his heart is too full for words. He can only stand and study the back of his wife as she sings with the others. And love her.

Chapter 69

The roar of the fire in the pot–bellied stove was the only sound in the Lewis' sitting room as Katie sat reading Elizabeth Barrett Browning.

How do I love thee? Let me count the ways.
I love thee to the depth and breadth and height
My soul can reach...[1]

Katie slammed the book shut, then shuddered when Daniel looked up from his newspaper. Drat it all! What was the matter with her, anyways? Why couldn't she see Thane no more? Why, from the beginnin she'd read them Portuguese Sonnets with him in mind. More than once she'd imagined his deep voice an flushed face as he whispered,

"How do I love thee? Let me count the ways..." [2]

Why, my goodness, she could purt nigh *see* thet chestnut mustache an them fine white teeth as he declared,

"I love thee with the passion put to use
In my old griefs, and with my childhood's
faith..." [3]

But not now. For in recent weeks chestnut curls had been replaced by charcoal waves and blue eyes supplanted by gray ones. A fine oval face was overshadowed by a heart–shaped one with a long jawline and jutting chin. And that shy, lopsided grin disappeared beneath a tender, curving smile. An drat it all, she didn't like it. She didn't take to havin her heart flip-flop this way.

Jumping up from the sofa, Katie let the book fall to her feet. Again, Daniel looked up from his paper.

"Katie," he asked gently, "is something the matter?"

"Course not." she retrieved the book then and laid it on the candlestand, trying to avoid her husband's gaze. Fact was, she felt all done in like jist lookin at him. He seemed so peaceful like readin thet paper while holdin a sleepin Benjamin on his lap. An thet one foot kept rockin Marie's cradle like she was somethin special.

"If I can help—"

"You can't!" Katie flounced from the room then, slamming the bedroom door behind her. In the darkness, she made her way to the window. Kneeling, she tried to see out. Drat it all, would this cold spell never end?

With a finger nail Katie scratched a small space in the frost on the glass. Peering through, she glimpsed an ebony sky, studded with winking stars. Wrapping her arms about herself, she rocked back and forth. What *was* the matter with her, anyways? Why my goodness, she should be glad Daniel had quit drinkin. Glad thet he spoke gently these days. Glad thet he cared fur her every need. But she wasn't. Fur this new Daniel was callin her to love. An she didn't want to answer. Not now, anyways. She'd rather jist be friends, the way they used to be.

"Katie?"

It was Daniel opening the door, lighting the lamp. Daniel bending over her, concern in his eyes.

"Why, Darling, you're freezing."

As he slipped his arms about her, Katie stiffened. Drat it all, now he'd want lovemakin again. An she'd a mind to say no. Fur lately she'd started seein thet as somethin special like. Somethin she enjoyed. An thet scared her. Really an truly it did.

It was March before the weather cleared. And when it did Katie decided to go out. Why my goodness, she'd been cooped up in them rooms so long she felt purt nigh crazy. She'd go to Aunt Jane's shop she would, an buy a new hat. One of them tall ones with lots of little feathers an a narrow brim. Thet'd make her feel a tad better, anyways.

Inside the millinery, Katie directed Benjamin to a corner where she placed Marie in his care. Glancing about, she saw that Mamie worked by herself today. Drat it all, she'd hoped to find Sally here. For despite her stout figure and graying hair, she was preferable to the moody Mamie. Why my goodness, Mamie was so touchy these days thet even Aunt Jane had to light into her ever now an again.

Turning her back to her sister, Katie studied the newest hats. There. Thet dark red one with them pink feathers. Standing on tiptoe, she had just touched the edge of the shelf when a voice startled her.

"*Nein*! Not *that* hat."

Whirling, Katie saw a stranger scowling at Mamie. Ugly she was, with thet awful frown on her face. An over thet hat too. Why my goodness, it was a purty thing with them bright green feathers an all thet lace. Course thet woman was wearin mostly black herself. An a second woman too. Though—

"Fur heaven sakes, don't scare me thet aways!" Mamie's green eyes shot sparks as she faced the stranger, hat in hand.

But it was the second woman who winced at Mamie's tone. Younger than the first one, she was. Better lookin too. Why my goodness, with them warm hazel eyes an thet buxom figure she was purt nigh beautiful. Only the warmth went out of them eyes when Mamie put back the feathered hat and got down a black bonnet with tiny white flowers.

"*Danke*." And the first woman took the bonnet and handed it to the second. When the hazel eyes grew moist, Katie couldn't stand it any longer. Marching across the room, she reached out her hand and smiled into those eyes.

"I'm Katie," she said. "You're new in town, ain't you?"

The woman smiled in return, a puzzled look on her pleasant face.

Drat it all, what was she thinkin of, anyways? Course this woman didn't understand her. She was German. Leastwise Katie reckoned thet's what she was. Why my goodness, there'd been talk fur weeks now about them folks over at Emma startin a school here. A church too.

Smiling even more broadly, Katie tapped her own chest. "I'm Katie," she repeated. "An this is Benjamin an Marie." She gestured to the corner where Benjamin was rocking a restless Marie.

"*Ich bin* Frieda. *Er ist* Wilhelm." She patted the ashbrown hair of the small boy standing beside her. Then nodding toward the older woman, she added. "*Sie ist* Gretchen, *meine Schwester*–"

"Why my goodness, I'm so glad to meet you. It must be somethin awful like livin in a new place an all. This is my Aunt Jane's shop. An this is my sister, Mamie." She gestured toward Mamie who smiled faintly as she tried on a hat for another customer.

Frieda smiled again, but that smile quickly faded as Gretchen gave her a light shove toward the door.

Katie was incensed. Why my goodness, what was the matter with thet Gretchen woman, anyways? Behavin somethin awful she was, takin on like other folks wasn't good enough fur her. Why, she'd a mind—

"Auf Wiedersehen."

Katie started at the wistful voice, then smiled and waved briefly as Frieda followed her sister out the door.

Chapter 70

Livingston shivered. And it wasn't from the cold. For despite the icy rain pelting the window, the room was warm. Daniel had seen to that. Come to think of it, Daniel had done a lot lately to help alleviate the aches in his joints. But this evening it wasn't his joints that pained him. It was his memories. Memories of a tall, thin man whose angular face rarely wore a smile. Memories of a deep voice leading the family in daily prayers. Memories of a man whose generosity stopped short of his son. Biting hard on his Havana, Livingston sighed as he reread the letter in his hands.

> *Dear Livingston,*
>
> *I take my seat this morning to write you concerning myself. I should like to come visit you this summer, if that is agreeable with you and Daniel. I would have proposed my visit sooner but I've been caring for my brother now, ever since Jeremiah passed on. Ira joined your father a month ago today.*
>
> *I am alone now, and it seems only right and proper that I should meet the only kin I have left. I trust this finds you in good health.*
>
> *Respectfully yours,*
>
> *Althea Lewis*

Livingston laid the letter on the candlestand and sighed. Lord, he didn't know what to say. Personally, he didn't want to meet his step–mother. He didn't want a visible reminder of his father. He didn't want to hear a lecture about how giving his father had been and how much he, Livingston, owed him in return. He didn't want to be told he should have stayed in Harrisonburg all those years ago.

Because he'd *had* to leave. Lord, but he'd been glad, more glad than he could say, to bid his father good–by that day. Ah yes, he'd been happy to go, relieved to leave behind the stern man who'd beat him for neglecting his little sister, Nettie. Relieved to shove aside memories of Nettie being trampled and his mother dying of heartbreak. Relieved to be on his own at last.

Even so, the bumpy stage ride from Harrisonburg to Romney that day in 1836 had been a painful one. For it was on that trip that Livingston laid aside his allusions about love. Personally, he was through caring. Hadn't he cared for his parents and Nettie? And hadn't he lost both his mother and his sister? And his father—Ah well, he'd *always* been lost to him.

Separation. The pain was unbearable. To love and lose—He couldn't endure the suffering that ensued. And yet, ironically, he had loved again. First his wife, Verna Marie, then his little daughter, Joy. And again, he'd lost them. For Joy had choked to death right before his very eyes. And his wife? He'd lost her bit by bit with each child they buried. And any feeling she'd had left was smothered when that damned darkie had raped her. All things considered, the final separation was perhaps the least painful of all. Even so, it had hurt. For he had finally lost the only woman he'd dared to love.

Biting hard on his Havana, Livingston cursed himself for being fool enough to love his son. But Daniel was turning out to be a fine man. A mighty fine man. And Livingston was proud of him. Even so, it scared him to care so much. Ah well, he would never love anyone else again. Certainly not a woman.

Spitting the stub of his Havana into the pot–bellied stove, Livingston noted again the letter from his stepmother. He might as well say she could come, he supposed. Then maybe she'd leave him alone so he could go on wishing that his father had never existed.

❖   ❖   ❖

Jane was worried. About her shop and her family. Pinning a bit of scalloped lace to the edge of a sleeve, she leaned closer to the lamp and sighed. Land sakes, thet Mamie had been impudent of late. Downright disrespectful she was, to her family an customers as well. And it was the latter which concerned Jane just now. For several of her best customers had taken their business elsewhere because of Mamie's sharp tongue. But speakin to thet girl didn't do a mite of good.

"Oh fur heaven sakes, Aunt Jane, stop bein so persnickety. Them women is too uppity fur their own good, anyways."

Jane sighed. She didn't cotton to Mamie's ways, yet she did feel sorry for the girl. A regular old maid she was, with no one to love her. An ailin too. Leastwise it seemed thet away to her. Why land sakes, Mamie hardly ever ate a proper meal nowadays. Jist picked at her food she did, protestin she wasn't hungry.

Snipping a thread, Jane pushed her specs more firmly on her nose and turned her attention to the other sleeve. Part of a trousseau this was, fur Amy Smith. My but she wished it was fur Mamie. Or fur Thomas' fiancée. Course, Thomas didn't have no lady friend jist now. Hadn't since Julia died. Still an all, if he was to marry again maybe he'd settle down an stop bein so difficult. Why land sakes, he'd carried on so when thet frost got them peach blossoms thet Jane had purt near lost herself an whipped his backside. Downright childish he was, ablamin everybody from God to Uriah Martin fur the mess things was in.

Taking a tiny stitch, Jane shook her head. My but thet Thomas was a mystery. When he wasn't arantin about them crops, he was asittin quiet like, smokin thet stinkin pipe an sippin corn liquor. Fact was, he seemed worse off then. Fur durin them silent times he seemed lost like, in another world, where nothin or no one could touch him.

Jane held up the dress then, trying to decide if the ruffles at the bottom needed one–inch or two–inch lace trim. Deciding on the two–inch, she took up a bolt and rethreaded her needle. Land sakes, she got mighty tired of all this hand work. Still an all, she needed somethin to keep her busy these evenins when she sat in the dinin room alone. Course there wasn't too many of them times. Why land sakes, Katie came over purt near every other night. Lonesome she was, fur home—an her pa. She'd draw up a chair beside his rocker an hang on his every word, like she was astarvin fur attention. An she wasn't. Why, purt near every one in town knew thet Daniel doted on her. Downright romantic he was, abuyin her gifts an atakin her places. Why land sakes, if Jane didn't have such a good man of her own she might even be jealous.

But Jane wasn't jealous. Not of Katie or no one else. Fur Michael was the best man in the whole world. Loved her aplenty, he did. Still an all, she worried about him. Worried because he worked too hard. Worried because he wasn't as spry as he used to be. Yet, when she urged him to slow down, he merely smiled.

"Aye, Mavoureen, I'm right tired, to be sure. But I'm happy, mind."

He would kiss her then, running his thick fingers through her unbound hair, across thet crimson scar on her cheek an down her petite body. And for a time Jane would forget that here was a man who was aging too fast.

But she didn't forget for long . Sometimes, as she lay on his arm after lovemaking, she would run her fingers through the heavy mat of hair on his barrel chest, wondering how she could ever live without him. Then laying her marked cheek against his stubbly one, she'd ask the good Lord to protect him, this man she loved with all her heart.

Chapter 71

Biting his Havana cigar, Livingston Lewis brought his buggy to a halt on Lexington Avenue. Climbing down, he looped the reins over a hitching post and rubbed his aching fingers. Lord, he hurt. His fingers, his knees, his entire being screamed with pain. And it had been such a short trip too. Of course he could have let Daniel do the driving. But he wasn't in the mood for company; he wanted to greet his stepmother alone.

The street was crowded as usual with numerous hack drivers vying for the space closest to the platform. Wincing, Livingston drew his watch from his waistcoat pocket. 7:40. The train would arrive in five minutes. There was nothing to do but wait. Whoo–ooo. Whoo–ooo.

Livingston heard the locomotive before he saw it. And then it was there, a black engine rounding the bend, steam pouring from its stack, its headlight gleaming orange as it reflected the setting sun. Screeching to a halt, the train shuddered as porters rushed to lay steps for disembarking passengers. Hack drivers danced and shouted, luring businessmen, politicians and families as they stepped onto the wooden platform.

Biting hard on his Havana, Livingston surveyed the three passenger cars. Let's see, what would she look like, this step–mother of his? Come to think of it, all he knew was that she was younger than his father. How much younger he didn't know. He must admit though, that he hoped she would look as his mother had, plump and matronly with salt and pepper hair.

The passengers dispersed, Livingston looked about, puzzled. He didn't see anyone left except a slender mulatto woman about his own age. Sighing, he turned to his buggy, angry with himself for getting the date wrong. Lord, all this agony for nothing. And he'd have to repeat it again

311

tomorrow. He—

"Livingston Lewis?" The soft feminine voice caused him to turn.

"Yes."

"I'm Althea, your father's widow." And the mulatto held out her hand.

"No!" Livingston gaped at the figure before him. A DARKIE! *His* father had married a darkie? Of course the older man had always championed the cause of slaves. But *marry* one? It was unthinkable.

"Excuse me, but you're about to lose your cigar." Again the voice was soft, with just a hint of amusement.

Savagely, Livingston clamped down on his Havana, nearly biting it in two. A darkie. For a moment he wished his father was still alive. So he could wring his neck.

A darkie. He'd know one anywhere. For, despite her slender figure and light skin, her features gave her away. Her hair, tucked neatly beneath a narrow–brimmed hat, was black and coarse with tiny curls escaping to frame her oval face. A face dominated by wide nostrils and generous lips. A darkie. Lord, what was he to do?

"You were expecting me." It was a statement.

"Of course." Then turning his back to his step–mother, Livingston struggled into the buggy. But if Althea felt slighted, she gave no hint. She simply gathered up her skirts and stepped up after him.

"I'll have Daniel collect your trunks later," Livingston spoke brusquely as he flicked the reins and the buggy began to move. The drive home was made in silence.

❖   ❖   ❖

It was the Fourth of July and so hot that Livingston's swollen fingers kept losing their grip on the reins as he guided the buggy up Miller Street. Puffing his Havana, he was glad, more glad than he could say, that the streets were deserted. For he couldn't bear to meet the quizzical expressions of townspeople should they see the tall darkie sitting in the buggy beside him.

It had been a week since Althea had arrived and he'd scarcely said two words to her. For she was such a far cry from the mother of his youth that he deliberately avoided her. No sir, he wasn't about to accept this—this *darkie* as a replacement for the woman he'd loved so completely. Even so, Althea had managed to fit in fine with the rest of his family. Daniel was especially kind to her. Katie too. But then that wasn't surprising. For Katie had been born into a slave–holding family. He had to admit though, he was a bit jealous of the children. For even they accepted her. Especially fourteen– month–old Marie whose rosebud mouth had rounded into an "oh" when Althea showed the quilts she had brought.

Ah yes, those quilts were beautiful. And she'd given Marie hers first, a flower–basket pattern with bright colors made just the size to fit her trundle bed. Benjamin's had been a dazzling kaleidoscope of scraps from solids to checks to plaids, while the one for Daniel and Katie had been a wedding–ring pattern pieced in pastel colors. But it was his own that drew the family's praise. For one glance told him it was scenes from his beloved Shenandoah Valley. He'd turned away then, biting hard on his cigar as he limped from the room.

Even so, he hadn't thanked her for it. But then why should he? Being good with her hands didn't erase the color of her skin. And he was sad, more sad than he could say, that she'd come to stay a fortnight. Another week like this was bound to drive him crazy. Personally, he wondered if he could even make it through this day. For today he could not avoid her. Today she was his to entertain. For Daniel had taken Katie and Benjamin to the Spring Grounds. And it was out of the question for Althea to accompany them. No, sir. For those Southern politicians wouldn't take kindly to a former slave parading about *their* grounds. And so he, Livingston, had harnessed a horse to the buggy so he could drive Althea to the north part of town. It was the only place he felt she belonged.

"Why do you insist on treating me as if I had been a slave?"

Althea's question was so unexpected he nearly dropped his Havana. Then getting a hold on himself, he glared at her. She was a pretty woman. A mighty pretty woman. But that didn't give her the right to put on airs. How dare she hold her head high as she bounced Marie on her knee? Whatever gave her the right to behave like whites? She was a darkie. And to think that his father had actually lived—

"You needn't bite that cigar in two. Just tell me why you think the worst of me."

"Because I *hate* darkies!" he snapped. "Just because my father championed the slaves—"

"But I was never a slave," she interrupted smoothly, then hurried on before he could reply. "I admit that I was born on a Virginia plantation. But it was my father's land. And *he* was a real "darkie" as you insist on calling us. It was my mother who was light. But regardless of the shades of their skins, my parents were kind people. They loved each other and their children. And they respected the forty or so slaves they owned."

Turnin, his face away from her, Livingston groaned. Ah yes, she was a free Negro. Lord, how could he have been so stupid as to not see that? For of course there had been no slaves in the Harrisonburg of his childhood. Even the old barber had been free. So why had he assumed—

"Mama died when I was eighteen." It was Althea's soft voice, revealing more of her background, more of herself. "Since I was the only girl, it was only right and proper for me to run the household. It wasn't hard really. For Papa was a good man. He just worried too much."

"How come you moved to Harrisonburg?"

"I didn't, until after the War. Like I said, my family was a good one. But the War changed everything. It didn't have to, I suppose. Maybe it wouldn't have if Papa hadn't been such a worrier. And he did worry; all the time. He was certain the Yankees would steal our crops and burn our home. Of course they never did." She paused, smiling briefly. Then smoothing Marie's dress, she went on. "He worried about the family too. You see, my younger brother had two sons who went off to fight for Virginia." Again she paused, looking off to her right. "My brother—my brother hung himself when word reached us that his oldest had died at Gettysburg. It was just as well I suppose, for the other one was killed the following year up by Chancellorsville. Papa—Papa took to his bed after that. And he died shortly after we received word of Lee's surrender."

Livingston said nothing. And for a moment the only sounds were the clop of horseshoes and Marie's delighted squeals as she played with scraps of fabric. They were nearing the African Christian Church when Althea went on.

"Ira and I moved to Harrisonburg in the spring of 1866. Ira set up his smithy and I my quilting frame. We got along just fine. I really didn't know I was lacking anything until I met Jeremiah." She turned to him then and smiled. "Your father was such a kind man. And he loved—"

"He did *not!*" Livingston spoke so savagely that the butt of his Havana flew from his mouth, landing in a gutter. Angry, he jerked the reins, turning the buggy onto Maude Street.

"I'm sorry you feel that way," Althea said, her lack of irritation fueling Livingston's anger. He was further irritated to realize he'd lost his cigar. Now he'd have to wait until he got home for another one. It was just as well he supposed, since he had to have help lighting them. Lord, he hated growing older, losing the full use of his body.

"You know, Livingston, I don't think you knew your father very well."

"Oh, I knew him, all right. Too well."

"Then you know he always loved people. All people."

"Not me, he didn't."

"Yes, especially you."

"No, he didn't. My father never cared one bit for me. Ah yes, he took *my* shoes and *my* supper to give to the poor. And he whipped *my* behind when Nettie got killed."

"I know. He told me those things. And lots more. Livingston, do you know your father named you himself?"

"Never told me."

"Well, he did. You see, Livingston means 'a loved son'."

"All right, so he named me. Then why did he treat me so abominably? Why?"

"I'm not sure, of course. But I think he saw you as part of himself. So when he gave your shoes away, in his mind it was himself doing the giving. And you know your father was generous to a fault."

"Ah, yes. And what about the whipping?"

"Oh, Livingston, don't you see? He was angry with himself that day. Angry that he hadn't protected his little girl. And so while he whipped you, it was his own soul he flailed."

Livingston groaned. Biting his lips together, he gave his attention to driving and turned the horse south again.

"You know, your father never really got over your leaving after your mother died. Of course he went on, helping others— preaching on Sundays." Althea paused, waving a fly from the face of the sleeping Marie.

"My father loved his pulpit," Livingston spoke matter–of–factly.

"I'm sure he did. And when they barred him from serving because he opposed slavery –" Althea looked off to the right again, a small sigh escaping her lips. It was several moments before she resumed speaking. "Jeremiah—Jeremiah was a broken man when I met him. Broken, but so very kind. Though he never returned to church, he was caring to the end."

Livingston sighed too. Lord, he wanted to cry for that kind old man. It seemed unfair that he had lost so much. Even so—

"Livingston, your father never forgot you. He spoke of you often. And Daniel. He wanted you both to be happy."

Biting his lips, Livingston concentrated on the dirt road ahead. Lord, what could he say that wouldn't sound condemning?

"You know, Livingston, even though I may seem more like a sister than a mother to you, I'd like to give you some motherly advice."

"Oh? And what's that?"

"Stop tiptoeing around those you love. Tell your son you love him. Share yourself with Katie and the children–"

"The way I shared myself with my mother and Nettie? The way I shared my life with Verna Marie? Lord, woman, do you *know* what you're asking?"

"I think so. I—"

But Livingston wasn't listening. He ignored the soft–spoken words as he turned back onto Lexington Avenue. Lord, he'd be glad to get home. To rid himself of this meddlesome woman. He'd be glad, more glad than he could say, to light up another Havana, lean back in his chair and forget this discussion had ever happened.

Chapter 72

Jane sighed as she guided satin fabric beneath the presser foot of her treadle machine. Land sakes, it was hot. Downright sultry, it was. And if her fingers kept astickin to this fabric, she'd ruin the dress fur sure. Then where would she be? Fur ever one in town knew Mrs. Mason was purt near the most persnickety woman this side of the Missouri River.

Pushing up her spectacles, Jane snipped thread, then carefully removed pins from the sleeve. Holding it up for a better view, she nodded. Fine. Now all it needed was a mite of pressin. An she'd a mind to put thet off till evenin. It was too blamed hot to heat her iron this afternoon. Picking up the second sleeve, Jane carefully matched notches, then pinned the seam together. She'd jist stitch this one then—

"Mrs. Fitzsimmons! Mrs. Fitzsimmons, come here quick! Fur God's sake HURRY!"

Startled, Jane flung down the sleeve and ran to the kitchen, her heart racing. Land sakes, what could be the matter, anyways? At the door, she gasped. No! It couldn't be. But it was. Michael was hurt. Mighty bad, it looked like. Ableedin like a stuck hog he was, an passed clear out. Mr. Cramer, a townsman she scarcely knew, was holdin him in his arms.

"Land sakes, bring him in here." And Jane led the way to their bedroom.

Gently, the burly Mr. Cramer laid Michael on the bed. Without a word Jane hurried back to her sewing and snatched up her sharpest shears. In the kitchen she grabbed half a dozen clean tea towels.

Back in the bedroom, Jane bent over her husband, nearly gagging at the sight and smell. For Michael's shredded apron was drenched with blood and waste. Grimacing, she cut away the apron and flung it aside. His shirt and trousers had to be cut, too, though carefully. For bits of fabric were imbedded in muscle and intestines.

"Land sakes, this is awful. What happened, anyways?"

"He was shoein Lightnin, he was. I told him to watch thet horse. But then he was careful, fur as thet's concerned. Reckon somethin must of scared old Lightnin. Anyways, he reared. Knocked the Mr. plumb off his feet, he did. An when thet foreleg came back down them nails went purt nigh through him. Young Fitzsimmons is gone fur the doc."

Frowning, Jane attempted to staunch the bloody flow with a towel. Land sakes, she wished Thomas would hurry. This was downright serious. Fur Michael's normally ruddy face was white as a sheet. An his breathin wasn't right. An the mess— All thet blood an feces thet wouldn't stop acomin—

"M—Mavoureen?"

"Land sakes," Jane scolded, "you jist keep quiet an lie still."

But Michael, his eyes fluttering, tried again. "Aye, Mavoureen, I'm right bad, mind. I—I— that is I'm thinkin you need to—to write me sister."

"Your sister?" Jane stopped sopping gore long enough to stare at him. "Land sakes, I didn't know you had one. Anyways, you'd best rest while I—"

"Allison." The whisper was urgent.

"In Rogersville?"

Michael nodded. "Tell her—tell her I love her. I—I always have, mind."

"Course you have. An I'll send thet letter right off, providin you git well. Land sakes, you jist rest now or I've a mind to smack you."

Michael, a faint smile playing across his moon–shaped face, lapsed into silence. Moments later, his eyes fluttered again.

"Mavoureen?" He attempted to raise his hand.

"Michael, please!" Jane covered the back of his hand with her own, caressing the hairs which curled there.

"Aye, Lass, I'm thinkin I'm not goin to mend. Meself, I—I've always loved folks the way the Good Book says to."

"Land sakes, course you have. An you're goin to go right on—"

But Michael wasn't finished. His thick shoulders heaving, he tried again.

"Aye, Lass, but only—only two really loved me, mind. You—you and Katie."

Jane could scarcely see the bloody rag in her hand for the tears.

"Land sakes, don't carry on thet away," she snapped. "Leastwise not now."

"Aye, Mavoureen, me own Mavoureen. I—"

It stopped then. The voice, the heaving shoulders, the breathing. Michael was dead.

"Guess the doc's too late after all."

Jane started at Mr. Cramer's voice. She'd forgotten he was there. Suddenly, she couldn't stand this steamy room with its horrid stench. Dropping the towel from her hand, she fled.

In the dining room, Jane drops into Michael's rocker, and stares through the window facing Main Street. The feeling now stealing over her is familiar. Why land sakes, course it is. Fur she set right here on another July day thirteen years ago. An watched her friend go away. An Claudia's leavin had changed her life furever.

An now, Michael's aleavin. Thet good man who'd stood on thet other July day wavin to his friend, Andrew, is atakin his own journey now. Fact is, he's agoin beyond the reach of them all. Never again will he tousle Katie's hair or sharpen tools fur Thomas or tell Benjamin a "wee little" story from Tennessee. Never again will he call her Mavoureen or run thick fingers through her hair or tell her she is bonny. Fur Michael is gone.

Caressing the crimson birthmark on her left cheek, Jane stares through the window into the bright sunlight beyond and weeps.

❖   ❖   ❖

Katie bites her bottom lip until she tastes blood. And still, her chin trembles; still, the tears flow unchecked. Standing before her bedroom bureau, she lets them fall as she clutches her K box to her heart.

Oh, My Pa, My Pa, why did you have to leave me fur, anyways? Why did you have to go before this new youngin is born? Don't you know I feel all done in like without you? Drat it all, I miss you somethin awful like. Really an truly I do.

Pressing her lips to the K box, Katie recalls the day My Pa gave it to her. After the War it was. "Aye, Lass, here's somethin fur your purties, mind." He'd tousled her hair then as she turned away and hurried upstairs. An it was on thet day she'd knelt before her bedroom window an watched the limbs of the maple tree swayin in the rain. An when the sun came out an them raindrops turned all sparkly like, she'd heard My Pa's soul callin to hers. She'd answered then, openin her arms to My Pa, lovin him with all her bein.

An now he's gone again. This man who tousled her hair when she cried at havin to quit school; this man who purt nigh cried on thet election day in 1868 when Thomas disgraced them all by insistin he had a right to vote; this man who lugged home gallons of spring water so My Ma could have a drink; this man who fashioned them kitchen utensils fur her new home; this man who smiled so proud like thet day Marie was born—this man is gone. Furever.

> *Under a spreading chestnut–tree*
> *The village smithy stands;*
> *The smith, a mighty man is he,*
> *With large and sinewy hands;*
> *And the muscles of his brawny arm*
> *Are strong as iron bands...*[1]

Remembering the poem from her childhood, Katie tries to smile. Thet was My Pa all right. Burly shoulders an thick hands; barrel–chested an moon–faced, he was. Strong too. Strong an tender. Fact is, it's his tenderness, his love fur life an people thet she remembers best.

> *Toiling,— rejoicing,— sorrowing,*
> *Onward through life he goes;*
> *Each morning sees some task begin,*
> *Each evening sees it close;*
> *Something attempted, something done,*
> *Has earned a night's repose.*
> *Thanks, thanks to thee, my worthy friend,*
> *For the lesson thou hast taught!*
> *Thus at the flaming forge of life*
> *Our fortunes must be wrought;*
> *Thus on its sounding anvil shaped*
> *Each burning deed and thought.*[2]

Oh, My Pa, My Pa, couldn't you have stayed here jist a little longer? Couldn't you have loved me jist a little more? Fur I'm comin all apart like without you. Really an truly I am.

Chapter 73

The warmth of citrine sunlight streaming into the sitting room caressed Livingston's face, causing him to stir. Sitting up slowly, he flexed his swollen fingers, welcoming the sun, though he knew it would be hot by midday. Already he could see beads of sweat forming on Benjamin's upper lip as he slept on a pallet on the floor. Already he could hear Daniel stirring in the front bedroom. For Daniel was to take Althea's trunks to the depot before he started work in the shop.

Althea. She was leaving today; going back to Harrisonburg. And he had to admit that he would miss her. Of course she'd made him angry at first. Angry and frightened and frustrated. Lord, how could he learn to love the man he'd hated all these years? And how could he learn to open himself to others? It was out of the question. Or it had been, until these past few days. Personally, he didn't know how she had done it, but somehow Althea had made him want to try. Like a patient teacher she had questioned him and instructed him and guided him toward loving. And now, she was leaving.

Ah yes, she was leaving. And he would miss her kind, caring ways; her thoughtfulness; and her refusal to be insulted. He'd miss having someone to reminisce with about Harrisonburg. He'd miss the sound of that soft, alluring voice and the sight of those gentle, competent hands. Hands which had created the quilt hanging over the end of the sofa.

Leaning forward, Livingston pulled the quilt toward him. Studying it, he had to admit it was beautiful. And it made him homesick, more homesick than he could say, for his childhood days in Virginia. For Althea had captured the essence of the Shenandoah Valley. There were the saffron yellows of summer wheat; the emerald greens of grasses and leaves; the varied roans of cattle and horses; the deep walnuts of upturned earth; the aqua greens of gently rolling hills; the indigo blues of softly peaked mountains—all done in tiny scraps of fabric. Lord, but he loved it. And her?

He could hear her now, moving softly about the kitchen. Closing his eyes, he could envision her lovely form as she measured coffee grounds, cut out biscuits and set the table. And he had to admit, he liked what he saw. A warm, gentle, desirable woman. A woman he could learn to love.

❖   ❖   ❖

Biting hard on his Havana, Livingston managed to climb down from the buggy. Then limping to the other side, he held up his arms for Althea. She stepped down lightly, barely leaning against him, as though to spare his swollen knee. Lord, but she was wonderful.

Taking her elbow, Livingston guided her to the platform, wishing that somehow the train would be late.

"It was kind of Daniel to bring my things down," Althea nodded toward her waiting trunks. "Especially since he's been so preoccupied with his father–in–law's passing. You know, Livingston, you have a thoughtful son. Definitely kin to his grandfather." She paused. "And his father."

Clamping down on his cigar, Livingston groaned. Lord, he didn't want her to go. He wanted to keep her here. He wanted to—

"Livingston, are you all right?"

"Of course I'm all right."

"Well you be sure now, to take care of those knees. Your hands too." And she lightly touched his swollen fingers.

"I will. Though, I must say I hate the thought of giving up my trade. It makes me sad, more sad than I can say, to abandon those lovely woods."

"I'm sorry too. But you do have Daniel, you know. And Katie."

Livingston nodded, unable to speak.

Whoo–whooo. Whoo–whooo.

The train was coming and Althea must leave. Separation. Lord, he didn't think he could bear it. But she was moving now, toward the rear passenger car, the short train of her traveling suit gliding graciously across the platform. Her foot was on the bottom step, when he broke.

"Wait. Oh, Lord, Althea wait!"

She stopped then, a question in her large, dark eyes.

"All aboard."

At the conductor's shout, Livingston hobbled faster. Hastily removing his straw hat and his Havana, he stopped beside her. Then reaching up, he pulled her lovely face down to meet his.

"Come again sometime. Please?" And he kissed her full, velvety lips.

"All abo–o–o–oard!"

Livingston stood back then, his hat and cigar dangling from swollen fingers as he watched the slender figure disappeared into the car. Seconds later, Althea was waving from the window, a warm smile lighting her lovely face. And then the train was moving, gathering speed, pouring steam. Whoo–whooo.

Groaning, Livingston turned away and limped toward his empty buggy. And he was halfway back up Spring Street before it occurred to him that *he* had kissed a darkie.

Chapter 74

Tramp. Tramp. Tramp. Hundreds of feet slapped the dust as Price's army marched north following their victory at Wilson's Creek. Bone–tired these fellers was, yet exhilarated. Hadn't they jist whupped thet bastard, Lyon? Tramp. Tramp. Tramp. Thomas scowled. He was sick an tired of this damn War. Sick an tired of fightin in this stinkin heat. He was sick an tired of rememberin his red bandanna tied about them bloody clumps of dun–colored hair.

Tramp. Tramp. Tramp. "Oh, Wade, what did you have to go an die fur? It didn't make a lick of difference nohow. Them Feds is still chasin us. Darn you, rascal, I need you. Purt near everone needs you. Your Pa, Julia—

Tramp. Tramp. Tramp. "Wade, oh, Wade, please come back. You're my best friend. Anyways, let's stop this silly fightin an skedaddle out of here."

Tramp. Tramp. Tramp. "Wade, listen. This is important like. We got to stop this here fightin."

Tramp. Tramp. Tramp. "Wade, please—I said STOP!"

Thomas sat up with a start. Glancing about, he saw he was sitting beneath the old oak tree. Dreamin about thet stinkin War , he was. An Wade. Shifting his legs, he puffed his pipe, his left sleeve brushing his eyes. Made a feller get all choked up like, rememberin. Course thet was all over now an he was safe in Brownsville. Minus an arm an his best friend, but safe.

Tramp. Tramp. Tramp. Thomas' mouth went dry with fear. Fur thet sound was *real*. Tramp. Tramp. Tramp. Them darn Feds was back. An they aimed to carry State's folks off. Leaping to his feet, Thomas crossed West Street and hurried down Main toward the sound of the marching. It was them all right, their blue coats an Springfield rifles shinin in the sun. An they was turnin down Bridge Street, marchin like they owned the place. An Katie an Benjamin was standin there watchin them.

"Git back!" Thomas panted as he neared his sister and his son. But Katie merely stared at him as though he was a mite silly. And Benjamin, his face alight with pleasure, pointed to the marching columns. "See, Father. See?"

But all Thomas saw was columns of blue–clad soldiers, marchin. Soldiers! Snatching his son with his left hand, Thomas jerked Benjamin backward. "Git back from there you little whippersnapper. You aim to git taken like My Pa did?"

"Thomas?" It was Katie.

But Thomas didn't hear. "Git back, I say!" And he reached for his sister.

But Katie, despite her increasing figure, spun away. "Thomas," she snapped, "what's wrong with you, anyways?"

Thomas glared at her. "What's wrong with *me?* Why, Katie, I mean to tell you them's soldiers. Feds they is, an we ain't safe."

"Oh, Thomas, fur goodness sakes. Them ain't Feds. They're police reserves from over by St. Louis. An they're goin to the Spring Grounds fur maneuvers."

"But Katie—"

"Oh, fur goodness sakes, Thomas, look at them. They ain't Feds. Besides, thet War's over an done with."

Thomas looked then. Really looked, and the stiffening went out of his legs. Course they wasn't Feds. Why, in all his born days he'd never seen a Fed wearin *light* blue trousers with white stripes runnin up the sides. Anyways, Katie was right, thet War was over. An My Pa had returned even if Wade hadn't. My Pa who had forbade him to hang thet CSA plaque in the dinin room. My Pa who loved peace an hated war.

"Thomas, are you all right?" It was Katie, touchin his left arm, lookin into his face.

"Course I'm all right." With that, Thomas jerked free and turned back toward home. Home, an thet blacksmith shop which stood empty. Home, where no man resided but himself. Home, where My Pa had so often touched his shoulder in a gesture of affection.

"Damn! Damn! Damn!" He swore then, as tears forced their way down his leathered cheeks. Fur he'd done it again. Like someone plumb stupid he'd gone an loved My Pa. An he hadn't aimed to. Fact was, he'd guarded his heart real careful like. Yet somehow, when he hadn't been thinkin, he'd answered when My Pa beckoned. An now My Pa was gone. Jist like Wade an Julia. An once again he was bleedin inside. Stuck real good he was, an hurtin like nobody's business.

Reaching into his pocket, Thomas drew out a blue bandanna and wiped his eyes. Damn, but he was sick an tired of hurtin. Sick an tired of carin an losin. Sick an tired enough not to love anyone again. Ever.

His lips in a taut line, Thomas shoved the bandanna back in his pocket. Then squaring his shoulders, he marched toward home where he picked up a wooden bucket off the back porch. He'd a mind to pick some corn fur supper.

Chapter 75

Stroking the bright birthmark on her left cheek, Jane stared at the lamp in the center of the kitchen table and shivered. September it was, an arainin to beat the band. September. Two months since Michael died, an it seemed purt near a lifetime. A lifetime of waitin fur them heavy footsteps to enter the kitchen of an evenin. A lifetime of waitin fur thet husky voice to say, "Aye, Mavoureen, you're a bonny lass, to be sure." A lifetime of goin to bed an gittin up alone.

Scratching her head, Jane sighed. Land sakes, she'd be agittin lice if she didn't wash her hair soon. But she didn't have the gumption. No gumption to comb her hair or take a bath or dress in the latest fashion. No gumption to pretend she was purty. Fact was, she barely had the strength to tend to her customers. Like thet satin dress she was astitchin fur Mrs. Johnson, she was acomin all unraveled at the seams. An she couldn't afford to. Why land sakes, business had been downright slow these last few weeks. Still an all, she couldn't blame her customers if they didn't cotton to the spittin Mamie or her own witch–like self. Why, she'd be flat out of business if it wasn't fur thet loyal Sally. But even Sally couldn't make amends furever. She'd jist have to take herself an Mamie in hand. But not now. She jist didn't have the gumption.

Course things would be a mite easier if Thomas would take to smithin. Leastwise then they'd have a little more acomin in. But Thomas was flat out against it. Why land sakes, he even had the idea of sellin Michael's tools an tearin down thet old shop. Well, she wouldn't stand fur it. Gave him a real tongue lashin, she did, in this very kitchen. "Land sakes, your Pa ain't hardly cold in the ground an you're afixin to sell off his things? Why, thet's downright shameful. An I've a mind to whup your backside fur even thinkin on such a thing. Now scat!"

Thomas had left then. But his taut lips an the stiffness in them legs told Jane she'd not heard the end of it. Land sakes, the impudence of thet man. An her atryin to make do with purt near nothin.

Course she could ask Katie fur help. But Katie had enough troubles of her own. Expectin her second youngin she was, an saddled with the care of old Mr. Lewis. Fur Daniel's pa was downright poorly. Why land sakes, she reckoned he never tended the shop no more. Leastwise thet's what Katie said. Still an all, you'd think *someone* could help. Fact was, Linda was carryin on a thrivin business. But she didn't cotton to them much nowadays. Like her pa, she'd taken to actin uppity, givin a cold shoulder to the rest of the family.

Scratching her head, Jane sighed. Maybe thet sister of Michael's could help out. Course Jane would have to read her letter first. An she'd been puttin thet off, awonderin if she'd done right to contact her in the first place. But Michael had said to, an so she had. And now, the answer lay at her fingertips, on the table. Picking up the envelope, Jane wondered again why Michael had waited until he was adyin to think of his sister. Well, she'd a mind to find out. Now. Taking a case knife, Jane slit the envelope and pulled out a sheet of paper. Then pushing her spectacles more firmly into place, she read:

Dear Jane,

> *You could have knocked me over with a turkey feather when I got your letter about Michael. I figured he'd done died a long time ago.*

> *He did fur us, mind. Me an Me Mom, thet is. Aye, we'd have throwed him out after Me Dad died, cept Me Dad left him thet smithy. Me Mom thought we needed him. Aye, what fur I don't know. The rascal was a pagan, to be sure. Never set foot inside a church long as I can remember.*

> *Me, I hated him. So after Me Mom died, I turned him out. Him an thet ugly slave of his. They were out West the last I heard. Most probably livin as wild as thet country out there.*

> *Aye, Me Dear, furgit about Michael. You're better off without him, to be sure.*

> *Allison Fitzsimmons*

For a moment Jane simply stared at the paper in her hand. Then angrily, she crushed it into a ball. Jumping from her chair, she rushed to the cookstove. Then, opening the small door on the left, she hurled the ball into the fire and slammed the door shut. The nerve of thet woman! Sayin them unkind things about her Michael. Why, she'd a mind to give her a good tongue lashin. Leastwise maybe then she wouldn't be actin so high an mighty. But of course she couldn't do thet. Why land sakes, she lived clear out in Tennessee.

Jane paused then before the mirror above the washstand. The mirror that Michael had looked in every morning when he shaved. Michael. Thet kind, gentle man who said he loved his sister. But why? Why pay any mind to a selfish person like thet?

"Aye, Mavoureen, you know I've always loved folks, the way the Good Book says to."

Jane started. Surely thet was Michael's voice. But it was only a memory she heard. The memory of a man who loved simply because God said to. An how many of them loved back?

"Aye, Mavoureen, only two really loved *me*, mind. You an Katie."

Frowning, Jane touched her left cheek. Michael loved, with no strings attached. It was enough thet the Good Book said to do it. An she? What was she adoin now, anyways?

Catching a glimpse of herself in the mirror, Jane winced. Land sakes, here I am afeelin downright sorry fur myself when what I should be adoin is thinkin of others. Lovin folks, like Thomas. An Mamie.

Turning up the lamp, Jane ladled cold water into the tea kettle. She'd fix a cup of tea, then make some plans fur tomorrow. She'd return to thet shop an tend to them customers like they was special folks. She'd talk to Linda an Katie an— oh, jist everone. Fur everone needed lovin.

When the kettle began to sing, Jane hummed along. Why land sakes, she was afeelin downright happy. An after tonight she'd feel even better. Fur tonight she was agoin to scrub her head an take a nice warm bath.

Chapter 76

On a gray October afternoon, Katie kneels before three tombstones. Tracing the letters on the smaller one, she sighs. My goodness, has it really been sixteen years since her brother went away? It don't seem like it. Yet there it is, plain as day:

PATRICK FITZSIMMONS
June 5, 1846—March 12, 1863.

Sixteen years since them dumb Feds killed Patrick an took My Pa away. Sixteen years of livin with only one brother. Sixteen years of watchin Mamie come apart like with grief. Even now, it seems like they should all be gatherin in the kitchen fur supper: My Pa, My Ma, Aunt Jane, Thomas(with *two* arms), Patrick, Mamie—

But they ain't. Fur Patrick is gone, an My Ma. Placing her hand on a larger stone, Katie bites her lower lip. Drat it all, why had My Ma taken on so over Patrick? She'd been no account fur nothin once them Feds had shot her youngin. An then, after Uncle James got killed, she'd gone clear off her rocker. Really an truly she had. Still, there'd been My Pa—

> *Under a spreading chestnut–tree*
> *The village smithy stands;*
> *The smith a mighty man is he,*
> *With large and sinewy hands;...* [1]

"Stop! Stop! Oh, please—" And Katie wraps her arms about herself, as though to shield herself from memories. But the images won't go away. The one of My Pa bouncing her on his knee while he tells a story about a "wee little lad who lived in a wee little house, in a wee little town in Tennessee". Or the one of My Pa tousling her hair as she cries fur them purty red ribbons Mamie burned up. Or more recently, the one of him rockin on the back porch, amused by Aunt Jane playin ma to baby Marie. They was all there. An they'd called her—called her away, to a place of givin an sharin. An what had she got fur all thet carin? My Pa went away, thet's what. An she—

"Hanne, oh, Hanne. *Meine* beautiful, *Hannechen!*"

At the unfamiliar words, Katie turns. What's this all about, anyways? Why, my goodness, you'd think whoever it is would at least speak English. Course thet is the German section over yonder. An it jist might be—Course it is. It's the purty young woman she met thet day in Aunt Jane's shop. An she's fallen over a fresh grave.

Getting to her feet Katie wipes her eyes with a handkerchief, chiding herself for still missing My Pa. Why my goodness, it's jist plain silly to be takin on this way. Still, her chin trembles as she picks her way across the cemetery. Bending, she touches a heaving shoulder.

"Gretchen?"

Jerking upright, the younger woman glares at her. "Frieda," she snaps.

"Oh my goodness, yes. Of course, Frieda." Katie sighs, looking into hazel eyes which brim with tears. In her whole life she reckons she's never felt so at loss fur words. What can she say, anyways?

"Your daughter?" she points toward the grave.

Frieda nods. Then reaching out, she touches Katies protruding belly. *"Miene Hannechen."*

Katie nods. Frieda has lost a youngin. A tiny girl. Leastwise, thet's what the stone says.

HANNE LOEBER

August 20, 1879—September 15, 1879

Suddenly, as Katie watches the tears glide down plump cheeks, she sees her own little Marie. And her heart breaks for Frieda.

"I'm so sorry."

Frieda stops crying then and attempts a wistful smile. Without thinking, Katie opens her arms.

"Danke. Danke schon."

Katie lets her own tears fall then as she hugs this new friend close. Frieda is a beautiful person. Really an truly she is.

❖   ❖   ❖

"Katie, what's wrong?" Daniel's voice barely concealed his impatience. For the third time that evening he'd attempted conversation, only to be rebuffed. Sighing, Daniel tossed the sheet aside, letting the breeze cool his naked chest. It was warm, too warm for October. So warm in fact, that some folks were worried fall would never come.

Daniel worried too. But not about the weather. He worried about Katie, pure and simple. For weeks now she had spurned his attempts at lovemaking. Thinking her present attitudes would blow over, he'd been patient. Yet, even his tenderest touch failed to arouse her.

"Katie?" he tried again. "Darling, what's wrong?"

"Nothin's wrong. I'm jist fine. Really an truly I am." With that she rolled away from him.

But Daniel knew better. Of course something was wrong. For despite the fact she didn't love him, Katie had never pulled away from him before. Until recently. But then no doubt, she'd decided that since she was already with child she didn't need him anymore. He supposed that was normal enough. Ah well, just so long as she wasn't seeing Thane. Or was she? No! He must not dwell on that.

Clenching his fists and breathing deeply, Daniel stared at the ceiling, trying to think of other things. His father's deteriorating health; Benjamin's increasing aptitude for furniture making; Marie's ability to wind him around her finger; the coming baby—he did hope it would be a boy this time; Katie's family—

Ah, of course. Katie was missing her father. Why hadn't he realized that in the first place?

"Katie?"

No answer.

"Katie? Darling, is it your father you're missing?"

No answer.

"It's all right to miss him, you know." Daniel touched her shoulder as he spoke. "The truth is, I—I missed my mother when she died. It was torture, pure torture, having to do without her. Even so—" His hand moved to the base of Katie's neck then and on to the silky smoothness of her cheek. God, how he loved the feel of her skin. His fingers crept downward again until they gently cupped her chin. It trembled.

"Katie?" he moved closer.

"Leave me alone." Katie grasped his wrist then and shoved his hand away.

"But, Darling, I only—"

"I *said* leave me alone!"

"But, Katie, I only want to share your grief, to love—"

"Drat it all, man, can't you see I'm all done in like? Now fur goodness sakes, jist leave me alone. I don't need you, anyways."

The words lashed his chest, curled about it and tightened. God, he wanted to hide. To retreat into his inner sanctuary, safe from the whip of Katie's rejection. But he couldn't. For the truth was, that on that Christmas Eve when he'd vowed again to love her, he'd meant it.

His fists clenched, Daniel breathed a prayer, "Oh, Christ, I need you, pure and simple. Be near me, love me and make it pleasure, pure pleasure, for me to love Katie." It grew quiet then. And gradually the warmth of the breeze, the rustle of leaves and the depths of his love worked their will. Daniel's fingers uncurled, his chest expanded. He slept.

Chapter 77

Jane shivered as the March wind whistled outside the dining room window. Land sakes, it was cold. Reached well below freezin last night an not much warmer today. Sighing, she drew her rocker closer to the fireplace and commenced hemming a dress. Land sakes, she was weary this evenin. Downright tired she was, an needin rest. But Mrs. Mason had been purt near rude this mornin when she marched into the shop askin if her dress was ready. Rude an a mite angry till Jane promised to have it finished by tomorrow. Still, Jane couldn't complain none. Hadn't business purt near doubled since she went back to mindin the shop herself?

Even so, Mamie still wasn't actin right. An she reckoned the child wasn't entirely to blame fur thet. Why land sakes, thet girl looked downright peaked nowadays. Eatin little an drinkin lots. Like right now. Slinkin across the kitchen floor she was, toward thet water pail when she'd done had a drink not three minutes ago.

"Mamie?"

"You call me?" And Mamie appeared in the doorway, a metal dipper in her hand.

"Course I called you. Land sakes, Girl, what you adrinkin again fur? Why, at this rate them springs will be dried up in no time."

"Oh fur heaven sakes, Aunt Jane, I'm thirsty."

"Course you are. An thin too. Purt near thin enough to blow away. Leastwise you would be if you was standin outside. Why land sakes, Girl, you got to start eatin."

"Please, Aunt Jane, don't take on so. I—I—" And Mamie burst into tears. The dipper hit the wood floor with a thud as she covered her face with trembling hands.

334

"Why land sakes, Girl, I didn't mean no harm. Come here an sit beside me." And Jane patted the hassock at her feet.

Without a word, Mamie padded across the floor and sat down. But the tears continued to fall, slipping through her fingers and splotching her flannel nightgown.

Running her hand over Mamie's auburn mane, Jane sighed. Why land sakes, even the girl's hair was alosin its shine. Whatever was the matter, anyways?

"Mamie? Girl, what's wrong?"

"Oh, Aunt Jane, I'm goin to die. I—I've—"

"Nonsense. You may be ahurtin but you ain't adyin. Why land sakes, you're still a youngin. Why, thirty-one ain't—"

"Oh, Aunt Jane, fur heaven sakes, stop your jawin." Mamie looked up then, her green eyes glittering in the firelight. "I—I *am too* goin to die. Doc says—he says I got diabetes."

"No."

"Yes. An it's a God–awful thing to have too. But please, don't be such a meanie. You're all I've got left."

"Why land sakes, Girl, I ain't no meanie. Leastwise I don't aim to be. Course to be downright truthful, I never did cotton to you the way your Ma did. Still an all, I love you.

"Course you do. But I guess—I guess I jist liked bein selfish. Carryin on real uppity I been. Only now, now I wish I'd done different."

"Well, providin you mean thet, you can change."

"Oh fur heaven sakes, Aunt Jane, stop pretendin. I can't change things *now*. It's too late."

"Course it ain't too late. Why land sakes, Girl, you ain't dead yet. You've got lots of time to change. So jist git busy right now an start lovin folks."

"No." Mamie shook her head. "I ain't lovin folks. I did thet a long time ago. An Patrick he—he—got killed."

"Course he did. But jist cause them Feds shot Patrick don't mean they killed everone around here. There's still Thomas, an Katie—"

"No. I ain't lovin Katie. So you can jist kiss thet notion good–by."

"Why land sakes, Girl, you're a real stick–in–the–mud ain't you? Why, I've a mind to whup your backside fur actin like thet."

"But, Aunt Jane, I loved—"

"Hush, Girl. I know you loved Patrick, an your Ma, an your Pa. An they all went off an left you. Why land sakes, I miss them too. Specially, your Pa. He—he—" Jane paused, touched her birthmarked cheek, then went on. "Your Pa loved me, Girl. An I loved him."

"But, Aunt Jane, it's so *hard!* Losin loved ones is most more than a body can take."

"Course it's hard. I ain't sayin its easy. But the fact, is it's the only way to live. Cause like thet Good Book says, you got to give away your heart if you aim to keep it. Now, have you a mind to change or not?"

"Oh, Aunt Jane, I don't know. I jist don't know." And sniffling, Mamie rose and hurried from the room.

Amber rays of sunlight filtered through muslin curtains as Jane sat sipping a cup of tea after supper. The kitchen was quiet, fur Mamie hadn't even bothered to come down, an Thomas was asmokin thet pipe an abroodin as usual. Land sakes, he looked downright tired this evenin. But then he ought to be, seein as how he'd been busy at thet smithy all day.

Sighing, Jane poured another cup of tea and set the strainer aside. She'd miss thet old shop when it was gone. Purt near as much as she missed Michael. Still an all, apples was a good cash crop. An them blossoms smelled downright heavenly along about May. Anyways, at least Thomas had some gumption nowadays. An thet was a mite better than watchin him mope fur hours on end.

"Aunt Jane."

Startled, Jane looked up to see Thomas standing beside her. Why land sakes, she'd been so busy athinkin, she hadn't seen him leave his chair.

"I found this in the smithy. Thought you might think it important like, seein as how you loved them niggers so much." And he laid a folded piece of paper beside her tea cup.

"Why land sakes, what is this, anyways? It's so old it's purt near yellow. Where'd you say you found it?"

But Thomas had gone, leaving her alone. Frowning, Jane shoved her glasses higher on her nose and unfolded the crackling paper. It was a verse. A very long verse and dated in 1830.

"Why land sakes, this was written fore I was even born. By Claudia's ma too, the first Rachel. Wonder what she said, anyways?"

> *Lord, if thou dost with equal eyes*
> *See all the sons of Adam rise,*
> *Why dost thou hide thy face from slaves*
> *Confined by fate to serve such knaves ?*
> *Stolen and sold in Africa,*

Transported to a America
Like hogs and sheep in market sold
To stand the heat and bear the cold
To work all day and half the night
And rise before the morning light.
Sustain the lash, endure the pain,
Exposed to storms of snow and rain,
Pinch'd both with hunger and with cold
If we complain we meet a scold....
When will Jehovah hear our cries?
When will the sons of freedom rise?
When will a Moses for us stand
And free us all from Pharaoh's hand?
What tho' our skin be black as jet,
Our hair be curld, our noses flat?
Must we for this no freedom have
Until we find it in the grave?
Yet while I thus my fate condole
Jesus, my Lord, possess my soul
For all the comfort that I have
While I am here confin'd a slave
Is that strong hope that I'm made free
By thy rich blood once shed for me.
My soul is free, it can't be sold
For all the gold that can be told.
And when my body drops in dust
My spirit in thy hand I trust.
And tho' no coffin I shall have,
Nor yet be laid into a grave,
The Lord will watch it from the skies
Till the great trumpet bid it rise.
Contentment, Lord, on me bestow
While I remain a slave below,
And while I suffer grief and wrong
May thy salvation be my song.[1]

Finished, Jane solemnly refolded the paper. Why land sakes, she could see thet first Rachel now. Beautiful she was, with them firm breasts an slender legs. An black eyes set in a cocoa face. Still an all, them eyes had been wells full of sorrow thet day Pa took her Dinah off to Glasgow to sell. Grievin she was, fur her oldest daughter.

An thet long trip to Missouri. Why land sakes, Jane had been so full of her own sorrow them days she'd paid no mind to Rachel. But she must have been sad. Why land sakes, Kentucky had been her home too.

Fact was, Missouri life was downright cruel to Rachel. After Pa was killed, her Adrian was sold straight off. Whisked away he was, with no thought fur his grievin wife. Course James had tended to thet. But it was Jordana who separated Rachel from her other children. Fur Jordana was amarryin an amovin into Brownsville. An she took Rachel along, leavin son Harry an daughter Claudia on the farm. What had thet slave thought of thet day as she waved good–by to the last of her family?

Poor Rachel. She'd died shortly after thet move. She never guessed her Harry would rape Mrs. Lewis an be hung fur it. She never guessed thet Claudia would marry Michael's Andrew an have a Rachel of her own.

Poor Rachel. She'd lived an died a slave. Freed only by death. An Claudia? How had she felt, anyways? Course Claudia'd been freed. Fact was, she'd been free enough to up an move away. Still an all, she'd looked as wretched as any slave thet day she climbed into the creakin wagon.

Rereading Rachel's poem, Jane was stunned. How naive, how down-right simple she'd been all these years. Course Claudia was free. But not as free as Jane. Why land sakes, she couldn't even *live* amongst them business folks in town. She couldn't jist shop anywhere she'd a mind to. An she couldn't do nothin to thet white man who'd raped *her* Rachel.

The sun had set by the time Jane refolded the verse for the last time. Laying it aside, she vowed to put it in a drawer somewheres. Keep it as a reminder of them other days.

Placing a hand on her left cheek, Jane stared at the yellowed paper and cried. My but she wished she'd understood better then. Wished she'd been kinder, more carin. She wished she hadn't been so impudent; so sure of herself. Mostly though, she wished she could see her jist once more— thet skinny little girl with caramel–colored skin an kinky hair, who had been her dearest friend.

Chapter 78

Sunlight poured through the sitting room window warming Katie's neck as she sat rocking baby Jeremiah. Running her hand across the brown fuzz on his head, she had a sudden longing to see Bonnie. Why my goodness, they had ever so much to talk about. Besides, Katie reckoned she jist wanted to show off this new youngin. Fur at three months, he was already somethin special like. Really an truly he was. Jist like Bonnie's new youngin was bound to be. Fur Bonnie was in the family way again.

> *Oh, Katie I'm so happy I could die. I'm goin to have another youngin! An the idea has purt near made me go silly. She'll be a right nice one too. (I jist know it'll be a girl.) Fact is, I can't hardly wait to show her off, take her fur buggy rides an watch her grow. Oh fur cryin out loud, there I go talkin loony again. Why, she ain't even due till August. Still, in all my life I ain't never been so happy.*

Katie smiled, remembering her animated friend. Somethin special was bound to happen to Bonnie. She jist hoped this new youngin would be all right.

The rattle of a newspaper broke into Katie's thoughts. Glancing up, she saw this week's *Herald* slip from Mr. Lewis' swollen fingers to the floor.

"Well, I must say things are really changing around here. I see they're shipping the Daisy off to St. Louis. Personally, I thought her an asset to our own Spring Grounds."

Katie nodded, then gave her entire attention to Jeremiah. Drat it all, what did she care about thet steamboat fur, anyways? Why my goodness, she only rode the thing once. On July Fourth, it was. An so hot she like to melted. Still, as they paddled their way down the Blackwater, she'd felt close to Daniel. Closer than she ever had. Why my goodness, she'd purt nigh swooned when his scarred hand had closed over hers as they stood on the deck together. After all, she reckoned he was the most handsome man there, wearin his new straw hat an all. Still, thet had been before My Pa—

No. She wouldn't think on My Pa. Leastwise not this mornin. Why my goodness, she had two youngins to mind an an old man to care fur. She reckoned she didn't have time fur mopin around. But drat it all, she missed him. Really an truly she did.

"Katie? Daughter, is something the matter?"

Startled, Katie looked up to meet her father–in–law's eyes. Gray they was, like Daniel's. An jist as full of love.

"No, course not. I'm fine. Really an truly I am. But I'll bet you're wantin somethin awful to hold this here youngin."

With that Katie crossed the room and placed the sleeping baby in his grandfather's arms. She took Livingston's cigar from his mouth then and tossed it into the pot–bellied stove.

"Thank you, Daughter. I must admit I like holding the boy. You and Daniel have made me happy, more happy than I can say." And he smiled at the child cuddled against his flannel shirt. "He'll make a fine man someday. A mighty fine man."

Sighing, Katie pulled her rocker closer. Drat it all, didn't neither of her youngins want *her?* After all, she was their ma. But fact was, they both preferred them men. Why my goodness, Marie had taken to Daniel right off like. An she'd be down there in thet shop this minute if Daniel would stand fur it. Course he wouldn't, so the youngin contented herself playin with them wooden blocks Daniel had made fur her. Katie frowned. She did worry about thet youngin now an again. Stubborn she was, jist plain stubborn. She wanted what she wanted an nothin else would do.

Jeremiah was a different turn though. Content like, he was. Why, she reckoned in his whole short life he hadn't fussed more than a handful of times. Still, he was Grandpa's youngin. Why my goodness, right now he had them dark eyes open an was smilin up at thet old man like he was somethin special like. Course Daniel's pa was a lot more lovin than he used to be. Kinder he was, more gentle like. In her whole life she'd never knowed anyone to change like he had. An she reckoned Althea had done it.

Althea. Katie shook her head. She jist couldn't figure thet one out. Why my goodness, it was plain as day thet Daniel's pa didn't take to

Negroes. Course this one was his step–ma. Still, he'd treated her somethin awful like them first few days she was here. Then slow like, he started changin. An since she'd gone back East, he'd been jist plain nice. Fact was, he seemed almost happy like, even if he was stuck up here in these quarters all the time. An he cared more fur Daniel too. Even hugged him once he had, on the day thet Jeremiah was born. An then they'd cried like a couple of youngins, while Daniel's long fingers pressed into his pa's back. Once she even thought she heard the older man say, "I love you, Son", to Daniel. But she couldn't be sure, seein as how done in she was an all.

Katie sighed. Seemed like jist about everbody was happy these days: Daniel, his pa, even Aunt Jane. An she wanted to be happy, too. Really an truly she did. But drat it all, she jist couldn't furgit about My Pa. An rememberin how he went still made her come all apart like. It jist wasn't no use. She reckoned she jist wasn't the sort to be kind an carin like. Leastwise not now. Anyways—But Katie wouldn't let herself think anymore. Instead, she turned away from Daniel's pa, hugged herself tightly and rocked.

❖   ❖   ❖

Daniel hummed softly as he strolled west on Lexington Avenue. For he had just purchased Walt Whitman's *Leaves of Grass*. Katie would love it, pure and simple. And maybe, just maybe, she would love him too. Ah well, it was worth a try anyway.

Pausing before Fuld and Hoffman's Dry Goods, he looked up. Up to where the afternoon sun cast an amber glow on a white–bricked wall. Katie. He could still see her as they danced in the hall behind that wall on New Year's night in 1877. The place had been crowded that night, but he had seen only Katie. And it had been pleasure, pure pleasure, to hold her lovely form in his arms. For Katie was beautiful, pure and simple. And her large, gray eyes, her petal–soft skin and her pink, silk gown had combined to capture his heart. And try as he might, he hadn't succeeded in reclaiming it.

Ah well, that was all behind him now. And the truth was, that in spite of the anguish she'd caused him, Katie was worth loving. Just to be in the same room with her, to study her lovely face as she nursed their new son filled him with a contentment that defied description.

Ah, Katie, my love, my love. Smiling softly, Daniel crossed the street and quickened his steps toward home.

Chapter 79

It was a warm, gloomy afternoon and Katie sighed as she settled into a rocker in the sitting room. Drat it all, why did the sun have to hide fur, anyways? Made it seem purt nigh like evenin. Still, she didn't light the lamp. For Daniel's pa rested easily in the overstuffed chair and she didn't want to disturb him. Or baby Jeremiah who slept in the cradle at his feet.

Opening the book in her hands, Katie leaned closer to the window. Walt Whitman. Why my goodness, she'd never even heard of him. Still, he must be somethin special like, seein as how he'd had all them poems published. Leastwise Daniel seemed to think so. An today she'd a mind to read him fur herself. An she reckoned she'd start right here with this one.

> *O Captain! my Captain! our fearful trip is done,*
> *The ship has weather'd every rack, the prize we sought is*
> *won.*
> *The port is near, the bells I hear, the people all exulting,*
> *While follow eyes the steady keel, the vessel*
> *grim and daring;*
> *But O heart! heart! heart!*
> *O the bleeding drops of red,*
> *Where on the deck my Captain lies,*
> *Fallen cold and dead...*
> *The ship is anchor'd safe and sound,*
> *its voyage closed and done,*
> *From fearful trip the victor ship comes in*
> *with object won:*
> *Exalt O shores, and ring O bells!*
> *But I with mournful tread,*

> *Walk the deck my Captain lies,*
> *Fallen cold and dead.*[1]

Biting her lip, Katie reread the last stanza. Thet was beautiful. Really an truly it was. Even if it was about thet stupid War an thet dumb Fed, Abe Lincoln. Made her feel purt nigh sad like, it did.

She turned the pages then to find a shorter verse. Here, this one. Why my goodness, this one had a mark beside it. A big check mark. Drat it all, someone had been messin with her new book. An if it was Benjamin she'd light right into him. Jist cause he'd been to school last year didn't give him no reason to be botherin *her* books. She'd talk to him right off like, at supper time. Take him in hand, she would. But fur now she'd jist read them lovely words.

> *O you whom I often and silently come where you are that I*
> *may be with you,*
> *As I walk by your side or sit near, or remain in the same*
> *room with you,*
> *Little you know the subtle electric fire that for your sake is*
> *playing within me.* [2]

Katie hugged herself, her chin trembling. Why my goodness, course Benjamin never marked thet poem. A man had. A man in love. An it made her go all trembly like, jist readin it. Fact was—

"Aunt Katie! Aunt Katie?" As though he knew she'd been thinking of him, Benjamin hurried up the steps.

"Sh—h," Katie placed a finger to her lips as the boy appeared in the doorway. When he instantly began to tip toe, she reached out a hand to touch him. She loved this youngin, really an truly she did. An she was sorry fur blamin him about thet mark. For though he remained a quiet child, Benjamin had become a real help to Daniel.

"Aunt Katie, a lady wants to see you," he whispered.

"Oh my goodness. Well, seein as how she's already here, tell her to come on up. I'll jist mix up some lemonade—"

Benjamin shook his head. "She can't come upstairs. Uncle Daniel said for you to come down." Then as if sensing her hesitation, he added, "I'll stay with Grandfather and the children."

"Thanks, Benjamin. You're a good youngin. Really an truly you are." Katie laid aside her book then and made her way downstairs. Why my goodness, who would be comin to see her, anyways? Course if it was Bonnie—Katie hurried the last few steps, then stopped. For the figure curled on a chair was certainly not her friend. She was too thin. Looked somethin awful like, she did. Why my goodness, she was purt nigh one of them skeleton things.

"Katie?"

"Mamie?"

The skeleton nodded and started to rise. Then falling back, she snapped. "Oh fur heaven sakes, look at me. I can't even git up no more."

"It's all right. Really an truly it is." Katie frowned as she seated herself in a vacant chair next to her sister. What was wrong with Mamie, anyways? Why my goodness, she looked all done in like. Not fit to be out visitin. Course it could be worse. If Daniel had customers— But he didn't. He remained in the background, expertly shaping a leg for someone's table.

"Katie? I know you're wonderin why I'm here. I ain't tryin to be a meanie or nothin." Mamie paused, then opened her handbag. "I—I jist wanted Marie to have this."

"Marie?" Katie frowned. Drat it all, what was Mamie up to this time? If she hurt Daniel's favorite—

"Oh fur heaven sakes don't look at me like thet! I ain't goin to scratch your precious youngin. I jist wanted—Oh, here—" And she pulled a length of ribbon from her bag. Red ribbon it was, an inch wide an shiny. Purt nigh a yard of it too.

Katie stared. Then digging both fists into her sides, she glared at her sister. "Drat it all, Mamie. I ain't goin to be done in by one of your tricks. Why, my goodness I've a mind to—"

"Oh, Katie, fur heaven sakes, stop bein so persnickety. I jist brought this fur Marie. Thet's all." Mamie sniffled then as she tossed the ribbon at Katie. "Take it an—an when thet youngin gits ready fur schoolin tie up thet hair with it."

Katie touched the ribbon on her lap, her mind whirling. What was Mamie meanin by this, anyways? Why, Marie wasn't near old enough fur schoolin.

"Please, Katie?"

Katie's mind jolted to a stop. And she saw on its screen the picture of a young girl. A good youngin she was, who loved schoolin. An she hummed as she tied narrow red ribbons on the ends of her braids. Ribbons she'd been right proud of.

"Katie?"

The green eyes looking at her were flooded with tears.

"Tell—tell Marie it's special like. Jist fur school wearin."

"Course I'll tell her. Why my goodness, she'll be purt nigh proud, havin a purty like this."

"Well, I guess I've been jawin long enough." And Mamie tried to stand.

"Here." Katie helped her then, conscious of her sister's thinness. Yet, Mamie seemed content as she weaved toward the door where she turned, smiling briefly.

"Katie, take good care of your man now. He's most special, you know."

Her chin trembling, Katie nodded. Why my goodness, what was she supposed to say, anyways? What did Mamie know—

But Mamie was already gone, padding softly down the boardwalk toward home.

Chapter 80

Brownsville, Missouri
July 29, 1880

Dear Althea,
I take my seat this afternoon to write you one last time...

Livingston winced as his fingers labored to guide the pen. Lord, but this was going to be painful, more painful than he had imagined. Even so, it would be worth the trouble. For Althea was a fine woman. A mighty fine woman.

Thank you for the box of Havanas. Your likeness...

Again his swollen fingers balked. Sweating, he forced them into action.

Your likeness on the lid is lovely. Almost as lovely as you
are in person. It makes me glad, more glad than I can say
to have it...

This time Livingston groaned, his fingers throbbing. "Oh, Lord," he breathed, "let me write just this once more." Biting hard on his new Havana, he pushed his fingers again.

I hope this finds you well. The family here is fine.
Daniel... Daniel enjoys his work and is kind. But person-
ally, I think he longs for Katie's love...Katie seems to
enjoy motherhood. And I must admit she's becoming a
first–rate cook... My father's namesake is growing. He
sits up by himself now. I wish you could see him... Little
Marie is still Daniel's special girl. At times I imagine a
young Daniel with another little girl riding his
shoulders...Ah well, my little Joy is forever with God

now...Benjamin is a fine lad, a mighty fine lad. He's six now and helps Daniel in the shop...

There's not much news around here that would be of interest to you. Though I did see that the M.E. Colored Church laid the corner stone for their new building a week or so ago... Our town continues to grow. The census of 1870 recorded 300 people. This year's, 1200...All things considered, I'm glad I settled here when I came West...

Althea, my days are numbered. My rheumy knees confine me to these living quarters now... And my fingers—they can scarcely guide this pen...Even so, I must thank you again for that lovely quilt you gave me. It is as close to Virginia as I will ever be again...

Althea, I love you. Forgive me, if you can, for not accepting you from the beginning...I simply didn't know a darkie could be so fine. And you, my dear, are a fine woman. A mighty fine woman...Forgive me too, if I seem to speak out of turn. I do not ask that you love me. For I'm a far cry from the caring man that my father was. But then you know that...Even so, I'm different from what I was before I met you...You see, Dear, from the day my Verna Marie was raped, I closed my heart to love...You helped me to open it again...

Althea, in a different time, under different conditions, I think we might have wed...But Brownsville is no place for you. And I'm too crippled to care for you properly...Even so, an old man is entitled to his dreams...

Take care of yourself, my dear. You are a special person. A very special person. I understand now, why my father made you his own...

> *Your humble servant,*
> *Livingston Lewis*

Chapter 81

Katie poured herself a cup of hot tea, then sat down to the kitchen table. My but it was cool. Specially fur August Why my goodness, folks was usually sweatin like troopers along about now. Still, she wasn't fixin to complain. Thet rain had been somethin wonderful. After all, they needed it. Really an truly they did.

Smiling, Katie took up the envelope that lay on the table. This would be Bonnie's announcement about thet new youngin. Slitting open the envelope with a case knife, Katie eagerly unfolded the letter.

Dear Katie,

> *I thought to have good news fur you, but fact is, I don't. Cause last week thet new little girl was stillborn. Oh, Katie, when I saw how still she was I purt near passed out. She was right beautiful too, with curly brown hair an a sweet rosebud mouth. An I was all set to call her "Katie". Fact is, I did whisper thet name once before they took her away.*

> *Oh, Katie, in all my life I've never hurt this bad. Why, I had my heart all set on takin her to church. Fact is, I thought to have her in thet infant class with all them purty red chairs. Only now, she's dead. An I'm purt near to go crazy because of it.*

> *Oh, Katie, why did God do me this way fur? Why?*

Katie bit her trembling lip until she tasted blood. It wasn't fair! Why my goodness, thet smilin, chattin, lovin Bonnie was hurtin somethin awful like. Hurtin purt nigh as much as thet German Frieda had hurt thet day in the cemetery. Only, Bonnie wasn't here. She couldn't jist walk right down the street an comfort Bonnie like she had Frieda.

Hugging herself, Katie tasted the salt of tears as she moaned aloud. "Oh, Bonnie, I miss you somethin terrible like. Really an truly I do."

❖   ❖   ❖

Katie finished pinning a fresh didy on Jeremiah, then returned him to his cradle. She left the gown off, though. Why my goodness, in jist a few weeks it had gone from purt nigh cold to downright hot.

Dropping the wet didy into the chamber pot, Katie turned to the bedroom. She reckoned she might as well rest too, seein as how she was all done in like. Fur days now she'd done nothin but worry about Bonnie. Drat it all, why did Bonnie have to live so far away fur? It felt jist plain awful not bein able to help her. Why my goodness, Bonnie *needed* her.

Pulling pins from her hair, Katie advanced to the bureau, then stopped. For there— No. It couldn't be. She'd jist took on so about Bonnie thet she imagined it. Still, Katie's chin quivered as she laid her hand over those bits of cardboard. They was *real*. Train tickets, they was. To Sedalia. Three of them, fur her an her two youngins.

Without bothering to refix her hair, Katie spun about and raced from the room. She hurried through the sitting room and bounded down the stairs. Daniel. She had to tell Daniel. She came to a halt at the sight of his dark head bent over a spindle he was sanding. Why my goodness, what would he think of her, bustin in on his work this way?

"Katie?" Daniel looked up, perplexed.

"Oh, Daniel, somethin wonderful jist happened. I got tickets. Tickets to see Bonnie—an—an—" Katie paused then, suddenly uncertain of her husband's reception. "Bonnie needs me somethin awful like," she added lamely.

"And the truth is, you need her too."

Something about the way Daniel voiced those words and the way his eyes took on tender tones, caused Katie to tremble.

"Oh my goodness, it was *you* thet got them, wasn't it?"

Daniel nodded, his eyes on the rag he was using to wipe dust from his fingers.

"But I can't go. Really an truly I can't. Why my goodness, I have to cook an care fur your pa. An seein as how Benjamin's in school most days—"

Daniel held up a hand as though to stop her. "Oh, Katie, of course you can go. Actually, I was already planning on it. Mrs. Cramer says she'll be more than glad to look in on us while you're gone."

"But—but fur how long? Why my goodness, Bonnie's feelin so poorly I—I—"

"Stay as long as you like, Darling. No doubt you two have a lot to catch up on."

"Course we do, seein as how it's been so long—" Katie broke off, her chin trembling. "Oh my goodness, it's jist plain silly of me to go on like this. I'm goin as soon as I can git packed. An Daniel, I do thank you. Really an truly I do. I jist don't know what else to say. I—I—"

"Think nothing of it, Katie. Just remember, I love you."

At his words, Katie closed her eyes and wrapped her arms about herself. Fur Daniel was callin again. Callin her to love. Oh drat it all, why didn't he jist leave her alone, anyways? Couldn't he see she didn't want lovin? After all, somethin awful might happen if she cared. He jist might walk away like Thane had. Or die like My Pa. An then where would she be? No. She couldn't. She jist couldn't.

"Katie, are you all right?"

Her eyes flew open and she glared at him. "Course I'm all right. I—" Katie bit her lip then to keep her chin from trembling. For Daniel was holding out his arms to her. An the wistful expression on his face said he needed her somethin awful like. Needed her to share her body, to share her heart, to share her life. An she needed *him* too. Really an truly she did.

Her arms fell limply to her sides at the realization. Why my goodness, she needed him purt nigh as much as he needed her. She needed the strength of his arms an his character. She needed the solidity of his frame an his goodness. An way down deep, she needed the security of thet love he kept special jist fur her. Katie smiled then, and stretching her own arms, she ran across the room to embrace him.

"Oh, Daniel, my wonderful, wonderful Daniel. I love you somethin awful like. Really an truly I do."

Daniel didn't answer. But as his lips met hers and clung, Katie felt his tears mingle with her own.

EPILOGUE
APRIL 18, 1882

THE CALL CONTINUES

"So God created man in his own image...male and female created he them...And God saw...(what) he had made, and behold, it was very good."

— *Genesis 1:27,31*

Epilogue

Katie buttoned the jacket of her crimson–colored suit, and sighed. My goodness, it was hot fur April, an so sticky she felt like she hadn't had a bath fur weeks. Still, it was nice gettin all dolled up on a weekday. An Aunt Jane did need her help, seein as how Sally was ailin an all. Course she had them youngins to care fur, but they wasn't no trouble. After all, baby Cecilia would nap in the buggy an Marie would mind Jeremiah.

At the thought of her oldest daughter, Katie frowned. Purt nigh four years old she was, an stubborn as all git out. Why my goodness, at dinner time she'd clenched them little fists an stuck out her bottom lip somethin fierce like. All because she didn't want to go to Aunt Jane's shop. Course Daniel had tended to her right off like. Took her right in hand he did, tellin her to mind her mother or he would paddle her bottom. After thet Marie had been good as gold. After all, Papa was somethin special like, someone to please.

Thoughts of her husband brought a smile to Katie's lips. Daniel. My goodness, but she loved him. Why, in the past year an a half she'd gone plain silly over him. She reckoned she'd never loved no one this much before. Thet's why she'd been a tad worried last evenin when she found him sittin in his pa's favorite chair, broodin. He had a peppermint stick in his hand and a far off look in his eyes.

"Daniel?"

He'd started when she touched his arm.

"Is somethin the matter?"

"No. Well yes, the truth is, I keep thinking of Harvey Fudd. I loved that man, pure and simple. Why, it seems like only yesterday that he was shoving wood into the stove until the shop radiated heat." He paused, toyed with the peppermint stick and smiled. "My father sweat in those days more than he ever did before or since. Even so, I think he liked the old man. I suppose because he meant so much to me."

Katie nodded, wishing she could share Daniel's feelings. But she couldn't. Why my goodness, she'd hardly knowed Mr. Fudd at all. Jist an old man always tradin somethin fur peppermint sticks was all she remembered. Still, if Daniel loved him, he must have been somethin special like.

Daniel had risen from the chair then and handed the candy to Marie. "I'm going for a walk," he said, then quietly slipped from the room. He'd returned an hour later in time to tell the children a bedtime story. And then he'd taken Katie's hand and led her to their own bed.

Katie smiled now, remembering. Fur Daniel had held her close like, an his lips had been soft as velvet when he whispered:

> *"How do I love thee? Let me count the ways.*
> *I love thee to the depth and breadth and height*
> *My soul can reach, when feeling out of sight*
> *For the ends of Being and ideal Grace.*
> *I love thee to the level of everyday's*
> *Most quiet need, by sun and candle–light.*
> *I love thee freely, as men strive for Right;*
> *I love thee purely, as they turn from Praise.*
> *I love thee with the passion put to use*
> *In my old griefs, and with my childhood's faith.*
> *I love thee with a love I seem to lose*
> *With my lost saints,—I love thee with the breath, Smiles,*
> *tears, of all my life!—and, if God choose, I shall but love*
> *thee better after death."*[1]

Those soft lips had kissed her fully then; her forehead, her eyes, her nose, her lips. And his hands had gently explored her body before he took her to himself. He was so tender, so loving that afterward she'd cried.

An she'd be bawlin now if she wasn't careful. Why my goodness, what was the matter with her, anyways? Here she was actin like a moonstruck schoolgirl stead of a married woman with four youngins to mind. Still, she smiled as she tucked a fresh handkerchief into her handbag. Fact was, she reckoned she'd never been as happy in her whole life as she was jist now. Lovin Daniel was wonderful. Really an truly it was.

Katie collected her children then and went downstairs. Daniel was busy with a customer, but he looked up long enough to smile at Katie and return the waves of Marie and Jeremiah.

Outside, the air was so close that Jeremiah dragged his feet and Cecilia whimpered. Her silk waist clinging to her perspiring body, Katie glanced at the sky. Dark clouds were gathering in the south. Drat it all, she didn't want it to storm. Leastwise not while she was clerkin fur Aunt Jane.

Passing the Central Hotel, Katie pushed the buggy toward the far side of the boardwalk so as not to bump into the old men who sat in chairs.

"Serves them right," one old feller said to another "Jesse had it comin."

"Aw, I don't know. Them James Boys ain't so bad. Seems to me only a coward would shoot a man in the back."

Jesse James dead? Why my goodness, Katie couldn't believe it. Fur thet polite man who'd taken dinner at her table seemed too young to die. She jist couldn't picture it any more than she'd been able to see President Garfield dead last fall. Why, them men was somethin special like. Still, they'd died.

Jist like Mamie an Daniel's pa had. Mamie'd gone first, in the fall of 1880. Jist too weak to keep on livin, she'd slipped into a coma an died. An she'd been buried in thet new cemetery north of town. Course the others had been moved to join her: Patrick, My Ma, My Pa. It seemed almost eerie like, seein them in thet new place. Still, they rested together.

Daniel's pa had passed on jist last summer. Died in his sleep he did, real peaceful like. An Daniel, his eyes moist with grief, had made the casket himself. He'd carved the wood with expert fingers, an lined it with love. But it was little Jeremiah who'd cried the hardest fur his beloved "Papaw".

"Mama, where are you goin, anyways?" It was Marie, pulling on the ruffles of her overskirt.

"Oh my goodness, I purt nigh walked right on by, didn't I?"

"Yes, you did." And Marie frowned as Katie maneuvered the buggy into Aunt Jane's shop.

Katie stared after the plump figure of Mrs. Mason as she disappeared through the door of the shop and sighed. My goodness, she was highfalutin as all git out. An jist as hard to please. Course Aunt Jane had warned her thet Mrs. Mason was difficult. Still, Katie'd been certain she could handle her, seein as how Aunt Jane was so busy stitchin up new things an all. But Katie hadn't done so well after all. Why my goodness, fur purt nigh an hour she'd tried on one hat after another only to have Mrs. Mason reject them. "The feather's too small on that one," or "The crown's a bit high on that one," or "Couldn't you get that one in purple instead of gray?" And now she was gone, leaving Katie with hats strewn about the counter and no sale.

Drat it all, why couldn't she have at least come on a cooler day? Katie frowned as she picked up a red hat, her fingers sticking to its ribbon band. Goodness, but she'd be glad when this afternoon was over. Why, in her whole life she—

"Katie!"

Katie whirled to see Thane Chapman in the doorway, his handsome face white below his thinning chestnut curls.

"Fur goodness sakes, Thane, don't scare me thet away. I'm purt nigh done in already—"

"Katie! This is no time fur chattin. There's an awful storm brewin out there. Now, git them youngins an hide behind thet counter."

When Katie hesitated, he stepped closer. "Gosh darn you, Katie, hurry. Go along. Now!" And he shoved her toward the counter before racing back outside.

Startled, Katie grabbed up Cecilia from the buggy and shooed the older two ahead of her. She opened her mouth to call Aunt Jane, but already the older woman was hurrying from the back room to snatch up Jeremiah. They'd barely crouched behind the counter when they heard the approach of a freight train.

"Choo–choo train. Woo–woo." Jeremiah grinned.

But thet wasn't no train. Why my goodness, there wasn't another one due before this evenin. Besides, the depot was up north an this was down south.

RUMBLE. SHATTER. SMASH.

"Oh my goodness, what was thet?"

ROAR. SPLINTER. *CRASH.*

"Mama? I'm scared!"

"Land sakes, sounds like the whole town's comin apart."

WOOSH. *SLAM*. THUD.

Silence.

And then the sound of raindrops. And voices. Screaming, moaning, wailing voices.

Oh my goodness, Benjamin an Daniel was out there somewheres. "Here." Katie thrust Cecilia into Aunt Jane's arms. "I'm goin to find Daniel."

Rushing through the doorway, Katie stops, unable to believe her eyes. My goodness, this is awful. Really an truly it is. Wood, glass, shingles, bricks, bits of cloth, pieces of furniture, dishes, fruit—everything is strewn about Main Street. Stores stand gaping, robbed of plate glass windows. Lots stand vacant, shorn of two and three story buildings. Buggies stand on end, stripped of wheels and hoods.

"Katie!"

It's Thane. Pawing through a heap of boards, he screams. "Katie, help me! Please, I can't find Linda."

But Katie hasn't time for Thane or her cousin. She has to find Daniel. An Benjamin. Oh my goodness, what if the school blowed down. Course it wouldn't. Anyways, she'd best git home first. Then turning toward the west, Katie screams. For even from here she can see that home is gone. The shop an living quarters, the Christian Church next door— all is gone.

"Daniel!" Picking up her skirts, Katie begins to run, trips over upturned boards and falls. Sobbing, she lurches to her feet and rushes on. But rain has turned the street to mud and her new high button shoes mire down. Jerking her feet free, she hurries on. And falls again. This time on broken glass. Oblivious to her muddy skirts and bleeding arm, she hauls herself to her feet and runs again. Drat it all, why can't she go faster, anyways?

At the corner of Bridge Street, she stops. Mounds of boards are everywhere. Why my goodness, how will she ever find Daniel? Picking her way among the rubble, she spies a hand lying in the mud. Palm down it is, an attached to an arm which disappears beneath a mountain of scattered wood.

"Daniel!" Falling to her knees, Katie grasps a timber and yanks.

"Need some help there, Lady?"

"Oh my goodness, yes. My husband's under there."

The old codger kneels then and lifts the scarred hand to place a finger on the inside of the wrist. Seconds later, he gently lays it back in the mud. Shaking his head, he looks at Katie.

"Waste of time, Lady. There's live ones to care fur."

"No!" Katie screams as the old man limps away.

"Daniel? I need you somethin awful like. Really an truly I do. Please, oh, please tell me you're not dead!" And Katie grasps the hand in both her own. But it is cold and still.

"Oh, Daniel." Sinking in the mud, Katie kisses his hand. For despite the scar tissue ridging its back, it is beautiful. Really an truly it is. Fur she's seen thet hand fashion many a chair leg, them long fingers brushin across the grain, checkin fur the tiniest flaw. Thet same hand has molded rockers, an tables, an cradles, an baby blocks. An a blanket chest, fur his new bride. Thet hand was all trembly like when it first offered a peppermint stick to Benjamin. An gentle when it stroked baby brows or an old man's swollen knuckles. It was gentle too, when them fingers traced the curves of her face on their weddin night. An last night—Last night thet hand caressed her body with a tenderness thet was beyond words. An now, thet hand is stilled.

"Daniel. Oh, my wonderful, wonderful Daniel."

Sobbing, Katie struggles to her feet. She has to git away from here. Why my goodness, she'll go plain crazy if she stays here one more minute. All done in she is, an fixin to come apart like inside. Lifting her skirts, she picks her way to the boardwalk and begins to run. Faster. Faster. Faster.

At the corner of West Street, she stops. And stares. For there across the street, is the home of her childhood. Still standing. With a cry of joy Katie races toward it. Without bothering to announce her presence, she rushes into the kitchen and up the stairs. In her old bedroom, she collapses before the open window facing Main Street.

"It's there. Oh my goodness, it's still there." And she laughs hysterically at the sight of the maple tree across the way. Other plain old trees may be twisted an yanked up by their roots, but not this one. Fur it's special. Really an truly it is. Why, fur her whole life she—

"Katie!"

It's Aunt Jane. Jumping to her feet, Katie rushes across the room.

"Benjamin? Where's Benjamin? He's all right, ain't he?"

"Land sakes, Child, course he's all right. He's downstairs right now with his pa."

"Thomas? He's all right then?"

"Course he is. But land sakes, Child, what's wrong with thet arm?" And Aunt Jane touches Katie's right arm where the jacket sleeve is torn away.

Katie winces. "It's all right. Really an truly it is. Jist a little scratch, anyways. Why my goodness, it even quit bleedin." Katie pauses, her chin trembling. "Daniel—Daniel's dead, Aunt Jane."

"I know, Child. Lots of folks is ahurtin jist now. Frieda got hit pretty bad. An she's askin fur you."

"Frieda?"

"Frieda Loeber, thet German gal who comes to the shop now an then. Anyways, she was at Kelley's Drug store when this thing hit. Thet youngin she was expectin is lost fur sure. But she jist might make it, providin folks can keep her spirits up. Thet's why—"

"No! I ain't goin. Let her own folks mind her."

"Why land sakes, Child, you're bein a real stick–in the mud. Course you'll go. Thet gal *needs* you.

"Well, I ain't goin. Drat it all, Aunt Jane, can't you understand? I jist lost Daniel. An—an I loved him somethin awful. Really an truly I did. But he's gone. An I'm left hurtin. An now, *you* have the gumption to ask me to mind a woman I don't hardly know. Well, I won't. Cause she might jist up an die. Then where would I be?"

"But Katie, she jist might live—"

Katie shakes her head. Then, digging her fists into her waist, she glares at her aunt. "Drat it all, Aunt Jane, what difference would thet make? If Frieda mends she'll jist go back to thet German family of hers an leave me like she never knowed me at all. So jist leave me alone. Cause I ain't goin."

With that Katie turns back to the window. Falling on her knees, she wraps her arms about herself, and rocks back and forth, sobbing. Drat it all, why can't folks jist leave her alone, anyways? She's jist plain tired of carin. Why my goodness, there was Thomas, Patrick, My Ma, My Pa, Linda, Thane, Bonnie, Daniel—she'd loved them all. An they'd left her. Ever one of them. Jist like Benjamin an Marie an Jeremiah an Cecilia an even Aunt Jane will. What? Oh my goodness, what is she thinkin of, anyways? Why my goodness, Benjamin will never—But of course he will. He'll grow up, marry an take himself away from her. Jist like them others have. An she reckons it's bound to happen with them other youngins an Aunt Jane too.

Wiping her tears on an already soggy handkerchief, Katie leans out the window. Looking towards the east, she bites her lip to keep her chin from trembling. Fur her husband is buried out there neath all thet rubble. Rubble from her home an her church.

Her church. Thet special place where she heard them beautiful words about God. God? Where's he now, anyways? Don't he know she's all done in like?

Sighing, Katie turns her gaze to the maple tree across the way. An it seems to her thet them top leaves reach purt nigh up to thet gray heaven above. An them lower limbs stretch their pale green arms toward the east an toward the west. Oh my goodness, why hadn't she seen thet before. Course God loves.

But why? Why care fur folks who'll jist go away an leave you hurtin inside? Why not jist stop lovin altogether?

Cause—Cause other folks is spirits too. Jist like herself. Hadn't she felt somethin of Daniel's soul when he read aloud from Browning or whispered her name in the dark? Hadn't she felt somethin inside herself grow deeper, richer, when the tender lights in them gray eyes was shinin on her? An hadn't she purt nigh busted with joy when he touched her face with them gentle hands?

An Frieda? Hadn't her eyes lighted up thet day in Aunt Jane's shop when Mamie had modeled thet purty hat with them bright green feathers an lace? An hadn't her face shone with pride as she patted her son's head an said, "*Er ist* Wilhem?". An thet other day, there in thet old cemetery, hadn't she clung to Katie an wept fur her youngin? Course she had. Fur Frieda is a spirit too. A bein made fur laughin an cryin an lovin. A bein who can make her own life somethin special like.

Course she can jist stay away if she's a mind to. She can jist make believe she never knowed thet German gal. She can jist sit here by herself, away from thet other bein an rock. An be lonely an miserable an unhappy.

But drat it all, she don't want thet. Why my goodness, she'd rather come all apart like now an again than miss all them special times.

Pulling herself back inside the window, Katie rises to her feet. Then gradually, she relaxes her fingers and lets her arms fall to her sides. Slowly, she turns around.

"Why land sakes, Child, I thought you'd never make up your mind. Come on now, we got work to do."

Katie crosses the room then, her chin still trembling. Biting her lip, she pauses for a moment. Then looking into Aunt Jane's eyes, she smiles. And holds out her hand.

AUTHOR'S
AFTERWARD

I have wanted to write a historical novel for most of my adult life. But it wasn't until a few years ago that I felt ready for such an undertaking. I had some story ideas, but I wasn't certain just where to set this novel.

Then in September, 1985, my family moved to Sweet Springs, Missouri. We hadn't been in town two weeks until I began to hear comments like: "You know, this used to be called Brownsville" (The name was changed to Sweet Springs in August, 1887). Or "Did you see that little pagoda down at the park? The spring is still behind there, you know." Or "One time there was this really bad tornado…" Well, comments like these served to fuel my imagination. Why not set my story right here? And so I did.

As with any work of this kind, I have far more people to thank than I can possibly do here. I especially though, wish to thank all those members and friends of the "Brown County" Historical Association. Not only have they welcomed me and my husband into their circle, they have given me lots of little tidbits for use in my book. Also, I wish to thank Jennie Aiken, the Sweet Springs Librarian, and her predecessor, Emma Margaret Meador. These two women have consistently gone out of their way to be of help to me. There is one other person who has given invaluable help: Joyce Agerton, of Pine Bluff, Arkansas, formerly from this area. Joyce, whose ancestors settled a small town just south of Sweet Springs called Dunksburg, has supplied me with old family letters, old poems, deeds and ballads. These were of tremendous help to me.

A number of historical societies have been most helpful. The State Historical Society of Missouri, located on the University of Missouri Campus, Columbia, has been invaluable. I have made frequent use of their

Reference Library and their Newspaper Room. Much of the Missouri history (including Brownsville news) used in this story came from The State Historical Society of Missouri. Outside Missouri, I owe thanks to several people and organizations. In Virginia, there is the Harrisonburg–Rockingham Historical Society. From them I received free newsletters and a *free* copy of *My Recollections of Rocktown–Now Known as Harrisonburg*, by Maria G. Carr. Livingston Lewis could not have been created without this last booklet. Also, I wish to thank Mary E. Pugh of the Hampshire County Public Library in Romney, West Virginia. Ms. Pugh put me in touch with a number of works concerning Hampshire County and Romney history. In Kentucky, my thanks go to Cecil E. Good of Glasgow for referring me to works concerning Barren County history. And finally, I wish to thank Opal Price Alvis of Rogersville, Tennessee, for supplying me with copies of works concerning the history of Rogersville and Hawkins County.

There remains but one group I wish to thank and that is my family. Though my son and daughter are now both grown, they deserve a share of credit for the success of this novel. Indeed, they did without many things during their growing up years so Mom could stay at home and scratch around on paper, learning to be a writer. I thank them both for their patience, their love and their understanding. Perhaps though, my husband, Chuck, deserves the most credit of all. For he has been with me since the first of my writing endeavors some fifteen years ago. He has supplied the family income during this time, working two jobs when necessary, so that I could be free to follow my dream of becoming a writer. Even more, he's given me constant emotional support. He believed I'd become a novelist when no one else did. And he believed in *me* when I was too discouraged to believe in myself. For this and so much more, I love him.

Lastly, I wish to thank my Creator. For it is he who gave me my love for words, my gift of imagination and the knowledge that people are worth loving. Indeed, without him I would have no life, no story to tell.

It is my earnest desire that every reader leave *The Call* convinced that loving is worth the pain of inevitable separation. God bless you, each one.

Chris Ahlemann
Sweet Springs, Missouri
August 31, 1991

HISTORICAL
NOTES

Historical Notes...

Prologue

The Fitzsimmons family, like all my characters, are fictitious. Their origins, however, are based on those of real people who settled in the Brownsville area. As I indicated in the story, Jordana's and Jane's folks (the Douglas family) came from Kentucky. Several early families to this area came from Barren County, Kentucky, and many brought slaves. Asa Pennington, the town's founder, built a grist mill on Davis Creek. He also built a log cabin with a blacksmith annex. The dirt path between the mill and the blacksmith shop became Main Street. Mr. Pennington later built a plank house next to his shop. The first Irishman, James Fitzpatrick, built a dry goods store which housed the first post office.

References concerning both the Mexican War and the Civil War are pretty much as stated. My characters' opinions, however, are meant to reflect *their* outlooks only. They do not necessarily represent my own, nor are they always accurate. For example, a Union man would view the Camp Jackson affair in a much different light than did Thomas Fitzsimmons.

Part I

Kentuckians were not the only people to settle Brownsville. A number of early families came from Virginia, several from Rockingham County. Though I found no specific reference to Harrisonburg itself, I felt it was representative enough of the county to use it for my story. The incident concerning the death of little Nettie Lewis is based on fact. There was a cattle stampede near the court house in Harrisonburg, Virginia, sometime in the late 1820s or early 1830s. Many people were injured, but no one was killed.

One early family, that of Issac Parsons, came to Brownsville from Romney. Located in Hampshire County, Romney is in present day West Virginia.

The cabinet making business operated by the Lewis men is based on that of North Carolina native Nathan F. Andrew, who set up shop on the corner of Bridge and Main Streets next to the Christian Church in 1871.

In addition to Kentuckians and Virginians, a few early settlers came from Tennessee. Since I was unable to pinpoint a specific location, other than simply East Tennessee, I decided to use Rogersville, in Hawkins County, as the basis for Michael Fitzsimmons' origin. There was in fact, at least one Irishman in early Rogersville.

To return to those references to Kentucky for a moment. Yes, there was a Big Spring in Glasgow (the seat of Barren County). This spring was located behind the present buildings on the northeast corner of Glasgow's Square between Main and Water Streets. A little stream still flows east along Water Street. The Big Spring was one of the main reasons land was appropriated from one John Gorin for the site of the county seat in 1799.

There was a good deal of bushwhacking activity carried on in the Brownsville area both during the Civil War and in the years immediately following. In an effort to curb these activities, Brownsville, along with several other towns in Saline County, formed what was known as an Honest Men's League. Thus in the spring of 1866, several honest, high-principled men in Brownsville were selected to assist law enforcement officials in keeping the peace in our town. Just how well this idea worked is pretty much unknown. It is known, however, that there was trouble at the polls in the election of 1868. The Drake Constitution of 1865 required a test oath to bar Southern sympathizers from holding public offices, voting, teaching, practicing law and preaching. Though the U. S. Supreme Court declared the oath unconstitutional, many local authorities required it anyway. Thus in November of 1868, many men of Saline County were barred from voting.

The rape of Verna Marie Lewis and subsequent hanging of the slave, Harry, are based on an incident in Saline County in 1859. A Negro named Jim was arrested for attempting to rape a respectable white lady. Jim was jailed in Marshall (the county seat) along with two other slaves, Holman and John (the former accused of assaulting a white man, the latter of murdering one). Holman and John had received sentences and Jim was awaiting his when a mob broke into the jail and dragged the three outside. John was tied to a stake and burned while Jim and Holman were hung. It is recorded that Jim struggled before dying.

Circuit Court Judge Russell Hicks, the presiding official at the trials, was so incensed by the lawless behavior of the local citizens, that he resigned his position on the spot.

Part II

The Lexington and St. Louis Railroad Company broke ground for a new line in Sedalia, Missouri, on May 12, 1869. The track reached Brownsville in 1871. And on Sunday, December 24 of that year, the first locomotive steamed into town just before noon. In 1878 the Lexington and St. Louis Railroad was leased to the Missouri Pacific Railway for thirty years. In 1880 a consolidation was effected which added the Lexington and St. Louis to the Missouri Pacific system.

The Sweet Springs, located just south of Brownsville, was discovered in 1841 by the young wife of John L. Yantis, D.D. An invalid for years, and in the third stage of pulmonary consumption, Mrs. Yantis had come to Brownsville to visit her family and die. Instead, one day as she rode on her brother–in–law's land, she came upon the spring, drank from it and lived.

Upon his wife's return to health, Dr. Yantis purchased the land surrounding the spring. Then in the late 1860s, Dr. Yantis granted a Colonel Walton of Lexington the right to start a boarding house and provide cottage accommodations. By 1871 "Sweet Springs" was established as *the* place to visit if one was in delicate health. As improvements were made on the grounds it was even prophesied that Sweet Springs was bound to become the Saratoga of the West.

Most of the people who came had been sympathizers to the Confederate cause during the War, leading at least one historian to speculate that Sweet Springs was established for the purpose of allowing the genteel Southerners of Missouri a place for leisure.

I have tried to describe the Spring Grounds as accurately as possible with one exception. The original Pagoda was built *directly over the spring*. A Black attendant would lower a tray of glasses into the pool and bring the water up for free distribution.

The Mexican influence in Brownsville was practically nonexistent. Yet, family histories indicate that many young men from the area went west in the California gold rush. While some of them stayed in the West, a good many returned. I find it believable then, that at least a few of the latter brought back Mexican wives or children.

Part III

The Ku Klux Klan was quite active in the Brownsville area following the Civil War. Lafayette County in particular was the scene of much unrest during this time. Though the Klan was not as active in Saline County, its presence was felt. Thus early in 1872 it was alleged that the Klan was involved in the killings of a number of Negroes. These allegations were later proven false. Still, because of the Klan's known harassment of citizens in Lafayette and Saline Counties, I felt the murder of Andrew and Claudia and their family by members of the Klan was justified.

The reference to Daniel working on a street crew comes from an ordinance passed by the Brownsville City Council in May, 1872 which said that all male citizens from 21 to 50 years should work on town streets or roads four days a year or pay a tax of $2.50.

The Smith & Wesson Schofield .45 revolver was first produced in 1875. I altered the year slightly for the purpose of my story. This, by the way, was said to be the outlaw Jesse James' favorite hand gun.

The briefly mentioned proposed "Brown County" was just about as briefly mentioned in Brownsville history. The only materials I was able to obtain concerning this proposal came from the files of Governor B. Gratz Brown (Missouri Governor 1871–1873) in the Missouri State Archives, Jefferson City. In about 1872 application was made to the General Assembly of the state of Missouri for the establishment of a new county. This county was to take in the corners of the adjoining counties Lafayette, Saline, Pettis, and Johnson. Brownsville was to be the county seat. The proposal did not pass and was quickly dismissed from the thoughts of many locals. However, there was some feeling of contention between some Marshall leaders (Marshall is the seat of Saline County) and those of Brownsville. Presumably, leaders from the other county seats felt a similar antipathy toward the "upstarts" who wanted their own county.

The two Brownsville newspapers mentioned were in fact real. *The Brownsville Banner* was the first paper in town. Little is known about it except that is ceased publication in 1875 and its office was on Miller Street. I was unable to find any copies of this paper. *The Brownsville Herald* came into existence in August of 1874. This weekly paper is still being published, though it is now the *Sweet Springs Herald*. Copies of the *Herald* dating back to the original are on file at the State Historical Society of Missouri building on the University of Missouri campus in Columbia.

The murder of James Douglas is based on that of a real murder in

Brownsville. A Kansas City man, Mr. Frank Barnum, was found murdered near the Spring Grounds on October 6, 1876. Though a reward of $500 was posted by the citizens of Brownsville, few leads were forthcoming. And though over a century has passed since the event, the case was never solved.

The railroad bonds alluded to had been issued in the amount of $400,000 by various counties throughout Missouri. However, in July 1872 the supreme court ruled the counties had no such authority, making the bonds worthless. Naturally, investors were angry. An incident occurred in Cass County where a group of about seventy masked and armed men stormed a train, dragged several county officials outside and shot them. State troops were sent in to stop further violence. But the murderers got away and were never caught.

The cyclone at Houstonia occurred on the afternoon of February 23, 1875. Though most of the business district was demolished, only two people were killed and three seriously injured. The people of Brownsville did rally to help out, providing money and provisions.

A note about this type of storm—technically, this was a tornado. However, since the broader term cyclone seems to have been more commonly used at the time, I preferred to use it in the text.

The attempted hanging of Harvey Fudd is based on a real incident. As with Harvey, the prosecuting attorney of Saline County stopped the proceedings, thus saving a man's life.

Yes, noted Missouri outlaw, Jesse James, was known to have been through Brownsville. At least two families claimed to have seen him and given him a meal. It is also rumored that he "holed up" in an old house in town for three days.

Part IV

On August 1, 1876, John Yantis sold the Sweet Spring Grounds to Leslie Marmaduke. During the next four years Leslie and his brother, Darwin, spent considerable sums of money expanding the facilities at the Grounds. The Sweet Springs Hotel was enlarged to accommodate 400 guests and contained a convention hall, parlor, and dining room. The Pagoda was renovated in much the way I described.

The Grounds reached their "hey–day" in the mid–1880's. When in 1884 John S. Marmaduke (former Confederate officer and brother to Leslie and Darwin) was elected Governor of Missouri, Sweet Springs became the scene of many political gatherings. In fact, since the State

Assembly met here for their summer session, Sweet Springs was dubbed the "little capital" of Missouri.

In the early 1890's the Spring Grounds was converted to a military academy. But more about that in my next book.

The fire described in chapter 65 is based on an actual one which happened on March 15, 1878. The real fire burned buildings on the corner of Main and Bridge Streets rather than the corner of Main and Spring. (This puts the location on the south side of Main rather than the north side as depicted in the story.) Three buildings were destroyed in a blaze that lasted from 3:00 A.M. to 9:00 A.M. Since there was no fire department in town at the time, a bucket brigade was used to bring things under control.

The cyclone in Richmond, Missouri (a small town located approximately 25 miles northwest of Lexington) took place on June 7, 1878. Approximately one third of the town was destroyed. Fourteen people were killed outright; 87 were seriously injured.

The German element in Missouri is one of mixed origins. Those settling in southeastern Lafayette County, however, came mainly from the state of Hanover. Lured by glowing reports from Gottfried Duden's work, *Report of a Journey to the Western States of North America*, they began arriving in 1838. In 1840 the Lutherans among this group started holding services. This then, was the founding of St. Paul's Evangelical Lutheran Church in what is present–day Concordia, Missouri. This church in turn started the Holy Cross Lutheran Church and school in Emma in December, 1864. And finally, in 1878, the congregation in Emma sponsored a school and church in Brownsville.

Though the towns of Concordia and Emma were basically German settlements, Brownsville, as depicted in my story, was not. Thus, these new people in town were seen as "intruders." *The Brownsville Herald*, December 6, 1878, refers to them simply as "the Germans". Nevertheless, the German Lutherans were in Brownsville to stay. I find this element of our town history fascinating and will develop it more fully in my next novel.

It may come as a surprise to some readers that Althea Lewis was a Negro, but had never been a slave. While free Negroes were a small percentage of the overall Black population (there were 488,070 in the United States in 1860), they were indeed an integral part of society. Some free Negroes were descendants of slaves who had earned their freedom during the colonial period of United States history. Others had simply been indentured servants, becoming free when their term of service expired.

Yes, it was possible for a free Negro to own slaves. He could not, however, own a white person. The freedom enjoyed by these Negroes was greatly curtailed after 1834. From this time on no Southern Negro was considered a United States citizen. This was true also in some of the Northern states.

Though I could find no mention of free Negroes fighting with troops from Virginia, I did find that a good many of these men from Louisiana and Mississippi enlisted in the Confederate Army. Thus, it seems believable that Althea's brothers could have fought for the South during the Civil War.

Epilogue

The brief mention of Jesse James' death is, of course, true. On April 3, 1882, Bob Ford, a cousin and member of the James' gang, shot Jesse in the back of the head while the outlaw was standing on a chair in his St. Joseph, Missouri, home dusting a picture. The bullet, from a Colt .45 revolver, was said to have entered Jesse's skull at the base and gone out through his forehead. He died instantly. Jesse was 34 years old. Though Jesse's older brother, Frank, fled at the time, on October 5 of that same year, he walked into Governor Crittenden's office in Jefferson City and turned himself in.

On April 18, 1882, at about 3:30 p.m. a cyclone raced through Brownsville. Coming from the southwest, the storm cut a path of approximately 100 yards wide diagonally across town. Many businesses on Main, Spring and Miller Streets and on Lexington Avenue were destroyed or badly damaged. The Christian Church and the Public School Building were destroyed. Fortunately, no pupils were in the school at the time. It seems that the superintendent saw the storm coming and dismissed early, warning students to "run home as fast as you can".

Unfortunately, not all persons were as lucky as the students. Eight people were killed outright. Three died later as a result of injuries sustained by the storm. Many others who suffered injury had taken refuge in the Kelley Drug Store on Lexington Avenue.

Though the cabinet shop of Nathan F. Andrew, located on the corner of Bridge and Main Streets, was not demolished as I indicated in the story, it was damaged and moved three feet off its foundation. Evidently it was torn down shortly after the cyclone, for the Christian Church dedicated a new building on the corner lot in April, 1883. (This building is still being used for services and is listed on the National Historic Register.)

Considered the worst cyclone is the history of Saline County, this storm of 1882 has remained one of the most noted events of take place in Brownsville (Sweet Springs), Missouri.

END
NOTES

PART I

Chapter 4

[1] from "Ballad of Joe Stiner" based on recollections of M. I. Mathis, Springfield, MO. First published, *Springfield Leader*, October 16, 1933. Note— this Civil War ballad depicts the victim as a Dutchman. However, in all likelihood Joe was German rather than Dutch. Because the German word for German is *deutsch*, many English speaking Americans interpreted this to mean they were Dutch. Also, the word Himmel as used in line 15 is the German word for heaven or sky. Perhaps though, the overall depiction of Joe as Union makes him seem more German than anything else. For the Germans who fought in Missouri, while Union, kept together so as not to lose their own identity.

[2] ibid.

[3] "A Walking and Talking" is an old song ballad from North Carolina.

[4] ibid.

Chapter 5

[1] "Darling Nellie Gray" is a Negro song, sung in old Kentucky.

Chapter 7

[1] from "The Village Blacksmith" by Henry Wadsworth Longfellow. First published, 1842.

[2] from Psalm 100 (KJV).

Chapter 8

[1] John 14:1 (KJV).

[2] from "There's a Land That Is Fairer Than Day" also known as "The Sweet By and By" . Words by Sanford F. Bennett (1836–1898). Music by Joseph P. Webster (1819–1875).

PART II

Chapter 16

[1] from "Sweet Hour of Prayer". Words by William W. Walford. Music by William B. Bradbury (1816–1868).

[2] ibid.

Chapter 18

[1] "Love's Philosophy" by Percy Bysshe Shelley (1792–1822).

Chapter 19

[1] from "Jesus, Lover of My Soul". Words by Charles Wesley (1707–1788). Music by Simeon B. Marsh (1798–1875).

Chapter 24

[1] "Pippa Passes" Song Number 2, by Robert Browning. First published, 1841.

Chapter 26

[1] from "The Disciples Marriage Service", *Christian Worship: A Service Book*, edited by G. Edwin Osborn (St. Louis, MO, The Bethany Press, 1953). Used by permission.

[2] Ephesians 5:25,33.

[3] from "The Disciples Marriage Service". See note one.

[4] from Song of Solomon, chapter 2 (KJV).

[5] ibid.

Chapter 27

[1] from Luke, chapter 2 (KJV).

PART III

Chapter 30

[1] from "A Psalm of Life" by Henry Wadsworth Longfellow. First published, 1839.

[2] from "The Charge of the Light Brigade" by Alfred, Lord Tennyson (1809–1882).

[3] from "Sweet and Low" by Alfred, Lord Tennyson (1809–1882).

[4] from "Cristina" by Robert Browning. First published, 1842.

[5] ibid.

[6] from Song of Solomon, chapter 2 (KJV).

Chapter 32

[1] A song ballad, hand–copied by a woman simply identified as Sallie on January 27, 1872. Original author and date unknown.

Chapter 34

[1] from the Civil War song, "The Battle Cry of Freedom" by George F. Root.

Chapter 35

[1] from Song of Solomon, chapter 2 (KJV).

[2] ibid.

Chapter 38

[1] ibid.

[2] ibid.

Chapter 41

[1] ibid.

[2] ibid.

Chapter 45

[1] from Psalm 23 (KJV).

[2] ibid.

[3] from "On Jordan's Stormy Banks". Words by Samuel Stennett, 1787. Tune, *Promised Land*, American Folk Hymn.

[4] Sonnet XXX by William Shakespeare.

Chapter 47

[1] from "First Love". *The Brownsville Herald* (Brownsville, MO), June 11, 1875.

Chapter 48
[1] from "A Poetical Slander on Missouri". *The Brownsville Herald* (Brownsville, MO), November 26, 1875.

Chapter 49
[1] from "Life" by Francis Bacon, Viscount St. Alban (1561–1626).

Chapter 50
[1] Article published in *The Brownsville Herald* (Brownsville, MO), October 22, 1875, under column entitled "Get the News!".

Chapter 51
[1] from Sonnet XXX by William Shakespeare.

PART IV

Chapter 54
[1] from "What a Friend We Have in Jesus". Words by Joseph Scriven (1820–1886). Music by Charles C. Converse (1832–1918).
[2] from Philippians 3:13 (KJV).
[3] from I Corinthians, chapter 11 (KJV).
[4] ibid.

Chapter 55
[1] from Song of Solomon, chapter 2 (KJV).

Chapter 56
[1] from "The Disciples Marriage Service". See chapter 26, note one.
[2] from Song of Solomon, chapter 2 (KJV).

Chapter 57
[1] from "Paul Revere's Ride" by Henry Wadsworth Longfellow. First published, 1863.
[2] from "Pippa Passes", Song Number One, by Robert Browning. First published, 1841.
[3] from "Annabel Lee" by Edgar Allan Poe. First published, about 1848.
[4] from "The Day Is Done" by Henry Wadsworth Longfellow (1807–1882).

Chapter 60

[1] from "Pippa Passes", Song Number Two, by Robert Browning. First published, 1841.

[2] ibid.

Chapter 62

[1] from "The Disciples Marriage Service". See chapter 26, note one.

[2] ibid.

[3] from Song of Solomon, chapter 2 (KJV).

[4] from "Two In the Campagna" by Robert Browning. First published, about 1855.

Chapter 67

[1] from "The Village Blacksmith" by Henry Wadsworth Longfellow. First published, 1842.

Chapter 68

[1] The words to "Away In a Manger" are anonymous and were first published in 1885. The music, written by James Ramsey Murray, was first used in 1887. I altered the years slightly for the purpose of my story.

[2] ibid.

[3] from John 1:14 (KJV).

[4] from "Joy To the World! The Lord Is Come". Words by Issac Watts (1674–1748). Music arranged by George F. Handel (1685–1759).

Chapter 69

[1] from "Sonnets From the Portuguese", Number XLIII by Elizabeth Barret Browning. First published, 1850.

[2] ibid.

[3] ibid.

Chapter 72

[1] from "The Village Blacksmith" by Henry Wadsworth Longfellow. First published, 1842.

[2] ibid.

Chapter 76
[1] ibid.

Chapter 77
[1] This verse is credited to a slave and written about 1817. The writer's name is unknown.

Chapter 79
[1] from "O Captain! My Captain!" by Walt Whitman. First published, 1871.
[2] "O You Whom I Often and Silently Come" by Walt Whitman. First published, 1867.

Epilogue
[1] "Sonnets From the Portuguese", Number XLIII by Elizabeth Barret Browning. First published, 1850.

BIBLIOGRAPHY

BOOKS

Bowman, John S. *American Furniture.* New York: Bison Books Corp., 1985.

Brannon, Selden W., ed. *Historic Hampshire.* Parsons, West Virginia: McClain Printing Company, 1976.

Breihan, Carl W. *The Complete and Authentic Life of Jesse James.* Revised Edition. New York: Frederick Fell, Inc., 1953.

Carr, Maria G. *My Recollections of Rocktown, Now Known as Harrisonburg.* Bridgewater, VA: Bridgewater Beacon Printing, Inc. Copyright 1984 by Harrisonburg–Rockingham Historical Society.

Carruth, Gorton. *The Encyclopedia of American Facts & Dates.* 8th edition. New York: Harper & Row Publishers, Inc., 1987.

Catton, Bruce. *The Civil War.* New York: American Heritage Press, Inc., 1985.

Commonwealth of Missouri, The. St. Louis: Bryan, Brand & Co., 1877.

Corson, Richard. *Fashions in Hair: The First Five Thousand Years.* New York: Hastings House, Publishers, 1965.

Craftsman in America, The. Washington, D.C.: National Geographic Society. Copyright, 1975.

Current, Richard N., Freidel, Frank and Williams, T. Harry. *American History: A Survey.* 2nd edition. New York: Alfred A. Knopf, 1963.

Davis, Alec. *Package and Print: The Development of Container and Label Design.* New York: Clarkson N. Potter, Inc. 1967.

Duff, Charles. *Spanish for Beginners.* New York: Barnes & Noble

Books, 1958.

Ehwa, Carl Jr. *The Book of Pipes and Tobacco.* New York: Random House, Inc., 1974.

Encyclopedia Americana. U. S. Constitution Bicentennial Commemorative Edition. Volumes 1–30.

Encyclopedia of Collectibles, The—Advertising Giveaways to War Memorabilia. Alexandria, Virginia: Time–Life Books, 1978–1980.

Encyclopedia of the History of St. Louis, Volume III. St. Louis: The Southern History Company, 1899.

Family Creative Workshop, The, Volume 16. New York: Plenary Publications International, Inc. Copyright, 1976.

Fitzgerald, Oscar P. *Three Centuries of American Furniture.* Englewood Cliffs, New Jersey: Printice–Hall, Inc. 1982.

Florin, Lambert. *Western Wagon Wheels.* New York: Bonanza Books, 1970.

Garraty, John A. *The American Nation: A History of the United States.* New York: Harper & Row, Publishers, Inc., American Heritage Publishing Co., Inc., 1966.

Goode, Cecil E. *Heart of the Barrens: Historical Sketches of Barren County, Kentucky.* Glasgow, Kentucky: Cecil E. Goode and The South Central Kentucky Historical and Genealogical Society, 1986.

Goode, Cecil E. and Gardner, Woodford L., Jr. editors. *Barren Count Heritage: A Pictorial History of Barren County, Kentucky.* Glasgow Kentucky: The South Central Kentucky Historical and Genealogical Society, Inc., 1980.

Heal's Catalogues 1853—1934. *Furnishings for the Middle Class.* New York: St. Martin's Press. 1972.

Historic Romney: 1762–1937. West Virginia Workers of the Federal Writers' Project, Works Progress Administration. Sponsored by The Town Council, Romney, 1937.

History of Pettis County, Missouri, 1882.

History of Saline County, Missouri, 1881. St. Louis: Missouri Historical Company, 1881.

History of Tennessee Illustrated. East Tennessee Edition. The Goodspeed Publishing Company, 1887.

Jackson, Eugene and Geiger, Adolph. *German Made Simple.* Garden City, New York: Doubleday & Company, Inc., 1965.

Jensen, Oliver; Kerr, Joan Paterson; and Belsky, Murray. *American Album.* New York: American Heritage, 1985.

Josephy, Alvin M., Jr. *The Civil War: War on the Frontier, The Trans–Mississippi West.* Alexandria, Virginia: Time–Life Books, 1986.

Kalman, Bobbie. *The Early Settler Life Series.* New York: Crabtree Publishing Company. Copyrights, 1981–1983.

Kamm, Minnie Watson. *Old China.* Michigan: Self–published, 1951.

Koller, Larry. *The Fireside Book of Guns.* New York: Simon and Shuster—A Ridge Press Book, 1959.

Lang, Hazel N. *Life in Pettis County 1815–1973.* 1975.

Lee, Ruth Webb. *Early American Pressed Glass.* Northboro, Massachusetts: Self–published. Enlarged and revised edition, 1946.

Lee, Ruth Webb. *Victorian Glass Handbook.* Massachusetts: Self–published, 1946.

Lester, Katherine Morris. *Historic Costume.* Peoria, Illinois: The Manual Arts Press, 1925.

Merit Students Encyclopedia. Volumes 1–20. United States: Crowell–Collier Educational Corporation, 1967–1970.

Mott, Frank Luther, ed. *Missouri Reader.* Columbia, Missouri: University of Missouri Press, 1964.

Nagel, Paul C. *Missouri: A Bicentennial History .* New York: W. W. Norton & Co, 1977.

Napton, William Barclay. *Past and Present of Saline County Missouri.* Indianapolis, IN: B. F. Bowen & Company, Publishers, 1910.

Peterson, Harold L. *The Remington Historical Treasury of American Guns.* New York: Thomas Nelson & Sons— A Ridge Press Book, 1966.

Reiter, Joan Swallow. *The Old West, The Women.* Alexandria, Virginia: Time–Life Books Inc., 1975.

Robertson, James I., Jr. *The Civil War: Tenting Tonight, The Soldier's Life.* Alexandria, Virginia: Time–Life Books, 1984.

Rogan, James W. *Sketches of Hawkins County, Tennessee.* Knoxville, Tennessee: The Presbyterian Witness, 1859.

Saline County History. 1967 edition. Published by the Saline County Historical Society, Marshall Missouri.

Schroeder, Joseph J., Jr. *The Wonderful World of Ladies Fashions.* Chicago: Follet Publishing Company, 1971.

Smith, J. Lawrence. *The High Alleghenies.* Tornado, West Virginia: Allegheny Vistas. Copyright, 1982.

Studwell, William E. *Christmas Carols: A Reference Guide.* New York: Garland Publishing, Inc., 1985.

Tarver, H. M. *The Negro in the History of the United States*. Austin, Texas: The State Printing Co., 1905.

Trachtman, Paul. *The Old West, The Gunfighters*. Edited by George Constable. Alexandria, Virginia: Time–Life Books, 1974.

Triplett, Frank. *The Life, Times and Treacherous Death of Jesse James*. Edited by Joseph Snell. New York: Promontory Press, 1970.

Wayland, John W. *A History of Rockingham County, Virginia*. Dayton, Virginia: Ruebush–Elkins Company, 1912.

We Americans. Washington, D. C. : National Geographic Society. Copyright, 1975.

Wheeler, Keith. *The Old West, The Townsmen*. Alexandria, Virginia: Time–Life Books, 1975.

Wilcox, R. Turner. *The Dictionary of Costume*. New York: Charles Scribner's Sons, 1969.

Wilder, Laura Ingalls. *Little House on the Prairie Series*. Revised edition, illustrated by Garth Williams. New York: Harper & Row Publishers, First Harper Trophy Book Printing, 1971.

Williams, Richard. *The Old West, The Loggers*. Alexandria, Virginia: Time–Life Books, 1976.

Williams, Walter. *The State of Missouri*. Columbia, Missouri: Press of E. W. Stephens, 1904.

Woodson, Carter G. *The Negro in Our History*. Eighth edition. Washington, D.C.: The Associated Publishers, Inc., 1945.

PERIODICALS, PAMPHLETS, and NEWSPAPERS

Armstrong, O.K. and Marjorie. "The Battle of Wilson's Creek", *Missouri Life*, July–August, 1977.

"Brownsville Cyclone", *The Sweet Springs Herald* (Sweet Springs, MO), April 17, 1914.

Brownsville Herald, The (Brownsville, MO), August 20, 1874–April 28, 1882.

Castel, Albert. "The Siege of Lexington", *Civil War Times Illustrated*, 1969. Reprint 1983.

"Civil War Letters of Bethiah Pyatt McKown, Part II, The", edited by James W. Goodrich. *Missouri Historical Review*, April, 1973.

Crawford, R. Clay. "Reminiscences of Rogersville", *Rogersville*

Herald (Rogersville, TN), May 29, 1901.

Dye, William E. "Battle of the Hemp Bales; The First Complete Story", *The Lexington Advertiser News: Special Battle Day Edition* (Lexington, MO), September, 1961.

Fellman, Michael. "Emancipation in Missouri", *Missouri Historical Review*, October, 1988.

Haddock, Neil. "Embattled Mansion", *Missouri Life*, March–June, 1977.

Hardeman, Nicholas P. "Bushwhacker Activity on the Missouri Border, Letters to Dr. Glen O. Hardeman, 1862–1865", *Missouri Historical Review*, April, 1964.

Hughes, John Starrett. "Lafayette County and the Aftermath of Slavery, 1861–1870", *Missouri Historical Review*, October, 1980.

"Interesting Facts about Early Life in Rogersville", *Rogersville Review* (Rogersville, TN), November 26, 1936.

Kakuske, Louis F. "Pursuit Through Arkansas", *Civil War Times*, February, 1975.

Medicine of the Civil War. National Library of Medicine.

Mendenhall, Willard Hall. "Life is Uncertain: 1862 Civil War Diary, Part II", *Missouri Historical Review*, October, 1984.

Pickle, Linda S. "Stereotypes and Reality: Nineteenth–Century German Women in Missouri". *Missouri Historical Review*, April, 1985.

Robbert, Louise Buenger. "Lutheran Families in St. Louis and Perry County", *Missouri Historical Review*, July, 1988.

"Survivor of 1882 Severe Cyclone at Sweet Springs Recounts Storm", *The Daily Democrat–News* (Marshall, MO), April 14, 1962.

"Sweet Springs of Yesteryear", *The Daily Democrat–News* (Marshall, MO), June 24, 1957.

MISCELLANEOUS

"Brown County". Map of proposed county on file Missouri State Archives, Jefferson City, Missouri.

Brownsville City Minutes, Brownsville, MO, January 6, 1871–June 7, 1880.

Bushwhacker's Annual, A Missouri History Calendar. Tenth Anniversary Edition, 1988.

Deed Record, Saline County (Marshall, MO), Volume 22, page 702.

First Christian Church: 130th Anniversary Booklet, Sweet Springs, Missouri. 1973.

Illustrated Atlas Map of Saline County, Missouri. Missouri Publishing Company, 1876.

Plat Book of Pettis County, Missouri. North West Publishing Company, 1896.

Plat Book of Saline County, Missouri. North West Publishing Company, 1896.

Presbyterian Scrapbook: Items of interest. Courtesy, Presbyterian Church, Sweet Springs, MO.

Vickery, William Madison. Unpublished letters 1859–1881. Courtesy of Joyce E. Agerton.